The Legend of the Leaf
A Cozy Mystery
L.L. Gray

Heroic Rose Publishing

Contents

Grab your FREE novella now!   VI

Dedication   VIII

1. Books, Bunnies, and Bad Omens   1

2. Truffles, Clues, and Curious News   9

3. Roots and Revelations   16

4. Well, Well, Well   24

5. The Weight of a Wish   31

6. Well, That Escalated Quickly   35

7. Secrets Beneath the Branches   38

8. Clean Bones, Dark Shadows   43

9. Out of the Forest, Into the Fire   49

10. Going Back to School   53

11. A Lab of Curiosities   62

12. Dwarves Don't Do Desk Jobs   67

13. Snoop First, Apologize Later   77

14. The Gnome Depot   83

15. No Rest for the Inquisitive   91

16. Luna Logic: Resistance is Futile   96

17.	Doughnuts and Dead Ends	103
18.	Second Breakfast and Secrets	109
19.	May the Road Rise Up…To Meet a Mystery	115
20.	The Ley of the Land	124
21.	The Scavenger's Creed	134
22.	Not All Gold Glitters	139
23.	Buried Fire and Fortune	145
24.	Grave Concerns	150
25.	An Unlikely Hoard	160
26.	A Bad Sort of Brilliant	167
27.	Locked Doors and Loose Ends	176
28.	Old Magic, New Leads	182
29.	Bling with a Backstory	187
30.	Majestic. Graceful. Absolutely Not Suspicious.	192
31.	A Tiny Dragon for Tea	199
32.	Red Flags and Ring Boxes	208
33.	Calling in Reinforcements	217
34.	Enthusiastic, But…	221
35.	A Run of Bad Luck	229
36.	Charlie Pending	236
37.	What's in a Name?	240
38.	Peer Reviewed and Panicked	245
39.	Chasing Charlie	253

40. Multiplying Problems   257

41. On the Loose   264

42. Will Luck Turn?   270

43. The Luck We Make   279

Grab your FREE novella now!   289

Thank you   291

Also By   293

About the Author   295

Acknowledgments   296

Legendary Acknowledgments   297

Grab your FREE novella now!

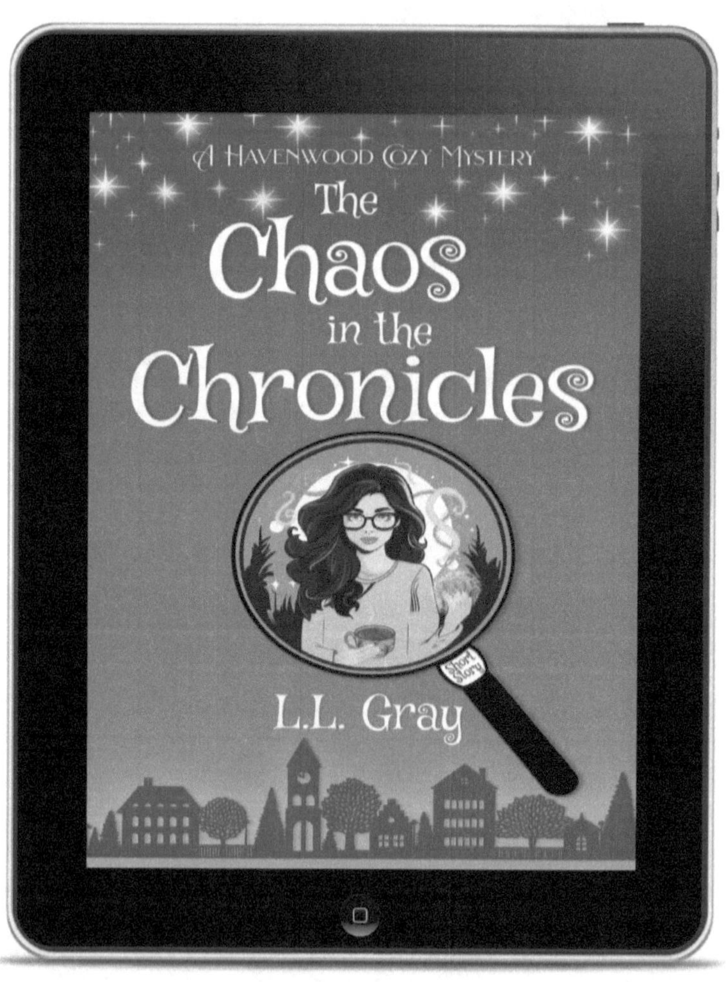

Want a free book?

Of course you do, what madness could possess someone to **not** want free books?
There's no catch - you do sign-up for my mailing list but you can unsubscribe at any time.
There's also no spam.
Ever.
Sign up here to get your free book!
https://www.subscribepage.io/havenwood

To book lovers everywhere.

May your luck be legendary,
your coffee bottomless,
and your shelves always full of treasure.

Books, Bunnies, and Bad Omens

I FLITTED AROUND SULLIVAN'S Spellbooks, my magical bookshop, straightening shelves and giving the shop one last critical once-over. The scent of aged paper and a hint of lavender polish hung in the air, wrapping around me like a calming embrace, but my nerves weren't so easily soothed. Today was a big day, and the atmosphere in the shop felt charged with the quiet hum of anticipation.

Everything needed to be perfect.

The spring thaw had embraced Havenwood in an unseasonably warm hug for early March, tempting locals and tourists alike to stroll down Arcadia Avenue. Whether it was the promise of blooming flowers or the buzz from my new arrangement with Mindy Hart, business was picking up. Spellbooks was already becoming a hub for book signings and promotional events, drawing a steady stream of curious visitors—some still asking questions about what happened during Garrett Grimshaw's book signing event.

I'd perfected my enigmatic smile as a response, but one thing was certain: people were talking about Sullivan's Spellbooks, and that meant business was thriving. So much so that I couldn't handle the shop by myself any longer.

I pulled a paperback from the counter, flipping it open once more. The cozy mystery I was promoting was a lighthearted, charming whodunit, perfect for a rainy afternoon. I'd read it already, but there was something about rereading a book and noticing all the clues the author layered in that really made me appreciate the cleverness of the storyteller.

However, this time, I found it hard to focus as I stared at the words on the page and my thoughts began to drift.

The shop around me faded...

A wishing well. I don't know how I knew the little well was more than just a way to fetch water. There was no shimmer of magic or a handy sign, but I knew in my bones, there was more to this well than met the eye.

It stood nestled in the woods, wrapped in creeping ivy and dappled sunlight. A familiar sight and one I'd seen countless times in the movies or in my imagination. A peaceful spot where people tossed coins and whispered their dreams into the water. I was certain I'd never set foot here before, but it felt like stepping into a memory I'd almost forgotten.

And it certainly wasn't a peaceful memory either.

The air felt wrong. The light was too golden, the warmth of the day too heavy. Even the trees stood unnaturally still, their branches reaching skyward as if frozen in time. My breath caught in my throat and my heart thundered loudly in my ears.

Something was out there. Waiting.

Hesitantly, I leaned forward, peering over the stone wall into the well's depths.

The water was still. Too still. A glassy, black mirror reflecting nothing. No ripple. No movement. Just endless, undisturbed darkness ringed in silent stone.

And then, a single splash.

It broke the silence, echoing loudly as if amplified by the curved stone walls of the well.

I couldn't tell what had made the splash. I looked around, but everything in the forest was still, quiet. Whatever had caused the splash hadn't fallen from my hand. Nor had it come from above.

My pulse quickened.

Something moved in the dark water below.

A sharp thump snapped me back to reality.

I jolted, blinking rapidly as the shop swam into focus.

Luna stretched lazily, her velvety ears twitching as she hopped out of her hutch by the front window. She flicked her tail once, then fixed me with a pointed look. "You looked like you were about to faint onto your precious display. If you're going to pass out, do it somewhere more dramatic. Preferably into the waiting arms of a handsome gentleman. Failing that, at least make good use of the reading nook."

I exhaled sharply, pressing a hand to my forehead. "I wasn't going to pass out."

"No? Because from where I was sitting, it looked like you were seeing ghosts." Luna twitched her nose, her voice laced with curiosity. "You sure you're not coming down with something?"

I hesitated, doing a quick mental evaluation of myself. Was I feeling ill? No, not really. But that daydream had been remarkably realistic. Ominous even. Perhaps it was the two consecutive late nights I'd spent reading thrillers into the wee hours of the morning. Was it my fault if the author wrote books that were impossible to put down?

"Well? Should I call someone?" Luna asked, tipping her head at me quizzically.

I held up a hand to forestall her. "It's nothing. I...just zoned out for a second."

"Zoning out, seeing ghosts. Next thing you'll tell me it's fate knocking on the door," Luna said, twitching an ear.

I gave a weak laugh. "If fate's got a plan, I'd love to see the draft notes. It sure looks like improv from where I'm standing."

Luna's nose wrinkled. "Fate has a sense of humor, all right. Just isn't always a funny one. Besides, if fate really wanted to be in charge, it wouldn't make so many poor decisions. When you've lived as long as I have, you eventually realize that fate has all the organizational skills of a squirrel with a caffeine addiction."

She paused, giving me a long, measuring look. The kind that made me feel like she could see straight through to the truth I'd rather not admit.

Then she flicked her ears and sniffed loudly. "Fluff and furballs, you're fussing like a hen before a storm. Nervous, are we?"

"Yeah, well, you know what's happening," I muttered, adjusting a stack of books that didn't actually need adjusting.

"I do. You've been talking and worrying about it nonstop. And let's be honest, we both know this should've happened ages ago," Luna said with a smug twitch of her whiskers. "You've been running yourself ragged long enough."

"Well, it's happening now," I replied, but my words trailed off as I glanced toward the door. I shook myself, forcing the lingering unease from my daydream to the back of my mind.

"And you're nervous," she said, hopping closer and fixing me with her sharp, knowing eyes. "It's natural. Kind of like when parents drop their kids off at kindergarten for the first time—this overwhelming mix of pride because your little one is growing up and sheer terror because you can't fix anything if it goes wrong."

I blinked at her, startled by the accuracy of her analogy. "That's surprisingly insightful, Luna. Yeah, it's exactly like that. Thank you for—"

"Well, snap out of it!"

"What? Wait a second. I thought we were bonding," I protested.

Luna huffed, flicking an ear in dismissal. "Don't be so silly. We've already bonded. And as your sensei, I know when you need a kick in the proverbial behind to get you going. This is the right step. Spellbooks is going to be just fine and so will you."

I opened my mouth to argue, but she held up a forefoot.

"No, no, don't start. I can already hear it. 'But what if—' 'And what if—' 'What if—'" She wiggled her ears dramatically. "You're turning into a broken record. Have some faith in yourself, Sullivan."

I sighed, running a hand through my hair. "I know. It's just—"

"You're nervous. I get it. But don't be. I wouldn't let anyone bully your little baby."

I choked back a laugh. "Bully my—Luna!"

"What?" she demanded with a haughty sniff. "You needed some tough love."

"You're impossible," I muttered.

Luna hopped closer, her voice softening just a little. "Listen, this is going to be the best thing that's happened here since you kicked that annoying cousin of yours to the curb."

"Hey, I didn't kick him anywhere," I protested.

"Okay, fine, you didn't physically kick him, which I'm still judging you for by the way. He totally deserved it, what with stealing Beatrice's rare books. But I suppose you can't be held entirely accountable for not taking the logical course of action. You hadn't earned your ninja headband yet, after all."

"I still haven't earned it," I pointed out dryly. "Something about a lack of proper ears?"

"True. An insurmountable obstacle, really. But if you keep doing what you have been doing, I'd be inclined to recommend you for honorary ninja rabbit status."

"Really?" I said.

"Give it a decade or two," Luna said, shrugging. "The point is, Spellbooks is going to be just fine, and so are you."

I let out a breath I hadn't realized I was holding and consciously forced my shoulders to unknot. "You'll let me know, won't you? If anything happens?"

Luna gave me a haughty look. "Are you asking me to *spy* for you?"

"I—" I bit my lip, unsure what the right answer was here.

Luna didn't wait. "Because I absolutely will. What did you think I'd do all day? Lounge in my hutch? Go play mahjong with Agatha? Please. If anyone was made to spy, it's me."

"Thanks, Luna," I said, relief washing over me. "But don't be too critical, okay? I'd really like this day to run smoothly."

"You're asking me not to be critical and to spy?" Luna sniffed in mock outrage. "Make up your mind, woman. That's just setting us both up for failure." She blew out a breath, making her shining whiskers twitch, before hopping down the hall toward her private small door which led outside.

"Where are you going? She'll be here any second," I called after the rabbit.

"Where do you think I'm going? I need a disguise. As all spies know, the mark should never see them coming. Now, what do you think would be better? The stilts or the ventriloquy dummy? Or maybe..." Her voice faded away as she hopped through her door.

As the little door swung shut behind her, Mr. Wigglesworth, my Maine Coon cat, stretched luxuriously in his bed, giving me an unimpressed look before padding over. He wound his way around my ankles, nearly knocking me off balance. Chuckling, I crouched, running a hand over his soft, luxurious fur.

"What do you think, buddy?" I asked him. "It's a big day. Are we ready for it?"

He purred, leaning into me.

I chuckled. "If only I had your confidence. But I suppose I've got to make the leap sometime."

A gentle knock sounded at the front door, startling me. I gave Mr. Wigglesworth one last scratch before hurrying to unlock it.

A warm breeze carried the scent of fresh earth and budding greenery as Cassandra Bellamy stepped into the shop. She'd tied her vibrant red hair back in a low ponytail, and her confident smile practically lit up the room.

"Oh, I'm so excited!" she exclaimed, her enthusiasm bubbling over as she clutched the strap of her messenger bag. "My first real day! I can't wait!"

I forced a smile, though my stomach was doing little butterfly loops. "Me too. I'm so glad you took me up on my offer to work here."

Cassandra glanced around, her gaze lingering on the shelves as if soaking in every detail. "You've been so kind, but the rest of Havenwood hasn't exactly rolled out the welcome mat," she admitted, her voice laced with wry humor. "Not that I blame anyone. Especially after what Lysandra Wraithmoor pulled last month. I just wish they knew I wasn't my mentor. But after cutting all ties with her, I needed a fresh start, and I'm hoping I can find it here."

"Havenwood is a special place, but I imagine it's a little sleepier than what you described about your former home."

Cassandra grimaced. "You mean being apprenticed to a bitter old mage who let revenge cloud her judgement and nearly destroyed the happiness of everyone who lives here?"

"Well, not all mages are bad, are they?" I asked.

She sighed and lifted a shoulder. "Maybe not, but every single one I met seemed more interested in learning spells and gaining power than enjoying their time on this earth. I don't love the climb-the-ladder mindset. I'm more interested in finding balance, I guess. Figuring out what my magic really means to me and how to use it to further my life, not sacrificing my wellbeing for the sake of the magic."

I nodded, though I couldn't fully empathize. My magic was limited at best. Although now that I was bonded to the heartwood tree as its guardian, I had my own learning curve when it came to magic.

"Well, I'm glad you're here," I said sincerely.

Cassandra's smile softened. "Anything you want to walk me through before you head out?"

I hesitated, glancing around the shop. "Well, we went over most everything in training."

"Great! I've got it then," Cassandra said, her confidence as steady as her smile.

I rubbed the back of my neck. "And Luna's promised to keep an eye on things. Just don't be alarmed if she shows up in costume. Or tries to test your reflexes."

"Strong-willed, independent women don't scare me, even if they come in rabbit form. Trust me, dealing with anyone after Lysandra will be a breeze, isn't that right, Mr. W?" She crouched to give the cat a scratch behind his ears in his favorite spot. His rumbling purr intensified as he leaned into the caress and closed his eyes in enjoyment.

If the cat was any judge of character, I'd done well in hiring Cassandra as my first employee at Spellbooks. However, I wasn't sure how much I could trust his judgement.

A second knock drew my attention to the door, where Bella cradled a large white box in one arm as she waved enthusiastically through the glass. I hurried to open the door for her.

"Hey, Harper! Hey, Cassandra!" Bella called as she entered.

"Hi, Bella. Good to see you again," Cassandra said, shooting her a friendly smile.

"Morning!" I said, giving her a quick hug after she set the box on the counter. Bella flicked the top open, displaying a mouthwatering array of treats. "Those look incredible," I breathed, my mouth watering at the sight.

"I brought pastries from the Enchanted Oasis and talked Mama and Papa into giving me the morning off. Harper, we're going out to celebrate. You've got your first employee! That's huge!"

"I was thinking I might stay and—"

"Nope," Bella said, cutting me off. "Cassandra has this under control. You two were lucky the stars aligned, and she needed a job just as you needed an employee. But now that she's here, you need to let her do her thing."

Maybe it was good luck, I thought, casting a glance toward Cassandra. At least, I hoped it was. I wasn't entirely convinced the universe hadn't mixed up someone else's good fortune with mine, but I'd take it either way.

Cassandra chimed in with a smile. "Bella's right. After all that training, I feel like I know Spellbooks better than my apartment. You two should go have fun. I'll call if I need you, Harper."

"Promise?" The word slipped out of me before I could think of a more adult response.

"Absolutely," Cassandra said seriously without even missing a beat.

Bella triumphantly shook my coat at me. "See? Come on, Harper. Take the training wheels off. Besides, remember this is Havenwood. What could possibly go wrong?"

I hesitated, my mind flashing back to the various mishaps I'd encountered over the last six months. Based on first-hand experience, quite a lot could go wrong. However, with the sun shining outside and Cassandra already arranging the pastry display while humming to herself, I had to admit Bella had a point.

"Everything's going to be fine," Bella insisted, shoving the coat into my hands.

I forced a smile, though my stomach was still fluttering. "You always know what's best."

"Of course I do," Bella said brightly. She wiggled her fingers at Cassandra in farewell while simultaneously steering me towards the door. "See you later. Have fun!"

And I hoped, more than anything, that Bella was right. But the ghost of that unsettling daydream clung to me like a shadow—silent, lurking, and ominous.

Truffles, Clues, and Curious News

THE RICH SCENT OF freshly ground coffee beans mingled with warm vanilla and the faintest trace of cinnamon as I took another sip from my mug, letting the velvety brew chase away the last traces of my tension. Sunlight streamed through the tall windows of Hocus Mochas, my new favorite coffee shop, painting golden pools across the wooden floors and glinting off the glass display case brimming with pastries and truffles.

Soft jazz played in the background, a lazy, undemanding melody that paired perfectly with the scent of caramelized sugar and dark roast. The space itself was a cozy blend of rustic charm and whimsical enchantment—a chalkboard menu hung behind the counter, covered in swirling script advertising seasonal specials, while dessert-themed coffee mugs lined the shelves. Small round tables filled the space, each with a flickering candle nestled inside enchanted glass globes that subtly changed color to match the music.

And the food? Absolute heaven.

I had to hand it to Bella. She knew the way to my heart, and it was through my stomach.

On my plate, the last bite of a buttery croissant dusted with cinnamon sugar practically begged to be savored. Bella, on the other hand, was methodically finishing off what remained of her maple pecan scone, its golden edges perfectly crisp, the interior soft and studded with candied nuts. Between us sat two steaming vanilla lattes, their frothy surfaces adorned with intricate designs.

All in all, this was the perfect way to spend my first morning away from Spellbooks now that I had an employee to take some shifts.

I leaned back in my chair, finally exhaling the last of my worries as I cradled my cup. Bella, catching the shift in my posture, smirked knowingly. I indulged in a long sip of coffee before giving her what she wanted to hear.

"You were right," I admitted.

Bella tilted her head, looking smug. "I usually am but humor me. What am I right about this time?"

I huffed a small laugh. "You're going to make me say it? Fine. This was exactly what I needed. If you hadn't shown up this morning, I'd probably still be at the shop, hovering and making Cassandra feel like she had a micromanaging boss who doesn't trust her on her first solo day." I sighed. "You were right. I was wrong. I appreciate it."

Bella tapped a finger against her chin in mock consideration. "I'm gonna need you to put this in writing so I can rub it in your face next time you don't believe me."

"Ha!" I snorted. "Not a chance."

I took another sip of coffee, but the warm, peaceful feeling was already slipping away. Some part of me still couldn't stop worrying—about the shop, about the future, about what came next.

"Uh oh," Bella said. "I know that expression. Where did your mind just go?"

"What if teaming up with Mindy changes everything?" I blurted out. "What if I just rewrote Spellbooks' whole destiny without realizing it? What if what I think is a good thing is really a disaster?"

Bella didn't miss a beat. "People act like destiny's got some grand master plan. From what I've seen, if fate even exists, it's more like a bored cat knocking things off a shelf to see what happens."

I snorted out a laugh despite myself. "If that's true, then maybe Mr. Wigglesworth might've been in charge of my fate this whole time." I paused, considering. "Actually...that would explain a lot."

Bella leaned back in her chair, smirking. "Maybe fate just likes to delegate. And if it handed the reins to your cat? Honestly, I've seen worse decision makers."

I grinned. "Wait. Are you saying fate told my cat to send me here?"

"To Havenwood or to Hocus Mochas?" Bella teased. "Because if it's the latter, it was definitely me. But, if you want to blame fate, then fate wants you to buy me a truffle."

I huffed. "Fate's got questionable priorities."

Bella shrugged cheerfully. "So do I. Works out great. Truffles are over there." She pointed dramatically over her shoulder at the display case, where rows of chocolates glistened under warm golden light.

"Seriously? You want truffles at 10:30 on a Monday morning?" I asked, raising an eyebrow.

Bella gasped in mock horror. "Harper Sullivan, are you questioning my dedication to joy? Chocolate brings me joy. And who are you? The Joy Police?"

"There should never be a limit on joy," I conceded immediately, setting my mug down. "Why don't we both get some truffles?"

We made our selections, each choosing two of the decadent treats. Bella went for a dark chocolate sea salt truffle and a pecan praline. They looked incredible, but I opted for a raspberry champagne truffle and a dark chocolate mint one.

Being best friends, we of course sampled each of the truffles, nibbling delicately at the sweet morsels and then debating their merits with the precision of literary professors dissecting a classic novel. Which was more decadent, which had the perfect balance of flavors, and whether the raspberry champagne truffle was a triumph of confectionary art or an unnecessary, over-the-top affectation that detracted from the complex flavors of the chocolate. Bella wasn't convinced. I, for one, found it utterly delightful.

As we savored our treats, I had to admit—once again—that Bella was right. Joy was meant to be experienced whenever possible, not just at "appropriate dessert times," whatever those were. Of course, I wasn't about to tell her that again today. Her ego didn't need any more fuel.

We were just about to launch into Truffle Voting: Round Two when the bell above the door jingled, announcing a new arrival.

At this time of day, Hocus Mochas wasn't exactly bustling. Two other people were at the counter, and the tables were mostly empty. Curious, I turned my head to see which townsperson or tourist had wandered in.

My jaw dropped.

I leapt to my feet, my heart giving an embarrassingly enthusiastic little flutter. "Gabriel!"

My boyfriend strolled toward us, casually handsome in a dark sweater and jeans, his signature amiable smile in place. As always, his presence felt warm and steady—like sunlight through leaves, familiar and golden.

"Morning, ladies," he said. "Fancy meeting you here."

Something about his tone—and the quick, knowing exchange of looks between him and Bella—had me narrowing my eyes. "Hang on. Did you two set this up?"

Bella raised a hand without an ounce of shame. "Guilty as charged, and I'm not even a little bit sorry, so don't expect an apology."

Gabriel chuckled, draping an arm around my shoulders and pressing a soft kiss to my temple. The warmth and sweetness of the simple gesture of it spread through me like honey dissolving into tea.

"Bella called me last night," he admitted, his warm brown eyes capturing mine. "We figured you might be feeling a little nervous, and since your apartment is right above Spellbooks, you'd probably be tempted to hover over Cassandra all day, which wouldn't be good for either of you."

Bella grinned. "So, we concocted the Harper Babysitting Plan."

Gabriel pointed at Bella. "Her words, not mine. I'm calling it a date."

Bella waved him off. "Whatever you call it, I'm tagging Gabriel in. I've got responsibilities back at the Oasis, so Gabriel's on duty for the next couple of hours while I go do real-life work. You two enjoy yourselves."

"Date. Not duty," Gabriel corrected.

"Date duty," Bella said with a shrug and a wink. "But with a knight in shining Armani, who'd want to argue?"

"I won't argue about spending the day with Gabriel, but I'm not a lady of leisure that can just afford to play hooky all day," I protested.

"You own a business, Harper, and you've gotten it to the point where you can afford to take a little time off. Which you should. Seriously." Bella tipped her head meaningfully at Gabriel in silent, but not at all subtle, encouragement.

She reached across the table and gave my hand a gentle squeeze. "You trusted us when everything was on the line. You can trust us now too. It's okay to breathe."

My throat tightened just a little. I nodded, quietly. "Okay. Breathing. I can do that."

Bella smiled, satisfied. "See? Progress. I knew there was a reasonable human buried under all that stubborn."

She flicked her hair with dramatic flair. "Anyway, I promised Mama and Papa I'd be back this afternoon. You two kids have fun. Don't do anything I wouldn't do and make sure you fill me in later. Especially if mischief is involved." She shot us both a conspiratorial smile before grabbing her things and heading out the door.

I watched her go before turning back to Gabriel, who was watching me. "You're planning things with my best friend behind my back now?" I asked, raising an eyebrow.

"That depends. Were you contemplating convincing me to sneak back to Spellbooks after this with you?" he asked, voice full of lazy amusement.

I huffed, taking another sip of coffee. "I was considering it."

His smile widened. "Well, you can take that off the table. Not happening. I've got plans for us."

I arched a brow. "Oh? And what exactly do these 'plans' involve?"

Gabriel leaned in slightly, his voice dipping just enough to send a pleasant little shiver down my spine.

"A great date always has a plan and surprises, so for now, that's all you get. But maybe—just maybe—some handholding." His thumb brushed over the back of my hand, warm and deliberate. "But only if you behave."

I swallowed, heart skipping a beat. The man was dangerously good at the whole boyfriend gig.

I cleared my throat, putting on a faux Southern accent like I'd seen debutantes use in the movies. "*Hand holding*? Why I do declare, Mr. Silverthorne!"

He raised an eyebrow, the corner of his lips twitching upwards and revealing a hidden dimple. "Are you saying no?"

I dropped the accent and shook my head immediately. "Not a chance."

"Good," he murmured, eyes twinkling. "Then finish your coffee, *amaryn*. We've got a date."

The word slipped out so effortlessly I almost missed it. Almost. "*Amaryn?*" I repeated under my breath, the unfamiliar syllables tickling the edge of my curiosity.

Gabriel's lips quirked into a smile, and for a second, something unreadable flickered in his eyes. Rather than explain, he startled me by abruptly changing the topic. "So, are you going to sit here all day, or are we actually going to start this adventure?"

I blinked, caught off guard. "Adventure?"

"Adventure, surprises, a little mystery—all of that and more is waiting for you just outside that door." He gestured towards the entrance.

A date. Not an obligation, not some scheme to keep me occupied, but a real date. I took a slow sip of my coffee, letting the warmth settle into me, and for the first time in what felt like ages, the world outside of Spellbooks—the one filled with truffles, good coffee, and Gabriel's lingering touch—felt like exactly where I was supposed to be.

I slid my arm through his, letting him guide me out of Hocus Mochas. "Lead the way."

Once we were in his sleek car and he'd started the engine, I glanced at him. "Okay, so where are we going? What are we doing? And tell me more about these surprises."

Gabriel smirked. "Ever the detective. All right, I'll give you some clues and let you solve the mystery yourself."

"Deal," I said, game for the challenge.

"Clue number one," he began. "We're not going to eat. At least not right away."

I laughed. "That's not a clue. That's just a statement. But I'm glad that you know me well enough to include food somewhere in the plan."

"Not my first rodeo," Gabriel said with a wink. "Clue number two: you've been so busy getting Spellbooks up and running, and dealing with Garrett Grimshaw, that I figured you might need a hobby now that you've got more free time."

"A hobby?" I raised an eyebrow. "Are you taking me to a craft store to pick out yarn and knitting needles?"

"Do you like to knit?" he asked curiously.

I shrugged. "Honestly? I've never tried, but I wouldn't be opposed to learning. It seems relaxing, especially with friends or a good TV show on in the background."

"So noted," Gabriel said. "But that's not today's plan, clue number three: there's someone who's been waiting to see you and someone else who's been a little neglected lately."

I blinked. "An old friend?"

"Maybe," he said, his tone teasing. "Do you want the last clue?"

I tilted my head, intrigued. "Absolutely."

Gabriel's grin widened. "Clue number four: we're going on a walk. Something about fresh air always helped me to get out of my head for a little while. Maybe it will do the same for you."

I sat back, thinking it over. "A hobby, an old friend, and a walk," I said, repeating the clues.

"And some food. Later on, of course," Gabriel added.

"Don't worry, I haven't forgotten. But the rest of it? Well, it's not much to go on, is it?"

"That's all you're getting."

"Come on. You can't really expect me to give you an answer based on just that," I argued playfully.

Gabriel ignored my antics. "You're the detective," he said with a grin. "Figure it out."

"And if I do?"

Gabriel ignored my antics. "You're the detective," he said with a grin. "Figure it out."

"And if I do?"

"You win a gold star sticker."

I scoffed, hand on my hip. "Excuse me, I deserve at least a platinum star."

His lips twitched as though he was holding back a laugh. "Ambitious. I like it."

I narrowed my eyes playfully. "So where's my platinum star, then?"

"Finish your coffee, amaryn," he said, his thumb brushing over my hand. "We've got a date—and you'll just have to trust me that the prize is worth it."

My heart did a little flip, and I knew I was grinning like a fool. Whatever surprise he had in store, I was ready.

Roots and Revelations

I leaned back in the plush seat of Gabriel's car as he cruised through Havenwood, the world outside a blur of spring greens and sunshine. His hand rested casually on the steering wheel, his other draped along the center console, inches from mine. I tried to focus on his clues, piecing together his cryptic hints about today's adventure, but his calm presence and the soft hum of his car's engine made it hard to think straight.

I glanced out the window, trying to focus. The sleepy town had fully embraced the morning, although it felt like Havenwood was almost emerging from an enchanted slumber. Tourists spilled out of bed-and-breakfasts in search of morning entertainment, while locals moved through their routines with unhurried ease, stopping to smile and wave at their neighbors. Havenwood wasn't just a town; it was a haven in every sense of the word.

"You've got your thinking face on," Gabriel teased, glancing at me with a smile that could melt glaciers.

"It's your fault," I replied. "You're being all mysterious and giving me riddles instead of answers."

Gabriel chuckled, his voice low and warm. "I thought you liked puzzles, Detective Sullivan."

I rolled my eyes, though my heart gave a pleasant flutter. "You're lucky you're charming."

"Lucky?" he said, feigning shock. "I think you mean skilled."

I ignored him, focusing instead on the clues he'd given. "A walk...an old friend," I murmured. "Are we going to Auntie Agatha's house?"

"Nope," Gabriel replied with a self-satisfied smirk.

"What about a walk to visit a friend? Maybe to see Isadora at the magic academy?"

"Not a chance," he said, shaking his head. "School is not a hobby, Harper. I gave years of my life to academia and don't need to relive it, thanks."

I frowned, casting my mind over mutual friends we might be visiting. Gabriel and I hadn't made many public appearances together yet, so the list of possibilities was short.

"Is it Martha? Are we going to the library?"

Gabriel shot me a side-eye look. "I'm not taking you out of a bookshop just to plop you into a library. That's not a hobby; it's just work in a different building."

"Books are never work," I argued.

"Tell that to authors, editors, and agents," he replied, his tone teasing.

Before I could retort, Gabriel eased the car into a parking lot. My mouth dropped open as I recognized where we were.

"The botanical gardens?" I asked, clapping my hands in delight. "Are we here to see Jeremiah?"

"Exactly," Gabriel said, his grin widening. "He's got something special planned for us today. But first—" He shifted, reaching into the backseat and pulling out two neatly wrapped packages I hadn't noticed before. "A little preparation," he said, offering them to me.

I blinked at the parcels. "What's this?"

Gabriel set them on my lap, his eyes sparkling with amusement. "Go on, open them. I hope you don't mind, and I hope you like the color," he said, "but I didn't want to spoil the surprise by telling you to pack for this. So, I took the liberty."

Excitement got the better of me as I ripped the wrapping paper off to reveal a shoe box and a set of thick socks.

"What's this?"

"Well," Gabriel said, "the plan today involves a little more than just a walk around the block. I didn't want you to get sore feet. Your shoes, while adorable, wouldn't hold up where I plan on taking you, and I didn't want you to get blisters," he said, brushing it off like it was no big deal. But the way his eyes softened told me otherwise.

I quickly swapped my ballet flats for the boots, wiggling my toes in their comfortable new home. "You know, most people would've just said, 'Good luck!' and laughed when I tripped over a root."

Gabriel chuckled. "What can I say? I'm not most people."

"No, you're definitely not," I murmured, more to myself than to him as I finished lacing up the boots. I had to admit—they were solid. Good ankle support, decent grip, and while they weren't the most romantic gift, the thought behind them made up for it.

"I'm even more excited now!" I said.

"Good," Gabriel said with a grin. "Come on, Jeremiah has the next part of your surprise ready."

As I headed toward the gates of the botanical garden, Gabriel moved to the back of the car and popped the trunk.

"What are you getting?" I asked.

"Just these," he said, hefting two daypacks. The larger one went over his shoulders, and he passed me the smaller one.

"When you said hike, you weren't kidding," I said, adjusting the straps.

"Nope," he replied. "We might be out for a few hours, so I made sure we're prepared. Snacks, water, and everything else we'll need."

"All right, I'm ready for this adventure," I said, excitement bubbling inside me.

We headed toward the garden gates, where Jeremiah stood waiting, his bark-like skin dappled in sunlight. His walnut-colored eyes glowed warmly as we approached, and his weathered face creased into a warm smile as he greeted us.

"Harper, Gabriel. Welcome."

"Hi, Jeremiah," I said, grinning. "Gabriel said you were part of this surprise?"

Jeremiah inclined his head. "A small part. Gabriel's plan was inspired, and I was happy to help."

I glanced between them, my heart swelling at the thought of the effort they'd put into making today special. "You two and Bella are unbelievable. Thank you so much for doing all of this for me."

Jeremiah smiled. "Big life changes are worth celebrating, Harper. We throw parties for births and weddings, but we often forget to honor smaller milestones—like a new job or a new chapter in life. That's what today is about."

I pressed a hand to my heart, deeply touched. "Thank you. That's...so kind."

Jeremiah nodded and gestured deeper into the gardens. "Shall we?"

Warmth filled me as we followed him through the public gardens and toward the greenhouses. I felt grounded, as though my roots were finally sinking into Havenwood's soil, giving me an anchor against whatever storms life might bring.

The vibrant blooms and lush greenery of the gardens were a feast for the senses. Gabriel stayed close, his hand brushing against mine as we walked. When we reached the greenhouses, Jeremiah surprised me by leading us around the side instead of inside. My breath caught as realization dawned.

"It's one of the heartwood saplings," I whispered.

Jeremiah nodded. "It's the youngest. The last one I planted. I thought you might like to connect with it today. With your newfound freedom, this seemed like a perfect time."

When we reached the sapling, its delicate branches swayed slightly as if in welcome, though no breeze stirred the air. I reached out through my connection towards the young tree. Unlike the sapling we'd planted at the site of the original heartwood, this one couldn't communicate with me in words and sentences. Instead, I felt warmth, welcome, and a hint of happiness in my mind.

"It's good to see you, too," I whispered to the baby tree through our mental connection.

Unaware of my communication with the tree, Jeremiah gestured at Gabriel, who handed me a pair of floral gardening gloves.

"What's this?" I asked, slipping on the gardening gloves and flexing my fingers against the thick lining.

"Protection," Gabriel said simply, his voice steady but carrying an undertone of caution.

"Protection from what?" I asked, frowning.

Gabriel tipped his head towards Jeremiah. The treant offered me a small vial of glowing emerald liquid. He cradled it carefully, as though it were something alive and either fragile or dangerous before extending it toward me.

"Gabriel is right to be cautious," Jeremiah said, his voice low and deliberate. "This is meant for the saplings, Harper. I've crafted it specifically for them. I've drawn on magical sources to provide unique nutrients they need to grow strong and steady. But such things are best handled with care. Magic, even well-intended, can take root in ways we don't always foresee."

I swallowed hard, a shiver running through me as I carefully accepted the vial with both hands. The liquid inside shimmered as though lit from within, swirling in slow, hypnotic currents.

"Got it. Gloves on. Careful handling," I said.

Jeremiah shot me a knowing glance. "When handled with respect and caution, magic can do wonderful things. Remember that, Harper."

Gabriel knelt beside the sapling, laying out a small trowel and a roll of cloth. "I'll dig the trench," he said, casting me a reassuring glance. "You pour the magical tonic around the sapling."

I nodded, kneeling carefully beside him and cradling the vial as I tilted it over the shallow trench Gabriel had dug. The liquid poured out in a thin, glimmering stream, soaking into the soil around the sapling's roots. I took the trowel from Gabriel and covered the small trench, patting the soil back into place.

"Well done," Jeremiah murmured.

"Am I safe now?" I asked, holding up my gloved hands.

The treant nodded. I sat back on my heels and tugged the gloves free, laying my palm on the sapling's trunk.

"There you go," I whispered. "I hope that helps you grow big and strong."

As the words left my tongue, something shifted in the air around me. The vibrant garden colors dulled, like a painter had washed them in gray, and the edges of my vision blurred.

The world fell away.

I was somewhere else.

A stone well stood before me, wrapped in ivy that seemed to twist and almost writhe unnaturally. Plants were supposed to stay rooted and still, weren't they? The air was heavy, charged with an oppressive stillness that pressed against my entire being.

The sound of something slithering through grass reached my ears. It was faint but undeniable, a soft, rhythmic rustle that sent a chill down my spine.

I tried to turn toward the sound but couldn't. The shadows pooling in and around the well, seemed to grow darker and deeper.

Then, a splash sounded.

The sound echoed loudly, and I flinched, my gaze snapping to the water. Rings of ripples expanded outward, distorting the surface. Something had fallen in—no, something was moving within the water.

I leaned forward instinctively, trying to see through the shifting ripples. Was it a fish? An animal?

A dark shape darted just beneath the surface, quick and serpentine, its motion so fluid it could have been water itself. My breath hitched as I peered into the well, but the inky surface of the water was perfectly still once more, giving nothing of its secrets away.

A shout sounded to my right.

I tried turning to look, but before I could focus, a hand landed on my shoulder and the vision shattered completely.

I gasped, falling forward on my hands and knees, my breath coming hard and sharp high in my chest. The vibrant garden swam back into focus: bright flowers, rich earth, the gentle sway of the sapling. Gabriel's hand tightened on my shoulder, steadying me. I was back in the garden, my hands pressing into the soil.

"Harper," he said, his brow furrowed in concern. "What happened? Are you all right?"

"I..." My voice faltered as I sat back on my heels, the weight of the vision lingering like a faint shadow. "I think so." The words came out thin and unconvincing.

Gabriel cupped my cheek, his gaze searching mine for answers I wasn't ready to give. "You don't look all right," he murmured, as he brushed soothing circles against my shoulder.

I managed a shaky smile. "I just...zoned out for a second. Maybe the magic threw me off balance or something." I shot Jeremiah a grateful look. "Those gloves were probably a good call."

Jeremiah nodded, his bark-like face etched with quiet concern. "The saplings are growing quickly," he said, his deep voice slow and deliberate. "But the young ones sometimes struggle as they try to find their place in this world. I imagine you may feel some of their growing pains as well, Harper, as you and the trees find your way through this bond."

My fingers curled instinctively into the soil, and I glanced at the sapling beside me. Its leaves shimmered faintly, catching the light in a way that felt almost too alive. Was that what I'd felt? The sapling reaching out in some way I didn't yet understand? I swallowed hard, not ready to share that thought aloud.

"I suppose we'll both have to get used to it," I said lightly, though my voice wavered. Gabriel shot me a concerned look, not missing a thing. I gave him a little reassuring smile, but it felt forced.

Jeremiah gave a slow, measured nod. "You will. Bonds like this require time, patience, and care—just as these saplings do. Listen when they speak, Harper. They may not have words yet, but they have much to teach you as you grow together."

I nodded, though I wasn't entirely sure what he meant. My heart was still pounding from the vision, and I couldn't shake the sensation of something slithering just beneath the surface of my thoughts. But now wasn't the time to linger on it. Not here, not in front of Gabriel and Jeremiah.

Gabriel's hand slid down to take mine, his fingers warm and grounding. "Why don't we check on the next sapling?" he suggested softly. "Maybe the fresh air and a little movement will help."

I forced another smile, squeezing his hand. "Good idea."

Jeremiah handed me the folded map and a bottle of the magical formula, his weathered fingers brushing mine briefly. "Take this," he said. "The saplings form a circle through the forest around Havenwood and some can be a little difficult to find."

I glanced at the map, my eyes widening as I counted the marks. "There are nine saplings now? I only helped plant a few."

Jeremiah's mouth curved in a knowing smile. "Numbers have power. Three is strong on its own. But three threes? That's stronger still. Besides, nine is a lucky number for my people. I thought it wouldn't hurt to add a few more in the effort to protect Havenwood. We all must do our part, after all."

I couldn't argue with him there, but looking at the map, it seemed like visiting each sapling might take us most of the day.

Gabriel nudged me, seeming to read my mind. "Look on the bright side. We'll get some exercise, and it'll keep your mind off the shop. Win-win."

I shot him a mock glare. "You planned this, didn't you?"

His grin was entirely too charming. "Of course."

Jeremiah's eyes softened, the lines at their corners deepening. "Visit them all and use the same amount of elixir we used on the first one here. It will help them grow into powerful protectors for our community."

I glanced at the hand-drawn markings, heart tugging with familiarity. As my finger traced the nearest circle, I reached inward toward the bond that tethered me to the main heartwood. In my mind's eye, the golden thread I always imagined connecting us seemed to sprout finer strands—like new roots branching out toward these saplings.

"Thank you," I murmured, not really knowing what else to say.

Jeremiah inclined his head in a gesture that felt almost like a blessing before retreating into the gardens. Gabriel turned to me, his hand still clasping mine.

"Ready?" he asked gently.

I nodded, letting him help me to my feet. The warmth of his touch steadied me, but the chill of the vision clung stubbornly to the edges of my mind. Whatever I'd seen, it felt important, though I couldn't yet make sense of it. Was it really the sapling trying to communicate with me? If so, what was it trying to say? The image had been simultaneously so clear and so confusing. For now, I could only hold on to Jeremiah's words to pay attention and listen.

Gabriel gave me an encouraging smile as he guided me toward the woods where the next sapling stood waiting for its magical elixir. The sun was warm, the garden alive with color and light. But somewhere, just out of reach, a shadow lingered.

Well, Well, Well

THE SUN FILTERED THROUGH the canopy above, casting dappled patterns on the forest floor. The path ahead twisted gently, bordered by wildflowers in shades of lavender and gold. A soft breeze carried the scent of pine and earth, mingling with the faint spicier notes of Gabriel's distinctive cologne clinging to his shirt. It was the kind of day that begged to be savored.

I adjusted the straps of my pack and glanced over at Gabriel, who was crouched beside one of the heartwood saplings, his movements deliberate and steady as he worked the trowel. He had a way of making even mundane tasks look graceful. I couldn't help but admire the way his dark hair fell across his forehead, the easy confidence in the way he knelt on the soft earth.

"You've got dirt on your face," I teased, as I knelt beside him to help.

Gabriel glanced up, his expression amused. "Really? Is it rugged and outdoorsy dirt, or more like I've-been-playing-in-a-sandbox dirt?"

"Somewhere between rugged and endearing," I replied, tugging off my glove and brushing a smudge off his cheek with my thumb.

His smile widened, and he captured my hand, pressing a kiss against my palm. "Careful, amaryn," he murmured. "If you keep complimenting me, I might start thinking you enjoy my company."

"Don't let it go to your head," I said. Then I paused at the unfamiliar word, my brow furrowing. "Amaryn?" I repeated, tilting my head as I studied him. "You keep saying that. What does it mean?"

Gabriel's lips curved into a soft smile, one that somehow felt entirely for me. "It means 'queen of my heart.' It's from my father's native language."

My chest tightened at the tenderness in his voice, and I swallowed, caught off guard. No one had ever spoken to me like that before, as if I were something sacred. It felt too big to hold, but at the same time, I didn't want to let it go.

"That's...really beautiful," I finally managed. "What language is it?"

Gabriel sat back on his heels, his gaze going a little distant. "Aetheryn. It isn't widely spoken, but the language is a beautiful one. Deep meanings and poetic flow."

"Aetheryn?" I asked. "I've never heard of it before. Do you still speak it with your dad?"

Gabriel's expression shifted, a flicker of something crossing his face. "Not often anymore. He had to return to his homeland years ago. It's...complicated. But the word stuck with me. It reminded me of how he always looked at my mom, like she was the center of his world."

I softened, leaning a little closer. "Can you tell me more about him? And about where he's from?"

Gabriel hesitated, his fingers brushing over mine. "People assume my mom married into the Silverthorne name, but she was born a Silverthorne. The name, the legacy, the responsibility to Havenwood—it's all hers. But my dad? He's...different."

"How so?" I asked.

Gabriel blew out a breath and ran his free hand through his hair. "I don't talk about him often because it's..."

"Complicated?" I offered when he trailed off. Gabriel nodded. I squeezed his fingers. "Look, we don't have to talk about it if it's too hard."

"No, it's not that. It's just..." Gabriel paused, taking a deep breath. "Well, my dad's not exactly human. He's Aetherborn, a being tied to magic itself."

"Aetherborn?" I asked. "I've never heard of them."

"Think of it like the fae but more primal, less bound by rules. His people are deeply connected to the raw forces that flow through everything. Magic, nature, life. They're all sort of...intertwined for the Aetherborn."

I blinked, stunned by the weight of his words. "That sounds...incredible."

"It is. But it also means his life and ours didn't always align. Aetherborn can't stay away from their homeland for long without consequences—draining their magic, unbalancing their connection to the Aether. He came and went as long as he could, but when I was about nineteen, he had to go back for what we thought would be just a season. It's been years now. He and my mom..." Gabriel trailed off, his voice softening. "Well, they're still together, still love each other, but it's like having parents on opposite sides of the globe before there were cell phones or planes. Hard to stay in touch, and even harder to visit."

"That must've been tough for you," I said, my heart squeezing at the thought of him growing up with such a distant connection to his father.

Gabriel shrugged, but the motion didn't carry his usual ease. "It wasn't easy. He always tried to come back when he could, and sometimes he did. But when he left the last time..." He glanced down briefly. "Well, we don't know how long he'll be gone this time. My mom did the best she could to compensate for his absence, especially when we were kids."

"That must've been hard on her and on you," I said carefully. "How did she handle it?"

Gabriel huffed a soft laugh. "She handled it by becoming Vivienne Silverthorne. All structure, no cracks. I think it's her way of keeping the family steady while he's gone. But...it's not the whole story. Not really."

I squeezed his hand gently, offering a smile. "Thank you for sharing that. I can see where you get your strength from. Both of your parents sound incredible."

For a moment, his thumb traced small, reassuring circles against my knuckles. "They were very lucky to find each other, and I guess I've been lucky. In my own way. And now, well...now I have my own amaryn."

My throat tightened again, but this time with something warm and unspoken. "You do," I said softly, giving his hand another squeeze.

Gabriel's grin returned. For a moment, the forest seemed to hold its breath around us, sunlight catching on the edges of the leaves like a golden promise. Then he nudged my shoulder gently, breaking the spell. "Well, amaryn, if you're done distracting me, we've got work to do."

I laughed, swatting at him lightly with my glove. "Me? Distracting you? Please. If anything, it's the other way around. Let's see if you can keep up."

He chuckled, shifting back to crouch beside the sapling. "Challenge accepted."

We worked in comfortable silence. The fresh earth smelled rich and alive, and a faint birdsong drifted through the trees. By the time we finished, a soft breeze had picked up, carrying with it the faint scent of wildflowers and pine.

Gabriel leaned back on his heels and wiped his hands on his jeans, his grin easy and proud. "You're a natural at this, you know."

I tilted my head, giving him a playful look. "What, pouring magical fertilizer around a tree? It's not exactly groundbreaking stuff, no pun intended."

He laughed, reaching over to pluck a stray leaf from my hair. "It's more than that. You look at home out here. Happy. Like this is exactly where you're meant to be."

I brushed another stray leaf off my shoulder. "Well, I have an excellent guide," I said lightly.

Gabriel's grin widened, but there was nothing teasing in his expression. "I'm just saying, you've got this way of making things bloom around you, amaryn. Spellbooks, Havenwood, the people who know you. Even these saplings are lucky to have you. As am I."

My throat tightened at the unexpected compliment. It felt like too much, like something I wasn't sure I deserved, and yet...I couldn't deny how much his words warmed me. "That's...well...how can anyone live up to that?" I said, my voice quieter than I intended.

"You already do. It's the truth," he said simply, handing me a water bottle from his pack. "And you deserved to hear it."

I took the bottle, our fingers brushing briefly. His steady gaze held mine for a moment longer, and I felt that familiar flutter low in my stomach—the one that always seemed to happen when Gabriel said something that reached right past my defenses.

"Well," I said, unscrewing the cap, "if this is your way of convincing me to spend more time outdoors, it's working."

"Good," he said with a soft laugh. "But for the record, this isn't about dragging you out here or Bella's master plan to distract you from Spellbooks. I just wanted to spend time with you. And I thought you might enjoy this."

"I am," I admitted, taking a sip of water. "The fresh air, the quiet...and the company."

He smiled. "Good. Because I still have some surprises up my sleeves."

I smiled back, feeling the tension from earlier melt away completely. "Well, then lead the way, Mr. Adventure. I'm all yours."

Gabriel's grin softened. "I like the sound of that."

We settled into a rhythm as we worked, the quiet punctuated by birdsong and the occasional rustle of leaves overhead. Gabriel dug small trenches around each sapling while I carefully poured the shimmering emerald elixir, watching as it soaked into the soil like sunlight captured in liquid form. The trees seemed to respond almost immediately, their leaves catching the light in a way that made them look like they were glowing from within.

We continued down the trail, our pace leisurely as we soaked in the forest's beauty. The conversation drifted easily between lighthearted banter and comfortable silence. It was the kind of moment I hadn't realized I needed—an escape from the constant buzz of the shop, the town, and the responsibilities that came with being the heartwoods' guardian.

As we moved from tree to tree, fertilizing the young heartwood saplings with Jeremiah's special blend, the hours seemed to melt away. I didn't even notice the time until my stomach betrayed me with a loud grumble.

Gabriel raised an eyebrow, a smirk tugging at the corner of his mouth. "I heard that. Is it time for lunch?"

Blushing, I pressed a hand to my stomach. "I think so. I could've sworn I was too full after Hocus Mochas to eat another bite, but here we are."

He shrugged. "We've been burning calories." Gabriel pulled out the map Jeremiah had given us. He unfolded it carefully, the edges worn from our frequent checks. "Looks like we've got one more sapling to visit," he said, tracing the path with his finger. "Shouldn't be too far from here. And lucky for you, I packed a picnic lunch. Can I tempt you with some food before we finish this last sapling?"

My stomach grumbled again at the mention of food and a blush crept up my cheeks. "I think that was my stomach agreeing for me."

Gabriel winked at me as he folded the map and slid it into his back pocket. "Well, Jacques outdid himself with the picnic. He insisted on nothing less than perfection, so I'd say we're in for a treat."

"Jacques?" I asked, my excitement bubbling. "The chef I met at the masquerade? You got *Jacques* to pack our lunch? Now I'm definitely hungry."

Gabriel shrugged modestly, though the glint of pride in his eyes betrayed him. "What can I say? I like to go all out for the people who matter."

I laughed. "Trying to win me over with food?"

Gabriel chuckled, holding out a hand to me. "Just stacking the odds in my favor. Come on, amaryn. Let's finish up so we can eat before your stomach starts singing a solo."

We picked up our pace, our steps falling into a comfortable rhythm as we followed the winding trail. The scent of wildflowers and pine hung in the air, and the sunlight filtering through the canopy dappled the ground with golden patches. I felt alive. Connected not just to the forest, but to the moment itself. Gabriel's presence only added to the magic of the day.

When the trail opened into a sunlit glade, I stopped short, my breath catching in my throat.

"Wow," I whispered, taking in the scene before me.

The clearing was like something out of a dream. Tall grass swayed gently in the breeze, and wildflowers painted the ground in vibrant bursts of red, yellow, and violet. The towering trees formed a protective circle, their branches arching overhead like the vaulted ceiling of a cathedral. In the center of the glade, sunlight bathed the scene in a soft, golden glow.

Gabriel grinned as he took in my awed expression. "Told you it was the perfect spot for a picnic."

"It's incredible," I said, my voice barely above a whisper. "How did you even find this place?"

"Jeremiah might've given me a hint or two," he admitted, setting down his bag and beginning to unpack the food. "Now, what do you think? This, or the table at Hocus Mochas?"

"This, obviously," I said, spinning slowly to take in every detail of the space. The sunlight filtering through the trees, the gentle rustle of leaves, the wildflowers carpeting the ground—it all felt like a scene plucked straight from a storybook. "It's perfect. But I reserve the right to bring truffles from Hocus Mochas next time we come."

"Deal," Gabriel said with a chuckle as he set out two plates.

I was about to comment on the sheer perfection of the day when my gaze snagged on something near the edge of the glade, and my stomach plummeted.

Nestled in the shadows of the trees stood a small well. Creeping ivy and moss covered its weathered stone along with a small wall that sat behind the well. The vines curled and twisted, appearing almost alive. Intricate patterns adorned the wooden beams supporting the roof, and the bucket hanging from the rope swayed in the breeze. Beside the well, its delicate branches arching over the slanted roof, was the final young heartwood sapling.

Gabriel caught the direction of my gaze and followed it, his expression shifting. "There's a legend around that well," he said quietly. "Locals say it grants wishes if your heart is in the right place and you offer a coin." He hesitated and then shrugged. "It never worked for me. Maybe I was asking for the wrong things."

The scene was enchanting and unsettlingly familiar. My breath caught, and a shiver ran down my spine as I stared at the well, unease coiling tight in my chest.

I froze, my pulse thudding loudly in my ears as realization struck like a thunderclap. This wasn't the first time I'd seen this place. The oppressive stillness, the twisting ivy, the shadows pooling around the well. It was all the same.

I'd seen this exact place before. Twice in my strange daydreams.

Once in Spellbooks and again when I touched the first heartwood sapling. Both times brought the same rising sense of dread that lingered in the corners of my mind, impossible to shake.

The air here seemed to shift, charged with something intangible that raised the fine hairs on my arms. Beneath the dappled sunlight's warmth was an edge, a quiet wrongness that whispered just below the surface.

My instincts prickled, a low, insistent hum of warning. This clearing wasn't meant for picnics or carefree moments, no matter how inviting it appeared.

What was going on? And why did this place make me feel like I was trespassing somewhere sacred—and dangerous?

The Weight of a Wish

"Harper?" Gabriel's voice cut through the haze of my thoughts, drawing me back to the glade.

I blinked and turned, finding him standing beside a red-and-white-checked blanket spread across the grass. My stomach flipped when I saw the feast he'd laid out.

"How did you—?" I stopped, glancing between him and the meticulously arranged picnic. "Gabriel, you should've asked me to help! You set all this up while I was daydreaming?"

He chuckled, brushing off my concern. "Relax, it didn't take very long. Besides, Jacques deserves most of the credit. I just carried the food and opened the boxes."

I shook my head, still feeling a little guilty as I walked over. "Still, you and Jacques have outdone yourselves. I don't think anyone has ever made me a picnic like this before."

"Then they haven't really treated you right. But don't worry, that's why I'm here," he said, flashing me a grin. "Now, sit. You've earned it."

I dropped onto the blanket, my curiosity overtaking my guilt. "All right, what did Jacques whip up this time?"

Gabriel began showing off the dishes with the flair of a showman. "First, we've got croissants stuffed with roast beef, caramelized onions, and horseradish aioli. Jacques called them 'a symphony of flavor.' And before you ask, yes, he told me I had to say that." He set them down, the golden, flaky layers practically shimmering in the sunlight.

I reached for one, unable to resist. "Jacques really doesn't do anything halfway, does he?"

"Nope. And he'd probably be offended if we suggested he try," Gabriel said with a laugh. "Next, there's a cucumber and dill salad—fresh and crisp, to balance out the richness. Oh, and roasted fingerling potatoes with rosemary and sea salt. Simple but perfect."

"And dessert?" I asked, already knowing Jacques wouldn't let that part slide.

"Triple berry tarts," Gabriel said, lifting a lid with dramatic flair. "Vanilla custard topped with raspberries, blueberries, and blackberries. Jacques insisted they'd be the perfect finale."

I couldn't suppress a delighted laugh. "He's a genius with food. You know that, right?"

Gabriel shrugged. "It's why my mother pays him the big bucks. I'm just happy to take advantage of his skills when it comes to picnics."

I turned to look at him, a smile tugging at my lips. "No issues here. And for the record, anytime you want to surprise me with a picnic like this, I'm all in."

"I'll keep that in mind," he said, chuckling as he slid a plate toward me.

I didn't need to be invited twice. Shamelessly, I loaded my plate with a little of everything, savoring each bite. The croissants were buttery and rich, the potatoes perfectly seasoned, and the tarts were divine—sweet but not cloying, the perfect blend of flavors.

By the time I leaned back, sighing in contentment, I was sure I couldn't eat another bite. "This is perfect," I said, lying on the checked blanket. I laced my fingers behind my head and stared up at the sunlight filtering through the leaves, the lingering sense of dread from earlier nearly forgotten. Maybe I'd just been hungry, and that had sent my mind into overdrive.

Gabriel lay down beside me, propping himself up on one elbow. "Glad to hear it. But I've got one more surprise."

I sat up, intrigued. "Another one? You're really setting the bar high."

"Just a little one." He reached into his pocket and held out two coins. "Thought we might test that legend."

I glanced toward the well, its ivy-draped silhouette still and waiting. "You're serious?"

He just smiled, dropping one coin into my palm. "Couldn't hurt, right?"

I hesitated, the weight of the coin suddenly heavier than it should've been. I knew better than to mess with magic I didn't understand. And I definitely hadn't forgotten what I saw in those visions. Something slithering beneath the surface of the water. Something watching.

But Gabriel was already standing, waiting for me with quiet expectation. If fate had brought me this far, maybe it knew what it was doing.

I took his offered hand, letting him pull me to my feet. "Well, I'm in. But only if you do it too."

"Of course." He gave my fingers the slightest squeeze.

Together, we walked to the well. Up close, its weathered stone walls seemed even older, the ivy curling tightly around the edges like it was clinging for dear life. The bucket swayed on its rope, though no breeze stirred the air.

I hesitated at the edge, glancing into the inky darkness below. The sense of dread that had nearly disappeared as I'd indulged in Jacques' roast beef sandwiches and berry tarts surged past the delicious food in my stomach and clogged my throat.

"What's wrong?" Gabriel asked, his voice soft.

I forced a chuckle, trying to shake off the odd sense of unease. "I, um, I guess I don't know what to wish for. Which, I guess, is a good problem to have."

Gabriel gave me his full attention. "What do you mean?"

"For so long, all I wanted was a place to put down roots. Dad's job kept us on the move, so I never had that stable, suburban childhood. Coming to Havenwood has been a dream come true. Spellbooks is thriving; I'm excited about my collaboration with Mindy. Then of course, there's Bella and you. Well, I feel like my life is perfect right now."

Gabriel gently placed a finger under my chin, his touch warm and steady. He waited until I met his eyes before pressing a sweet kiss to my forehead. "You've worked hard for this. But wishes aren't just about what you need. They're about what you want." His eyes lit with warmth as he bent his head, capturing my lips in a way that left me a little breathless.

Before I could go too weak at the knees, he pulled back, his eyes twinkling as he lifted his coin. "Let me show you how it's done."

"I thought that's what you were doing already," I murmured, the words slipping out of me.

He chuckled and winked. Then he closed his eyes, made his wish, and tossed his coin into the well.

"What did you wish for?" I asked.

He smiled and wagged a finger. "Not telling. Otherwise, it won't come true."

"Fine," I grumbled.

I closed my eyes, taking a deep breath as I thought of my wish. It wasn't complicated: more time with my friends, more adventures, more joy. Smiling, I tossed my coin into the well and watched it fall, the soft splash echoing up from the darkness below.

Gabriel stepped closer, his shoulder brushing mine lightly. "Feel any different?"

I grinned. "I guess we'll have to wait and see."

He chuckled, heading back to the packs and pulling out my gloves. "Come on, let's finish what we came here for."

Together, we approached the heartwood sapling. Its delicate branches seemed to sway faintly, as if in welcome, though the air in the glade was still. There was something almost expectant about the atmosphere now, like the forest itself was holding its breath.

"I'll dig, you pour," Gabriel said, crouching beside the sapling with the trowel in hand. The soft sound of earth being turned mixed with the gentle rustle of leaves overhead.

I tilted the bottle carefully, letting the shimmering liquid spill into the trench. It soaked into the soil immediately, disappearing as though the sapling were drinking it eagerly.

Gabriel patted the dirt back into place and sat back on his heels, brushing his hands against his jeans. "There. Teamwork at its finest."

I hesitated, my gaze drawn to the sapling's smooth bark. There was something about it—a faint hum beneath my skin, a whisper in the back of my mind. My fingertips brushed against the bark, cool and smooth to the touch. The moment my palm rested fully against it, the world seemed to lurch, the vibrant glade around me dissolving into shadow.

Well, That Escalated Quickly

The forest glade wavered, the warmth of the sunlight dissolving into a haze of shadow and unease. This time, I was sure. The vision had the distinct flavor of the communication I shared with the heartwood, but this was somehow younger, like the difference between grape juice and properly aged wine. It must be the sapling trying to communicate with me. Its awareness brushed against mine like an eager, inexperienced storyteller. Its impressions were raw and vivid, like freshly painted colors that hadn't yet blended.

A man stumbled into the clearing, sagging against the edge of the wishing well. His coarse, brown jacket snagged on the ivy twisting around the rough stone. His breathing came in uneven bursts, loud enough to disturb the quiet rhythm of the glade. In his trembling hands, he clutched a cage. Light flickered off the metal bars, and within, dark, restless shapes shifted, pressed tightly against their confines, blurred and indistinct from this angle.

His movements were erratic, his legs faltering as though they could give out at any moment. He leaned heavily on the well, his knuckles white as his grip on the cage slipped. The sapling didn't understand his fear, but it registered the ripples of panic that radiated from him like a tide, flooding through the clearing.

Then came a faint sound—soft, almost imperceptible. The crunch of a leaf. A twig snapping. The man froze, his head jerking toward the noise. His breath hitched, each exhale coming sharp and shallow, almost as though he thought the very act of breathing might betray him.

The sapling detected nothing beyond the man's terror, but his fear was palpable, almost suffocating. He clutched the cage tighter, his eyes darting to the tree line, searching for something the sapling couldn't see. He took a step back—and too quickly. His boot snagged on a root.

The cage slipped from his grasp.

It struck the stone lip of the well, teetering precariously before the door sprang open, and it tumbled into the abyss. Down, down it fell, the vibrations of metal striking stone rippled through the glade, faint but jarring. The final sound, a splash followed by a faint gurgle, reverberated through the glade. Whatever had been inside was gone, swallowed by the inky darkness below.

The man staggered, his knees buckling beneath him. He lurched toward the edge of the clearing, crashing into the rough bark of a pine tree. His breath rasped, each sound more strained than the last. He stumbled into a dense thicket of evergreen bushes, their branches snagging his coat as he fell to his hands and knees.

He struggled to rise, one hand braced against the ground, the other clutching his chest. His breath slowed, faltering. He collapsed onto his side on the soft, damp earth, his body half-hidden beneath the trailing branches. For a moment, he seemed to settle, his chest rising and falling in uneven gasps.

Then he went still.

His weight shifted, toppling him fully onto his back. The evergreen branches bent under the motion, their shadows swallowing him whole. From where the sapling stood, the trees obscured the man's form entirely, as though the glade itself had taken him in.

But the glade wasn't empty.

The sapling's awareness prickled, drawn toward the well. A shimmer distorted the sunlight, bending it at an unnatural angle. Ivy curled along the stones, stirring without wind. Shifting like something unseen had brushed past.

A sudden sound broke the hush. Not quite a slap. More like the whisper of something dragging across stone. Then a voice. Hoarse. Ragged. Too close.

The presence jerked away. Footsteps crashed through the underbrush, retreating fast and leaving only the glade's oppressive silence in its wake.

The sapling strained, its awareness reaching out, desperate to understand. The ripple had vanished, the presence it hinted at now beyond its perception. The forest grew quiet once more, unnaturally so, as though every creature held its breath.

And then, breaking the stillness, came the mournful cry of a mockingbird. Its lonely call drifted across the clearing, carrying a sorrow that felt impossibly deep for a single bird.

Secrets Beneath the Branches

THE VISION SHATTERED, AND I came back to myself with a sharp gasp. The forest glade wavered, the warmth of the sunlight dissolving the haze of shadow and unease. My breath came fast and shallow as I tore my hand from the sapling's bark, stumbling back a step. My knees buckled and my pulse raced as though I'd been running for miles. The vision lingered in my mind like a vivid, unwelcome dream, refusing to fade.

"Amaryn! Harper?" Gabriel's voice was a lifeline, tugging me back towards a sense of normality. A moment later, his hands gripped my shoulders gently as he searched my face. "What's wrong? What happened?"

"I—" My voice faltered, the words stuck somewhere between my throat and my chest. I shook my head, trying to clear the lingering dread. "I'm fine. I think. Just...give me a second."

Gabriel frowned, his concern plain as he studied me. "You don't look fine. What happened? Do I need to call a doctor?" Gabriel demanded, pulling out his phone.

I placed a hand on his, forestalling the motion. "No, it's just...hard to explain."

"I've lived in Havenwood most of my life. I just told you my dad isn't exactly human. Trust me, my tolerance for strange is pretty high."

I took a shaky breath, straightening as best I could. My pulse still raced, my palms clammy as the vision replayed in fragments. "The sapling. I think it was trying to talk to me."

"Talk to you? Like the main heartwood?" Gabriel asked, his brows pulling together.

"Yes, but not the same way. That heartwood uses words that are clear and easy to understand. This was…" I paused, pressing my fingers to my temple. "I don't know. Images. Feelings. Disjointed. Overwhelming."

I glanced at the sapling, its delicate branches swaying innocently in the breeze. The contrast between its serene appearance and the dark, chaotic vision it had shown me made my stomach churn.

"What did you see?" Gabriel pressed.

I swallowed hard. "A man… He fell. Something was watching."

Gabriel's expression darkened. "That's unsettling."

"It's more than that." I rubbed my palms against my jeans. "I didn't know the saplings could do that. Remember things like that. I thought only the first one, the one we planted where the old heartwood stood, could reach out. I figured its consciousness had transferred or it was a network or something. But maybe they all have their own."

Gabriel's hand rested on my arm, his touch warm and steadying. "Maybe the original heartwood has some answers. Why don't you reach out and ask? It might be able to shed some light on the situation."

I nearly facepalmed myself. He was right, of course. It was a testament to my distraction that I hadn't even considered reaching out to the tree. I closed my eyes and turned my attention inward, reaching for the ancient presence that had become a part of me.

"Umm, heartwood? Are you there?" I asked in my mind.

"Yes, Harper. How can I help?" The familiar voice was low, ancient, and resonant.

The words tumbled out. *"This might sound strange, but I think one of the saplings tried to communicate with me. It showed me something. A vision of sorts."*

The heartwood's reply came slowly, thoughtful. *"Unusual, but not unexpected. Their connection to the ley lines accelerates their development. This communication is a sign of awareness, though still rudimentary. Images and raw emotions, not words."*

"It didn't feel rudimentary," I said. *"It was vivid. Clear."*

"Because it was a memory, not a thought," the heartwood said. *"The sapling is too young to interpret what it sees. But it can remember. Whatever it showed you left a mark. A disturbance strong enough to linger."*

I relayed the vision as best I could. The man. The fall. The sense of something watching. A silence followed, heavy and still.

Finally, the heartwood answered. *"Yes. What you saw was real."*

A chill skittered down my spine. *"So, it really happened?"*

"The sapling cannot lie. You should proceed carefully. And Harper? Be vigilant. If the saplings are this aware, they are vulnerable, too. Their growth is a gift but also a responsibility."

I opened my eyes, the heartwood's words settling uncomfortably in my mind. Gabriel stared at me, concern etched across his features. "What did it say?"

"That the saplings are growing faster than anyone expected," I said. "And that what I saw actually happened. It was a memory. A disturbing memory from the sapling I saw was most likely the tree reaching out in distress."

"Tell me more?" Gabriel asked.

Gabriel was a good listener and didn't interrupt, letting me tell the story at my pace. I sketched out the flashes I'd seen before, then described this one in detail. When I finished, my shoulders sagged, and I blew out a breath.

Gabriel brushed a loose strand of hair from my face, his touch reassuring. "That's a lot to take in. Maybe you should take a minute. Sit down, catch your breath."

"No," I said, straightening my shoulders. "If the sapling is reaching out, then we need to help it. It's my responsibility as the guardian of the heartwoods."

Gabriel glanced toward the well, his jaw tightening. "Then we need to figure out what happened here. As part of your role as guardian and to make sure the rest of Havenwood isn't in danger from this unseen presence."

The glade seemed to hold its breath as we circled the well, every sound amplified against the oppressive silence. The soft crunch of leaves beneath our boots was the only sound. My gaze swept the clearing, searching for anything—anything—to make sense of the sapling's vision. I couldn't shake the unease clinging to me, as if the vision's shadows had seeped into the air around us.

Cautiously, I put the well behind me, trying to remember the exact direction the man had gone. There was dense underbrush. He'd been running, stumbling away from the well before falling to his knees. A little spark of hope lit inside me as I scanned the empty glade. Maybe he'd gotten up and left. Perhaps the sapling's memory had just cut off before—

Then I saw it.

"Gabriel," I whispered, my voice barely audible. "Over there."

Beneath the shadow of the evergreen branches lay the unmistakable remains of a person. My breath caught in my throat as I stepped closer, the skeletal form half-hidden beneath the trailing limbs of an evergreen tree. The clothing, still intact despite the condition of the body, seemed wildly out of place. The skeleton wore a man's tweed jacket with elbow patches, khaki trousers, and polished Oxfords. Not exactly hiking attire. The forest floor around him seemed undisturbed, as though he'd simply lain down and never gotten back up.

"Oh my," The words escaped unbidden, a breathless whisper that vanished into the stillness. My hands trembled as I clenched them into fists, my nails biting into my palms in a desperate attempt to steady myself. It felt surreal, like I'd stepped into someone else's nightmare. The vision had shown me this exact moment but seeing it with my own eyes made my stomach churn.

Gabriel knelt beside the body, his expression grim. "How long do you think he's been here? For the sapling to have witnessed this, it has to be within the last month or so, right? Isn't that when you and Jeremiah transferred them all to the forest for replanting?"

"Some of them," I murmured, still staring at the remains. "Jeremiah handled a few sites on his own, especially the ones deeper in. I didn't see this glade."

That detail settled uncomfortably in my chest. I shook my head, trying to reconcile the vision. "It can't have been more than a week ago. There was no snow or frost in what I saw, and the thaw just started."

Gabriel glanced at the skeleton, his frown deepening. "Then how do we explain this? A week isn't enough time for decomposition to make it this far, is it?" He gestured toward the bones, his voice tinged with disbelief. "Even if animals got to him...it just doesn't add up."

"I don't know. It doesn't make sense. None of this makes any sense," I said, my voice shaking as I hugged my arms around myself. My knees felt weak, and I had to force myself to stay upright.

Gabriel stood, pulling out his phone. "Agreed. But we are out of our depth. We need to call the sheriff."

As he stepped away, I remained frozen in place, staring at the skeleton. My mind churned with fragments of the vision: the man's fear, the cage tumbling into darkness, the shimmer of something unseen. A whisper of wind stirred the leaves, and I shivered.

Swallowing hard, I forced myself to shift, inching around the edge of the remains. I didn't dare touch anything, but I needed answers. My stomach churned as I scanned the remains. Who was he? What was he doing out here in the middle of the woods? What had happened to him? A hint of deep purple around the neck caught my eye. It didn't match the palette of his otherwise neutral attire. Carefully, I tugged it free, revealing a lanyard with a name tag attached.

"Dr. Malcolm Fenwick, Professor of Natural Sciences at Eastford University," I murmured, my voice barely above a whisper. The photo on the badge showed a man in his early to mid-fifties, smiling into the camera and oblivious to the fate that awaited him in this glade.

The forest seemed to grow quieter, the stillness pressing in around us. The glade that had once felt serene now felt like a tomb. The vision hadn't prepared me for this. For the shock, the confusion, the unsettling stillness that clung to the clearing like a shroud. And as I stared at the remains of Dr. Fenwick, two thoughts consumed me:

What could possibly turn a man into a skeleton in less than a week? And was it still out here, waiting?

Clean Bones, Dark Shadows

I COULDN'T SHAKE THE image of the stark white skull, its surface catching glints of light like polished porcelain. It stayed with me as Gabriel guided me away from the scene, his hand warm and steady on my arm. He sat me down on the picnic blanket, kneeling in front of me with a berry tart in his hand.

"Eat," he said gently, his tone leaving no room for argument. "Sugar helps when you're...shaken up."

The tart, vibrant and sticky with juice, sat untouched in my hand. My world felt tilted, like reality itself had been knocked askew. Gabriel stepped back a few feet. I overheard him talking to someone—his mother, I thought—his voice low but urgent. Every few seconds, his gaze flicked to me, as though attempting to anchor me to the present with his concern.

But it wasn't working.

My breaths came fast and shallow, the forest edges blurring. I squeezed my eyes shut, but the image only sharpened. The white bones covered by the clothes that were still perfectly intact. How could that happen in a week? How could something that wrong exist in a place like this? The tart slipped in my fingers, syrup smearing across my palm.

"I can't…" The words barely escaped my lips.

"Harper," Gabriel's voice broke through the haze. He crouched in front of me again, his eyes searching mine. "You're okay, amaryn. Just breathe."

"I've never…" I swallowed, my throat dry. "I've never seen anything like that before. It's like…like something out of a movie."

His hands covered mine, grounding me with their warmth. I focused on the strength in his grip, willing myself to hold on to that steadiness.

"You're not alone. I'm right here," he assured me.

The heartwood stirred at the edge of my awareness, its voice like the rustling of leaves in a gentle breeze.

"He's right. You aren't alone. Let me help." The heartwood's voice was strong and confident. I leaned into that feeling, unable to even put words into a coherent sentence.

A subtle warmth spread through me, gentle and steady, like the first rays of sunlight breaking through a storm. My breaths slowed, the trembling in my hands easing as the heartwood's presence wrapped around me like a comforting embrace. Magic seeped into me, warming me from the inside out and banishing the lingering chill that had settled into my core. The tension in my chest loosened, and the shadows pressing at the edges of my vision retreated. I slowly unclenched my hands, wiping the crushed tart on the grass.

"Better?" Gabriel asked, his brow furrowed with concern as he offered me a napkin.

I nodded, my vision slowly clearing. I took the napkin and scrubbed the sticky juice from my fingers. "A little. Thank you."

"Good." He cupped my jaw and pressed a kiss to my forehead before rising. "Stay here. The sheriff will be here soon. I'm going to double-check the path to make sure he doesn't miss us."

I watched him walk away, his form disappearing behind the trees. My gaze drifted back toward the glade. It was like I couldn't stop staring at where Malcolm Fenwick's remains lay. Questions churned in my mind, chaotic and relentless. Why had he been out here in the first place? Had he been studying something—plants, wildlife, maybe even the unique microclimate that Professor Edmund Hawke had been researching just last month? Had Dr. Fenwick heard about Havenwood's strange magic and come here to investigate?

It wasn't impossible. Scientists and professors were always chasing mysteries, weren't they? Maybe he thought he'd stumbled onto something groundbreaking. But why did he bring a cage? And what had been inside it?

My gaze flicked to the wishing well. What if the professor hadn't been here for the plants or the wildlife? What if the well was the reason? The thought prickled at the edge of my mind like an itch I couldn't quite reach.

I shivered, rubbing my arms as though I could scrub away the clinging foreboding that had settled over the glade.

I forcibly turned my thoughts back to Dr. Fenwick. His skeleton looked like something out of a classroom, polished and clinical, but that just made the discovery more disturbing. If this had happened within the last week, how could he have decayed to nothing but bones so quickly? And why were his clothes still intact? Relatively clean and unweathered, like they'd been left out for a day, maybe two at most. Could something have accelerated the process? Magic, perhaps? This was Havenwood, after all.

But what refused to leave me alone—the one thought that wound itself tightly around my heart and *squeezed*—was the look on his face in the vision. That sheer, unrelenting panic. What had scared him so much? What had chased him into this glade before he collapsed?

And was it still out there?

The sound of footsteps crunching through the forest pulled my attention. Sheriff Jackson followed Gabriel into the glade, his mouth set in grim determination under his impressive moustache. His piercing eyes scanned the scene, taking everything in with quiet efficiency. It might have been my imagination or the fact that I knew the sheriff was a werewolf, but even in the daylight, he seemed to carry a dangerous edge to him, a quiet intensity that commanded attention and primally warned of the presence of a predator at the same time.

"Harper," Sheriff Jackson said, his voice low and calm. His sharp gaze captured mine, his steel-gray eyes searching. "I hear you've had quite a shock. Gabriel's filled me in. How are you holding up?"

I swallowed hard, the chill of the recent discovery still clinging to me like a second skin. Before I could answer, Gabriel appeared at my side again and offered his hand. I didn't hesitate. His fingers closed around mine, warm and steady, as he helped me to my feet.

"I'm okay," I managed, though the quaver in my voice betrayed me. I straightened, forcing myself to meet the sheriff's gaze. "I'll be fine."

The sheriff nodded, his expression unreadable, though something softened in his stance. "Good," he said. "Take it slow, though. No need to push yourself." He pulled on a pair of gloves with practiced efficiency. The sharp snap of the latex cut through the quiet of the glade, bringing things back into focus for me. "Alright, then. Show me," the sheriff commanded.

Gabriel led the way, his hand brushing mine briefly as we moved toward the clearing. I tried to focus on his steady presence, but my heart thudded in my chest as we approached the remains.

Sheriff Jackson crouched low near the skeleton, his nostrils flaring slightly as he moved closer. It was subtle—likely unnoticeable to anyone who didn't know his secret. But I did. He was using his werewolf senses. He didn't flinch or hesitate, his sharp gaze sweeping over the scene with the precision of a predator surveying its surroundings. His nostrils flared as he slowly moved along the path where Dr. Fenwick had fallen.

"Fresh clothes, no scent of decay" he muttered, more to himself than us. "Clean bones. No obvious signs of scavengers. Limited insect activity." His nostrils flared again, and his head tilted, as though listening to something beyond my perception.

Then, without warning, he dropped lower, brushing the ground with his fingers. He inhaled deeply, his movements smooth and deliberate. My pulse quickened, my mind racing. Was there something beyond our senses that the sheriff could scent?

Gabriel must've had the same thought. "Do you smell something?" he asked.

The sheriff rose slowly, his movements smooth and measured, like a wolf sensing a threat. "There's a scent," he said, his tone clipped. "Not human. Animal. Reptilian, maybe. It's faint, but it's wrong."

"Wrong?" I echoed, my stomach tightening.

"Abnormal. Strange. Something I've never smelled before, and that's saying something."

Gabriel spoke up. "What could be out here that you are unfamiliar with?"

The sheriff didn't answer immediately. Instead, he circled the spot where the skeleton lay hidden in the brush, his head tilting, nostrils flaring as he tested the air with his preternatural senses.

When he spoke again, his voice was low, almost a growl. "And it's not just the scent. Look at the bones. They're too clean. No scavenger marks, no signs of decay. No insect population boom. Nothing natural. Something strange is going on here. Not to mention the clothes."

"What about the clothes?" Gabriel prompted.

The sheriff gestured sharply. "No weathering, no tears, no sign of animals or elements. By my best guess, they haven't been out here long. A day or two, maybe three. But the bones..." He trailed off, his jaw tightening.

I swallowed hard, my eyes darting between the skeleton and the sheriff. "So...what are you saying?"

"I'm saying this doesn't add up," he said, his gaze narrowing. "It's like nature skipped a step. Or was forced to."

The words sent a chill racing down my spine. I rubbed my arms again. My gaze flicked toward the wishing well, its shadowed depths suddenly feeling alive.

"Sheriff," I said softly, "you said something about an animal scent. Could it be tied to the well? Maybe to whatever scared him?"

I didn't mention the vision. Not yet. I wasn't sure how to explain it or even if I should. He gave me a long look. Not exactly suspicious, but thoughtful. Like he knew there was more I wasn't saying. He didn't press. Just nodded, filing it away. Havenwood had its share of secrets, and he'd learned when to let them breathe.

His gaze followed mine, his expression hardening. He stepped closer to the well, his movements quiet despite the crunch of leaves beneath his boots. He sniffed the air again, this time near the stone rim, and let out an indistinct sound that was somewhere between a hum and a growl.

"Possibly," he said, turning back to us. "But whatever it is, it's long gone. For now."

"For now?" Gabriel asked, his voice sharp.

The sheriff gave Gabriel a steady look, something unreadable flickering in his eyes. "It's an old forest, Gabriel. And not everything in it plays by the rules."

A chill swept through me, though the March air had nothing to do with it. "What do you mean?" I asked, my voice quiet.

The sheriff hesitated, his eyes flicking to the well for the briefest of moments before returning to mine. "There are things...old things...tied to this forest. Most of them are long gone, or so I thought." He trailed off, his mouth pressing into a thin line. From the set of his jaw, I knew I wouldn't get any more out of him, not now anyway. The sheriff could be a stubborn man when he put his mind to it.

Gabriel frowned, his brow furrowing as he studied the sheriff. "You thought *what* was all gone?"

The sheriff didn't answer directly. Instead, he straightened, his gaze sweeping the glade as if he expected the trees themselves to respond. "I'll secure the scene and call in a forensic team," he said finally, his tone brooking no argument. "But you both need to be careful. Stay out of these woods. At least until I've had time to sort this out."

His words carried more weight than his usual caution. They felt less like a suggestion and more like a warning.

"What do you think it is?" I asked, the question escaping before I could stop myself.

His eyes met mine, sharp and piercing. "Something I hoped we'd never see again."

The sheriff turned away abruptly, his focus shifting to the task at hand as though he'd already said too much.

Gabriel stepped closer to me, his arm brushing mine. "Let's give him some space," he murmured, his voice low, but his eyes lingered on the sheriff.

As Gabriel guided me away from the clearing, my gaze drifted back to the well. Its shadowed depths seemed darker now, like they were watching, waiting.

What had scared Malcolm Fenwick so much that he'd run into this glade? What had chased him here?

Gabriel's hand settled lightly on my back, pulling me from my spiraling thoughts. "Come on," he said gently. "We'll let the sheriff do his job."

But as I followed Gabriel out of the glade, the sheriff's words echoed in my mind.

'Something I hoped we'd never see again.'

What was he talking about? It could be anything. And in a place like Havenwood, where old magic still breathed beneath the roots, things didn't always stay buried forever.

Out of the Forest, Into the Fire

THE CAR DOOR SHUT with a soft click, muffling the sound of the wind rustling through the trees. We'd left it tucked just off the old walking trail, close enough to the glade to make a relatively quick exit. I leaned back against the seat, the cool leather pressing against my shoulders, and let out a long breath I hadn't realized I'd been holding. Outside, the forest loomed, its shadows creeping closer as the afternoon sun dipped lower. Even though we were leaving it behind, it felt like the forest wasn't quite ready to let us go.

Gabriel slid into the driver's seat, his movements steady and deliberate. He glanced at me as he started the car, the low rumble of the engine breaking the silence. "Are you okay?"

I nodded, though I wasn't sure if I was trying to convince him or myself. "Yeah. Just...a lot to process." My gaze flicked to the rearview mirror, where the trees seemed to close ranks, swallowing the path we'd taken. "Let's just go."

He didn't argue, shifting the car into gear as the gravel crunched beneath the tires. The woods disappeared in the rearview mirror. I stared out the window, watching as the forest gave way to fields and scattered houses, the golden light of the afternoon sun washing over everything, but it couldn't wash away what I'd just seen.

Havenwood was supposed to be safe. A haven. But after today, I wasn't so sure.

"What if we're wrong about this place?" The question slipped out before I could stop it.

Gabriel shot me a quick glance. "Wrong how?"

I hesitated, unsure how to put it into words. "I mean, what if Havenwood isn't as safe as we thought? What if things like...that," I gestured vaguely back toward the woods, "aren't as rare as we'd like to believe?"

He frowned, his fingers tightening on the steering wheel. "Havenwood has always been different, Harper. You know that better than anyone. But it's not dangerous—not in the way you're thinking. There are unique people who live here which means strange things sometimes happen, but no one who lives in town is out to hurt anyone. Believe me."

"And what about those who don't live in town?" I asked.

Gabriel glanced in his rearview mirror. "Despite what the sheriff seemed to think, I don't know of anything truly dangerous living in the forest. Neither does my mother. I know. I checked with her. If anyone would know about a lurking threat to Havenwood or its inhabitants, it would be her. She wouldn't let anything bad happen to anyone in her town. Trust me."

I nodded, wanting to believe him. But the memory of the skeleton in the woods refused to leave me. "I just hate not knowing," I admitted. "What if whatever did that to poor Dr. Fenwick is still out there? What if it's not finished?"

Gabriel reached over, threading his fingers through mine. "Then we'll figure it out. Together."

I squeezed his hand, taking comfort in his steady presence. We drove in silence for a few minutes, the hum of the engine and the rhythmic thrum of the tires filling the space between us. The open sky felt both liberating and unsettling after the oppressive closeness of the forest. Gabriel reached over to adjust the temperature, the casual motion a small reminder that, for all the strangeness we'd just left behind, the rest of the world still existed. That normalcy was still out there—somewhere.

Finally, he broke the silence. "So, where to?"

"Eastford," I said without hesitation, my voice steadier than I expected. "Dr. Fenwick worked there. If we're going to figure out what he was doing in Havenwood, that's the place to start."

Gabriel raised a brow, eyes flicking to me before returning to the road. "You sure about this?"

I nodded, trying to sound braver than I felt. "The sheriff said to stay out of the forest. He didn't say anything about chasing leads."

Gabriel tapped the steering wheel lightly. "He didn't say anything about detours, either. I could still take you for coffee instead."

I smirked, the tension easing just a little. "Eastford isn't the forest. We could kill two birds with one stone. Coffee and a little sleuthing. Besides, what could go wrong at a university?"

Gabriel let out a low chuckle. "Famous last words."

"Don't jinx us," I muttered, though his teasing tone helped loosen the tight knot in my chest. "This is just... information-gathering. That's all. We're not chasing anything."

"Except answers," Gabriel pointed out.

"Exactly. Whatever Fenwick was doing out here, wouldn't it be better to know? What if whatever did this strikes again? If there really is something out there, it could've been you or me it attacked next. What if the next victim is a tourist? Worse, what if it's not?" My stomach dropped at the thought of discovering Bella in Dr. Fenwick's place.

"That's not going to happen," Gabriel said, threading his fingers through mine.

I took a deep breath, forcing my stomach to calm its roiling. "No. No, it's not. Because we are going to Eastford to get some answers. The sooner we can help the sheriff figure out what's going on, the sooner we can put this whole thing behind us."

"Are you sure you want to go out there now?" Gabriel asked. "We could wait until tomorrow, give ourselves time to regroup."

"No," I said, my fingers tightening around his. "I don't know about you, but I'm not great at sitting around and waiting for answers to come to me."

He smiled, the tension in his jaw easing. "And here I was hoping for a quiet evening with you."

I raised an eyebrow. "After what we just discovered, did you really think I'd sit still?"

He let out a soft laugh and gave my hand a gentle squeeze. "Not for a second. Let's go find those answers."

As we pulled onto the highway, leaving Havenwood's forested edges behind, I couldn't help but glance at the trees one last time. The shadows seemed to shift, reaching out toward us as we sped toward the neighboring town. Just a trick of the light, I told myself. Probably.

My fingers curled tighter in my lap. I hadn't been this far from the heartwood since becoming its guardian. Could it still hear me from here?

"I'm leaving town for a bit," I thought, reaching out for the thread of magic that connected us. *"Keep an eye on the saplings and on Havenwood. Let me know if anything feels off."*

The connection thinned like a stretched, shimmering thread, but it held. A pulse echoed back, a slow, steady thrum like a heartbeat in deep earth.

"I will watch."

I exhaled softly and turned to the road ahead. Whatever answers waited for us in Eastford, I just hoped they wouldn't raise even more questions.

Going Back to School

EASTFORD UNIVERSITY WAS NOTHING like I'd expected.

Maybe I'd envisioned something more like the sprawling, ivy-covered institutions I'd seen in Europe, or maybe a gothic, foreboding campus straight out of a ghost story. Given recent events, my brain had even entertained the dramatic idea of a mist-shrouded place where skeletons wandered the halls and spirits flickered in the windows.

Instead, Eastford University sprawled across several well-kept city blocks in a town only marginally larger than Havenwood. The main campus quad was alive with students enjoying the unseasonably warm March weather. The paved paths were simple but well-kept, leading past a wide, gurgling fountain that sparkled in the sunlight. A handful of students lingered around the fountain, its soft babble underscoring the casual buzz of laughter and conversation.

Somewhere to our left, a group of college students tossed a Frisbee back and forth, their laughter occasionally punctuated by shouts of encouragement or dismay. One of them threw a little too hard, and the Frisbee veered wildly off course, arcing through the air before landing squarely in the fountain with a loud splash. A few students nearby laughed, and one player threw up his hands in mock defeat before trudging over to fish it out.

The scene was so ordinary, so perfectly collegiate, that it almost made me forget why we were here.

Almost.

The academic buildings, distinctly older than the dorms, clustered together behind the main quad. The centerpiece was a four-story brick structure topped with a rounded cupola and an ancient bell tower. The old bell sat silent, but I had a feeling it had witnessed its fair share of university pranks and late-night shenanigans over the decades. The main hall's weathered facade gave it a quiet dignity. The science building sat just beyond it, although it was less ivy-clad castle and more pragmatically modern.

"Well, this is almost disappointingly normal," Gabriel said, gesturing toward the scene.

"Disappointed we didn't find a campus haunted by skeleton professors?" I teased as I tapped my phone, double-checking the map I'd pulled up during our drive. "The science building is past the bell tower and the fountain."

"Got it," Gabriel said, stepping out of the car. He stretched, scanning the quad. "But for the record, I wouldn't rule out haunted Frisbees just yet. Did you see the look on that guy's face when he realized he'd have to climb into the fountain?"

I snorted, the corner of my mouth twitching upward despite myself. "Maybe he made a wish first. Let's hope it was worth getting wet for."

Gabriel grinned, the sun catching in his eyes. "Ready to find some answers?"

"Let's do it," I said, though the playful moment didn't quite banish the nagging unease in the back of my mind. Together, we stepped onto the paved path, weaving through students as we crossed the quad. The hum of life around us was a stark contrast to the oppressive quiet of the forest earlier.

Gabriel must've noticed because he nudged me gently. "Alright, what's going on in that head of yours?"

"I don't know," I admitted. "It's just...this place feels so, well, normal. It's hard to imagine Dr. Fenwick working here and ending up in Havenwood. But if there's even a chance the university is connected, I think we should explore it. After all, it's the only lead we've got."

Gabriel gave a slow nod. "So you think there's something tying the two places together?"

I frowned, tucking my hair behind my ear. "Maybe. Or maybe I just want there to be. Something to make sense of all this."

Gabriel nodded thoughtfully, his gaze scanning the cheerful university students scattered across the campus quad. "Well, you're right about one thing—this place isn't exactly brimming with danger. If we're going to get answers, it might as well be in the safety of a science lab. At least he wasn't a professor of chemistry, so we don't have to worry about any explosions."

A small smile tugged at my lips. "You always see the silver lining."

"What are boyfriends for?" he quipped, slipping his hand into mine. "Besides, I'm not worried. What's the worst that can happen? We stumble into a lecture on the migratory patterns of squirrels?"

I laughed softly, some of the tension easing from my shoulders. "Do squirrels migrate?" I asked.

"They would if they heard of Honey DeLuca's scones," Gabriel deadpanned.

I shook my head. "Now you're tempting fate."

The science building loomed ahead, its modern glass doors a jarring contrast to the historic architecture surrounding it. Gabriel reached for the handle, pausing as he glanced back at me. His brow furrowed slightly. "You've got that look again."

"What look?" I asked.

"That 'something's bothering me, but I don't want to talk about it' look," he said, his tone gentle but pointed.

I hesitated, the weight of his question settling on my chest. "It's hard not to think about what we found," I admitted. "I've never...I mean, it wasn't even just that he was dead. It was how. It doesn't make sense."

Gabriel nodded slowly, his hand still on the door handle. "It was strange," he said, his voice quieter now. "But it's not like you were responsible for what happened to him."

I bit my lip, debating whether to tell him the truth. But I'd dragged him out here, and he deserved an answer. "Fine," I admitted. "When I tossed my coin into the wishing well, I wished for an adventure that would bring all my friends together."

Gabriel blinked at me, his expression unreadable for a moment before he asked, "And you think the wishing well responded with a dead body?"

I winced. "Okay, when you put it that way, it sounds...illogical."

He raised an eyebrow, clearly fighting back a grin. "That's putting it lightly, amaryn. But if wishing wells do work like that, then we're going to have to start vetting your wishes more carefully," he teased. "But seriously, you didn't cause this."

I nodded, his words easing some of the tension I hadn't realized I was holding. "Thanks."

"Anytime." He reached for my hand, pressing a quick kiss to my knuckles before opening the glass doors with a flourish. "Now, let's see if Eastford's science department holds the answers. After you, Detective Sullivan."

The cool, sterile air of the building greeted us, carrying the faint scent of chemicals and freshly polished floors. The hum of lab equipment buzzed faintly in the distance, underscoring the quiet scrape of our hiking boots on the tiles. A directory stood just inside the entrance, listing faculty offices and departments, its sections neatly color-coded for easy navigation.

"So, where's his office?" Gabriel asked.

I scanned the faculty directory. "Hang on. Here are the Natural Sciences...Chemistry, Biology, okay, here we go." I skimmed through the list. "Dr. Maxine Charlotte Annabelle Victoria Winterbourne...wow, that's a name. Then Dr. Malcolm Fenwick, Ecology, Room 307."

We climbed the staircase to the third floor, passing doors labeled with bold caution signs: LIVE SPECIMENS INSIDE, BIOHAZARD MATERIALS, and one ominous DO NOT ENTER WITHOUT AUTHORIZATION. The faint smell of something vaguely antiseptic mixed with the tang of metal, reminding me we were in a space where experiments weren't just encouraged—they were the main event.

As we reached the ecology department, a sleek directory sign listed the names and titles of all the professors in easy-to-read rows. Gabriel squinted at Dr. Fenwick's name in the middle of the list. "What does 'Professor of Applied Ecological Systems' even mean?" he asked.

Before I could reply, the sound of measured footsteps approached. A woman appeared, her crisp white lab coat tailored to perfection over a sleek black sheath dress. Her heels, tall but practical, clicked rhythmically against the tile, the only sound in the quiet corridor. She carried a stack of notebooks, each perfectly aligned, and her sharp, no-nonsense gaze swept over us from behind a pair of understated but elegant glasses. Her polished appearance matched the air of authority she radiated, as though she'd never encountered a question she couldn't answer.

"Applied ecological systems," she said in a tone dripping with academic superiority, "is the study of ecosystems, species interactions, and how organisms adapt to environmental challenges."

I blinked. "Uh...thanks."

The woman studied us pointedly. "You don't look like students."

"That's because we aren't. We're, um, associates of Dr. Fenwick," I said, stumbling over the words. Lying really wasn't my thing.

"Associates, hmm? How come he's never mentioned you before?" the woman asked cautiously, looking between us.

"We're fairly recent acquaintances," Gabriel said smoothly. "And you are?"

The woman narrowed her eyes and then shifted the notebooks to the crook of her left arm. "Dr. Winterbourne," she said, extending her free hand.

"Gabriel Silverthorne," he replied. "And this is Harper Sullivan."

"Nice to meet you," I said, shaking hands as well. "We're looking for Dr. Fenwick's office. Do you know where that is?"

Dr. Winterbourne sniffed. "If you're looking for him, I don't think he's in. He missed this morning's classes, and I had to cover for him at the last minute. As if I could afford to hold the hands of undergrads at the moment with my busy schedule," she said, drumming her fingers on the stack of notebooks in her arms. "If you find him, tell him to report to my office immediately."

"That must be frustrating. If we see him, we'll pass on the message," Gabriel said sympathetically.

"Speaking of messages, we might just slip one under his office door if he's not in. You know, to let him know we stopped by," I said, hoping I hit the tone just right so as not to arouse Dr. Winterbourne's suspicions. "Could you point us in the right direction please?"

Dr. Winterbourne tipped her head down the hall. "Two doors down on your left. You can't miss it." She gave us a polite smile before continuing on her way, her heels clicking noisily against the tile.

Gabriel and I exchanged glances. "That was surprisingly easy," I murmured.

"Don't jinx it," he whispered back.

We followed the hall as directed and immediately understood what Dr. Winterbourne had meant. Dr. Fenwick's office was impossible to miss. While the other doors in the corridor were plain and utilitarian, his space was a burst of organized chaos. Photos, maps, and display boards plastered the wall outside his door almost like an impromptu museum of his career.

Snapshots of him with rare animals, often in exotic, far-flung locations, vied for space with maps covered in scrawled notes. He smiled in jungles, deserts, frozen tundras, and even what looked like a cavern filled with bioluminescent fungi. Pinned to one corner of the wall was a laminated article titled The Eco-Trailblazer: Malcolm Fenwick's Quest to Save the Rare and Forgotten.

Gabriel let out a low whistle. "Looks like he was a big deal in his field."

I nodded, my eyes scanning the collage. "He must've traveled constantly. Do you think these are all his students or colleagues?"

"Possibly both." Gabriel gestured at a photo near the center. "That one looks important."

The picture he indicated featured Malcolm posing with an older woman in rugged expedition gear. They stood in what appeared to be a dense rainforest, the woman holding up a clipboard with a triumphant grin.

"Maybe his research partner or mentor?" I guessed. The caption beneath the photo read: Dr. Fenwick and Dr. Bethany Langley, tracking endangered amphibians in the Amazon Basin.

"Well, at least he wasn't boring," Gabriel remarked, scanning the wall. "But I can't tell if he was brilliant or just couldn't sit still."

"Probably both," I said, stepping closer to the door itself. The nameplate read Dr. Malcolm Fenwick, Professor of Natural Sciences. I reached for the handle, only to find it locked.

"Figures," Gabriel said. "Looks like we're not getting in this way."

"Well, the note under the door won't do us any good either. It's not like he's around to receive it," I pointed out.

"Fair enough. What do you suggest then?" Gabriel asked.

I held up my hand and wiggled my fingers at him. "Magic."

Gabriel blew out a breath, running a hand through his hair. Finally, he nodded. "I don't see a better option. Go ahead but make it quick. I don't want to get caught breaking and entering."

I nodded, placing my hand on the doorknob and drawing on my metal magic. Gabriel turned his back to me, scanning the hallway for signs of anyone approaching.

"Hurry up," he muttered under his breath, his eyes flicking between the empty corridor and me.

"I'm trying," I whispered back, my focus on the lock. "It's not exactly cooperating."

The lock was surprisingly intricate, far more complex than I'd expected for a university office. Typically, these locks were about as sophisticated as the ones you'd find on a bathroom door. Pretty basic and easy to bypass. This one, however, was stubborn, its tumblers resisting my magic as if they had a will of their own.

"Harper," Gabriel half-sang, half-whispered, his tone urgent. The sound of footsteps caught my ear. And they were getting closer.

"One second," I whispered, closing my eyes to concentrate fully. With my magic, I felt the internal mechanics, nudging and prodding until the tumblers reluctantly gave way, one by one.

Finally, there was a satisfying click.

"Got it," I said with a note of triumph, stepping back just as Gabriel let out a low curse.

"Hi there," Gabriel said brightly, his tone suddenly cheerful.

I turned sharply, following his gaze down the hallway to see a woman striding toward us with quick, purposeful steps. She wore a slightly rumpled blazer over a button-down shirt, paired with practical loafers that tapped softly against the floor. Her short-cropped hair framed angular features, her sharp eyes darting between Gabriel, me, and the door with an expression of guarded suspicion. The way she clutched a thick stack of papers and a tablet suggested she was perpetually in motion, juggling a thousand tasks at once, each more pressing than the last.

"Can I help you?" she asked, her tone clipped and wary.

I put on my best disarming smile, gesturing toward the door. "We were looking for Dr. Fenwick, but when we knocked, there wasn't an answer. Have you seen him, by chance?"

Her eyes narrowed slightly. "Dr. Fenwick hasn't been in today," she said, glancing pointedly at the doorknob I was still holding. "And who, exactly, are you?"

I hesitated for a split second, caught off guard by her intensity, but Gabriel stepped in smoothly, his voice warm and professional. "We recently became aware of Dr. Fenwick's work here and wanted to have a word with him if possible. I'm Gabriel Silverthorne."

Her brow shot up at the name, the faintest glimmer of recognition passing over her face. "Silverthorne," she repeated. "As in *Vivienne* Silverthorne?"

Gabriel inclined his head, the corner of his mouth lifting in a polite smile. "She's my mother."

The tension in her posture melted almost immediately. "Dr. Elise Harlow," she said, shaking his hand. "Vivienne Silverthorne. Now there's a name. I've read some of her work. Brilliant mind." She glanced at me, her tone turning a touch more curious. "And you are?"

"Harper Sullivan," I said, offering a friendly nod. "I own Sullivan's Spellbooks in Havenwood."

Her eyes flicked between us, curiosity sparking behind her glasses. "Spellbooks," she murmured, her tone softening. "I've heard of that place. A bookshop that trades in magical tomes, isn't it?"

"Among other things," I replied lightly, keeping my tone casual and trying to hide my surprise. Although if Dr. Harlow knew of Vivienne Silverthorne, it stood to reason she was aware of the magical world as well.

Dr. Harlow glanced down the hallway as if ensuring no one else was listening, then leaned in slightly. "I rarely talk about this openly," she said in a hushed tone. "There are a handful of us who work with magical research, but we keep a low profile. Most of the faculty aren't aware, and those who are tend to look the other way."

Gabriel's expression softened. "You don't have to worry with us. My family's been involved in magical studies for generations. As has Harper's." He gestured toward me. "Havenwood isn't exactly known for being mundane."

A hint of a smile tugged at her lips, and for the first time, she looked at ease. "I know. It's refreshing to have an open conversation," she said, almost wistfully. "Most people here wouldn't know a spell circle from a coffee ring. It gets lonely, keeping that part of yourself hidden. But Dr. Fenwick understands. He isn't just a scientist, you see. He's a wizard. One of the best I've ever met."

I blinked. "A wizard?" Somehow, I hadn't expected the revelation to sound so ordinary with the backdrop of the completely normal science lab.

Dr. Harlow nodded. "A brilliant one. His gifts aren't flashy, but he found power in his methodical processes. He believes that blending magic and science could uncover answers no one else would've imagined. It's why I came here to work with him. My gift is minor, barely enough to matter by comparison, but he saw potential in me."

She exhaled slowly, worry unmistakable in her expression. "He's usually such a presence around here. For him to just disappear, it's...unsettling. I tried to report it, but they brushed it off. Apparently, adults have the right to go missing for a day if they want to. I couldn't exactly add that he's a wizard without sounding unhinged. Most people think he's playing hooky or out sick, but I'm worried. Especially now."

"Why is that?" I asked.

Dr. Harlow worried the strap of her lanyard between her fingers. "I don't know. It's just a feeling. He wouldn't leave without saying something. Not without a reason. And there's no one else I can really talk to."

"Well, you don't have to keep this to yourself anymore. We're happy to help if we can," Gabriel said firmly.

Her shoulders sagged slightly, the weight of her guardedness visibly lifting. "I appreciate that," she said quietly. "Really, I do."

Gabriel nodded toward the door. "Would it be possible to talk somewhere more private? It might help us understand what's been going on. Especially if you could fill us in on what he's been working on."

"Of course. Follow me," Dr. Harlow said, spinning on her heel as she tugged her purple lanyard up, fumbling with a small keychain hanging behind her ID. She led us down the hall and to a lab, using not only her badge and a fingerprint but also a small key to open the door.

I pointed at the security system. "Isn't that a little over the top for a university lab?" I asked.

"Just wait until you see what's inside," Dr. Harlow replied, pushing the door wide.

What I saw next took my breath away.

A Lab of Curiosities

Dr. Fenwick's lab was a mesmerizing blend of science and magic, a space that seemed to defy conventional academia. The moment I stepped inside, the room opened up like a living diorama of ecosystems from around the world. Bioluminescent terrariums lined the walls, glowing with an ethereal blue-green light. Each tank contained vibrant miniature habitats. There were lush rainforests, arid deserts, and misty wetlands, each teeming with fantastical animals I'd never seen before.

To my left, an enormous cylindrical tank stretched from floor to ceiling, filled with crystal-clear water. Inside, shimmering silver fish darted between coral structures, their fins trailing iridescent streams of light. They moved in perfect synchronization, their motions almost hypnotic. Perched near the top of the tank was a sleek, otter-like creature with silvery fur that rippled like liquid metal. It turned its head toward us, its intelligent golden eyes locking onto mine before it dove effortlessly into the water.

Suspended above us, glowing orbs floated like weightless lanterns, each containing tiny, fluttering winged creatures that might have been a cross between hummingbirds and fairies. Their wings left glittering trails in the air, like stardust, as they flitted between the orbs.

Long worktables dominated the center of the lab, covered in papers, diagrams, and jars filled with preserved specimens. Some jars held creatures that were distinctly mundane. One held a toad, and another contained a newt. One jar contained a tiny glowing sea star that shimmered faintly even underwater. Another housed a translucent spider the size of a quarter, its web glimmering with threads of liquid silver.

In the far corner of the lab, a massive glass enclosure took up an entire wall. Inside was a dense jungle of vines and moss-covered branches, home to a group of small, six-legged creatures resembling lizards but with feather-like frills along their spines. One of them skittered up a tree trunk, its frills vibrating slightly as it emitted a melodic trill that reverberated softly through the room.

"What are these?" Gabriel asked, his voice low with awe.

Dr. Harlow smiled faintly, gesturing to the various enclosures. "This is Dr. Fenwick's collection of magical and mundane hybrids. The smaller specimens are part of his controlled breeding experiments, while the larger ones are more advanced projects. He always said his goal was to explore the limits of coexistence between the magical and non-magical worlds."

I hesitated. There was something unsettling about the way she'd phrased that, even if her tone was admiring. Looking around, it felt a little like I was looking at a mad scientist's lab meets magical menagerie, and I couldn't decide if it was cool or creepy. Maybe both.

A smaller, reinforced enclosure stood to one side, separate from the others. Its glass walls were thick, with intricate runes etched along the edges that shimmered faintly with protective magic. Inside, a trio of long, sinuous creatures that looked like they were half snake, half earthworm coiled together in restless motion.

"What are these?" I asked, crouching to get a better look at the animals.

"Wyrms," Dr. Harlow said, her voice tinged with a mix of pride and frustration. "W-y-r-m-s. No relation to the earthworm, although I always thought there was a little bit of a physical resemblance. No, these creatures are related to dragons, if you can believe it. Although they're more scavenger than predator. They're fascinating creatures. Efficient, nearly indestructible, but also incredibly difficult to work with."

They looked like serpents at first glance, their sleek, scaled bodies shimmering in hues of brown and gold that seemed to shift as they moved. But their heads were more dragon-like, with small horns curling back from their skulls and ridged jaws that opened briefly to reveal rows of needle-like teeth. As one wyrm slithered toward the edge of the enclosure, its tongue flicked out, tasting the air. It fixed its eyes, which were a luminous, unsettling shade of orange, directly on me.

I shivered and took a step back. "What makes them so challenging?" I asked, unable to look away from the wyrm.

"They eat almost anything," Dr. Harlow said with a sigh. "Organic matter, non-organic matter...if you leave it in there long enough, they'll find a way to consume it. But their preferred diet is meat. Dr. Fenwick liked to say they're nature's cleanup crew. A clutch of wyrms can strip the flesh from a bull in a matter of hours."

I swallowed hard, glancing at the reinforced glass. "That's, uh...efficient." I said, trying not to wince. "If they'll eat anything, how do you keep them from chewing through the enclosure?" My mind flashed back to the skeleton in the woods. "Or...um...other things?"

Dr. Harlow gave a small, distracted shrug. "They have preferences. Flesh is easiest for them to digest. Plastic, metal, fabric, and even bone takes longer and seems to provide less nutrients for them. But they will eat anything if they're hungry enough."

I glanced back at the shimmering runes etched into the thick glass. "And this case is enough to keep them in?"

She followed my gaze, her expression unreadable. "They're magically reinforced. Dr. Fenwick designed the wards himself."

"Still unnerving," I murmured.

Dr. Harlow nodded. "You get used to them. Sort of. But that's also what makes them so difficult to breed. Every time Dr. Fenwick attempted to pair them with another species, they consumed their mate before anything could happen. He's been focused on trying to harness their potential without the...complications."

Gabriel raised an eyebrow. "And the university allows him to conduct experiments like this here? With magical creatures?"

Dr. Harlow hesitated, then nodded. "Dr. Fenwick has an incredible reputation in both magical and mundane academic circles. He is meticulous about keeping his projects legal and ethical, and he's careful to frame his work as ecological research with potential humanitarian benefits. As long as he operates within those guidelines, the powers that be here at the university are content to look the other way."

Gabriel frowned, obviously not liking the answer. "And this was his main project?"

"For the past few months, yes," Dr. Harlow replied. "He believes the wyrms could be the solution to the world's waste problem. Imagine a creature that can consume landfill waste and leave behind something harmless or even useful." She gestured toward a digital display showing data about their metabolic processes. "If he succeeds, it could revolutionize waste management."

On the far wall, a digital display cycled through data on several ongoing experiments. One screen played a simulation of a modified wyrm hybrid breaking down a plastic bottle into shimmering particles of harmless energy. Another screen displayed a rotating 3D model labeled "waste-clearing hybrid," showcasing an ambitious project aimed at solving global pollution by engineering a creature capable of metabolizing waste into benign, even beneficial, byproducts.

"But he wasn't making much progress?" I pressed gently.

Her shoulders sagged slightly. "Not as much as he hopes. He gets frustrated, but he refuses to give up. He keeps saying the potential outweighs the setbacks."

"This lab is incredible, but working on something like this also might be risky, right?" I said, glancing again at the wyrms.

Dr. Harlow nodded. "Dr. Fenwick is always cautious. He understands the risks better than anyone, which is why he always pairs magical creatures with mundane ones. It ensures the hybrids can't reproduce, so any experiment has an expiration date. He calls it his 'fail-safe.'"

"Sounds lonely," I observed, considering the creatures in the lab in a new light.

"But smart," Gabriel added.

"And necessary," Dr. Harlow confirmed. "No one wants a dragon-chimera hybrid set loose on the world. Or a manticore-kraken mix."

"I certainly don't," Gabriel said.

"How many people are doing this kind of work?" I asked, trying to sound casual. My gaze lingered on a large, iridescent spider in a nearby enclosure, its many eyes glittering as though it were watching me.

"Not many," Dr. Harlow replied, her tone both proud and defensive. "This isn't exactly a mainstream field. Most researchers stay within established lines of study that are safer, more predictable. But Dr. Fenwick has a boldness that sets him apart. People respect him for it, even if it makes him a target for misunderstandings."

The word hung in the air like a warning, and I couldn't help but glance at Gabriel. He gave the faintest shake of his head, silently telling me to tread carefully.

"What kind of misunderstandings?" I asked.

Dr. Harlow shifted, her voice softening. "He's a pioneer, a genius. I was honored to get the opportunity to work with him."

Gabriel raised an eyebrow. "I imagine not everyone was thrilled about his methods?"

Dr. Harlow nodded. "Some aren't. Crossing magical and mundane species isn't illegal, exactly, but it's...controversial. It's risky. But Dr. Fenwick doesn't believe in limiting himself. He thinks magic and science should push boundaries, not obey them. However, the last time someone tried, it ended with..." She trailed off, her fingers tightening around the edge of a desk.

"What happened?" I asked as a chill ran down my spine.

She sighed. "Let's just say the result was... catastrophic. It created something so destructive that it took a coordinated effort to contain and neutralize it. But Dr. Fenwick isn't reckless. He knows the limits."

Her words hung in the air, tinged with both admiration and uncertainty. I couldn't shake the feeling that, for all the promise of this lab, there were shadows lurking beneath the surface—questions and risks that no amount of caution could entirely dispel.

Dwarves Don't Do Desk Jobs

Elise led us out of Dr. Fenwick's lab, her expression strained but polite. Gabriel and I both promised to reach out if we discovered anything useful about the professor's work, and Elise thanked us with a distracted nod.

Just as we stepped into the hallway, the sound of hurried footsteps echoed behind us, followed by a muffled, "Wait! Wait!"

Before any of us could react, Officer Reggie barreled down the hall, clipboard clutched to his chest. He skidded to a stop but not before nearly colliding with Gabriel, who had to grab the wall to steady himself. Reggie's hat tipped precariously forward, and he fumbled to straighten it, his face flushed.

"Oh! Hey!" Reggie exclaimed, visibly relieved to have caught up with us. "Good catch, Gabriel. Sorry about that. These shoes aren't great for traction." He grinned sheepishly, patting his chest to calm himself. "I didn't expect to see you here. Are you testing out your shoes for traction too?" The police officer eyed Gabriel's hiking boots. "Those look like they'd give great traction."

"They do," Gabriel said with a chuckle.

"You two know each other?" Dr. Harlow asked as she took in the disheveled officer.

Gabriel clapped Officer Reggie on the shoulder. "This fine man is a member of the Havenwood Police Department. Officer Reggie, may I introduce Dr. Elise Harlow. Dr. Harlow, Officer Reggie."

Reggie's eyes went wide. "You're Dr. Harlow? Assistant to Dr. Fenwick?"

Elise blinked, her brow furrowing. "Yes, that's correct. Can I help you with something?"

"Well..." Reggie flipped open his notepad with exaggerated care, almost dropping it in the process. "I've been sent over to check in on the situation up here. Something about a missing professor?"

Dr. Harlow blinked, her brow furrowing. "Yes, that's right. But I thought the police couldn't open an investigation this soon."

The officer puffed up proudly. "I'm here on Sheriff Jackson's specific orders. He even asked me to follow up in person." I could read between the lines of this particular assignment. Either Sheriff Jackson didn't have anyone else he could trust at this hour, or he didn't think investigating Fenwick's research would lead anywhere. Officer Reggie was notorious for being sweet and bumbling in equal measure. Given that Sheriff Jackson's other officers were a centaur named Bill, who didn't fit in a squad car, and a vampire named Johanna, who seemed to get crankier in direct correlation to how much sunlight there was, I was leaning towards the former.

Sensing an opportunity, I gave Reggie my brightest smile. "Officer, it sounds like you could use some privacy to speak with Dr. Harlow. Gabriel and I will just step out of your way."

Reggie blinked, momentarily distracted. "Oh, uh, sure. But hang on, do you see my pencil? I could've sworn I brought one with me." He patted himself all over, searching for the lost writing implement.

"Here you go," Gabriel said smoothly, stepping forward and plucking it from behind Reggie's ear before handing it back to the scatterbrained police officer.

"Aw, thanks a million! The sheriff always says I'd forget my head if it wasn't attached. I told him that if he was so worried about it, maybe I should find a way to wear my pencil too. He always walks away, muttering something about temptations, but I never understand what he's talking about."

"Don't worry about it too much," Gabriel said, clapping him on the shoulder. "You know how the sheriff can be."

"Don't I just! He's getting grumblier by the week. Dr. Harlow, quick question! Where can a fella get a good cup of coffee around here?"

"Does that have to do with the investigation?" Dr. Harlow asked in surprise.

"Maybe. You never know where you'll uncover a lead," Reggie said, shooting her a wink and tapping the side of his nose. "Follow up question, you work with that Dr. Max lady too, right?"

Dr. Harlow paused mid-step, her brow furrowing. "Dr. Max?"

"Yeah, the boss of the department?" Reggie nodded enthusiastically. "She was on the contact list too, but I haven't found her yet."

Dr. Harlow's expression shifted to one of mild exasperation. "Oh, you mean Dr. Winterbourne. And for the record, she prefers Charlotte to Maxine. I don't think anyone has ever dared to call her Dr. Max before. Between us, I'd strongly advise sticking with 'Dr. Winterbourne' unless you're particularly brave."

Reggie chuckled nervously. "Got it. Dr. Winterbourne it is."

Dr. Harlow's polite demeanor wavered as she smiled tightly. "Officer Reggie, why don't we continue this conversation in the staff lounge? It's more comfortable, and I can grab you that coffee you mentioned."

Reggie brightened immediately. "Now that's hospitality! I knew I'd come to the right place."

"This way," the research assistant said, gesturing down the hall. Her clipped tone left little room for argument, but Reggie seemed oblivious, falling into step beside her with his usual cheerful enthusiasm.

As they turned the corner, Reggie started patting his pockets again. "Oh, no! Sorry, one more thing! I've got a whole list of questions from the sheriff. Probably in my other notebook...which I think I left in the squad car."

Dr. Harlow gave a tight smile. "Let me help you find that notebook, shall I?"

"That'd be swell! Thanks," Reggie said cheerfully as they headed down the hall away from us.

I forced a bright smile and gave them a little wave, but my stomach was doing slow, uneasy flips. Why hadn't Sheriff Jackson told Reggie to announce Dr. Fenwick's death?

Gabriel must've sensed my unease too, because as soon as they disappeared around the corner, he murmured under his breath, "Let's not linger."

"Agreed," I said, spinning on my heel and hurrying in the opposite direction.

Gabriel sighed, matching my pace. "Reggie, Reggie, Reggie." He shook his head. "He's such a nice guy. Why did he become a cop?"

I shrugged. "It doesn't seem like the best fit. I think he'd be much better suited to something else. Like the library. I bet he'd make a great librarian."

Gabriel laughed. "He'd drive Martha crazy. He'd put cookbooks next to history books and romances in non-fiction."

I laughed too. "I can see it now."

Gabriel's grin faded. "He's a good man. Great at festivals and parades. But..."

"Not the best detective," I finished for him.

"Exactly," he said, staring down the empty hallway at where Reggie and Dr. Harlow had disappeared.

I glanced at Gabriel, feeling a mischievous spark. "Come on," I whispered, tugging his hand.

"What are you doing?" he hissed.

"Now's our chance," I said, hurrying to Dr. Fenwick's office. "I unlocked it earlier, remember? We've already done the hard part."

"Harper, this is a bad idea," Gabriel warned.

"Given what we just learned about his research, do you want to leave his office unlocked?" I asked.

"Well, no," Gabriel admitted, his resistance wavering.

"Exactly," I said. "Come on. There might be a clue inside."

"Harper!"

But I slipped through the door. I heard Gabriel grunt, but he followed me a moment later.

The office was dark and musty like it hadn't been aired out in quite some time. It smelled faintly of old parchment and something earthy, like damp moss. The door clicked softly shut behind us, and Gabriel muttered under his breath.

A gruff voice barked from across the room. "Hey! What are you doing here?"

I jumped, startled, and spun to see a short, stocky figure step from the shadows behind the desk. He was barely half my height, burly despite his stature, with long hair tied back in a low ponytail and a beard reaching halfway down his chest. He reminded me of Mason Forham, Havenwood's dwarven auto mechanic, gruff but good-natured. This newcomer? There was no warmth in his sharp gaze, just suspicion. Hands planted firmly on his hips, he sized us up like we were intruders in his territory.

"The professor isn't here," he said, his tone sharp. "What're you two kids doing, sneaking around like this?"

"Who are you?" I asked, still recovering from the shock.

"Name doesn't matter much," he replied, his voice gruff. "What matters is Fenwick ain't here, and you two need to go."

Something about him put me on edge. Gabriel must have sensed it too because he spoke up, his tone even but laced with subtle authority. "Actually, we're here for a meeting with Dr. Fenwick."

The man crossed his arms, unimpressed. "He ain't here, so maybe you should try coming back later."

"It's really important we talk to him," I said. "If we miss him, it could cause some serious complications."

The man narrowed his eyes. "Well, I ain't seen him. And I don't know why you're pokin' around here like you own the place. What makes you think I know where he is?"

"Because you're in his office," I shot back. "Are you his secretary or something?"

He barked out a laugh. "Runar Ironvein is nobody's secretary," he said, clearly offended. "And I don't do desk jobs. Do I look like that kind of guy?" He waved at himself with two large, calloused hands. I had to hand it to him. He looked more like he could be a lumberjack than a secretary, but looks could be deceiving.

Gabriel smiled politely, though there was an icy edge to it. "If Dr. Fenwick isn't here, perhaps we should all go talk to Dr. Winterbourne. She might know where he is, and I'm sure she'd be curious to hear what brought you to his office."

At the mention of Dr. Winterbourne, Runar stiffened. He scooped up some loose papers from Fenwick's desk, shoving them haphazardly into his bag. Others scattered across the desk, a few fluttering to the floor. He muttered a sharp curse, snatching up what he could easily reach. His movements were frantic, almost panicked. Then he barreled across the room and elbowed past us without so much as a glance. The dwarf yanked the door open and bolted into the hall, boots pounding against the tile.

"Well, that was suspicious," I said, staring at the disarray he'd left behind.

Gabriel locked the door behind him and turned to me. "Let's see if we can figure out what he was looking at."

"Hey, I thought you were against snooping," I teased.

"I'm against breaking and entering," Gabriel corrected. "But since we're already in, we might as well make it count."

Dr. Fenwick's desk was an exercise in precision. The pencils were perfectly aligned, and their tips were sharpened to a uniform point. A row of pens was organized by color, and neatly stacked folders filled the file organizer.

All of which made the scattered papers stand out in stark contrast. They looked like receipts and were spread across the desk in a messy fan, a few lying crumpled on the floor where Runar had dropped them.

"These must've been what Runar was looking at, but why?" I murmured, snapping a photo with my phone.

"What are they for? Maybe that will give us a clue." Gabriel said from where he was scanning books on the bookshelf.

I sorted through the slips, organizing them by date. "Looks like purchases for lab supplies. Animal feed, terrarium parts, that sort of thing."

Gabriel moved beside me, peering at the papers. "Let me have a look," he said.

As Gabriel flipped through the receipts, I turned slowly in place, scanning the office. It was neat. Almost too neat. But someone had definitely been here. Was it Runar Ironvein or someone else?

One of the lower desk drawers sat just slightly ajar. A folder inside was crooked, like it had been shoved back in hastily. The chair near the bookcase was pulled out at an odd angle, and while the teacup on the side table was stone cold, a faint scuff broke through the thin layer of dust nearby. Not much, but enough to say someone had stood there. Recently.

And unless Dr. Fenwick had returned from the grave to make himself a midnight snack and forgotten to clean up after, that someone wasn't him.

My gaze landed on the bookcase. I straightened and frowned. The office was immaculate. Everything was squared, sorted, catalogued. Which made the gap on the shelf behind the chair even more obvious. Several books were missing, yanked out so hastily that the ones on either side had tilted inward.

My stomach twisted. Someone had taken them. Was that someone Ironvein? The coincidence was too great to overlook. He must've capitalized on the open door. I swallowed hard. That one was on me. But why would he have taken the books? What was so important about them?

"Wait," Gabriel said, reaching down. "There's another receipt on the floor."

I hurried over as Gabriel smoothed it out on the desk. The paper was crumpled at the corner, and the upper corner was jagged, like it had been ripped free of a larger stack. The date was recent, but the item line had been heavily scratched out with dark ink.

"Do you think this is important?" I asked.

"Possibly," Gabriel flicked the torn corner with his finger.

"Then maybe it'll give us a clue." I read the vendor's name aloud. "Northvale Exports. And—wow—that's a lot of money." I tapped the total. "Hey, look here, under the memo. It says, 'new subjects.' Do you think this has something to do with his wyrms?"

"That's a good theory. Maybe it will give us some insight into Fenwick's work," Gabriel said.

I snapped a photo of the receipt. "Have you ever heard of Northvale Exports?"

Gabriel frowned. "Nope. But we can run an internet search when we're out of here. For now, let's get out before someone catches us."

"Good plan," I said, stuffing my phone back in my pocket. Gabriel opened the door and peeked into the hallway.

"The coast is clear," he whispered. "How fast can you relock it?"

"Faster than I unlocked it," I assured him.

We slipped out, and I quickly secured the door. Gabriel took my hand. I expected him to run away as fast as we could. Instead, we strolled casually down the hallway as if we didn't have a care in the world.

"Don't we want to hurry?" I whispered.

"Nope," Gabriel murmured, nodding in greeting as an academic-looking man glanced up at us once and then back down at his papers. "Running makes you look guilty and draws attention. The trick is to look like you belong. Like you have every right to be where you are."

Despite my heart thundering loudly in my ears, I matched his steady pace, walking casually down the halls of the university science building. He was right. No one looked twice at us.

Once we were outside, I exhaled a shaky breath. "Do you think anyone noticed? Do they have security cameras? I didn't even think to check."

"I didn't either, but it's too late now," Gabriel said with a little shrug. "We'll have to cross our fingers that they don't have a reason to go back through the security footage. However, I definitely want to know more about Runar Ironvein and his connection to Dr. Fenwick."

"Agreed," I said. "And figure out what his interest is in this Northvale Export place."

"And we should call the sheriff to fill him in on what we found," Gabriel added.

"Couldn't we leave the update to Officer Reggie?" I suggested. The sheriff could be gruff at the best of times, and I didn't want to get on his bad side, especially if he thought we were poking our noses into his investigation.

Gabriel shook his head grimly. "Although he's a good man, I wouldn't put it past Reggie to forget more than just his notebook. Letting the sheriff know what we found can only help him sort out the mess."

"I suppose you're right," I said, even though my stomach was doing little flip-flops at the thought of calling the sheriff to tell him we'd been snooping around.

We walked across the university quad, the warm sunlight doing little to calm the nervous energy coursing through me. Students lounged in clusters on the grass, completely oblivious to the tangled mess surrounding Dr. Fenwick.

"Do you think Runar's connected to Dr. Fenwick's disappearance?" I finally asked, glancing at Gabriel.

"Possibly," he said. "But if he is, I doubt he's working alone. He doesn't strike me as the type to be interested in academia. If he's involved, I'm betting someone else is pulling strings. But if Fenwick was dealing with questionable types like Runar Ironvein, it's not hard to imagine a few grudges along the way."

I frowned, replaying the encounter with Runar in my mind. "He was nervous the moment you mentioned Dr. Winterbourne. Why do you think that is?"

"Could be anything," Gabriel replied, his voice low. "She's Fenwick's boss. Perhaps she has connections here at the university. Maybe he just didn't want to be noticed. Whatever it is, I think we need to pass his name onto the sheriff. There may be something going on here, something more than meets the eye."

"Like what?"

"I'm not sure yet. Perhaps someone was after Fenwick's research or even the man himself."

The thought sent a chill up my spine. Whatever was going on, this wasn't random. I doubted Fenwick hadn't just wandered into the woods and died. Someone might've wanted him gone.

"I'll call Sheriff Jackson as soon as we're back on the road," Gabriel said, breaking into my thoughts. "But I think we need to follow this receipt trail. Whoever sold Fenwick those supplies might know what he was working on."

"And what he was working on might tell us why someone wanted him out of the way," I added.

Gabriel nodded, his expression grim. "Exactly. At the very least, we need to figure out why Runar was so interested in that particular receipt from Northvale Exports."

As we reached the car, I glanced back at the sprawling campus. The picture-perfect image of student life clashed with the growing sense of unease in my chest. Something was brewing beneath the surface; I was certain. But how to uncover it?

Sliding into the passenger seat, I pulled out my phone. "Let's split up the tasks," I said. "You call the sheriff, and I'll see if I can track down that distributor online. With any luck, we'll have something concrete by the time we get back to Havenwood."

Gabriel started the car, the engine purring to life. "Good plan. And Harper?"

"Yeah?"

"Let's keep this between us for now," he said, his tone serious. "The fewer people involved, the better."

I nodded. This wasn't just about finding answers anymore. It was about justice. Whoever was behind this wasn't just clever. They were dangerous.

As we pulled away from the university, students wandered past the entrance, laughing and clutching coffee cups like nothing was wrong.

I pressed a hand to my chest, trying to slow the nervous flutter in my ribcage. Breaking into Dr. Fenwick's office, stumbling across an angry dwarf, rifling through secret research—

I sank back in my seat, but the unease didn't budge. My gut told me this wasn't just about one professor or a few dusty files. Something was shifting beneath the surface.

And I had the sinking feeling we'd just kicked a hornet's nest.

Snoop First, Apologize Later

As Gabriel merged into traffic heading for the highway and Haven-wood, I tapped on my phone, searching for leads on the receipt we'd found in Dr. Fenwick's office.

"Oh!" The surprised sound escaped me almost involuntarily.

Gabriel glanced over at me. "What is it?"

I swiped through the limited results. "Northvale Exports has no web-site. Just a shady-looking listing and a phone number. That's not normal. Who doesn't have a website these days?"

"Try the number," Gabriel suggested.

I tapped the number and pressed call. The line disconnected imme-diately, and an automated message played: "This number is no longer in service."

"Disconnected," I said, frowning at the phone.

Gabriel's expression darkened. "That's a bad sign."

"Why's that?" I asked.

"Well, I can only think of two reasons a phone line would be discon-nected, especially with the receipt being dated, what? A month ago?"

I glanced at the date. "A little longer, but roughly, yeah. Do you think they've gone out of business in such a short time?"

"No. I think they're hiding something," Gabriel said. "Disconnected number, no website? That's not just poor customer service. That's a trail going cold on purpose."

I double-checked the receipt. "Look. There's an address listed under the phone number."

"Do you think that's where Runar was heading?" Gabriel asked.

"Probably. I can't see another reason this receipt would be separate from the others. If you wanted to, we could go check out the address."

Gabriel hesitated, tipping his head back and forth as he weighed the options. "It's a good idea and I really want to see what's out there," he finally said, "but I also think we should let someone know what we're doing. Just in case." Gabriel pressed a button on the screen on the dash and scrolled through some numbers before selecting Sheriff Jackson's name. I tensed as he dialed the sheriff through his car's speaker system. It took only one ring before Sheriff Jackson picked up, his voice as gruff as ever.

"Silverthorne." The sheriff's terse greeting rumbled around the car. "Didn't expect to hear from you again so soon."

"Hi, Sheriff," Gabriel said, glancing at me. "You're on speaker with Harper. We just came from Eastford University."

"Didn't I tell you to mind your business?" the sheriff grumbled.

I winced, glancing at Gabriel, but he didn't hesitate. "We thought we could help out. Any updates on Dr. Fenwick's case?"

There was a pause, then the sheriff growled. "I thought I told you two to leave this to the police."

I winced, but Gabriel didn't miss a beat. "Sheriff, you and I both know that body didn't end up in the woods by accident. Someone wanted him dead. A man doesn't turn into a skeleton in just a few days without assistance."

"A few days? How can you be so sure of the timeline?" the sheriff asked sharply.

"Because no one missed him at the university until today, which means whatever happened to him happened sometime between his last classes on Friday and when we discovered him today. You've got to admit, Sheriff, three days is not a lot of time. We thought there might be more clues here that could help us understand what happened."

"I agree with that analysis which is why I sent an officer out there." Sheriff Jackson exhaled sharply. "You two should've stayed out of it."

"We weren't trying to interfere," Gabriel said quickly. "We just wanted to help. We didn't know you'd sent Officer Reggie."

"We ran into him actually," I offered.

"Oh? I trust everything was fine?" the sheriff asked.

"Well, he was trying, but he forgot his notebook full of questions in the car," Gabriel said.

"He's a good kid," Sheriff Jackson said, defensive now. "Gets along with people. Gets them to let down their guard. People talk to him."

Given the sheriff's tone, I chose not to point out that Reggie had nearly tripped over his own feet today. Instead, I murmured, "He's very enthusiastic."

The sheriff grunted. "Besides, without a bigger vehicle, it would've taken Bill a lot longer to run out to Eastford. Centaurs are fast, but he has to keep to the back trails, and then there's the issue of the obfuscation spells being local to Havenwood. And it's too sunny for Johanna today. Besides, she's already been pulling extra shifts. Reggie's baby's been sick, so we've been covering for him. And let me tell you, a testy vampire is no fun."

"I can imagine," Gabriel said with a slight smile. "Look, Sheriff, we didn't mean to step on toes, but something about all this doesn't sit right. You know what I mean? At the moment, Dr. Fenwick's colleagues don't even know he's deceased. They think he's sick or possibly missing. We didn't think it was our place to break the news."

Sheriff Jackson grunted. "Probably wise. Even though we found his ID, I'd rather confirm everything before we make any announcements. Don't want to traumatize his friends or family unnecessarily and there's no need to stir up panic when we don't know what we're dealing with yet."

I exhaled, gripping my phone tighter. That last sentence echoed in my head.

We don't know what we were dealing with.

Not yet.

And whoever was behind it might still be close.

Still watching.

Still dangerous.

Gabriel cleared his throat. "Speaking of that, it might be worth making the trip yourself. Just in case."

The sheriff sighed. "Yeah. Probably a good idea anyway. I should be the one to notify next of kin, once I get confirmation from running his dental records. And it wouldn't hurt to sniff around the university. See if anything's off."

I spoke up. "Do you think his death has something to do with his work here at the university?"

The sheriff answered immediately, his voice brisk. "Statistically, most victims know their assailants unless they are caught in a wrong-time-wrong-place scenario. Given it was the middle of the woods, and he wasn't in hiking gear, I'm going to guess he knew his attacker." The sheriff let out a slow breath. "But if Fenwick was tangled up in something bigger, we need to figure out what. Fast."

Gabriel took the opportunity to smooth things over, his voice even. "Sheriff, I get you don't want civilians interfering, but we've already found something useful. Dr. Fenwick was working with wyrms."

"Worms? Like the kind you go fishing with?" The sheriff sounded confused.

Gabriel shook his head even though the sheriff couldn't see it. "No, not earthworms. Wyrms, w-y-r-m-s. They're scavenger creatures, distantly related to dragons. He was trying to genetically modify them for waste disposal. He wanted to create a species that could safely consume garbage and break it down into non-toxic material."

Sheriff Jackson swore under his breath. "You're telling me the dead guy was messing around with bio-engineering?"

"Not just bio-engineering. Combining magic and science," I said. "Apparently, Dr. Fenwick was one of the few researchers trying to bridge the gap between the two. His experiments weren't just theoretical, either. He was well-known for his magical-mundane cross breeding experiments."

Sheriff Jackson didn't answer right away. I could practically hear the gears grinding. Finally, he exhaled hard. "Yeah... that kind of work makes enemies."

Gabriel's tone remained steady. "At the moment, that's our theory. That someone killed him over what he was trying to create. Either they wanted to stop him or wanted to take credit for his work."

"Not just that," the sheriff said. "You've got magical purists who think mixing bloodlines is sacrilege. Animal rights folks who'd protest breeding anything sentient in a lab. Even eco-extremists who'd see new species as invasive threats. Not to mention anyone with a vendetta against Dr. Fenwick himself. A lot of people could've had reason to want to get the doc out of the way."

My stomach clenched. I hadn't even considered half of those possibilities. This whole thing was layered, tangled, and vast. I didn't even know what kind of person I was looking for.

Why did I think I could solve something like this?

Before I could spiral further, Gabriel jumped in. "If it helps, we ran into someone else you might want to check out. A dwarf named Runar Ironvein was snooping in Dr. Fenwick's supposedly locked office. We didn't want to betray why we were there, so we made up an excuse, but something about the guy was definitely shifty."

"Good to know. Did you find anything else?" the sheriff asked.

I interjected, scrolling through the limited information on my phone. "Not much actually. We found what we think Runar was looking at. Some old receipts. There was one he left behind with a supplier called Northvale Exports. But from what I can see, there's no online presence and no working phone number. Luckily, we found an address on the receipt."

"Sounds shady," the sheriff growled.

"That's what we thought," I said. I shot Gabriel a questioning look, and he nodded encouragingly. "We were thinking of checking it out. Especially since the receipts seemed to be what this Runar guy was interested in."

There was a pause. Then Sheriff Jackson grumbled, "Look, I should tell you to stay out of this but if I did, you'd just ignore me anyway."

"Glad we understand each other," Gabriel said dryly.

"Fine. But be careful and stick together," the sheriff warned. "I don't like the feel of this. If Fenwick was killed over his research, whoever did it might not be done cleaning up loose ends."

The line clicked off, leaving silence between us. I exhaled, my shoulders relaxing as the tension in the car eased.

Gabriel shot me a knowing look. "See? Not so bad."

I huffed. "You call that not so bad? He practically chewed us out."

"He chewed me out. You just got guilt-tripped."

"Same thing," I muttered, though the corner of my mouth twitched. "But to be honest, I didn't expect it to go as well as it did. I half-expected him to order us back to Havenwood."

Gabriel's grin widened. "The sheriff and my family have an understanding. See, my brother and I work for the town. Technically, we're 'consultants,' which allows us a whole lot of leeway. He knows I can handle myself. And there's no way I'm putting you in danger either."

I studied him for a moment, considering that. It made sense. Gabriel was careful, methodical. He wouldn't have survived long in a family like his without knowing how to navigate trouble. And yet, trouble had a way of finding us anyway.

I tapped my fingers against my knee, glancing down at the receipt. The address caught my eye, and a familiar tingle of curiosity sparked in my chest.

"Well," I said, straightening in my seat. "Should I put this address into the GPS then?"

Gabriel's lips twitched. "I thought you were feeling guilty about snooping."

I smirked. "This isn't snooping. It's practically our civic duty."

Gabriel chuckled. "All right, you caught me. I'm curious. Let's see where this leads." He turned on his blinker, merging into another lane. "Answers, here we come."

The Gnome Depot

GABRIEL AND I SAT in the car, eyeing the Northvale Exports building. The green paint was peeling in long strips down the siding, and the whole place looked so dull and forgettable that I would've thought it was abandoned if I hadn't triple-checked the address.

"This is it?" I asked, checking my phone again. "It looks...underwhelming."

Gabriel's lips lifted in amusement. "What were you expecting? A grand magical bazaar?"

"Well, maybe something with a little flair," I admitted, tapping my phone against my leg. "And the lack of information online is just weird. I took a fairly deep dive on the way over here. There's no website, no reviews, not even an outdated blog. It's like they're allergic to the twenty-first century."

"Some people like to stay off the radar," Gabriel said, his gaze sweeping the building. "Especially if what they're selling is...sensitive."

"Sensitive?" I raised an eyebrow. "Magical wyrms aren't illegal, are they?"

"Not that I know of, but I'd guess wyrms are rare. And rare things attract attention." He nodded toward the rows of security cameras mounted on every corner of the building. "And paranoia."

I followed his gaze. There were at least six cameras on the outside alone, all pointing at different angles like mechanical sentinels. "Paranoid is right," I muttered.

We climbed out of the car, the air cooler than I expected. A faint smell of diesel and something chemical hung in the air. The scent seemed to stick to my skin, making me feel itchy. As we approached the steel door, I couldn't shake the sense that we were being watched by more than just the plethora of cameras. Gabriel must have noticed it too, because his steps slowed slightly, his eyes scanning the area.

"Well?" I whispered.

"We're here. Might as well see who's home," Gabriel responded softly.

I nodded and rapped my knuckles against the steel door. The sound barely echoed, swallowed by the dense metal. Nothing. I knocked again, harder this time. Still nothing.

"Maybe no one's here," I said, glancing back at Gabriel.

"It's the middle of a workday," he pointed out. "And with all these cameras? Someone's watching."

Before I could respond, a harsh buzz crackled through the intercom beside the door. A gruff, clipped voice followed, laced with impatience. "Whaddaya want?"

I leaned closer to the speaker. "We're colleagues of Dr. Fenwick. He recommended your place to us."

A long pause. Too long.

"Never heard of you. Go away."

Gabriel stepped in, his voice smooth, diplomatic. "Dr. Fenwick spoke highly of this place. Said it was the only supplier he trusted for his research. We're interested in the same field of study."

Another pause, then a heavy sigh.

"Wait there."

The intercom clicked off. I glanced at Gabriel. "Not bad," I murmured. "Very authoritative."

"I aim to impress," he said with a grin.

A few seconds later, the steel door groaned as it swung open, revealing the squat figure of a gnome. He stood only three and a half feet tall, but there was something slick and stubborn about him like a grease stain that refused to come out. His wiry gray hair jutted from beneath a battered newsboy cap like frayed steel wool. His vest was stained with oil, and his rolled-up sleeves revealed sinewy forearms covered in faded tattoos. The scent of scorched metal and damp fur clung to him. His beady eyes flicked between us, scanning us with the wary sharpness of someone used to slinking through shadows.

"I'm Grumbert," he said gruffly. "You said you know the doc?"

"Yes," I replied, keeping my tone polite. "He told us this was the best place to find what we're looking for."

Grumbert's chest puffed up slightly, pride flickering behind his suspicion. "Fenwick's a valued client," he admitted. "Always pays top dollar." He eyed us again, then stepped back, tilting his head toward the dim interior.

"Come in," he said. "But don't touch nothing if you value walking out of here with all your fingers and toes."

The moment we stepped inside, a chill ran down my spine. The warehouse had the sterile, impersonal feel of a laboratory, the air sharp with disinfectant and the low hum of machinery vibrating beneath my feet. But that all faded the moment I caught sight of the cages.

The sheer number of them hit me like a punch to the gut. They were crammed together, stacked two or three high in some places, a haphazard maze of containment. Some creatures rustled or chirped as we passed, but most remained unnervingly still, their eyes tracking our every move. The space felt more like a hoarder's den than a proper facility—overcrowded, suffocating, and, despite the pristine glass and polished steel, deeply wrong.

"Impressive collection," I said, though I couldn't quite keep the unease from my voice. The enclosures were clean, sure, but far too small. A pair of phoenix chicks huddled in the corner of a glass cage, their dull feathers a stark contrast to the vibrant plumage they should have had. Nearby, an eel-like creature shimmered faintly in a cramped tank, its coils wound so tightly that it could barely move.

Gabriel's jaw tightened, his gaze sweeping over the rows of containment units, his expression darkening. He didn't have to say it. This place was a violation.

Grumbert either didn't notice my discomfort or ignored it. "Only the best," he said proudly, patting the side of an enclosure as he led us deeper into the space. "I treat my stock better than royalty."

Gabriel shot me a look. He wasn't buying it either.

As we wound through the labyrinth of cages and tanks, Grumbert rattled off the virtues of his rarest acquisitions. I let him talk, nodding encouragingly at times, before steering the conversation in the direction we needed.

"We heard Dr. Fenwick bought something recently—wyrms, was it?" I asked, keeping my tone light.

Grumbert scratched his chin, his thick brows knitting together. "Wyrms? That wasn't his last purchase."

My heart skipped. "Oh? I thought we'd talked to him about it last month." I really was terrible at lying. My face flushed as I scrambled for something to say.

"It was two months ago," Gabriel interjected. "You must've forgotten after, well, that thing with your mother."

I fluttered a hand by my head. "Was it really two months? Oh my, how time flies."

Grumbert snorted. "Time flies, but my records don't. If Fenwick bought wyrms recently, it wasn't from me." He gave me a sharp look, eyes gleaming beneath his bushy brows. "Last I sold to him was...well, that's privileged information. Client confidentiality and all that."

Gabriel leaned against a nearby crate, arms crossed, his stance deceptively relaxed. "Confidentiality's a noble concept. But let's be honest, Grumbert—if Fenwick was working on something important and he trusted you as his supplier, wouldn't you want to make sure it was being handled properly?"

Grumbert's mouth twitched, something between amusement and irritation. "Handled properly? That's rich. You two aren't researchers."

Gabriel straightened slightly, adjusting his stance as if re-evaluating his approach. "No, we're not. We're also not asking for every detail, just confirmation. What was Fenwick working on?" Gabriel pressed.

Grumbert's eyes narrowed. "You're poking your noses where they don't belong."

"We're just doing our job," Gabriel said.

"What are ya? Some kind of private investigators?" Grumbert scoffed.

"Something like that," Gabriel said smoothly. "But about Dr. Fenwick's work—"

"Why is everybody so obsessed with ol' Malcolm's hobbies today?" Grumbert snapped.

"What do you mean?" I demanded.

"First it was that Ironvein fella, now you two. What's a guy gotta do to get a little peace around here?"

My brows lifted. "Ironvein? As in Runar Ironvein?"

Grumbert's expression soured instantly. He straightened, arms folding tight across his chest. "That dwarf was a menace. Stormed in here, shouting threats, demanding to see my records. Forced me to show him everything. He took nothing, but he snapped pictures of my logs and left in a rush out the back just as you two got here."

Gabriel and I exchanged a glance. "What was he looking for?" Gabriel asked carefully.

Grumbert scowled. "Not a clue. But whatever it was, he wasn't happy when he found it."

Gabriel tilted his head. "That's funny. I thought you said your records were confidential."

Grumbert flinched, just slightly, but covered it with a growl. "I didn't have a choice. He wasn't exactly polite about it. I feared for my life with that angry dwarf towering over me, shouting threats in my face."

Gabriel allowed the silence to stretch. Then he exhaled and reached into his pocket, casually thumbing through his phone. "You know, that's very interesting," he mused.

Grumbert's eyes darted to the phone, his expression tightening. "What are you doing?"

Gabriel smiled easily. "Oh, just checking in with the sheriff. I'm sure he'd be very interested in hearing how you've been threatened today. Sheriff Jackson doesn't take well to that kind of behavior around here."

"Sheriff *Jackson*?" Grumbert squeaked.

"Oh, so you do know him. Of course you do. Everyone knows about the werewolf sheriff from Havenwood." Gabriel let the words hang, his smirk growing when he saw the gnome shifting from foot to foot.

Grumbert's eyes widened, and his already ruddy complexion paled. "Now, hold on," he sputtered. "There's no need to go calling in *him*."

"Didn't say I was calling him," Gabriel said, still scrolling. "Just...checking my messages." He tapped the phone's screen lazily. "Let's make this easy. You give us what you know about Runar Ironvein, and I put my phone away. Otherwise..." He let the sentence trail off meaningfully.

Grumbert let out a low string of curses in a language I didn't recognize. He reached into a drawer and pulled out a small white business card, flicking it onto the counter. "That's all I got. Take it and go."

I stepped forward and picked it up. *Runar Ironvein—Acquisitions* was printed neatly on the front, along with a phone number. I started to set it down, but something on the back caught my eye. A faint green and gold smudge, like an old ink transfer. I couldn't make it out in the dim light, but it gave me a weird feeling.

I slipped the card into my pocket. Just in case.

"Mind if we check your security footage?" Gabriel asked.

Grumbert let out a short, barking laugh. "You've got nerve, I'll give you that. I don't let just anyone poke through my system."

Gabriel's lips twitched. "Well, let me put it this way—I check your system, or Sheriff Jackson does. Your call."

Grumbert let out a long, weary sigh. "Fine," he muttered. "But don't touch nothing."

He led us to a small, cluttered back room where a bank of monitors flickered in shades of gray. I resisted the urge to wrinkle my nose at the musty scent of old paper and machine oil.

The gnome grumbled under his breath as his fingers flew across a keyboard. The footage sped forward, and we watched Runar barge in, rifle through records, snap his pictures, and then storm out. But it was what came next that made my pulse spike.

The cameras caught him lingering outside. Watching. Watching *us*. He stood with his back pressed to the wall, peeking around the corner cautiously until Grumbert swung the steel door open for us and we entered the building. As soon as the heavy door closed behind us, Runar made a break for his car and sped off.

Gabriel let out a slow breath. "He was keeping tabs on us."

Grumbert's mouth twisted. "And stole half my records doing it. Slippery little rat grabbed the last few pages of my shipment lists and left me with nothing but soot smudges and broken bindings."

My heart sank. "So, the most recent shipment list is..."

"Gone," the gnome said, glaring at the screen where Runar had disappeared.

Gabriel's jaw tightened. "The sheriff will want to hear about this." He reached toward me, gently guiding me toward the door.

Grumbert darted in front of us. "Now, hold on. No need to go stirring up trouble where there ain't any."

"We're not stirring up anything," Gabriel said, voice calm but unyielding. "You were robbed and threatened in your place of business. That is trouble."

"I handle my own problems," Grumbert muttered, just a little too quickly. "Don't need nobody poking around. Especially not Jackson."

Gabriel raised an eyebrow. "If you've got nothing to hide, why wouldn't you want the sheriff to bring this Ironvein fellow to justice and return your logs?"

Grumbert stepped into our path again, eyes narrowed. "Don't call him. You hear me? I handle my business."

Gabriel didn't answer. Just guided me around him, raised a hand in vague acknowledgment, and kept walking.

As we passed the rows of enclosures, I glimpsed scaled wings curled in a too-small crate and a pair of intelligent eyes tracking us through the gloom. My stomach twisted.

I didn't trust myself to speak. I just walked faster. Gabriel matched my pace. The moment we stepped outside, the air felt sharper and cleaner. I could finally take a full breath again. We didn't say a word until we reached the car; the warehouse looming behind us.

As soon as the car door shut, Gabriel pulled out his phone.

I frowned. "What are you doing?"

He glanced at me. "Calling the sheriff."

I stiffened. "Are you sure that's a good idea?"

Gabriel slid into the driver's seat, jaw tight. "Grumbert's obviously running a black-market trade. If you hadn't been there, I might've dragged him in by the ear and dealt with the fallout later."

I blinked at the sudden edge in his voice.

He didn't soften. "People like him make my blood boil. Caging sentient creatures like they're collectibles? Selling them off to who knows where? If I'd stood there another minute, I might've done something stupid."

I didn't doubt it.

He tapped the call button. "The sheriff needs to shut him down. Now."

I looked out the window as Gabriel relayed everything to the sheriff, his voice clipped and efficient. The sun was sinking behind the warehouse, casting long shadows that stretched like claws across the cracked pavement. From the sharp edge in Gabriel's tone and the muffled bursts of frustration crackling from the other end, I could tell the sheriff wasn't taking the news lightly.

By the time Gabriel ended the call, I wouldn't have traded places with Grumbert for all the gold in a dragon's hoard.

Gabriel hung up and exhaled, slow and measured, but the tension still radiated off him like heat off asphalt.

"All good?" I asked quietly.

He nodded, his hands gripping the steering wheel. "The sheriff's calling in backup. Some kind of magical task force will be here within the hour. With any luck, they'll tear the place apart."

He didn't move to start the car.

I glanced at him. "We're not leaving?"

Gabriel's gaze stayed locked on the warehouse. "Not yet. If Grumbert gets wind of what's coming, I wouldn't put it past him to start moving creatures out the back. I'm not giving him the chance."

I followed his line of sight. The building squatted under the bruised-colored sky, like it knew the walls were about to close in. A flicker of movement behind one of the darkened windows sent a chill down my spine.

I exhaled slowly, watching the last of the light fade. Hopefully, the animals inside would be taken care of soon, but without clear answers on what Dr. Fenwick was really doing in that place last month, it still felt like a loose end. A dangerous one.

Today had taught me something I hadn't quite wanted to learn.

You can't prepare for the unexpected.

You just have to hope luck is on your side when it hits.

No Rest for the Inquisitive

The warehouse stayed unnervingly quiet until the sheriff arrived.

No movement from inside. No sounds. Just that heavy, watchful silence, like the building itself was holding its breath.

When the marked cruiser finally pulled in, Gabriel got out to speak with the sheriff, keeping his voice low and clipped. I couldn't hear what they said, but whatever it was, it ended with a firm nod and a glance back at the warehouse.

He opened the car door a moment later. "He's waiting for the task force," he said. "But once they arrive, it's going to get loud. I told them we'd clear out before the doors come down."

As he pulled back onto the road, I let out a long breath and leaned my head against the seat. The tension still thrummed beneath my skin, but at least the animals inside the warehouse were getting help.

If only the same could be said for Dr. Fenwick.

"Alright," Gabriel said, his voice cutting through the quiet. "Where to next?"

I reached into my coat pocket to grab my phone, and a small rectangle fluttered out with it, landing on my lap. Runar's business card. I almost shoved it back in without thinking, but then I caught a glimmer of something on the back. That same faint green and gold smudge I'd noticed earlier, like an old ink transfer. In the low light of the car, I angled it toward the window, trying to catch the fading sun.

As the light skimmed the card, the blurred mark sharpened into a partial logo. It looked like a tilted clover and the edge of looping script.

"Gabriel," I said, holding it up. "Does this mean anything to you?"

He flicked a glance over the card when we were safely stopped at a light, a frown furrowing his brow. "That's the logo for The Clover's Charm. It's a pub on the outskirts of Havenwood."

"What would Runar have been doing there?" I asked.

"I don't know," Gabriel murmured, easing the car forward.

"Well, should we go? If Runar was there, it can't be a coincidence. What was he doing at the distributor's place? Why does he keep turning up like a bad penny? He has to be involved somehow—"

Gabriel gave me a sidelong look, amused. "You know, you might set a world record for rapid-fire questions, amaryn."

I waved him off. "You can make fun of me after we figure this out."

"What about Cassandra?" Gabriel asked.

"Cassandra?" I repeated blankly. My hand flew to my mouth. "Oh no, her shift is nearly over! I can't leave her to close alone. How did it get to be so late already?"

Gabriel grinned. "And here you thought you'd be bored today."

I shrugged. "Maybe it's you. Maybe it's the wish I made at the wishing well. But I have to hand it to you, Mr. Silverthorne—this day has been anything but boring."

"I aim to please," he said smoothly, though his smile quickly faded. "But to answer your question about Runar. I don't think we should chase after him, at least not yet. He's clearly shady. Threatening the gnome, running out the back to avoid us, possibly breaking into Dr. Fenwick's office, and who knows what else. He's not someone we should confront unprepared."

"I agree," I said.

Gabriel tapped the wheel. "So. What's next?"

I leaned back with a sigh. "Honestly? I need to check on Cassandra. I feel like a terrible boss leaving her alone all day."

He shot me a reassuring look. "I'm sure she's fine. You wouldn't have hired her if she wasn't capable. Besides, I'm sure Bella's thrilled her distraction plan worked."

I rolled my eyes but couldn't suppress a smile. "Knowing her, she'll never let me live it down that she was right. Again. But I doubt even she expected the day to end with a body in the woods."

"Nope, that was an entirely unexpected turn," Gabriel said, his countenance darkening. "Honestly, not the way I would've wanted to end an otherwise lovely day with you."

"Not my first choice either, but at least I haven't worried about Spellbooks or Cassandra. Until now that is. All I really want to do is get back, make sure everything's still standing, and that Luna hasn't...I don't know...kicked any doors in."

Gabriel arched an eyebrow. "Can she even do that?"

I hesitated. "I mean, she's a rabbit with ninja training. I wouldn't put it past her."

"Fair point," he admitted. "I know better than to challenge opinionated rabbits."

"Wise man," I said with a smirk.

"So," he continued, "while you check in with Cassandra, I'm going to swing by my mother's office. She'll want an update, and with Johanna on duty now, they might be able to fast-track confirmation on the skeleton."

I nodded slowly. "Do you really think it could be Dr. Fenwick? Or did someone just take his lanyard?"

Gabriel's frown deepened. "Normally, someone doesn't turn into a skeleton in just a few days. But this is Havenwood..." He shrugged, the gesture equal parts frustration and unease.

"If it's not Fenwick, then who is it? And where is he?"

"Those are the million-dollar questions," he said grimly.

"Well, I don't have a million dollars, but I'd still like some answers."

"You and me both," he said, offering a tired smile.

The conversation drifted to lighter topics, but my mind kept circling back to Dr. Fenwick, Runar, and that skeleton in the woods. By the time Gabriel dropped me off at Spellbooks, I was ready for a break from my dark thoughts.

The bell jingled as I stepped into the shop, and the familiar scent of aged paper, ink, and a faint trace of rich coffee wrapped around me like a well-worn blanket. Spellbooks always smelled like magic, like stories waiting to be told. The warm glow of the lights bathed the shelves in soft amber light, making the polished wooden floors gleam.

Cassandra looked up from behind the counter, her face brightening as she saw me. The sight of her, standing confidently in my shop, arranging displays like she'd been here forever, settled some of my nerves. The normalcy of the moment banished all other thoughts from my mind after the whirlwind of the day.

"Harper!" She gestured around with an excited sweep of her hand. "I hope you like the displays. I tried to make everything neat for an easy close tonight and a smooth opening tomorrow."

I glanced around, genuinely impressed. The shelves sparkled, the floors gleamed, and her displays were artfully arranged. Even the counter looked immaculate, stacked with customer orders tied with twine. "It looks amazing," I said honestly.

"Thanks! With the warmer weather, I even propped open the front door for a bit. A few browsers wandered in, which was nice." She beamed.

"That's the hope," I said, shrugging out of my coat. "Especially with this partnership I'm working on with that publicist in New York."

"Mindy Hart, right?" Cassandra snapped her fingers. "She actually called the shop earlier and left a message. Something about checking your email."

I pulled out my cell phone, noticing a missed call. "Huh. She called me, too." I tapped her number and held the phone to my ear. No answer. I left a quick voicemail and promised to follow up later.

Cassandra grabbed her coat from the peg. "Well, I had so much fun today, and I'm actually looking forward to tomorrow. Never thought I'd say that about work!"

"I'm glad you're here," I said sincerely. "You've been such a great fit already. I was prepared to feel bad for leaving you alone all day, but it looks like you've thrived."

Cassandra put her hands on her hips and looked around the shop proudly. "It's been great. Thanks for taking a chance on me," she said, her voice soft. "I really needed this."

After she left, the shop settled into its familiar evening hush, the kind that carried a sense of comfort rather than emptiness. The only sounds were the occasional creaks of the old wooden shelves adjusting to the quiet or the faint hum of Spellbooks saying hello.

A soft thump announced Luna's arrival as she leapt onto the counter, her white fur gleaming under the warm light. She stretched luxuriously before sitting primly on the counter.

"Well?" I asked, propping my chin in my hand.

Luna twitched her nose. "I'll admit it. She's good for Spellbooks."

"Wow. High praise coming from you. Are you sure you're feeling okay? Not coming down with something?" I said with a grin.

Luna gave me a look so dry it could have turned parchment to dust. "I can rescind my approval if you'd prefer."

"No, no, I'll take the rare moment of validation," I said, grinning.

"What can I say? I'm an old softy," Luna mused, stroking her whiskers with an air of nonchalance. "But seriously. Good hire. For you, for Spellbooks, and for her."

"Thanks, Luna," I murmured, reaching down to scratch behind Mr. Wigglesworth's ears as he padded over, purring loudly.

For the first time all day, I allowed myself to exhale completely, letting the warmth of home settle in my bones. Whatever chaos tomorrow would bring, at least I had this—Spellbooks, Luna, Mr. Wigglesworth, and a new employee who fit right in.

I pulled my phone from my pocket, intending to check the time, and Runar's business card slid out with it. I caught it mid-fall and turned it over in my hands. Gabriel said the logo belonged to The Clover's Charm. I'd never heard of the place. Maybe I could check it out.

Curiosity tugged at me. I opened my maps app and typed in The Clover's Charm.

Forty-eight minutes on foot. Not exactly ideal. I looked out the window. The streetlamps cast long, watery shadows across Arcadia Avenue, and the breeze whispered against the glass as if it were looking for a way in.

I shivered at the thought.

Not tonight. Not with skeletons in the woods and too many questions still waiting in the dark.

Tomorrow would be soon enough.

Luna Logic: Resistance is Futile

My morning was a leisurely one, with all thoughts of missing professors and skeletons pushed far from my mind as I settled into my usual routine. There was something comforting about opening the shop, going through the familiar motions of setting things up for the day.

I set down Mr. Wigglesworth's food in his bowl, giving him an extra scratch behind the ears. He meowed pitifully, glancing between me and the meager scoop I'd given him, his fluffy tail twitching in protest.

I chuckled, crouching down to give him my full attention. "You know what the vet said," I admonished. "You're getting too big, buddy. We've got to put you on a diet. It's for your own good."

Mr. Wigglesworth, ever the drama queen, let out a long, suffering sigh before finally padding over to his bowl and digging in as if it were the greatest hardship of his nine lives. I rolled my eyes.

"I know, buddy," I said dryly. "The horror. The injustice. You'll survive, I promise."

I turned toward Luna, ready to set out her food, but she was already hopping out of her hutch like a rabbit on a mission.

"Come on, kid, we've got places to go and people to see. Let's hop to it."

I raised an eyebrow, glancing after her in amused surprise. "What are you talking about?"

She shot me a look. "The Clover's Charm, obviously. Don't you remember telling me all about your adventures last night?"

I rolled my eyes. "Of course I do. You wouldn't let me go to bed until I gave you every detail."

"And it's a good thing, too," she said smugly, twitching her whiskers. "Otherwise, you'd be waking up with no strategy and only half a clue what to do next. And trust me, if Patrick Murphy's involved, you'll want backup. That man could talk the fur off a werewolf."

"Umm, who's Patrick Murphy again?" The name rang a bell, but after the whirlwind of yesterday, I couldn't place it.

This time it was Luna who rolled her eyes. "The owner of The Clover's Charm? Honestly Harper, what would you do without me?"

"Probably get more sleep," I muttered, but I couldn't help but smile. She wasn't wrong. I'd given her a full play-by-play the night before, every twist, turn, and stray observation, and Luna had absorbed it all like a particularly snarky sponge.

Luna let out an exaggerated groan. "Come on, Harper. If you're going to amount to anything as an investigator, amateur or otherwise, you have to chase up leads. The little things. That's what makes or breaks a case, isn't it?"

I shook my head, smiling. "You're absolutely right. But as far as little things go, I checked out The Clover's Charm online. They don't open until ten. We've got at least an hour and a half before we can even think about heading over there."

Luna wrinkled her nose. "Well, you don't want to hit the morning rush."

I shot her a flat look. "Morning rush? On a Tuesday?"

"You never know," she sniffed. "The place could've picked up in popularity."

I snorted. "From what you described, The Clover's Charm doesn't seem like an early morning spot."

Luna flicked an ear. "Who knows? Maybe Patrick had an epiphany. A change of heart. Maybe he woke up one morning and decided to rebrand.

Maybe he hasn't changed. But that doesn't mean we should waste time sitting around twiddling our thumbs."

I crossed my arms. "And what do you propose we do?"

She gave me a slow, knowing smirk. "We strategize. We prepare. And by prepare, I mean coffee. Preferably with a side of breakfast."

I chuckled. "You just want an excuse to go to the Oasis."

"I'm a creature of habit," she said airily. "And of excellent taste."

I glanced at the clock. We had time to kill before The Clover's Charm opened and, honestly? Coffee and breakfast didn't sound like the worst idea.

I pressed a hand to the wall, speaking to the shop. "Hey, Spellbooks. I know you said things were fine with Cassandra yesterday, but she's coming back today. Are you okay with that?"

A deep rumble pulsed through the walls, and there was a scratch of chalk against the board. I held my breath, hoping the shop was in an agreeable mood.

The word appeared, written in slow, deliberate strokes.

Yes.

It was then swiftly underlined for emphasis.

I exhaled, patting the wall. "Got it."

At the sound of keys in the front door, I moved to wipe the board clean, but the shop beat me to it, the words vanishing as though they'd never been there.

Cassandra breezed into the shop with a cheerful, "Hi, Harper! Morning, Luna!"

"Hi, Cassandra," I said, returning her enthusiasm. "Ready for day two?"

"So ready." She slipped out of her coat and hung it neatly on the peg. Then, hesitantly, she added, "Hey, Harper, I had a question..."

I turned toward her, my attention sharpening. "Yeah? What's up?"

She tucked a strand of hair behind her ear, shifting on her feet. "I, um...I hate to ask, but would you be able to cover for me this afternoon? I know I've only been in Havenwood a couple of weeks, but my apartment's got some maintenances issue they've been putting off, and now they're finally sending someone to fix it. But, of course, it has to be today."

I waved a hand. "No problem. You need to be there, right?"

Relief flooded her expression. "Yeah. They won't even give me a time, just that it'll be 'sometime between two and five,' which isn't helpful." She sighed. "I wouldn't ask if it wasn't important."

"Cassandra, it's fine," I reassured her. "I'd want my plumbing—or whatever it is—fixed too."

She let out a grateful laugh. "You're the best. And, um…" She hesitated again, biting her lip. "While I've got you, I have another question."

"Fire away," I said with a smile.

She hesitated before taking a deep breath. "I've been thinking a lot about my former mentor."

I nodded, keeping my expression neutral. Cassandra's former mentor, Lysandra Wraithmoor, was a powerful weather mage who, not so long ago, attempted to unleash chaos on Havenwood. The town wasn't exactly ready to forgive and forget. Not when someone tried to mess with their hard-fought sanctuary. It was no wonder Cassandra had been met with some skepticism, to say the least.

Cassandra shifted her weight. "I know Lysandra wasn't who I thought she was. I get that now. But I think some people here are lumping me in with her."

I didn't say anything. There wasn't much I could say without lying. From what I'd seen of how certain people in town treated her, she wasn't wrong.

Cassandra hesitated, then squared her shoulders. "It's made me think, though. About what I missed growing up. What I want to do differently."

I tilted my head, curious about where this was going.

"I know your granny kept some rare books here. Things you wouldn't find in your average shop, magical or otherwise. And I know this might seem like an odd request, but…" She trailed off, suddenly uncertain.

I held my breath. Was this the other shoe? Was Cassandra about to ask for a forbidden text or ancient grimoire? Had this been her game all along?

"Do you have anything on magical ethics?" she asked in a rush.

That threw me. I'd braced for something darker. More self-serving. But *ethics*?

"I want to do my own research," she continued, voice steadier now. "Figure out how I want to use my magic going forward. The library won't let me near anything deeper than beginner charms, and… well, I want more than that."

I offered a reassuring smile and surreptitiously patted the wall, letting Spellbooks know it was safe to help. "That sounds like a very reasonable request. I'll check our inventory. If we've got anything, I'll grab it for you before I leave."

Cassandra's face lit up. "Really? Thank you, Harper. You have no idea how much that means. I'm lucky you gave me a chance. Especially when no one else would," Cassandra added quietly, tucking a strand of hair behind her ear.

I smiled, hearing Granny Bea's voice echo in my mind. "Luck might open a door," I said gently, "but walking through it? That's all you. And from what I've seen, you don't need luck to succeed."

The words tumbled out easily. It was something Granny used to say whenever I second-guessed myself. I'd always taken it as one of her cozy little aphorisms. But now, watching Cassandra, I wondered if she'd meant more by it. Maybe luck wasn't about chance at all. Maybe it was about choice.

Luna gave a soft snort from the floor. "Fluff and furballs. What are you two talking about? Luck's just another name for being stubborn enough to keep trying until the odds finally give up."

Cassandra let out a soft laugh, the tension easing from her shoulders. "Then here's hoping I'm stubborn enough to keep going even when times are tough," she said, her smile shy but genuine.

I chuckled, feeling a little lighter myself. As Cassandra settled in to work, organizing her papers with renewed determination, I headed upstairs, Luna hopping along beside me.

"She's got a good heart," Luna muttered. "Too bad Vivienne won't give her a fair shake."

I sighed. "I get it, though. Lysandra tried to kill both Vivienne and Gabriel. And you know how Vivienne operates. I'm not sure she's met a rule she doesn't like. If someone wants to mess with Havenwood, watch out. But someone messing with her family?" I blew out a breath and shook my head. "This isn't something we can fix for Cassandra. She and Vivienne are going to have to reach some sort of truce on their own."

"Still," Luna grumbled, "doesn't mean it's fair for Vivienne to be holding a grudge against her when it's her mentor who went nuts."

I reached the top of the stairs and glanced over my shoulder, making sure Cassandra hadn't followed. Then, I pressed my palm to the wall. "Spellbooks, do we have anything on magical ethics?" I whispered.

A soft vibration hummed against my fingertips, followed by the scrape of a book shimmying out of its position, directing me to the exact shelf I needed.

"Thanks," I murmured, patting the wall before heading downstairs with the book in hand.

Cassandra took it with both hands, pressing it to her chest. "You're the best."

"Anytime," I said.

As I checked the time, considering what to do next, my phone rang. Gabriel's name flashed across the screen.

I answered with a smile. "I don't need rescuing today, I promise."

Gabriel chuckled, but there was something off in his tone—something that made my stomach tighten.

"Glad to hear it. But that's not why I'm calling."

I straightened. "What's wrong?"

"The sheriff wants to talk to us," he said. "He says the sooner, the better."

A thread of unease wove through me. "He doesn't think we had anything to do with yesterday, does he?"

"I'm not sure," Gabriel reassured me. "But he sounded pretty shaken. Whatever he found, it's big."

I grabbed my keys. "I'll be ready."

Luna hopped onto the counter. "What's going on?"

"The sheriff called Gabriel," I said under my breath. "He wants to talk to us."

Luna's ears twitched. "Well, I'm coming."

I sighed. "Luna—"

She held up a paw. "We both know how this goes. You go, you get caught up in things, and I don't hear a word about it until later. Nope. Not happening this time."

Before I could argue, she wriggled behind the counter and dragged out a tote bag—one that had very clearly been customized for her travel comfort, complete with a plush lining and an embroidered moon.

A knock sounded at the front door. I looked up to see Gabriel.

This wasn't the time to get into an extended argument with a stubborn rabbit. I gave up without a fight. "Fine. Hop in."

Luna smirked. "Good choice."

With Luna settled, I grabbed my things and stepped outside to meet Gabriel.

He glanced at the tote, then at me. "Extra company?" he asked, raising a brow.

I sighed. "Long story."

Gabriel chuckled, opening the car door. "I wouldn't fight that battle."

"Smart man," Luna sniffed as I eased her into the backseat.

And with that, we were off to find out what the sheriff had uncovered.

Doughnuts and Dead Ends

THE SCENT OF OLD paper, floor polish, and something vaguely metallic hit me the moment we stepped into the Havenwood police station. Not exactly the most welcoming blend, but it was quickly joined by a far more pleasant one as Officer Reggie ambled in after us, carrying a large pink bakery box.

Behind the desk, Johanna looked like she'd lost a fight with the morning and wasn't taking it well. The blinds were drawn tight behind her, and the overhead lights in her corner had been dimmed to a low, moody glow. Her usually crisp ponytail drooped to one side, and she was gripping a pen like she might stab the next person who spoke.

"Rough morning?" I asked, already knowing the answer.

Johanna let out a slow, deliberate exhale through her nose. "No. Rough night," she corrected, voice dripping with irritation. "Because I worked the night shift. And then, thanks to somebody—" she shot a pointed glare at Reggie, "I had to stay late to cover the desk."

"Hey, in my defense, I was up all night, too. Just, you know, not for work," Officer Reggie protested, looking entirely too chipper for someone allegedly short on sleep.

Johanna folded her arms and glowered, her fangs descending just enough to make her point.

Reggie took an instinctive step back and lifted the brightly colored doughnut box like a shield. "If it makes it better, I brought doughnuts?"

Johanna's glare didn't waver. "It would be better if the jelly filling came with a side of O-positive," she deadpanned.

Reggie deflated a little. "Oh. Right. Vampire." He scrubbed a hand through his hair, cheeks flushing. "Sleep deprivation must be catching up to me."

Johanna rolled her eyes. "It's fine. They frown on blood at the front desk. Something about 'optics.'"

Gabriel shot Reggie a sympathetic look. "Let me guess—baby stuff?"

Reggie's entire face softened. "Little guy refused to sleep. I tried everything. Rocking, walking, lullabies. Nothing worked. But then, at three in the morning? He just passed out like a flipped switch. Just the cutest thing. Couldn't help but watch him for a while. So peaceful, you know?" He shook his head with a small, baffled smile. "Kids, man. Absolute mysteries."

Johanna snorted. "If only you could apply that problem-solving ability to literally anything work-related."

"I remembered to bring doughnuts. That's work-related," Reggie pointed out.

"That's work-adjacent," she muttered, already heading for the back room. "Now that you're here, I'm going to bed."

"Okay," Reggie called as she walked toward the back of the precinct. "Thanks again, Johanna!"

She lifted an arm in acknowledgement, but didn't turn.

Luna's ears twitched as she peeked over the edge of my tote bag. "If there's Boston cream in there, I call dibs now that the angry vampire is gone."

"Sure, Luna, here you go," Reggie said, grabbing a napkin and putting a chocolate-covered doughnut on the desk. I carefully lifted Luna out of the tote and set her next to her morning treat.

Reggie offered us the box. "What about you two? Would you like a doughnut?"

Gabriel shook his head, but I grabbed a Boston cream for myself. Sugar and caffeine: breakfast of champions. And I was already there. Now I just needed the coffee.

Then, just as I was taking a bite, the door to Sheriff Jackson's office swung open behind the officer.

"Reggie!" the sheriff growled

Reggie yelped and nearly dropped the doughnut box.

"Quit flapping your mouth and show them back." The sheriff's eyes lit on the pink box. "Oh, you brought doughnuts? I'll take a maple glazed, and a black coffee. On the double."

Reggie scrambled toward the coffeepot as Gabriel grabbed a napkin, plucked a maple glazed from the box, and passed it over to the sheriff as we headed into his office. Luna cleared her throat pointedly, and I scooped up her half-finished doughnut as she hopped inside after us.

As soon as he had his coffee and had shut the door behind Reggie, Sheriff Jackson wasted no time. He set a recording device in the center of the table and fixed us both with a level stare. "All right. I know we've done this informally, but I need you to walk me through everything that happened yesterday. From the beginning."

We gave him the rundown while he steadily worked his way through his maple glazed. Together, we covered every moment from finding the remains to confronting Grumbert. Jackson didn't interrupt, but I could tell he was clocking every detail, his sharp eyes missing nothing.

When we finished, he reached for his notebook, then paused, switching off the recording device. "This is strictly off the record, but I thought you should know. I got confirmation from my forensics guy. The bones in the woods? They're Dr. Fenwick's."

My breath caught. Gabriel's expression darkened. "Are you sure?" he asked.

"One hundred percent," Sheriff Jackson confirmed. "My guy's a sylph. Best in the business and his turnaround is fast. Faster than any human lab. So officially? We're still waiting. But between us, that's Dr. Fenwick."

Gabriel nodded, taking the information in stride. "And cause of death?"

Sheriff Jackson's expression tightened. "That's trickier. My guy says there's no sign of major trauma on the bones. No breaks, no stab wounds, no defensive injuries. Just scavenger damage. Which means...whatever killed him didn't leave a mark we can see now."

"So, it could've been natural," I said slowly, "or magical. Poison. Anything internal."

"Exactly," the sheriff said. "No way to confirm without more evidence and since all of the soft tissue is gone..." he trailed off with a helpless shrug.

I frowned. "Meaning we have no obvious cause of death."

"None," Sheriff Jackson confirmed. "And unless something new turns up, we may never have one. Whoever—" He paused, correcting himself, "Whoever or whatever caused his death either planned to destroy the evidence, or just got lucky."

A few days ago, I would've chalked it up to just that—luck. Good or bad, depending on whose side you were on. But now? I wasn't so sure.

"However, I also have an update," Sheriff Jackson continued, slapping another folder down on the table with satisfaction. "Thanks to a tip from two stalwart citizens, an illegal magical animal trade has been completely shut down."

"You shut down Grumbert?" Gabriel asked.

The sheriff nodded. I felt an unexpected surge of relief after the unfortunate news from before. This was the best news of the day. Maybe even the week.

The sheriff continued, "We've started the process of relocating all the creatures he was holding."

That should've been positive, but a knot of unease still sat in my stomach as another thought crashed in. "Did you find out anything about what animals Dr. Fenwick purchased from him? After the wyrms I mean?" I asked.

Sheriff Jackson studied me for a beat, then his mustache twitched with the smallest hint of approval. He opened his desk drawer and pulled out a thin ledger, which he slid across the desk toward me. "See for yourself."

I flipped it open and scanned the handwritten entries. A list of sales, trades, and acquisitions. Some of them were familiar. Names of creatures I recognized, mostly from fantasy books, not from real life. Others were complete mysteries.

And then—

I stopped.

Gabriel peered over my shoulder. "What is it?"

I tapped a line near the bottom of the page. It showed Dr. Fenwick's most recent purchase.

"What's this?" I asked, glancing up first at Gabriel and then at the sheriff.

The sheriff shook his head. "That," he said grimly, "is what I was hoping you could tell me."

I stared down at the word, unease prickling up my spine.

Auravores.

And Dr. Fenwick had purchased a male and a female. Despite not knowing anything about the creatures, something about the name sent a shiver of instinctive dread through me.

Luna, who had been steadily working her way through her doughnut, suddenly stopped chewing. That alone was concerning.

"That's not a comforting name," she muttered.

"Do you know what they are?" I asked immediately.

Luna shook her head slowly. "No, but think about the etymology of the word. The suffix comes from Latin vorare, meaning 'to devour.'"

Gabriel frowned. "I've heard of carnivores, herbivores, and omnivores, but auravore?"

"It eats auras?" I guessed, my mouth suddenly dry. "Like... the colored light energy field thingy?"

Luna snorted. "That's one way to put it. Certain humans can sense magic, but don't have proof it exists. Auras are what they called the faint impressions of that magical energy they could sense but couldn't prove and the name kind of stuck."

"An auravore eats people's magic?" I asked, suddenly uneasy.

"Maybe," Luna said slowly. "But the problem is I've never heard of an auravore. And if I haven't, that's not a good sign."

Sheriff Jackson grimaced. "Me either. On top of that, Grumbert isn't talking. I'm hoping one of you can shed some light on this beastie."

Slowly, each of us shook our heads, making eye contact with each other as we did so. My stomach sank. What did it mean if none of us had even heard of this creature, let alone what it was capable of?

Gabriel leaned forward. "So, we have an unknown creature, purchased by a dead man, from an illegal dealer...and no one knows what it is?"

Sheriff Jackson nodded. "That about sums it up. When Martha Morningstar at the library hadn't heard of them, I was hoping one of you might fill in the gaps. Failing that, the Silverthornes and Beatrice Sullivan had two of the best independent collections of magical tomes in town. Maybe there's something in one of your family's books that I haven't been able to uncover yet."

Gabriel raised an eyebrow. "What about Dr. Harlow? If anyone would know what Dr. Fenwick was doing—"

Sheriff Jackson shook his head. "Can't risk it. Asking the wrong questions could tip her off about Fenwick and raise suspicions at the university about how fast we get results here in Havenwood."

I bit the inside of my cheek, the unease returning. If Martha didn't know and Dr. Harlow hadn't even been asked, then yeah. We were officially on our own.

That realization settled like a stone in my gut. Granny Bea had spent decades collecting rare magical texts. The Silverthornes had even older tomes. Sheriff Jackson hadn't brought us in out of politeness. He'd been strategic. When it came to magical oddities, Gabriel and I had access others didn't.

The sheriff leaned forward, resting his forearms on the desk, and fixed us both with a hard look. "And just so we're clear, you're consultants on this. Look through your resources, but that's it. No chasing this down on your own. No poking things that might bite. Definitely no sharing with the humans. You find something, you bring it to me. Got it?"

Gabriel nodded, his expression serious. "Understood."

I managed what I hoped passed for a cooperative smile. "Of course. Wouldn't dream of it."

Sheriff Jackson's eyes narrowed slightly, as if weighing whether or not he believed me. But Luna coughed, drawing all of our attention as she licked a bit of chocolate off her paw and muttered, "Fluff and furballs, I hate to say it, but we really need better hobbies."

A breath of laughter escaped me, quick and sharp, but it didn't settle the dread winding tight in my chest. My restless fingers drummed against the edge of the table.

Because if this auravore creature wasn't in Spellbooks' collection either, then we weren't just up against something rare.

We were up against something unknown.

And that was never a good thing.

Second Breakfast and Secrets

GABRIEL GLANCED OVER AT me as we drove away from the police station, his brow furrowed. "Are you okay, amaryn? You're quieter than usual."

I forced out a chuckle. "Out of the three of us being quiet, we should probably be most worried about Luna."

A dramatic huff sounded from the back seat. "I just know when to let people process things," Luna said, her voice laden with the kind of wisdom only years of rabbit-hood could bring. "Restraint comes with age and experience. You'll get there eventually, you young whippersnappers."

Despite my heavy thoughts, I smiled. Luna's grumpy, self-assured nature had a way of cutting through tension like a well-aimed knife through a crumbly scone—swift, decisive, and leaving a bit of a mess in its wake.

Still, I couldn't ignore the lingering questions in my mind. "What do you think happened? To Dr. Fenwick I mean," I asked, my voice quieter now.

Gabriel shook his head. "I don't know. The sheriff didn't seem to know either. The lack of traumatic damage to the bones is interesting."

"Radish ruckus! The absence of evidence isn't evidence," Luna stated with a sniff.

"No, but it gives us direction," I pointed out. "At least we know Dr. Fenwick didn't just fall and crack his skull or break his leg and die of exposure."

Gabriel made the same intuitive leap I had. "Whatever happened to him damaged his soft tissue. Since it's no longer there, we don't know what it was."

I nodded. "That's what I'm thinking. And, from what I saw it was fast."

"Are we thinking natural causes?" Gabriel asked. "Maybe a heart attack, stroke, or brain aneurysm?"

I hesitated. "Maybe. But in the vision the heartwood shared, he ran and *then* clutched his chest. What do you think that means?"

Luna piped up. "Check his medical records. If he was healthy before he keeled over, my money's on poison."

"Luna!" I gasped. "You shouldn't bet on a man's cause of death."

"Why? It's not like he's going to get mad at me. And if I end up solving his murder, he might even thank me." Luna fanned herself with a paw. "Not that I'm in it for the glory, of course."

I was about to respond when I felt the car slowing. I glanced up in surprise. I'd been so caught up in the conversation that I hadn't even realized where we were.

The familiar pink-and-white storefront of Pixie Pastries greeted me. A hand-painted sign featuring a mischievous little pixie dusting cinnamon over a tray of golden pastries sat on the sidewalk outside the shop. The scent that drifted through the air as I opened the car door was pure temptation. Rich butter, warm vanilla, and just a whisper of spice, like the promise of something magical waiting inside. For the first time that morning, I felt some of the tension in my shoulders ease.

I turned to Gabriel, grateful. "Pixie Pastries? For a morning treat?"

His lips curled into a small smile. "Well, I figured we could both use a dose of normality. And Pixie Pastries, while not exactly normal by most standards, definitely helps settle my nerves."

"Mine too."

"That, and they have a cheese and egg croissant sandwich with bacon jam that is out of this world," Gabriel said, shooting me a wink.

"What? How come I haven't discovered this yet?" I asked, my mouth already watering.

As we stepped through the door, the warmth of the bakery wrapped around me, carrying with it the comforting hum of quiet chatter and the gentle clink of ceramic mugs against saucers. The display case at the counter was a feast for the eyes. Rows of flaky croissants, their golden layers crisp and delicate, sat beside plump fruit Danishes glazed to a glossy sheen. Miniature tarts filled with custard and topped with jewel-like berries were arranged in perfect rows, while a towering cake, half-frosted with shimmering lavender buttercream, stood like a centerpiece of edible art.

Gabriel, ever the purist, went for plain black coffee, its deep, roasted scent rising in the steam curling from his cup. I, however, was immediately drawn to their St. Patrick's Day special—The Shamrock Swirl Latte.

The barista handed over a mug brimming with creamy Irish coffee, sans the whiskey, unfortunately. Hints of honeyed vanilla swirled through the coffee, and an impossibly thick layer of matcha-infused foam topped the concoction. Gold sprinkles twinkled across the surface, and, in the very center, an enchanted design bloomed. It was a delicate four-leaf clover, traced in shimmering green sugar. The scent was warm and slightly sweet, with just the right balance of roasted espresso and earthy matcha, like a lucky charm in liquid form. As I wrapped my hands around the cup, I took a deep inhale, letting the aroma settle into my soul like the promise of good fortune.

We slid into a corner booth to enjoy our drinks, the high-backed seat offering just enough privacy to keep curious eyes at bay since Luna was with us. Despite already grabbing breakfast at Spellbooks and a police station doughnut, second breakfast was practically a requirement. Especially when it was being served at Pixie Pastries. Gabriel wasn't kidding about the croissant and egg sandwich. The croissant itself was a masterpiece. Its crisp outer shell giving way to an impossibly soft, buttery interior. Inside, the eggs were fluffy and rich, layered with a tangy, melty cheese that stretched with each bite. But the real showstopper was the bacon jam. It was something I never would've dreamed up by myself, but now that it was in my life, it was in my life for good. Sweet and smoky, with just a whisper of heat that made every bite linger on the tongue. I never wanted this breakfast to end!

The waitress, a Havenwood local named Martina, didn't even raise an eyebrow when Luna ordered a salad. Not just any salad either, but the Pixie Pastries monthly special called The Emerald Garden. A stunning mix of peppery arugula, crisp butter lettuce, and thinly sliced radishes, all tossed in a light honey-lemon vinaigrette. Delicate curls of fennel added a whisper of sweetness, while toasted walnuts and crumbles of tangy goat cheese lent it an undeniable elegance. The plate was finished with a scattering of edible flowers and a drizzle of something that shimmered just a little too much to be entirely mundane.

When Luna's salad arrived, I quietly set the plate on the bench beside me, where she could dig in without drawing too much attention. Havenwood's subtle enchantments would do the rest, nudging tourists' eyes away from anything too unusual. Luna took one look at her plate and sighed happily, tapping a foot against the edge of the table. "Now this is how one does second breakfast."

I eyed the artfully plated greens as she popped a radish slice into her mouth with a look of pure satisfaction. For a fleeting moment, I questioned my croissant and bacon jam sandwich. But only for a second.

We took our time, savoring the normalcy of the moment, but eventually Gabriel leaned forward, his tone shifting.

"I hate to leave you in the lurch today, amaryn, but I've got some things to handle." He hesitated, his expression darkening slightly. "This situation with Dr. Fenwick's body being discovered in Havenwood only complicates things. My mother will want to hear about these updates if the sheriff hasn't told her already. Knowing her, she'll probably send Lucas and me into the woods to reinforce the magical defenses. Just in case."

"That makes sense," I said, even though I hated the idea of not seeing him for the rest of the day. Yesterday had been a gift, but I knew reality was waiting. Gabriel had town duties to attend to, and I needed to get back to Spellbooks. "Keeping Havenwood safe is priority number one, especially with tourists making up so much of our economy."

"Exactly." Gabriel paused. "Do you want me to drop you at Spellbooks?"

I considered it, but I still had a little time before Cassandra needed me back at the shop and I really didn't want to be a micro-managing boss. An idea occurred and I said, "Actually...would you mind dropping me at the Enchanted Oasis instead?"

He blinked. "Bella's?"

I nodded. "Yeah. I want to check in on her. And..." I took a breath. "I was thinking of swinging by The Clover's Charm."

Gabriel's brows lifted. "To eat? Or to find the dwarf with the world's worst attitude?"

"Both?" I offered weakly.

He didn't say anything at first. Then he sighed. "Fine but promise me you'll stay safe and won't go chasing anyone off into the woods. And you won't do anything reckless."

I smiled, feeling the knot in my chest loosen just a little. "Scout's honor."

Luna scoffed. "You were never a scout."

"Okay, bookstore girl promise, then," I said with a chuckle.

Gabriel stood and offered me his hand. "I'd feel much better if Luna and Bella went with you. And if you find Runar, call me. Don't engage until either Lucas or I are there."

I nodded. "Promise."

Luna sniffed. "Miracles do happen. Look at her, making responsible choices and everything."

I rolled my eyes, but the smile tugging at my lips was genuine. Gabriel gave my hand a light squeeze, then reached for his keys.

"Come on," he said. "Let's get you to the Oasis before Luna decides to start critiquing my driving again."

"I've seen squirrels with better lane discipline," Luna muttered, hopping down. "And they don't even have thumbs."

Gabriel gave a faint smile. "Your feedback is noted."

Luna tossed her ears back like a diva with a silk scarf. "Good. I prefer to be memorable."

We stepped out into the late morning sun, the breeze tugging playfully at my hair as we made our way to Gabriel's car. The warmth of his hand lingered long after he let go to open the passenger door for me.

Gabriel pulled up in front of the Enchanted Oasis and put the car in park. Sunlight streamed through the windshield, casting a warm golden light across the front garden, where a few lingering guests ambled down the porch steps with takeaway cups in hand.

He turned to me with a small smile. "Be safe, okay? And call me if you find him."

"I will," I said, meaning it.

Gabriel studied me for a beat longer, then leaned in and pressed a soft kiss to my forehead. "See you later, amaryn."

Warmth bloomed in my chest. "You too."

Luna let out a loud, exaggerated sigh. "Well, that was disgustingly sweet," she said, twitching her nose. "You're lucky I don't have teeth sensitive to sugar."

I rolled my eyes as I got out of the car, adjusting the strap of her tote. "Jealous?"

"Please." She sniffed. "Can we get on with our day?"

Gabriel glanced over his shoulder at Luna. "You've got it. But try to keep her out of trouble, okay?"

Luna gave him a long, considering look. "No promises. But I'll aim for nothing requiring stitches."

With a final shake of his head, he pulled away.

I watched the car disappear down the road, then turned toward the Enchanted Oasis. Through the wide front windows, I spotted Antonio cleaning up the last of the breakfast dishes. He caught my eye and waved me in.

Luna cleared her throat as I walked up the steps to the porch. "Now that you're done making heart eyes at your boyfriend, can we talk about priorities?"

I arched a brow. "Like lunch?"

"Exactly. Preferably with a side of suspicious dwarf."

"You just had breakfast," I pointed out.

"Which only confirmed how much potential today has," she said, nose twitching. "Besides, you promised no reckless solo sleuthing. This is research with snacks."

"Snacks are strategic now?" I asked.

Luna flicked an ear. "Snacks are always strategic. And if that research happens to include dessert at The Clover's Charm? Well, it would be irresponsible not to follow up."

I pushed the door open and stepped inside. "Let me talk Bella into it first. I really don't want to have to walk all the way out there."

Luna nodded. "I approve. She's an excellent driver. Absolutely no squirrel tendencies. Which is more than I can say for that Silverthorne boy. And she also has impeccable taste in pastries. A solid lunch/investigative partner all around."

I smiled. "My thoughts exactly."

I fully intended to give The Clover's Charm's lunch specials my undivided attention. And if that food just so happened to come with answers?

Even better.

May the Road Rise Up...To Meet a Mystery

I MADE MY WAY through the front hall, past the breakfast nook, where a few late-morning guests lingered over their coffee. The warm scent of yeasty dough and cinnamon wrapped around me like a hug, a clear sign that Honey had been baking again.

Knocking softly on the kitchen door, I pushed it open and peeked inside.

"Harper!" Bella called, her face lighting up as soon as she saw me.

Honey looked up from where she was vigorously whisking something in a bowl. "Oh, I didn't know you were coming, or I would've made more."

Bella rolled her eyes, already hurrying over to greet me with a hug. "Come on, Mama, you know there's already enough food to feed an entire army."

"One never wants to be unprepared," Honey declared, lifting her chin slightly.

Bella let out an exasperated sigh. "You have never knowingly under-catered a single event in your life."

"And I don't intend to start now," Honey said matter-of-factly.

I chuckled. "It smells incredible in here. What are you working on?"

"Do you have any tea by chance?" Luna asked, poking her head out of the tote.

"Oh, Luna!" Bella turned, finally noticing the rabbit perched in her bag. "I didn't see you there."

Luna sniffed. "With Cassandra holding down the fort at Spellbooks, I figured it was a good day to stretch my legs."

Bella smirked. "I see an awful lot of sitting for someone who's stretching."

Luna's head snapped up. "Radish ruckus! I don't want any sass from you, young lady."

"I thought you enjoyed sass," Bella teased.

Luna wrinkled her nose. "My own. I don't need anybody else's. I've got plenty to go around, thank you very much."

Bella chuckled. "Well, I've learned from the best."

"Obviously." Luna fluffed her fur smugly.

"I'm glad you're here, Luna," Honey said, wiping her hands on her apron. "I need a second opinion on something. I've been testing a few treats for St. Patrick's Day, and I want to know which one is the best."

She slid two plates in front of me, and despite having just eaten, my stomach rumbled in appreciation. Honey's food had that effect on people.

Luna and I both sampled the treats. One was a Baileys-infused cheesecake with a chocolate-chip cookie crust, and the other was a slice of warm Irish apple cake drizzled with golden whiskey caramel. Both were decadent, rich, and full of Honey's unique magic.

"Harper?" Honey prompted as soon as I'd tasted both.

I sighed dramatically. "How do you expect me to choose between them?"

Luna swallowed her bite of cheesecake. "Easy. You put both on the menu."

Honey laughed. "Luna has spoken. Never let it be said I ignored the wisdom of rabbits."

Luna's whiskers twitched. "It won't because you won't." She winked at Honey.

Before Honey could press me for a final verdict, I cleared my throat. "Actually, I came to steal Bella for lunch. She's been looking out for me, and it's the least I can do to return the favor." I pressed a hand to my stomach. "Although my lunch idea might need to come after a long walk. I'm too full right now to eat another bite."

Bella glanced at the clock. "Actually, I have to finish up a couple of things around here. Would an hour give your stomach time to settle?"

"It wouldn't hurt. Is there anything I can do to help?" I offered.

She shook her head. "It's mostly inventory stuff, plus finalizing a few guest reservations. Nothing exciting. Why don't you make yourself comfortable in the breakfast room? Knowing you, I'm sure you have an e-book or ten downloaded on your phone. Enjoy the quiet while it lasts."

Honey clapped her hands together. "Wonderful idea! Luna, darling, come keep me company while Harper loses herself in her latest novel. I'll put on a pot of tea, and we can have a nice long chat."

Luna's ears twitched. "Will there be biscuits?"

I shot her a surprised look. "How do you still have room?" I asked incredulously.

Luna smirked. "I'm a magical rabbit. By the shiny whiskers of Lady Fluffy McHoppington, this really shouldn't surprise you anymore." She turned to look at Honey. "Now about those biscuits?"

Honey tsked. "Have I ever failed you?"

"Point taken," Luna said, hopping out of her tote. "Harper, try not to get into too much trouble while I'm gone."

I rolled my eyes but didn't argue. Once Bella disappeared into the office and Honey led Luna toward the kitchen, I settled at a corner table in the breakfast room. After pouring myself a cup of coffee from the carafe on the buffet, I pulled out my phone, but I didn't open my latest book. Not that I had anything against the M.C. Beaton book I was reading. In fact, I found the lead character, Agatha Raisin, quite endearing. However, thoughts of Dr. Fenwick and the mysterious entry for auravores swirled around my head, distracting me.

Time to put my detective hat on.

I opened the notes app on my phone and started a new list:

— What was Dr. Fenwick doing in the woods?

— What happened between Friday's lectures and Monday's discovery?

— And seriously...what is an auravore?

I sipped my coffee as I contemplated the questions. Unfortunately, the first two weren't likely to have Google-able answers, but that last one might. I set the mug aside and pulled up my browser, typing "auravore" into the search bar.

Nothing.

No cryptid records. No magical bestiaries. No shady blog posts with sketchy illustrations and all-caps warnings.

I scrolled. Kept scrolling. Then I typed in every conceivable spelling, combination, and keyword search I could think of.

Still nothing.

Even the rarest magical creatures had some sort of footprint. This? It was as if the term didn't exist. Not even as a whisper.

I took a sip of coffee and wrinkled my nose. Cold. I pushed the mug aside and sat back in my chair; the unease coiled tighter in my stomach. Maybe it wasn't a creature. Maybe it was a code word, or a nickname, or just a mistake in Grumbert's ledger. But something about the word stuck in my brain like a splinter I couldn't ignore. However, that didn't change my empty search results.

Okay, time to pivot.

I typed in Dr. Fenwick's name next, trying to dig into his research. A few journal articles popped up, mostly dry taxonomic ramblings about magical cryptids. Nothing in the past two years. No conference lectures. No papers. Not even a mention on a blog.

Had he stopped publishing? Or had his work shifted somewhere less... public?

I opened a fresh note and tapped out a list of suspects.

— Runar Ironvein: shady. In the professor's office. Might've been using my lock-picking distraction to sneak in. Definitely has secrets.

— Grumbert: tied up in mess after mess. Enough to make him desperate? Murderous? Hard to say.

— Dr. Elise Harlow: visibly upset at the university. Genuine? Maybe. But what if she wasn't?

I paused, my thumb hovering over the screen.

Could she have followed him? Confronted him? Done something in a moment of anger? But if that were the case, why Havenwood? Was it a way to cover her tracks, to distance herself from the crime? Possibly. But something about that didn't sit right. I frowned and added a string of question marks after her name.

The problem wasn't a lack of suspects. It was the lack of motive. None of them had an obvious reason for wanting Dr. Fenwick dead, or at least, not one I'd uncovered yet. And then there was the most unsettling question of all:

Had the auravores been involved?

What if they weren't just rare? What if they were dangerous? What if they were *deadly*?

The thought hit like a cold draft under the door. I took another sip of coffee, the chill of it matching the icy dread creeping up my spine. I stared at the screen, willing the search results to shift, to offer some breadcrumb I'd missed. Some stroke of luck that would make it all click.

Nothing happened.

No stroke of brilliance, no pieces of the puzzle snapping into place.

By the time Bella reappeared, I'd finished my cold cup of coffee but hadn't found a single answer. I only had more questions, and the sinking realization that the safety I'd always counted on in Havenwood might not be so solid after all.

I looked up as she leaned against the doorframe, swiping her hair up into a ponytail. "Sorry about that. That inventory took way longer than expected."

"Busy day?" I asked.

Bella groaned. "You have no idea. We just got a last-minute reservation request for a bridal party, and I had to shuffle some things around. I swear, if one more person tries to book a last-minute event, I might turn Luna loose on them."

"That's a terrifying thought," I teased.

"But effective," Bella said, with a twinkle in her eyes. "Come up with me while I change, and then we can go?"

"Sure," I said, pushing to my feet. "I can offer unhelpful fashion commentary while you pick an outfit."

"I'd expect nothing less," Bella shot back, leading me upstairs.

The Enchanted Oasis had some of the most thoughtful design choices I'd ever seen. Carved banisters featuring fairy-tale creatures, hidden nooks with enchanted lighting, and bookshelves tucked under every step of the staircase. I'd always wanted to take an afternoon to browse through the guest-donated books, but today was not that day.

Bella's room was bright and airy, with an entire wall of windows overlooking the garden. Sunlight streamed through, catching on the shelves lined with trinkets and books and making the space effortlessly warm and inviting, just like Bella herself.

She rummaged through her closet, pulling out a lightweight jacket. "So, how's Cassandra doing? Is Spellbooks still standing?" she asked.

"She's settling in well," I said, leaning against the bedpost. "She's really nice and seems to want to put down roots. I can relate."

Bella glanced over, her expression thoughtful. "How's that going for her? What with her crazy mentor and all? I didn't think she'd pick Havenwood of all places to settle down after what Lysandra Wraithmoor pulled last month."

"I think she's finding it hard," I admitted. "But I wish people would see that she's not Lysandra."

Bella shot me a sympathetic look. "You know small towns and their rumor mills. If someone sneezes weird on a Tuesday, it's news by Wednesday brunch." She gave my arm a reassuring squeeze. "But they'll come around. You just have a bigger heart than most."

I huffed a small laugh. "Or maybe I just have epically bad judgement."

"Not a chance," Bella said firmly. "Speaking of, how are you adjusting to having an employee? Must be weird not having to do every little thing yourself."

I shrugged. "It's nice to have a little bit of freedom during the day, but I expect things are going to get busier. Mindy Hart is bringing that book tour through soon, so I'll have my hands full."

Bella made a face. "Oh, yikes. What are we talking about? Another staged kidnapping?" she asked, referencing the famous author, Garrett Grimshaw's, failed publicity stunt.

"Hopefully not. But I think we can safely expect a hoard of book-loving tourists who all want the same limited-edition signed copies and ask really bizarre questions about the shop's 'vibe,'" I said, making air quotes.

Bella snorted. "I can already hear Luna's commentary."

"She'll either thrive or attempt to stage a coup. But speaking of settling in, how's Alex doing in Vegas?"

Bella hesitated. I didn't miss the way she focused a little too hard on adjusting her sleeve. "I think he's doing well. We were supposed to have a call yesterday, but he got pulled away. From what I can gather from the sporadic texts, the days are long and brutal, but he's learning a ton, and, apparently, he's impressing his instructors."

"That's good, isn't it?" I asked, trying to keep my tone light.

I knew Bella had complicated feelings about Alex's residency. The top performer in his program would be offered a permanent position at a high-end Vegas restaurant, and if he caught the attention of one of the celebrity chefs there, it could open even more doors.

Doors that would lead him away from Havenwood.

With Bella's heart set on staying here, the idea of another long-distance struggle loomed large.

"Yeah." Bella sighed. "I'm making plans to visit him next month."

"That's great!" I said. "I bet you'd love Vegas."

"It might be a little lonely," Bella admitted. "He'll be working most of the time, and I'll just be…there."

I squeezed her shoulder. "You know, now that I have an employee, I could probably manage a long weekend off if you wanted some company."

Bella's head snapped up, her eyes filling with hope. "Really?"

"Of course, I'd be happy to keep you company! I'd love to help you conquer the poker tables. Maybe even catch a show or two. Whatever you want."

Bella practically tackled me in a hug. "Harper, you are the absolute best!"

I chuckled. "Let's see how Cassandra settles in for a couple of weeks, let me get past this book launch, and then we'll plan it."

Bella pulled back, grinning. "You just made my day."

"Good. That means I don't have to share my emergency chocolate stash."

Her eyes widened. "You have one and you've been holding out on me?"

"Let's just say ever since I discovered Hocus Mochas, the drawer under the register has never been the same."

She laughed, then glanced at the clock and winced. "Sorry for making you wait so long. You must be starving."

"No worries. I had a lot to eat this morning. Besides, it gave me some time to catch up on some research."

Bella's gaze sharpened. "Research?"

I hesitated.

Bella crossed her arms. "Harper. I'm happy to play Dr. Watson to your Holmes, but you're going to need to fill me in."

I grinned. "Grab your purse. I'll explain on the way. And, while, I appreciate the comparison, I'm not sure I'm Holmes-level smart. And I really hope I'm not that neurotic."

"You do run a sentient bookshop, live with a talking rabbit, have a gargoyle guarding your rare book collection, and a massive Maine Coon as your shop mascot," Bella said dryly. "So, normal isn't exactly in the cards for you, babe."

"Fair," I admitted with a laugh. Then I lowered my voice. "But speaking of not being exactly normal, with the sheriff being a werewolf, I really don't want him coming after me if he thinks I'm gossiping."

Bella smirked, tipping her head with exaggerated seriousness. "Relax. You're not gossiping—you're invoking Rule One of the Best Friend's Forever Charter. BFF privileges cover all adventures, secrets, and occasional reckless decisions."

"I'm not sure that's a real thing," I said wryly. "But as long as the sheriff never finds out..."

"That's Rule Two," Bella shot back, lips twitching. "Never spill your best friend's secrets to a grumpy werewolf."

I laughed, shaking my head. "Fine. I'll tell you on the way."

Bella linked her arm through mine, pulling me towards the stairs. "I can't wait. Let's grab the ninja rabbit and head out."

Downstairs, Luna was still perched at the kitchen table, savoring the last crumbs of a pastry. Honey sipped her tea, watching the rabbit with amused patience.

"Finally," Luna said, flicking an ear as we approached. "I was beginning to think you two fell into a wardrobe somewhere."

Bella smirked. "You'd like that, wouldn't you?"

"Depends," Luna mused. "Is it the Narnia kind or the kind where I get a gold crown and endless desserts?"

I scooped up her tote, giving her a knowing look. "You're already living that dream, aren't you?"

Luna sniffed as she hopped inside. "I don't see any crowns. But there's no time to quibble. We have a very important and completely innocent lunch to attend."

I rolled my eyes at the rabbit before saying goodbye to Honey and following Bella outside.

Bella shot us a suspicious look. "Why do I feel like I just walked into a trap?"

I gave her my most innocent smile. "What? Can't a girl take her best friend out for a meal?"

Luna snorted. "Oh, absolutely. A meal. Nothing more."

We climbed into the car, and as she started the engine, Bella shot me a sidelong glance. "So, where exactly are we headed?"

I buckled my seatbelt. "Someplace new. I heard The Clover's Charm has a good reputation."

Bella's lips curled into a knowing smile. "If I didn't know any better, I'd say you're chasing down a lead."

"Let's just say that good food and good information often go hand in hand."

The Ley of the Land

As THE CAR PULLED onto the main road, I launched into everything that had happened that Bella didn't know yet, from Sheriff Jackson's warning to the mystery of the auravores. Bella listened, her eyes sharp on the road, nodding along as I filled her in. Luna, for once, let me get through my entire recap with minimal interruptions, though I caught her ears twitching with restrained commentary.

By the time we neared the edge of town, Bella let out a slow breath and shook her head.

"Only you would turn lunch at the Duck into an investigation."

I blinked. "The what?"

Bella glanced at me. "The Duck. You know, this place?"

She gestured toward the windshield just as we pulled into a gravel lot. A wooden sign swung gently in the breeze, carved with an elegant golden shamrock and the name: The Clover's Charm.

I stared out the window. "That's a shamrock. Not a duck."

"I didn't say it made sense," Bella said, grinning. "Locals call it the Duck because the owner's signature brew is Lucky Duck Ale. Supposedly, he was out fishing, fell into the lake, and was rescued by a duck."

I turned to gape at her. "Like... paddled over and pulled him to shore?"

Luna snorted from the tote bag in my lap. "No one knows. Some say it quacked motivationally until help arrived. Some say he hallucinated it. Some say the duck taught him to brew. Regardless, that man hasn't shut up about the duck since."

"Wait—he actually calls the duck his muse?" I asked.

"Allegedly." Luna's ears twitched. "Though I maintain that unless it wore a tiny beret and posed dramatically, it doesn't qualify."

Bella laughed. "He says he saw it and knew he had to make the beer that became the pub's signature."

"Because nothing says, 'life epiphany' like a web-footed bird," Luna muttered.

I gave her a look. "You say that like it's not possible."

"Oh, it's possible," she said airily. "Epiphanies often come from the strangest of places. One of the best teahouses I've ever been to was run by a magical armadillo on the dark side of the moon. He spouts prophetic limericks with every pot he serves."

I stared at her. "You're kidding."

She waved a paw. "Not even a little. But that's a story for when there's more caffeine and less disbelief."

Bella cleared her throat, wisely steering us back on topic. "Anyway, locals rarely use the pub's real name anymore. It's kind of a Havenwood inside joke."

I glanced around at the cozy-looking building and the carved sign. "No wonder I'd never heard of it. Why don't they just change the name from The Clover's Charm to the Lucky Duck?"

"We don't do normal here," Luna said. "Besides, it's tradition to make newcomers feel slightly confused and mildly judged."

"That's not the reason," Bella muttered as she eased the car to a stop.

"How do you know? Did the duck tell you?" Luna shot back. "Because you should never trust ducks. After cats and squirrels, they are naturally the most untrustworthy of creatures."

"Naturally?" I asked.

Luna nodded solemnly. "Ducks are chaos with feathers. Just ask any-one who's tried to cross a pond with a sandwich."

Bella rolled her eyes and switched off the car. "Ignore her. She once lost a staring contest to a goose and has held a grudge against poultry ever since."

"I did not lose," Luna huffed. "I blinked strategically."

I stepped out of the car, momentarily stunned by the view. The pub looked like it had been plucked straight out of a postcard for the Irish countryside. A low, whitewashed stone wall surrounded the property, crisscrossed with creeping vines. The thatched roof, which had to be magically reinforced to deal with the Connecticut winters, looked golden in the afternoon light. Hanging baskets overflowed with trailing ivy and delicate white blossoms, framing the weathered oak door that stood slightly ajar. The pub radiated warmth, its old-world charm wrapped in a welcoming glow.

A large whiskey barrel near the entrance held a chalkboard sign, its curling script inviting us inside:

"Stew, Stout, and Stories – All Are Welcome (Unless You Start Trouble!)"

Luna sniffed. "I like a place that sets expectations up front."

Bella smirked. "Good food, good drinks, and an implied bar brawl clause? I can see why you'd be interested."

"I'm only interested in the stew," Luna said primly. "And possibly heckling the beer duck."

As I stepped onto the stone pathway leading to the entrance, a warm, inviting scent wrapped around me. Freshly baked soda bread mingled with the rich, savory aroma of slow-simmered stew. My stomach gave a low, appreciative growl. If the food was even half as good as the atmosphere, we were in for a treat.

I was glad I'd wisely given myself time to digest before lunch. Any sooner, and I might not have had the stomach space for what promised to be a meal worth savoring. Still, I made a mental note to come back again, preferably on an entirely empty stomach.

Bella led the way into The Clover's Charm, I mean, the Duck. I followed close behind, Luna snug in her bag over my shoulder.

The pub exuded warmth, the kind that wrapped around you like an old, well-loved sweater. The polished wooden floors gleamed under the soft glow of hanging lanterns, while the rich green walls were adorned with intricate golden Celtic knots and framed photos of rolling Irish landscapes. A stone hearth crackled at the back of the room, casting flickering golden light across the tables topped with small vases filled with sprigs of clover.

A deep, jovial voice with a distinctive Irish lilt boomed from behind the bar. "Bella DeLuca, as I live and breathe! When did ya go and grow up on me?"

A broad-shouldered man emerged, wiping his hands on a bar towel. He had auburn hair threaded with silver at the temples, a strong jawline, and the kind of easygoing smile that suggested he was perpetually in on a good joke. His eyes twinkled as he spread his arms wide in welcome.

"Patrick Murphy," Bella said with a grin, stepping into his hug. "Are you keeping out of trouble?"

"Ah now, what would be the fun in that?" Patrick gave her a squeeze before turning his attention to me. "And who's this, then?"

"Harper Sullivan," I said, extending a hand.

His grip was firm and warm. "Sullivan, is it? Any relation to Beatrice Sullivan, the grand lady of Spellbooks, may she rest in peace?"

I nodded. "She was my great-grandmother. I run the shop now."

Patrick let out a low whistle. "Ah, good on ya, then! Havenwood wouldn't be the same without that shop. A pleasure to meet ya, Harper. I hope this won't be yer last time visiting."

"I'm already looking forward to coming back," I said honestly.

"And what brings ye both in today? Just lunch, or am I being treated to an unannounced book club meeting?"

"Mostly lunch," Bella said. "I figured it was high time Harper experienced one of your legendary meals."

"Ah, say no more." Patrick gave us a wink. "Let me get things sorted up here, and I'll join ye in a bit. Can I get ye both a pint?"

I shook my head. "Just water, thanks."

"Same for me," Bella added. "I still have to get back to work later."

A small, indignant sniff came from my shoulder.

"Patrick Murphy, I hope you're not ignoring me in your offer of a pint."

Patrick barked out a laugh as Luna poked her head out of her bag. "Luna! Didn't see ya there, lass." He leaned forward on the bar, resting an elbow on the worn wood. "Now, d'ye want the usual, or should I surprise ye?"

"The usual, naturally," Luna said, sniffing haughtily. "And you'd best not water it down this time."

Patrick held up his hands in mock surrender. "I'd never dream of it! A half-pint now, and another waiting behind the bar for later. Deal?"

Luna gave a satisfied nod. "Much appreciated. You've always been a good egg."

"Coming from ye, that's high praise, that is," Patrick said, grabbing menus. "Now, d'ye want a table or the bar?"

I glanced around. The pub had a cozy, lived-in feel, with rustic wooden tables scattered across the main floor and a small stage in one corner, likely for live music in the evenings. A second-floor balcony wrapped around the main room, offering a view of the dance floor below.

"The bar's good," I decided.

Patrick handed us menus, grinning. "Take yer time. No rush. Good food, good company — that's the best luck you'll find this side of the rainbow."

Bella sniffed the air appreciatively. "Is that your famous Irish stew I smell?"

"It is, indeed," Patrick said with a grin.

She leaned forward eagerly. "Do you have some soda bread and butter?"

"That I do, lass."

"Perfect. A large bowl for me then," Bella said.

Luna followed suit. "Same here."

"I'll have a small bowl," I said, patting my stomach. "I foolishly had a large breakfast."

Patrick's grin widened. "Ah, ye'll know better for next time." He tapped the side of his nose. "Ye ladies sit tight. I'll have yer lunch out in a moment."

As Patrick disappeared into the kitchen, the door behind us swung open.

A woman strode in, her posture upright, her expression unreadable. She was on the shorter side, with cropped black hair styled in a cute, spiky fashion, and luminous blue eyes that seemed to take in everything at once. Her dark green sweater contrasted sharply with her pale skin, the deep hue making her seem almost otherworldly in the dim light of the pub.

Something about her commanded attention. Not in an obvious way, but in the effortless manner of someone who knew how to hold a room without trying. The kind of presence that made people take note without quite understanding why.

Patrick returned a few minutes later, setting down the steaming bowls of Irish stew, thick slices of warm soda bread, and a generous dish of creamy Irish butter. "There you go, ladies. Just like my ma used to make." He caught sight of the newcomer and excused himself with an easy smile. "Let me see to our new guest, and then I'll be back to check on you."

He made his way over, greeting her with a familiarity that suggested he knew exactly who she was. Their conversation was too low to catch, but the subtle lift of Patrick's brow and the small, knowing smirk she offered in return spoke volumes.

Patrick disappeared into the back and returned a moment later with another bowl of stew and a thick slice of soda bread. He set it down in front of her, and she nodded her thanks before turning her attention to her phone.

Despite the casual posture, there was an alertness about her. An effortless awareness of everything happening in the room. The way her fingers tapped against the side of her glass seemed absentminded, but there was a rhythm to it, a quiet beat that suggested she was listening, cataloging, waiting. But for what?

Patrick poured himself a pint, made his way back over, and leaned against the bar with an easy smile. "Well now, how's the stew treatin' ye?"

I gestured at my bowl with my spoon. "It's excellent!"

Patrick grinned. "Ah, that's what I like to hear. Nothin' like a bit of comfort food to set the world right." He took a slow sip of his pint, then turned his attention back to me. "So, Miss Sullivan, tell me yer story. How's it that ye found yerself in Havenwood?"

I smiled. "Oh, you know, family, fresh starts, and a love of books. Granny Bea left me the shop, and I figured it was time to put down roots."

Patrick nodded knowingly. "That's the story of most of us here, one way or another. The ones that stay, anyhow." His gaze flicked to Bella, then back to me, with a hint of curiosity behind the warmth. "And out of all the places ye could've stopped for lunch, what brought ye to The Clover's Charm?"

Luna didn't miss a beat. "Because I have excellent taste."

Patrick let out a rich chuckle, but Bella leaned in, resting an elbow on the bar. "Harper loves a good story, you know, what with owning a bookshop and all. I was hoping you might regale us with one of yours."

From the corner of my eye, I noticed the woman down the bar subtly leaning in.

Patrick grinned, raising his glass. "Now, that's a fine compliment. Did ye have a particular tale in mind, or am I free to choose?"

"Storyteller's prerogative," Bella said with a wink.

Patrick stroked his chin, considering. "Well then, since we're so close to St. Patrick's Day, it only seems right to tell a tale of the man himself." Patrick's grin widened, and he raised his glass in a small salute. "If St. Paddy were here, he'd tell you that destiny has a funny way of working out, usually right after you've given up and ordered a drink."

He chuckled, the sound low and rich, then leaned on the bar with that familiar storyteller's gleam in his eye.

"Now, you've heard the tale, I'm sure," he began, his tone low and conspiratorial. "They say St. Patrick drove the snakes out of Ireland, that he stood upon the cliffs and, with the power of his faith, banished every last slithering thing into the sea. A fine story, that. But let me tell ye the version you won't find in any old church records."

Luna's ears pricked up. "I do enjoy uncovering the secrets of history."

Patrick gave her a wink. "Then settle in, lass, because this is one ye won't want to miss."

His voice dropped just a touch, taking on the lilting rhythm of an old Irish tale. "He didn't just drive out the snakes. He banished the *dragons*."

Patrick let that sink in for a moment before continuing.

"Long ago, when Ireland was still wild and untamed, the land pulsed with magic. The hills whispered secrets, the rivers burbled their songs, and, beneath the green earth, the great serpents of old made their home.

"These weren't the little garden snakes ye might find in yer boot if ye were unlucky. No, these were the great ones. The wyrms, the wyverns, the drakes, and the fire-breathers of legend. Some soared on vast wings that turned the sky to shadow, their scales gleaming like fire-forged steel. Others slithered through the rivers and bogs, carving deep channels into the land. Some, their spined crests sharp as iron, prowled the cliffs and caves, watching with knowing eyes as the world changed around them.

"For centuries, the dragons and their kin ruled unchecked, their magic woven into the very bedrock of Ireland. Some watched over it, tied to its fate. Others grew restless, hungry for dominion.

"But none were more feared than Caoranach.

"She was no ordinary dragon. She was an Oilliphéist, a terror from the old world. Some said she was born from the embers of the first fire, others swore she slithered forth from the darkness before time itself began. Wherever she went, the land cracked open, lakes formed in the prints of her feet and mist curled from her breath, thick with enchantment. Her emerald eyes gleamed like cursed jewels, and those who met her gaze were never quite the same again.

"At last, Patrick came to Lough Derg, where the last and most dangerous of all the dragons lay curled beneath the waves.

"Caoranach rose from the water, vast and terrible, her scales gleaming in the moonlight. 'Ye are no druid,' she hissed, her voice shaking the very air. 'No warrior. No king. And yet ye come to challenge me? No blade can pierce my scales, no shield can guard from my fire. Lay down yer weapons and I will grant ye a swift death.'

"Patrick stood firm, planting his staff into the earth as the wind howled around him. 'I come not with iron, nor blade, nor shield,' he said, his voice steady as the rising sun. 'I do not seek to wound, nor to strike, nor to fall before ye in fear. I come with light, with truth, and with the power to send ye back to the depths where ye belong.'

"Caoranach narrowed her great, slitted eyes, her tongue flicking out to taste the truth of his words on the wind. Something in them unsettled her. He didn't flinch. He didn't reach for a weapon. He simply stood. Unmoved and unwavering, as if the storm howling over the heather bent for him. That stillness, that quiet defiance, wormed its way beneath her scales.

"Fear, unfamiliar and furious, coiled in her heart. So, she struck first.

"The battle between them raged for three days and three nights. The land trembled as the two forces clashed. The air burned with her fire, the earth cracked beneath her fury, and the rivers swelled with her wrath. But Patrick did not falter. His words carried the weight of power, a force not of the sword, but of faith. Unyielding, unwavering, absolute.

"Caoranach struck back with all the fury of her kind. Her claws raked deep trenches into the hills, carving great gouges into the land that would one day cradle the rivers. Her tail lashed as Patrick forced her back, sheering the very earth away, sending entire swaths of land crashing into the sea and shaping what men would one day call the Cliffs of Moher. With every step she retreated, the land beneath her twisted and cracked, reshaped by her rage. Lakes swelled where her feet struck the earth, the ground forever marked by her presence. Her breath rolled in thick waves, shrouding the land in mist that never quite lifted from the hollows and valleys she left behind.

"But Patrick did not falter. On the third night, he raised his staff high, and the heavens themselves seemed to answer. A force unseen, vast and unrelenting, surged through the land. Caoranach howled, thrashing against it. She fought, she clawed, she roared, but the power was too strong.

"With one final, furious bellow, she was driven into the sea, her massive form vanishing beneath the crashing waves. Patrick, weary but victorious, raised his staff one last time, sealing the land so that no great dragon would ever rise again.

"But the power of the dragons did not leave the Emerald Isle. At least, not entirely. For magic does not simply vanish.

"Where the dragons fell, their lifeblood seeped into the earth. The great lines of energy, invisible yet thrumming with power, took shape in the places where their magic lingered. What men would one day call ley lines were born from the bones of dragons, their power running through the earth like veins, ensuring that Ireland would always be a land of mystery, power, and legend."

Patrick Murphy leaned back, a twinkle in his eye. "And if it wasn't fate that shaped the land that day, well maybe it was just a bit of good Irish luck, riding the winds."

He sat back, swirling his pint, his voice softening now that the tale was done. "And that, my friends, is why Ireland is steeped in magic. Not just because of the fairies or the leprechauns, but because of the dragons whose power was buried in the land itself. Their bones still hum beneath the hills. Their magic became the ley lines, forming rivers of raw power, threading through the earth like veins. They're still there to this day, powering all the fantastical stories you hear from Ireland. As long as we don't bleed them dry, that is."

The others murmured in appreciation, but I absently traced the rim of my glass. Ley lines. I knew them well. I felt them hum beneath my feet in Havenwood, shifting and pulsing like the town's hidden heartbeat. As guardian of the heartwood, I'd learned to sense them, even wield them in small ways using the heartwood as a conduit. But this? The origins of ley lines being rooted in dragon magic?

That was new.

And if dragons had formed the ley lines in Ireland, could the same be true for Havenwood?

I stared into my stew, but I didn't focus on the rich broth or the tender chunks of meat. My mind was miles away, turning over Patrick's words, fitting them against the puzzle that had been forming since discovering Dr. Fenwick's skeleton. Could dragons be tied to our own ley lines? And if they were, did that somehow link them to the wyrms Dr. Fenwick had been studying? Was that why he was in the forest surrounding Havenwood?

A flicker of unease rippled through me.

Had he known something about our ley lines? Something no one else had pieced together? And if so...was that why he was dead?

I dug my spoon into the stew, but I had no appetite anymore.

Had Dr. Fenwick been onto something that got him killed?

The Scavenger's Creed

A COMFORTABLE LULL SETTLED over us, the pub's warmth wrapping around me like a soothing blanket. The only sounds were the occasional clink of glass from behind the bar and the faint, sweet lilt of an Irish fiddle playing softly from a corner speaker. I should have been content to let the story sit, to appreciate it for the tale it was. But my mind churned with questions, each one twisting into the next.

I took a slow sip of water, playing it casual. "So, Patrick," I said, setting the glass down, "you've clearly heard your fair share of dragon lore. I'm curious. Do you think all of them were really as dangerous as the stories make them out to be?"

Patrick chuckled, the sound low and knowing. "Ah, dragons. Folk love to paint 'em all with the same brush. Great beasts burnin' down castles and stealing gold. But the truth's never that tidy."

I hesitated and then chose my words carefully. "Do you know more about the different types of dragons?"

Patrick leaned back and drummed his fingers on the bar. "Now that's a fine question. There're all sorts of dragonkin, ye see. The great, fire-breathin' beasts of legend, the hoarders, the tricksters, the guardians. But then ye get into the nastier sort. The ones that don't leave treasure behind, only ruin. The list of dragonkin is long and as wonderful as it is terrible. Did you have a specific one in mind?"

I shifted in my seat, trying to play off the sudden thrum of nerves tightening in my chest. My fingers curled against my knee, and I gave a small shrug. "You mentioned one I hadn't heard of much before. Wyrms? What are those?"

Patrick's expression darkened slightly, but he covered it with a sip of his drink. "Ah, the wyrms. Nasty creatures, those. I'd wager that if St. Patrick was going to evict any dragonkin from Ireland, the wyrms deserved it the most."

Luna flicked her ears. "Fluff and furballs! Now, that's a bold claim. Why single them out?"

Patrick puffed out a breath. "Because unlike your classic dragons, wyrms aren't noble. They don't have the intelligence of the greater kind, nor do they breathe fire or weave spells. They don't have the grandeur, and they certainly don't have the self-restraint. They crawl and burrow, twist through places they don't belong. Folk used to say if you heard the earth whispering, it was a wyrm beneath your feet. They're pure instinct and vicious as the day is long."

I shuddered. "And that's why St. Patrick was so determined to get rid of them?"

He leaned in slightly, lowering his voice as if sharing a particularly grim secret. "See, wyrms are scavengers. Where the great dragons hunted and ruled the skies, wyrms slithered in the shadows, waiting for the battles to end, for the mighty to fall. They'd burrow through the earth, claw their way through the dead, feasting before the vultures ever got a chance. They're the undertakers of dragonkin, taking what's left behind. Their numbers grew too fast, and they had a bad habit of overrunning places where death was common. Battlefields, old ruins, even graveyards. If left unchecked, they'd have turned the whole of Ireland into a feast."

Bella wrinkled her nose. "That's...charming."

Patrick chuckled. "Oh, don't let it put ye off yer meal. They've their place, same as any creature. Without 'em, the land would be littered with disease, bodies left to fester. Wyrms make sure nothing goes to waste. They burrow deep, always lingering near ley lines, though why that is, no one's rightly sure. Some say they're drawn to the old energy. Others reckon they just like warm places to nest."

A chill crept down my spine. Wyrms weren't hoarders of treasure, nor were they the type to spin riddles or bargain like their greater kin. They were patient. Opportunistic. They waited.

Were they out there, waiting even now?

The thought unsettled me more than I cared to admit. If Dr. Fenwick had been researching something tied to the ley lines, to the wyrms, what exactly had he uncovered? And, more importantly, had it gotten him killed?

Bella made a face. "And here I was, worried about regular snakes."

Her voice cut clean through the haze, snapping me back to the present. Right. I wasn't here for a mythology lesson. I was here for answers. Specifically, ones that might lead me to Runar Ironvein.

Patrick lifted his pint. "And that, ladies, is why we toast to St. Paddy every year. He did the Emerald Isle a great many favors, wyrms and snakes included." He shot us a grin. "Which reminds me, I do hope ye plan on coming back for our St. Patrick's Day celebrations."

I gave a polite nod, already shifting gears. Time to steer the conversation somewhere more useful. "Patrick, I came across someone recently. A kind of a passing acquaintance. He actually recommended this place to me."

Patrick leaned in. "Oh? Who might that be?"

"His name's Runar Ironvein. Ever heard of him?"

The easy warmth in Patrick's expression vanished instantly. His fingers curled around his pint, and he muttered something in Irish before fixing me with a sharp look. "Aye, I've heard of him. And I'll tell ye right now, he's not the sort a nice lass like yerself should be associating with, if you catch my meaning.

I frowned at the vehemence of his words. "Why do you say that?"

Patrick's grip tightened around his glass. "Because Runar Ironvein is a wolf in sheep's clothing. Better yet, he's a wyrm in a dwarf's skin. A scavenger. A good-for-nothing who takes, takes, takes, and never leaves anything but ruin."

Luna tapped her back foot. "Bit harsh, isn't it?"

"Harsh but accurate," Patrick shot back. "I wouldn't trust him as far as I could throw him, and with this bum shoulder, that isn't far." He clapped a hand over his shoulder and rolled it dramatically.

Bella glanced between us, brows knitting together. "I've never heard you talk about someone like that before. What happened between the two of you?"

Patrick let out a low, sharp breath, shaking his head. "That's not a story meant for polite company. But let me just say this: that dwarf better not show his face around here ever again if he knows what's good for him. Not after what he pulled last month." He scoffed, rubbing a hand over his face and then shooting me a confused look. "I can't believe he'd go about giving recommendations for my pub. We didn't exactly part on the best of terms."

A prickle of unease crawled up my spine. "Oh. Well, um...he actually gave me the recommendation a while back, but I've just been super busy at the bookshop." I could feel Bella's eyes on me. My lying skills were abysmal at best.

Patrick narrowed his gaze slightly, but if he saw through me, he didn't call me out. He sighed and tossed his bar towel over his shoulder. "Iron-vein's always digging. Always wanting to get his hands on the next big score no matter what the cost to anyone else."

I frowned. "Are you saying he's a thief?"

Patrick let out a low scoff, drumming his fingers against the bar. "Aye. A thief with no conscience and no shame. But the problem with a man like him? He doesn't stop. Even when he's been warned."

Luna twitched her whiskers. "Sounds like there's bad blood between the two of you."

Patrick's scowl deepened. "Let's just say, that dwarf never stays out of trouble for long."

"Really? Did he take something from you?" Bella asked carefully.

Patrick exhaled, rubbing the back of his neck. "Not from me, no. But there are things in this world that don't belong in the wrong hands. Things that—"

The bell over the pub door jangled.

A group of customers swept in, their laughter and conversation rolling through the room like a gust of warm air. The sound shattered the tension, scattering it to the shadowed corners of my mind, but not far enough to be forgotten.

Patrick flicked a glance over his shoulder, then let out a breath. "Hold that thought, lass. Let me get these folks sorted," he said, already slipping back into the role of welcoming barkeep as he hurried to greet his new guests.

I exhaled, exchanging a look with Bella.

"Well," she murmured, reaching for her drink. "That was unexpectedly intense."

Luna flicked an ear. "You're telling me. Patrick was one pint away from hexing the man's name into the floorboards."

Runar Ironvein.

What exactly had he done to earn Patrick's fury? Why had he been poking around Dr. Fenwick's office? And more importantly—had he been looking for something?

Or had he already found it?

Not All Gold Glitters

THE WARMTH OF THE pub still wrapped around us. The fire crackled cheerfully in the hearth, while the golden glow reflected off the polished wood and gleaming bottles behind the bar. But despite the inviting space, something about Patrick's words lingered, sharp and unsettling.

I ran a finger along the rim of my glass, my thoughts circling back to what he'd said about Runar Ironvein. Patrick had practically cursed his name. He called the dwarf a thief. I ran back through what I knew of Runar. He hadn't seemed to take anything of value either at Northvale Exports or in Dr. Fenwick's office, but maybe I'd missed something. Maybe I needed to take another look. Maybe—

"Excuse me."

I turned, startled.

The woman from down the bar had slid onto the stool next to me. There was a small hop in her movement as the seat was just a bit too high for her. She had the kind of coloring that stood out. raven-dark hair, luminous blue eyes, and the unmistakable air of someone who had stories to tell.

But that wasn't what caught my attention.

It was the slight point to her ears. I wondered if she was some sort of fae. I didn't want to press as it wasn't considered polite to ask such things outright, but I had a gut feeling she wasn't entirely human.

The woman exhaled, glancing between us. "Look, I normally wouldn't just walk up and introduce myself like this. There'd be a bit of banter first. Share a drink or two. But..." She tilted her head slightly. "I couldn't help but overhear your interest in Runar Ironvein."

I tensed. "What about him?"

"I get it," she said softly. "You don't know me. But I just heard about this Runar character this morning. Shady business. It didn't sit right. I went for a drive to clear my head and ended up here. Call it instinct, call it luck, but I think I was meant to find you."

A flicker of alarm prickled at the back of my spine, quick and sharp. "Sorry, but...who are you?"

She smiled and extended a hand. "The name's Sloane O'Shea."

"It's nice to meet you," I said, shaking Sloane's hand. Her grip was firm, steady. "I'm Harper Sullivan, this is Bella DeLuca, and, um...," I trailed off, uncertain whether to introduce Luna. The obfuscation charms around Havenwood usually kept her hidden from those unaware of the magical world, and I wasn't sure who or what Sloane O'Shea was.

"Nice to meet you all," Sloane said, giving us a courteous nod.

"Are you visiting?" Bella asked. "I don't think I've seen you around before."

Sloane leaned an elbow on the bar, the picture of casual ease. "I run a bar down in New Orleans," she said, her accent carrying a faint Southern lilt beneath the Irish roots. "But I'm up visiting my cousin for a bit. He runs a shop here in town. Maybe you know him? Liam O'Shaughnessy?"

Bella smiled warmly. "I do. It's nice to make your acquaintance. I hope you enjoy your visit to Havenwood."

To my surprise, Sloane turned to Luna and extended her hand toward the rabbit. "Pleasure to meet you. You don't see many moon rabbits around these days."

Luna twitched her ears. "Oh, someone with manners. I'm Luna and it's nice to be noticed." She sniffed. "Usually, people just mistake me for the White Rabbit from Alice in Wonderland."

Sloane smirked. "I would never. I know greatness when I see it. And moon rabbits are exceptionally rare."

Luna leaned forward, eyes twinkling. "Not as rare as seeing a leprechaun in public," she countered.

I blinked. Luna was a *moon rabbit,* and this lady was a leprechaun? I'd only heard whispers of the former and never expected to see the latter just hanging out in Havenwood. What was going on here today?

Sloane merely lifted a brow. "Ah, but nobody expects a leprechaun to casually walk up and order a pint, now do they? After all, we're all supposed to be red-haired, bearded men in green waistcoats, dancing jigs and singing about pots of gold."

I couldn't help but chuckle. She had a point. If Luna hadn't mentioned it, I wouldn't have pegged Sloane as a leprechaun. My guess would have been some kind of fae, but leprechaun wouldn't have even made the first page of possibilities.

Still, one thing didn't add up. "If you're just up here visiting your cousin," I asked, "how do you know Runar Ironvein?"

Sloane tapped her fingers on the bar. "He's actually the reason I'm here. Indirectly, anyway."

Bella shot her a skeptical glance. "What do you mean?"

Patrick bustled past, dropping off drinks at a nearby table. Sloane waited for him to move away before she continued.

"My cousin Liam runs an antique shop here in Havenwood. He's always raved about this place, so I figured I'd finally come visit." She glanced around. "It's got its charm. Not as lively as New Orleans, mind you."

"Few places can be," Luna murmured. "The jazz alone puts it in a league of its own."

Sloane pressed a hand to her heart. "Doesn't it just?" She exhaled and straightened. "Anyway, this isn't just a family visit. This Runar fellow has been in and out of my cousin's shop for a while, selling odd bits and pieces. But lately? He's been in there a *lot.*"

Bella frowned. "How often are we talking?"

"At least three or four times a week, until recently," Sloane said seriously. "Liam started to get suspicious when the dwarf dropped off an unexpectedly large haul yesterday."

That sent a small ripple of unease through me. "And your cousin is worried?"

Sloane nodded. "Liam's starting to get suspicious. Runar always has a bill of sale, but something about it doesn't sit right. He thinks they might be forged."

Patrick passed by again, shooting us a thumbs-up. "Are you ladies doing okay? Can I get you anything?"

Bella recovered first, offering a smooth smile. "All good, Patrick."

"Alrighty then. I'll just put this order in the kitchen and be back with you." He disappeared behind the bar.

I barely heard the exchange, my thoughts already racing. Patrick's warning about Runar echoed in my mind. What was the dwarf up to?

As soon as Patrick was out of earshot, Sloane lowered her voice. "It's not just any item. One of the things Runar sold Liam..." She hesitated, choosing her words carefully. "Liam recognized it."

A cold prickle ran down my spine. "And?"

Sloane's fingers tightened on the edge of the bar. "And there's no way Runar had a legitimate bill of sale for this one."

Bella frowned. "Why?"

Sloane took a slow, measured breath. "Because it belonged to a friend of Liam's. A friend who died nearly ten years ago."

The room seemed to shrink around us. I exchanged a worried glance with Bella.

"Okay..." I said, treading carefully. "But maybe it was part of an estate sale? Or one of your cousin's friend's heirs sold it without him knowing?"

"I suggested the same thing," Sloane said. "But Liam swears that can't be the case."

"Why not?" I asked.

Sloane's gaze flicked around the room, then back to us. Her voice dropped. "This isn't something I'd normally share out in the open."

She reached into her jacket and pulled out a small gold coin. She set it on the bar and tapped it gently three times. A faint shimmer rippled around us like a heatwave, muffling the background noise.

Luna's ears twitched at the shimmer. "Well. That's not your average party trick."

Sloane glanced between us again. "I know this all seems a bit sudden. I normally wouldn't share something this personal with strangers. But when your magic is tied to luck, you learn to trust it."

Sloane rapped her knuckles lightly on the bar. "What are the odds we'd end up in the same pub at the same time, asking after the same dwarf?" She gave a wry smile. "It doesn't feel like coincidence. So the question is, can I trust you?"

Luna tilted her head, her voice sharp. "That depends. Can we trust you?"

Sloane gave a slow nod. "Fair enough. Let's start with a little faith on both sides."

She looked up, her gaze steady. "What I'm about to tell you needs to stay a secret, but without it, you won't understand the danger. Can you keep it to yourselves?"

Bella and I nodded instantly. Luna's voice softened. "All of us here in Havenwood strive to keep this a refuge for magical creatures. You and your secret are safe here."

Sloane hesitated, meeting each of our gazes. Whatever she saw there must've convinced her. When she spoke again, it was barely above a whisper. "People think leprechauns have pots of gold and cause mischief. Which we do, but we also have a gift not many other folks possess. We can make our own luck. Literally."

I blinked in surprise, my mind racing to catch up. Wait. *Magical luck? As in... a real, actual power?*

Unable to help myself, I asked. "What? How does that work?

Sloane continued. "Luck usually moves in a balance. Some of it good, some bad. Leprechauns can generate luck. Not much at a time, mind you. Just enough to smooth the path, so to speak. Eventually, our kind discovered we could infuse an item with our luck. A charm. An object we bond with emotionally and magically. Not everyone does it, but for those who do, it's personal."

"So, you think Runar stole a leprechaun's lucky charm?" I asked, confused as I tried to process this new information.

Sloane shook her head. "No. Worse."

Bella leaned in. "Worse how?"

Sloane sighed. "If a leprechaun willingly gives their charm away, that's one thing. The luck will eventually run out and that's that. But if they lose it or it's taken from them? Then the luck doesn't just vanish."

I didn't like where this was going. "What happens?"

Sloane's expression was grim. "Once the luck runs out, it turns. What once absorbed luck begins draining it instead."

A chill coiled around my ribs, and I sucked in a breath. "Like a black hole for luck?"

"Exactly," Sloane said. "Instead of bringing fortune, it sucks it up like a sponge, leaving only bad luck in its wake."

Bella sat back. "Okay. That sounds...terrifying."

Sloane's expression was unreadable. "It's more than that. Depending on how long the charm was tied to the leprechaun, the curse can range from stubbed toes and lost keys to..." She met my gaze. "Exploding engines, car crashes, and other extreme forms of bad luck."

Bella sat back. "Okay. That escalated."

I exhaled slowly. "This isn't just mild inconvenience we're talking about. This is real danger. But I don't understand how this links back to your cousin."

Sloane nodded. "This bad luck charm is why Liam is worried. His friend's wedding ring was his charm. He wore it every day for decades, constantly pouring love and luck into it. And when his wife died, he never took it off. Said he'd been married to one woman, and that was it for him. Before he passed last year, he insisted he be buried with it. He was so tied emotionally to that ring that he never would have been able to give it away and sever the tie between it and him."

A cold shiver slid down my spine. If the ring had been buried with him, then Runar wasn't just a treasure hunter. He was a grave robber.

I swallowed. "And you're saying..."

Sloane's jaw tightened. "Runar sold that ring to my cousin. After ten years without a leprechaun pouring luck into it?"

I finished for her. "It's now an active bad luck curse."

Sloane's nod was slow, deliberate. "Liam knew what to do. He immediately put it in a lead-lined box that blocks the magic. For the time being, the bad luck is nullified. But he wants answers, which is why he called me to come up here and lend a hand. I tracked the dwarf to this pub and the question I have for Runar Ironvein is: how did he get that cursed ring?"

Buried Fire and Fortune

SLOANE'S WORDS HUNG IN the air. My mind reeled with questions, each one stacking on top of the other like a precarious house of cards. Before I could voice any of them, she tapped the coin once, palmed it smoothly, and slipped it into her pocket just as Patrick Murphy strolled over, clapping his hands with a cheery grin.

"Ladies, I see you've made a new friend," the barman said.

Sloane returned his smile, extending a hand. "Sloane O'Shea. Visiting from out of town. I'm Liam O'Shaughnessy's cousin."

Patrick's friendly expression didn't waver, but something flickered behind his eyes. "Ah, I know Liam well. Good lad." He shook her hand firmly, then turned back to Luna, Bella, and me. "Now, can I tempt ye with dessert? The bread pudding today is particularly fine."

I pressed a hand to my stomach, shaking my head. "I don't think I could eat another bite. Honestly, Patrick, that stew was delicious." I pulled out my purse and slid some cash across the bar to pay for our lunch, along with a generous tip.

"Absolutely," Bella agreed. "And now that Harper's been here once, I have no doubt she'll be back. Often."

"Oh, one hundred percent," I said enthusiastically.

Patrick beamed. "You're welcome anytime. Lovely to see you. Enjoy the rest of your day." He waved and turned back toward the bar, leaving us to gather our things.

To my surprise, Sloane stood as well. "Look," she said, lowering her voice slightly. "I don't mean to impose, but I don't want my cousin to get in trouble because of this Ironvein guy. Liam wants answers about his friend's ring and is worried Runar has skipped town. If you have a lead on where the dwarf might be, it would be a huge help."

I hesitated, then shrugged. "Honestly, I don't know. I ran into him in Eastford at the university. He was poking around places he shouldn't have been."

Sloane sighed. "That tracks."

"We followed him for a while," I continued, "but he slipped away. The only lead we had was a business card that brought us here." I glanced toward the bar. "And it doesn't seem like Patrick Murphy is a fan."

"No, it does not," Sloane muttered, throwing a glance over her shoulder before lowering her voice further. "Listen, I know this might be a stretch and I hate to impose, but would you be willing to come with me to my cousin's shop? He's worried Runar might be into something nefarious, and I can't extend my vacation indefinitely. I want to make sure I don't leave Liam on his own and he tends to keep to himself. It would make me feel so much better knowing that someone else is watching out for my cousin while I'm in New Orleans."

I exchanged a glance with Bella, who gave me a slight nod. "Of course," I said to Sloane. "That's what Havenwood is about, right? Helping each other when trouble comes knocking."

"Absolutely," Luna chimed in from her place in the tote.

Bella's expression grew more serious. "And if your cousin is right and that ring was buried with his friend, then Runar Ironvein isn't just a treasure hunter. He's a grave robber."

A shadow passed over Sloane's face. "That's exactly what I'm afraid of. A person like that has no scruples and if he's coming into Liam's shop?" She exhaled and shook her head grimly as we stepped outside, the crisp air a stark contrast to the pub's cozy warmth.

We walked in silence for a few paces, gravel crunching underfoot.

I tugged my coat tighter. "It feels like we've wandered into a patch of really bad luck."

Sloane let out a dry chuckle. "Luck's great and all, but I've seen more messes fixed with duct tape and desperation than fate ever sorted out."

I shot her a sideways glance. "Coming from someone who can control luck, that's a surprising attitude."

She shrugged easily. "No one controls luck. I've just learned how to lean into the curves. Besides, luck is fickle. But effort? Effort shows up when you need it. You can sit around waiting for fate to call, or you can go build your own phone line. Take it from me, the phone line is usually the better option."

She was right. It wasn't about waiting for the stars to line up anymore. It was about grabbing them and dragging them into place.

I straightened my shoulders. "We're not waiting around. I'd rather get to the bottom of this than sit here hoping Runar trips over his own shoelaces. We should go check on Liam."

Bella nodded immediately. "Agreed."

Luna wrinkled her nose. "That's the spirit. Never sit around like a damsel in distress waiting for luck to save you. If I had waited for luck, I'd still be stuck in a hutch with a raccoon named Gary."

I blinked. "Wait. What?"

Luna sniffed. "It's a long story which involves apple pie, a teleportation spell, and very poor life choices." She muttered under her breath, "In my defense, Gary started it." She straightened, ears twitching. "Moving on."

Sloane's smile returned, though it didn't quite reach her eyes. She tossed her keys lightly into one hand, her voice steady. "Exactly. Sometimes making your own luck just starts with showing up."

I gave a firm nod. "We'll show up for Liam. That's the Havenwood way."

Sloane's smile softened, the tension in her posture easing a little. "Now I see why Liam always raves about this place. Do you know where the Pot o' Gold is?"

Bella nodded, digging in her purse for her keys. "Yes. We'll meet you over there."

Sloane shot us a thumbs up and headed toward what looked like a rental car. Bella and I exchanged a determined glance before following.

As we pulled out of the parking lot, I glanced over at my best friend. "That was a lot to process. What do you think?" I asked.

Bella let out a breath. "I think we've heard an awful lot about dragons and treasure today. Not exactly what I expected from lunch."

I snorted. "Havenwood. Always expect the unexpected."

As the trees blurred past, I frowned out the window and mulled over what I'd learned today. Patrick's stories of ancient magic, buried power, and old battles sounded more like bedtime tales than history. But then again, I'd just met a leprechaun, so what did I know. Could ley lines really be remnants of dragon magic? Echoes of something older? If so, what did that mean for Havenwood? Had dragons lived here too?

Luna and Bella both knew about the ley lines. It had been impossible to hide the information from them with everything that happened around the time I became the guardian of the heartwood.

"Do you think any of what Patrick said could be true?" I asked quietly. "About dragons and...everything?"

Luna spoke up from the back. "There's always some truth in the old myths. You just have to know where to look."

I tapped my fingers against my knee. "If that's true, then what does that mean for the heartwood?" Both Luna and Bella knew I was its guardian—that I drew from the magic running beneath Havenwood. "Have I been using dragon magic this whole time?"

Bella considered that. "That's...kind of a wild thought and something I hadn't considered. Although, before this year, I thought they were just fantasy anyway."

Luna scoffed. "Maybe you should stop over-analyzing every magical inheritance you get and accept that you have a knack for collecting problems like some people collect stray cats."

I twisted in my seat to glare at her. "That's rich coming from you."

Luna glared at me. "I am not a problem. I am a privilege."

I rolled my eyes. "That's not what I meant. Over-analyzing is your thing, but when it comes to magic, it seems like you are content to just shrug and smile."

Luna sniffed. "That's because it's *magic*. If it could be rationalized, we'd call it science. So yes, sometimes you just have to nod and smile."

Bella chuckled but then sobered. "Still, it's something to think about. Especially with Harper being the guardian and all."

I stared out the windshield, my thoughts circling like moths around a candle. Havenwood's ley lines were powerful. There was no denying that. But if they were once dragon magic, then that raised some bigger questions.

Had dragons once lived here? And if so...what happened to them?

The car bumped slightly as Bella turned onto a side street, jostling me from my thoughts.

"Okay," I said, dragging my mind back to the present. "What about this ring Runar sold to Liam? I've heard of haunted objects, but a leprechaun's lucky charm turning into a bad luck magnet? That's new."

"New, but not impossible," Luna pointed out. "And if Liam is worried enough to bring it up, it's worth looking into."

Bella glanced at me. "Do we trust Sloane?"

I hesitated. "She's Liam's cousin, and she just got here. So far, she seems honest."

Bella gave a short nod, keeping her eyes on the road. "Do you think Liam's right?" she asked. "About the grave-robbing?"

I frowned. "I think that's the most obvious conclusion."

Luna tipped her head. "Sometimes the most obvious solution isn't the right one. In Havenwood, looking at things through a normal lens can actually distract you from seeing the real truth."

I narrowed my eyes. "What are you talking about?"

She shot me a knowing look. "Oh, I don't know. A certain sentient bookshop springs to mind."

I huffed. "That's different."

"Is it?" Bella asked. "For years, everyone assumed your great-granny just had a knack for picking the perfect book for every customer. Given our magical community, it made sense. She was a witch, after all. Nobody questioned it. But the truth was, Spellbooks itself was choosing the books."

I sighed, rubbing my temples. "So, what you're saying is we might have to rethink everything we think we know."

Luna smirked. "Welcome to Havenwood."

Grave Concerns

From the street, the Pot o' Gold had the air of a place that had been collecting secrets for centuries. Through the large front window, I glimpsed worn wooden shelves groaning under the weight of trinkets, brass candlesticks, and delicate china. Glass display cases lined the walls, glinting in the dim light, filled with brooches, pocket watches, and rings that seemed to hum with hidden stories. A grandfather clock loomed in the corner, its pendulum swinging on a slightly off-beat rhythm, as if it wasn't marking this time, but some other, older measure of it.

Sloane pushed the door open, and the bell above it gave a hollow clang. The cozy, cluttered charm I'd glimpsed from the outside wrapped around me as we stepped in. The scent of aged paper and polished oak mingled with something earthier, but beneath it lurked something...else. Through my connection with the heartwood, I could feel magic shifting through the space, curling around certain objects. The place wasn't just a shop. It was a vault of sorts, a carefully curated collection of magic-infused artifacts, some benign, some...less so.

"Liam? Are you in?" Sloane called.

A man emerged from behind the counter, wiping his hands on a cloth. Short and stocky, with his wavy red hair a tousled mess, he had the sharp, knowing green eyes of someone who missed nothing. He clocked us immediately, his expression shifting to something more guarded.

"Sloane," he grumbled. "What trouble have ye gotten into today?"

"Seriously," she said dryly, folding her arms. "I went out for lunch and made some friends. What makes you think I'm a trouble magnet?'"

Liam snorted. "That thing about a banshee haunting a jazz club down in New Orleans springs to mind."

"That's a great story," she shot back. "Not proof that trouble follows me."

"Agree to disagree." Liam shook his head, then turned his attention to the rest of us. His gaze lingered on Luna, a flicker of recognition crossing his face.

"Been a long time, Luna," he said.

Luna gave him a knowing look. "Not long enough for you to have paid back that favor you owe me."

Liam winced. "Ah. You'd have to bring that up."

Sloane rolled her eyes. "You owe Luna a favor? What did you do?"

"Fluff and furballs! What didn't he do? If you're looking for luck, don't borrow any from him. His luck's always a double-edged sword. Why, I remember—"

Liam cleared his throat, cutting her off. "Nothing that needs discussing at the moment. Besides, you know as well as I do that luck's the universe's way of keeping things interesting."

Luna huffed, twitching an ear. "Don't give me that. *You* know as well as I do smart people don't sit around waiting for luck. They stack the deck when nobody's looking."

Bella pinched the bridge of her nose. "What? No. That's not how that goes."

I arched an eyebrow at the rabbit. "Remind me not to play poker with you."

Liam shifted his attention to me and Bella. "I'm Liam O'Shaughnessy. And you two are?"

"Harper Sullivan," I introduced myself. "And this is Bella DeLuca."

Liam shook our hands. "DeLuca? The family that runs the Enchanted Oasis?"

"The same," Bella said.

"I'll have to swing by. It's been an age since I had one of yer mother's scones with a spot o' tea," Liam said.

"She'd be happy to welcome you," Bella replied with a warm smile.

Liam turned to me. "Sullivan, eh? Any relation to Beatrice?"

"She was my great-granny. I took over Sullivan's Spellbooks when she passed."

"Ah, a shame that was. She was a grand lady and a better neighbor." Liam studied me for a beat longer than I liked, his sharp gaze flicking over me like he was sizing me up. Then he huffed and leaned back against the counter. "Right. And what brings ye lot here?"

I hesitated and then decided to go for the direct route. "Runar Ironvein."

The air in the shop changed. Not literally, but the warmth dimmed slightly, and the easy banter between Sloane and Liam evaporated.

Liam crossed his arms. "Him."

The way he spat the word made it clear exactly how he felt.

"Yeah," I said carefully. "We ran into Sloane and realized we both had an interest in tracking him down. She filled us in on what happened. We were hoping to talk with you about him."

"Maybe take a look at some of the things he's brought in recently. They might give us some sort of insight into where he's been or possibly where he's going," Bella added.

Liam exhaled through his nose, clearly debating whether he wanted to entertain this. His gaze flicked between Sloane, Bella, and me, then to Luna, as if weighing something unspoken.

Sloane nudged his shoulder. "Come on, Liam. If we wanted to waste your time, we'd have brought bad whiskey."

Without a word, he strode past us, flipping the sign on the door to "Closed" and sliding the lock into place. Then he pulled all the shades down.

Luna flicked an ear. "Cabbage catastrophe, that's not ominous at all."

Liam ignored her. He moved to the counter, reaching beneath it and pressing something I couldn't see. A moment later, the shelves behind him shifted. A low, mechanical hum filled the air as the neatly arranged antique books and trinkets rotated away, revealing a hidden room beyond the counter.

The temperature seemed to drop, and the thread of magic I had sensed earlier tightened, curling through the air like an unseen current. The room was smaller than I had expected. Heavy iron shelving and locked glass cases lined the walls. Unlike the antiques outside, these objects weren't for public display.

They weren't just old.

They were powerful.

Liam pressed another button on the wall, and the shelves rotated again, sealing off the main shop. To my surprise, it also cut off my connection to the heartwood tree. The sensation hit me like a sudden drop in elevation. I sucked in a breath, instinctively reaching for the tether that had been there, thrumming steadily beneath my awareness since February.

It wasn't broken, just...silent.

I glanced at the walls, wondering how much of the magic-containing lead must be present to do such a thing.

Liam crossed his arms, surveying the space. "I don't let just anyone back here. This is where I keep the more...delicate acquisitions. The kind that don't belong on display because in the wrong hands, they'd do a lot more than collect dust." His sharp gaze settled on me. "And if you lot are sniffing around Runar Ironvein, then I have a feeling you know exactly the kind of mess he likes to stir up."

Sloane folded her arms. "Liam, we don't have time for dramatics. They're here to help. Just show them what he brought in."

Liam muttered something under his breath but moved to a large iron safe tucked into the corner. He twisted the combination lock while pressing his other hand to the top and humming a lilting tune. The mechanism clicked open with a soft hiss of released magic.

He pulled out a metal tray lined with silk and set it on a heavy worktable in the center of the room. Neatly arranged across it were various trinkets: vintage watches, delicate brooches, ornate rings, and a pocket compass inlaid with opal. All items that could stand the test of time, their craftsmanship exquisite and, I guessed, were also infused with magic. Next to it, he set a small box of dull gray metal. I could see faint, protective runes were inscribed on the box's surface.

"This was everything Runar brought in?" I asked incredulously.

"Yes," Liam said grimly. "All of it. Every last piece."

"It seems like a lot," Bella said, peering closely at a brooch. I noticed she didn't touch it.

"Normally it's a handful of curios, easy enough to log. But this haul?" Liam rubbed the back of his neck. "Dozens of pieces, all with enchantments layered in different ways. Sorting through them takes time, and I won't put anything on the shelf until I'm sure it's safe. Last thing I need is some trinket exploding in a customer's hands."

"Can't you just, you know, remove the magic?" I asked, eyeing a silver pendant warily.

Liam huffed out a soft laugh. "Sure. If you've got a fortune to burn and the patience of a saint. Every enchantment has its own quirks. Sometimes you can nullify a spell if you know the original crafting process. If that's not an option, legend has it you might manage such a feat with a blessed spell weaver's silk thread, a relic enchanted under a full solstice moon by a coven of benevolent witches, or another such rare magical item." He snorted. "But good luck finding something with that level of power in my shop. You'd have better odds catching a unicorn." He rested a hand on the small lead box. "But when I saw that, I knew I needed to confront him."

Liam pressed his palm against the lid of the box, murmuring something under his breath. The lock unlatched with a quiet click, and Liam carefully opened the box. Inside, resting on a scrap of deep blue velvet, was a simple gold ring. It looked unassuming, almost plain. But the moment the lid lifted, a shiver ran down my spine.

Even without my connection to the heartwood, I could sense a wrongness to the ring, as if the air itself recoiled from it.

"This," Liam said, voice tight, "was my friend's wedding ring. The same one he was buried with ten years ago."

Luna wrinkled her nose. "How can you be sure? I mean, not to be rude, but cursed rings have been around for ages. Just ask Tolkien."

I shot her a flat look. "One ring to rule them all" was not the comforting comparison I'd been hoping for.

Liam pulled a pen from his pocket and tilted the ring, pointing to the inside of the band. "Look here. It's engraved with their wedding date. His initials and his wife's. They had matching rings, and I remember the day we took them to Elowen Wispdale to have them inscribed. Trust me, this is his ring."

Silence stretched between us.

I swallowed hard. "And Runar sold it to you?"

Liam's expression darkened. "Aye. That rat had a bill of sale for the whole lot, but once I saw this ring, I knew there's no way it was real." Liam rested a hand on the small lead box, his expression dark. "Once I realized what I was looking at, I knew I needed backup. So I called my cousin Sloane. If anyone can track a trail, it's her."

Sloane crossed her arms. "That's why I'm here," she said, shooting Liam a glance. "He reached out when he started getting suspicious, and I don't ignore family. I've got a knack for finding people when I put my mind to it." She gestured toward the box. "But after Liam found this, Runar vanished. The dwarf never came back."

"Interesting," Luna murmured, peering closer at the items on the tray.

Sloane shrugged. "I didn't have much to go on. And then, what do I hear at the bar but you asking around about Runar? I figured luck was finally on my side. If we're all after the same dwarf, we might as well pool our resources."

Bella's gaze flicked over the rest of the items laid out before us. "And all of this came from Runar too?" She hesitated. "Is it safe to touch?"

Luna scoffed. "You have got to be kidding me. I'm not touching anything in a hidden vault filled with magical junk. You never know what else might be cursed."

Liam shook his head. "I've checked most of it out. A lot are simple charms. Good luck tokens, protective wards, that sort of thing. Nothing dangerous so far, but with this much coming in at once, I've had to be thorough." He gestured towards the pile of watches, brooches, and pendants.

I crouched down, inspecting the items without laying a finger on them. The collection was eclectic, but one thing stood out—everything here was built to last. Metal, stone, glass. No paper, no cloth, nothing fragile. Just things that could survive time.

"Do you know where he got these?" Bella asked.

Liam lifted a shoulder. "If you believe that bill of sale, an estate sale. However, I find that extremely unlikely. My friend was clear in his wishes. He wanted his ring buried with him to always link him and his wife."

"That's sweet in a morbid way," Luna said.

Before the snarky rabbit could say anything that might offend, I quickly jumped in. "Was there anything else he brought in?" I asked.

"Yeah," Liam said. "But I wanted to check them for spells before putting them on the shelf. I just haven't gotten around to them yet."

"Could we see them?" I asked eagerly.

Liam nodded and returned to the safe, retrieving a few more items. I noticed Runar opted for things that were relatively small and easy to slip into a pocket or a bag.

"These came in the same lot," Liam muttered, setting them beside the book. "Didn't think much of 'em at first, but now? Well, I hope they help, but I don't see how much they will offer you in way of tracking Runar down."

There was a velvet-lined case containing a neatly arranged collection of old coins, some clearly historical, others marked with arcane runes that shimmered faintly under the lights. Next to the coins was a pair of gold cufflinks, stamped with Eastford University's insignia. The next item was a sleek fountain pen with an ornate silver clip. A pocket watch rested nearby, its hands frozen at midnight, and a silver locket on a delicate chain lay unopened, glinting in the light. Then my eyes landed on the book Liam had brought out with the rest of the items from the safe.

I frowned, leaning in closer. There, stamped across the front in stark, unmistakable lettering, was **PROOF COPY**.

My breath caught. The author's name caught my eye in large, bold font along the bottom of the page.

Dr. Malcolm Fenwick.

I pointed at the book. "Do you mind if I take a look?"

Liam nudged it closer. "Go ahead."

I flipped it open, skimming the pages. They were filled with detailed descriptions of magical creatures—their habitats, diets, behaviors. My fingers tightened on the cover. A strange chill settled over me. If Runar had taken this from the university, had Dr. Fenwick given it to him or, as Patrick had implied, did he have sticky fingers? And if he had stolen it, could that have led to an altercation between the two? Was Runar responsible for Dr. Fenwick's death?

But if that was the case, why were either of them in the woods around Havenwood? And how to explain Dr. Fenwick going from a live professor on Friday to a skeleton by Monday afternoon? Something still didn't add up here, but I had a feeling Runar might hold the answers I sought.

Liam must've been watching me closely because he asked, "Something wrong, lass? Ye look a little pale."

I swallowed hard, scrambling for a cover. I wasn't ready to explain about Dr. Fenwick. "I've, um, heard of Dr. Fenwick before, but I didn't know he was an author."

Liam huffed. "If he was, he wasn't a famous one. I took a peek at it. Really niche stuff. An academic tome on magical creatures. Not much of a market for that, let me tell you."

My mind flashed back to the wyrms. "Do you mind if I borrow this?" I asked.

Liam waved a hand. "Take it. No one's lining up to buy it. If a buyer turns up, I'll give ya a call. Just return it when yer done."

I scooped up the book, my mind racing. Runar Ironvein had Dr. Fenwick's book. That meant something. I just didn't know what.

Luna shifted in her bag to get a better look at Dr. Fenwick's book. "If Runar had this, what else did he take?"

Liam snorted. "I'm not sure, but he's got a nose for valuable objects, even ones most folk wouldn't realize are worth anything."

Bella crossed her arms. "If he's turning up with books from Dr. Fenwick, a dead man's ring, and whatever else he sold Liam, then where is he getting this stuff?"

Liam's expression darkened. "That's the real question, isn't it?"

Sloane spoke up. "I told you, cousin. I don't like the way he's been sniffing around lately. If he's grave-robbing or worse, someone needs to put a stop to it."

Liam nodded. "Agreed. But how?"

My stomach churned. "Do you have any way of contacting him?"

Liam let out a sharp laugh. "If I did, I'd have words with him myself. No, he shows up when he wants to. Doesn't leave a trail. He's as slippery as they come."

Bella frowned. "Then how do we track someone who doesn't want to be found?"

Sloane tapped a finger against the counter. "We set a trap."

Luna twitched an ear. "Oh, sure. Let's just put an enormous pile of gold and a giant net in the middle of the town square and wait for him to show up."

Bella shot her a look. "Not exactly subtle."

I exhaled. "Besides, if Runar was that easy to bait, someone else would have caught him by now." I turned to Liam. "You said he brings things in but never leaves a trail. Does he ever drop hints? Mention places he's been, things he's looking for?"

Liam shook his head. "Not that I've noticed."

I picked up one cufflink emblazoned with the university's insignia, holding it up to the light. "If he's been stealing things from the university, maybe he left a clue behind there." I set the cufflink down next to the silver fountain pen.

Sloane snapped and pointed at me. "That's a great idea. I could drive out there and take a look."

Liam shot her a look. "I know you say you can handle yourself, but you going after him on your own makes me nervous. Better to wait until I close up the shop and then we can head out there together."

Sloane sighed but nodded. "Fine."

"Or I could go with you," I suggested.

Bella and Luna both swiveled to face me, identical incredulous looks on their faces.

"Harper," Bella started.

I held up a hand before she could argue. "It'll have to be tomorrow, though. I need to get back to my shop today. But if we go during the day when all the students are around, we should be fine, right?"

Sloane looked at me, then nodded. "I'm sure it'll be plenty safe. Shall I pick you up in the morning?"

"Perfect," I said before Bella or Luna could launch a protest.

Sloane reached into her pocket and pulled out her phone, passing it to me. "Here. Let's trade numbers in case anything comes up."

I quickly entered my number before handing the phone to Bella, who arched an eyebrow but didn't argue. She added her info and then passed it back to Sloane.

"If Runar shows up, you'll be the first to know," Sloane promised, slipping the phone into her pocket.

Liam folded his arms. "And if he sets foot in this shop again, I won't let him slip through my fingers. You'll hear from me the second he does."

Bella blew out a breath. "So... now we wait, and hope fate feels like being helpful?"

Luna rolled her eyes. "Please. Fate's about as reliable as a sugar-glider on espresso. I trust prep work."

Liam chuckled, a glint of humor in his gaze. "I agree with the wise rabbit. Fate's grand in fairy tales. But out here? It's elbow grease and a bit of stubbornness that'll win the day."

Bella threw an arm around my shoulders. "Good thing we're not short on either."

I hugged the book to my chest, warmth blooming through the knot of nerves in my stomach.

We weren't sitting around waiting for luck anymore. We were making our own.

Fate could wait. We had work to do.

An Unlikely Hoard

Bella's grip on the wheel tightened as she drove through Havenwood, heading back toward Spellbooks to drop me off in time to relieve Cassandra. She shot me another skeptical glance. "I want it on the record that I don't love the idea of you and Sloane chasing after this dwarf."

"Neither do I," Luna added, nestled comfortably in the back seat. "I prefer plans that don't involve you potentially getting yourself into trouble."

I took a deep breath, repeating the same argument I'd been making since we got in the car. "I'm not going alone. Sloane will be with me, and we're going in broad daylight when the place is full of students."

Luna snorted softly. "And what exactly are you hoping to find? A sign taped to a door that says, 'Runar Ironvein was here?'"

I twisted and shot a smile at Luna in the back. "That would be convenient. Think he'll be that considerate?"

Bella let out a breath, clearly trying to keep her frustration in check. "Harper, you don't even know if he left anything behind. And if he did take something from Dr. Fenwick, that means he was at the university before this all went down. What if you're walking into something bigger than we realize?"

"I'll be careful," I promised. "Besides, we need more information, and this is our best lead."

Luna flicked an ear. "Fine. But if you get yourself cursed, kidnapped, or in some sort of other cabbage catastrophe, I reserve the right to say, 'I told you so.'"

"Noted," I said with a soft chuckle.

Silence stretched between us, tangible enough to taste. Almost. But by the time we pulled up to Spellbooks, Bella's frown had softened into something more resigned than outright disapproving. I could tell she wasn't thrilled, but at least she wasn't actively trying to talk me out of it anymore. A minor victory.

Bella put the car in park and turned to me. "Just...promise me you'll be careful?"

I met her gaze. "Always."

She nodded, not looking entirely convinced, but she let it go. "Alright. I need to get back to the Oasis. Call me if anything changes." She gave us a quick wave before pulling away, leaving us on Arcadia Avenue outside of Spellbooks.

Mr. Wigglesworth was waiting for me at the door, his thick tail curling around his paws as he regarded me with a knowing gaze. I scratched behind his ears, earning a satisfied rumble as Cassandra called a greeting.

"Hey, Harper! Thanks so much for covering for me today. You really are the best boss," she said.

Boss. I liked the sound of that.

"I know how these things can go. It's really not a problem," I reassured her. "You go on and get that apartment sorted."

Relief spread across her face. "Thank you. I really appreciate it."

"Seriously, it's fine," I assured her. "I'll hold down the fort."

"I owe you one," she said, grabbing her coat. "See you tomorrow!"

She hurried out, and I settled in at the counter, opening Dr. Fenwick's book. The proof copy felt weighty in my hands, the pages crisp and untouched. I ran a thumb along the spine, exhaling slowly.

Alright, Dr. Fenwick. Let's see what was so important that someone was willing to steal it.

What I found inside went far beyond the general folklore you'd find online. This wasn't just another compendium of magical creatures. It was a carefully researched academic study, with classifications, behavioral analyses, and detailed ecological impacts.

Before moving to Havenwood, I'd assumed magical creatures were all flash and folklore—phoenixes, fairies, and the like. But the way Dr. Fenwick wrote, it was clear that there was an entire magical ecosystem intertwined with the mundane one, hidden beneath the surface of the human world. Not just magical beings living among us, but species with actual functions. Predators, prey, scavengers. A whole web of life I'd never really thought to question.

Most of the wyrm information lined up with what Dr. Harlow had told us about Dr. Fenwick's research. Wyrms were a scavenger species. Not exactly the brainiacs of the magical world, but they played an important role. They fed on decomposing organic material and, in rare circumstances, even synthetic materials like plastics. Their metabolic processes produced a nutrient-rich byproduct that enhanced soil fertility. Dr. Fenwick suggested they could be harnessed as a potential efficient form of magical waste management. It was strange to see it all laid out so matter-of-factly, like reading about badgers or stumbling across a field guide on magical composting.

Dr. Fenwick had been researching sustainable magical solutions for modern waste problems. But if he proposed turning a semi-sentient species into magical janitors, that might've sparked more than academic outrage. To some, it could've looked like exploitation or, at the very least, raised serious ethical questions. And if someone believed he was crossing a moral line, how far would they go to stop him?

At least the entry detailing their affinity for ley lines gave one possible solution for why Dr. Fenwick was in the forest surrounding Havenwood. He could've been conducting experiments. Had he been testing their limits? Trying to see just how much they could break down? But that would mean taking wyrms out into the wild. Based on what I just read, I didn't want to encounter these creatures accidentally.

Before I could follow that thought any further, the bell above the door chimed, and I straightened, slipping into shopkeeper mode as a customer wandered in.

"Let me know if you need any recommendations," I called, still half-lost in my thoughts. The customer gave a polite nod before perusing the shelves, and I forced myself to focus on the present, greeting another regular who came in right behind them.

Minutes blurred into an hour as I rang up books, answered a few questions, and fetched a special order from the back. It wasn't until there was a lull between customers that I finally exhaled and pulled the book out from where I'd hastily stashed it under the counter. The words blurred as I tried to focus.

Coffee. I needed coffee.

I put on a fresh pot, my mind still circling wyrms, Dr. Fenwick, and what exactly he'd been trying to accomplish before he died. Looking at the sketch of the wyrm in the book made me shiver. Definitely not a creature I'd want to run into if I could avoid it. In fact, I wouldn't have linked them to dragons at all if—

Dragons.

I nearly facepalmed myself. Why hadn't I thought of this before? Ignatius!

The tiny, book-loving dragon who occasionally nested in Spellbooks was nothing like the scavenging wyrms. He preferred paper to gold and wouldn't hurt a fly, although he would demand a perfectly cooked steak from the butcher if given the chance. Now that he had learned to control his fire-breathing, he was meticulous about never scorching a book.

Still, if wyrms were related to dragons, maybe Ignatius could shed some light on them. Why hadn't I thought of that before?

Excited by the idea, I leapt to my feet, grabbed a notebook and pen, and jotted down Dr. Fenwick's name at the top of a blank page. Beneath it, I wrote:

Wyrms—possible connection to ley lines?

Ignatius—potentially more information on wyrms.

I paused, tapping the pen against the paper. Ignatius was the obvious dragon expert, but I had a responsibility to Spellbooks. One I felt even more keenly since Cassandra had started. I couldn't run out to Mason's auto shop to find Ignatius for a chat. Not when I was supposed to be working. Once the shop closed, maybe I could head over to see Ignatius.

Pleased with my plan, I sent a quick text to Mason to see if I could swing by later to chat with the tiny dragon. He replied almost instantly, but said they were out of town until tomorrow. Something about a supply run or a forge delivery. Well, chatting with my dragon friend would have to wait then. I sighed and turned my attention back to Dr. Fenwick's unpublished book. Maybe there was something else interesting in there.

I opened to the back of the book, hoping to find an index. Maybe that would help me narrow down my search rather than aimlessly flipping through pages. My heart stuttered when I saw the following entry:

Auravores.

That was it. That was the other creature the sheriff had asked me to look into. I'd hit a complete dead end trying to research it online. No records, no folklore, not even a sketchy forum post. But here it was, printed on the page in black and white. I found the page number for the entry and settled in with my coffee to read.

Auravores (Auravorae Mustelaphis Arcanis)

Common Names

Known variously as treasure-sniffers, magical ferrets, or ley-line seekers, auravores have long been the subject of rumor and speculation. Their elusive nature has ensured that reliable information remains scarce, and for many years they were thought to be extinct.

Physical Characteristics

Auravores resemble oversized ferrets, with sleek, sinuous bodies built for burrowing. Their ashy black fur is streaked with molten-gold markings that shimmer when exposed to strong magical currents. The creatures' amber eyes, slitted like those of a cat, work remarkably well even in the dimmest light. Their claws are fine but sharp, well adapted to handling fragile enchanted objects, while their prehensile tails are capable of gripping or manipulating items with surprising dexterity. Most unusual is the marsupial-like pouch on the underside of the body, which is frequently used to store objects of value.

Behavior and Abilities

Highly intelligent and instinctive hoarders, auravores are irresistibly drawn to enchanted objects, often sensing residual auras long after the magic has faded. They demonstrate a remarkable capacity for navigation and are able to follow faint magical traces across great distances. Though generally non-aggressive, they are adept at using their surroundings to escape threats, suggesting an evolutionary advantage in cunning rather than combat. Scholars continue to debate whether auravores simply collect magic or actively consume it. Some accounts suggest that at least a portion of their population has adapted to feed on ambient magic, shifting their ecological role toward something more predatory.

Ecology and Environment

Auravores are most often encountered in places saturated with magic such as ancient ruins, forgotten shrines, and sites of prolonged enchantment. They are gifted tunnelers, constructing elaborate burrow systems that sometimes intersect with ruined magical structures. In their relentless collecting, they have been known to create hidden troves of enchanted objects, some of which remain undiscovered for centuries. Historically, their range was widespread, but loss of magical habitats and the over-harvesting of enchanted resources have left their current population uncertain. Some theorists argue that auravores once helped regulate magical ecosystems by redistributing ambient energy, though if populations are indeed recovering, it remains to be seen whether they will reclaim this role or evolve into something far less benign.

I sipped my coffee, absorbing the information.

Maybe Dr. Fenwick had abandoned the wyrms entirely. They were aggressive and difficult to control. Dr. Harlow had implied they might be far too volatile for any practical use. Maybe he'd shifted his focus to something like an auravore. But to what end? They didn't fit his waste disposal goals at all. So why had he gone in search of the rare creatures?

And who else knew he was looking into them?

My mind drifted back to Runar Ironvein. He had been in Dr. Fenwick's office. He'd started turning up with more enchanted objects than ever before. And then, he was looking for Grumbert and stolen shipment pages from his logs.

That couldn't be just a coincidence.

I tightened my grip on my pen. Had Runar discovered the existence of auravores and tried to pull Dr. Fenwick into some kind of treasure-hunting scheme? Had they been working together and had a falling out? Could the cage I saw in the vision from the heartwood have contained the rare creatures? Could that fight have led to the professor's death and possibly the disappearance of the auravores? If so, that could explain why Runar had gone in search of Grumbert. He needed new auravores to sniff out treasure.

I flipped open my notebook and scribbled a few quick notes.

Auravores—research further. How rare? Any known sightings in the area?

Runar Ironvein—suspicious. Possibly behind Dr. Fenwick's death? Hunting auravores? Stealing magical artifacts?

I started to close the book, then hesitated. Sheriff Jackson had asked me to look into auravores, and here was the first real information I'd uncovered. I snapped a photo of the entry, biting my lip as I stared at the screen. How much about ley lines did he know? How much could I share?

I decided caution was my friend and sent the photo to Gabriel. As a Silverthorne, he would know how to handle sensitive magical intel, and he already knew about ley lines.

Found a book Fenwick wrote. Will explain later. Not sure if I should pass it along to the sheriff as it mentions ley lines. Take a look at the photo?

Gabriel's reply popped up almost instantly. *Don't worry. I'll handle it.*

That was something, at least. One less worry weighing on my mind.

I turned back to my notes. This was all theory. Just scattered pieces of a puzzle I hadn't quite solved. I didn't know for sure what connected them, but my gut told me something did. And tomorrow, I was going to find out when Sloane and I went to the university. Maybe there, I'd find answers to some of my questions.

Or maybe I'd be walking straight into the same trap that had caught Dr. Fenwick.

A Bad Sort of Brilliant

I WOKE EARLY AND hurried through my morning, setting out food for Mr. Wigglesworth and Luna, and chatting with Spellbooks, but my mind was elsewhere. When I tried to make a third pot of coffee, Luna's ears pricked up.

"Radish ruckus! Not even you need that much caffeine. What's got your mind in knots?" the rabbit asked.

"Oh, I'm just distracted."

It wasn't a complete lie. I was getting the shop ready for Cassandra. But in truth, my thoughts were tangled in wyrms, auravores, and all the unanswered questions surrounding Dr. Fenwick's death.

"Mm hmm." Luna rolled her eyes. "Well, when you want to talk about it, I'll get you sorted out in no time."

"I have no doubt," I said with a chuckle.

Cassandra arrived not long after, her usual burst of energy filling the shop as she scratched behind Mr. Wigglesworth's ears and exchanged light banter with a few customers.

"Hey," she said, catching me watching her. "Is everything okay? You're not upset about yesterday, are you?"

"No! Not at all. Did they fix the issue with your apartment?" I asked.

Relief washed over Cassandra's face. "Yes, thank goodness. No more cold showers for me. But are you sure everything is okay with you?"

I hesitated, biting the inside of my cheek. Cassandra was nice, but we weren't at the point in our friendship where I was ready to dump a pile of magical mysteries and murder investigations on her.

Instead, I went with, "Oh, just a lot on my mind with this upcoming promotion."

She clapped her hands together, rubbing them like she was about to tackle a challenge. "Okay, boss, point me in the right direction and tell me how I can help."

I grinned. "Let's start with the ad campaign."

For a while, Cassandra and I worked together on organizing a new shipment and designing a series of promotional ads to post around town, in the newspaper, and on social media. It was a productive morning, broken only by a few early customers, most of whom were more interested in Honey's biscotti-of-the-day than the books themselves.

By the time Sloane pulled up outside, I felt like I had a solid handle on the business side of things. Cassandra waved cheerfully as I grabbed my bag and slipped into the passenger seat.

The car ride to Eastford University was anything but dull. Sloane, it turned out, was a natural storyteller, regaling me with tales of her adventures in New Orleans and beyond. She had a flair for the dramatic that I found both amusing and oddly comforting. If she didn't live so far away, I had a feeling we would have been fast friends.

As she eased the car to a stop outside the university, I glanced out the window. By the time we reached Eastford University, the morning was already slipping away. The university was quieter than I'd expected.

"Why's it so dead?" I asked, peering out the window as Sloane eased the car into a parking spot.

Sloane smirked. "It's a university, Harper. The kids who have class are in class. Everyone else is probably sleeping or just now getting breakfast."

I raised an eyebrow. "Breakfast? At eleven?"

"They're basically teenagers. Adult teenagers. Limited responsibilities and all the potential to get into trouble. What do you expect?"

I thought of Master Sergeant Edward Sullivan and shook my head. "Even being on my own, I didn't sleep in this late. And I was way too scared to party all night and miss a single class."

Sloane shot me a knowing look. "Your mom was a taskmaster, huh?"

"My dad," I corrected with a small shrug. "For better or worse, he made sure I knew and respected my responsibilities."

She nodded approvingly. "Well, whatever he did, it worked. You're a business owner with your head on straight. Not too crazy."

I smirked. "You should see my spreadsheet color coding. That's where the real madness begins."

Sloane let out a laugh as she switched off the car. "So, do you think your dad could come scare some sense into this Runar Ironvein?"

"If anyone could, it'd be my dad. But he's stationed overseas."

Her expression sobered slightly, but she nodded. "Guess that means it's up to us. Where do we start?"

I grabbed my backpack, having opted for something a little more student-like than my usual purse, and slung it over my shoulder. "Dr. Fenwick's office. Maybe his assistant can give us some insight. Or we might get lucky and bump into Runar again."

"I doubt it, but I don't have a better plan," she said, pushing open the door. "Lead the way."

We crossed the quad, blending in with a small group of students heading toward the science building. Entering after them, I led Sloane upstairs to the ecology department.

The last time I'd been here, the place had been quiet, the usual hum of academia filling the halls.

Not today.

Raised voices echoed down the corridor.

"If you didn't take it, then who did?" a sharp, shrill voice demanded.

Sloane and I exchanged a look, instinctively slowing our steps to avoid walking straight into the middle of whatever was happening. Peeking around the corner, I spotted Dr. Winterbourne standing with her hands on her hips, her back to us. Across from her stood Dr. Harlow, her face blotchy and tear-streaked.

"I don't know, ma'am," Dr. Harlow said, voice shaking. "The last time I remember seeing it, you were in Dr. Fenwick's office, having your meeting with him. I don't remember seeing it since then. Have you checked his office?"

Dr. Winterbourne's lips thinned. "It's locked. Ever since he decided not to show up for work this week."

Dr. Harlow swallowed hard. "Well...maybe you left it in your office?"

Winterbourne cut her off with a sharp glare. "Don't be absurd. Of course, I checked my office first. Do you think I'd be so foolish as to not check my own office?"

Her voice dripped with disdain, but there was something else beneath it. Frustration, yes, but also something more.

"I'll warn you now, Dr. Harlow," Winterbourne continued. "If my father's pen turns up in your possession, this will not go favorably for you on your annual report."

"I would never take it!" Dr. Harlow's face crumpled further, her hands trembling at her sides. "Please, ma'am, I—"

"I'll find that fountain pen," Dr. Winterbourne snapped. "It was a gift from my father, and I am not about to let it go missing. Not on my watch."

With that, she spun on her heel and stormed down the hallway, disappearing around the corner.

I shot a glance at Sloane, who shrugged.

"Who was that?" she mouthed.

"Head of department," I mouthed back.

Dr. Harlow's quiet sniffles turned into full-blown, hiccupping sobs.

"Follow my lead," I whispered. Sloane and I stepped around the corner. I feigned surprise at seeing Dr. Elise Harlow and hurried over, keeping my voice gentle. "Dr. Harlow? Is everything okay?"

She jerked upright, hastily swiping at her tears, her face blotchy and distressed. "It's nothing. I'm fine. Don't worry about me," she said in a rush, though the way her voice trembled made it clear that wasn't true.

Sloane touched her arm lightly. "Hey, it's alright. Want to grab a coffee? Talk about it?"

Dr. Harlow shook her head so quickly that her messy curls fell in her eyes. She shoved the hair back with a distracted hand. "I can't. My boss's boss misplaced something, and I have to find it as soon as possible."

"What is it?" I asked. "Maybe we can help."

Elise hesitated, then gave me a watery smile. "That's really nice of you, especially since we just met. But this is my problem."

"Trust me, I've dealt with my fair share of difficult people in my business," Sloane said, folding her arms. "But I bet we can help if we put our minds to it. Just tell us what's going on."

Elise swallowed hard and wiped under her eyes, smearing her mascara a little. "Dr. Winterbourne. She's my boss's boss. Her father was a tenured professor here years ago. A tough man by all accounts. He gave her this silver fountain pen when she became a professor, and she treasures it above almost anything else." Her voice wobbled. "But it's missing. And she thinks I took it."

Sloane shot me a quick glance, and I could almost hear her unspoken thought. A silver fountain pen...like the one we saw at Liam's shop? Could Runar have taken it when he was here?

Elise swallowed back another sob, giving an odd little hiccupping cough. Distress was written all over her face. Before she could spiral further, I reached for her hand and gave it a reassuring squeeze.

"Hey, it's okay. We'll figure this out." I glanced at Sloane beside me, then added gently, "This is my friend Sloane. She's great at solving puzzles." Sloane gave Elise a soft smile, and I turned back to her. "Do you remember the last time you saw the pen?"

Elise dabbed at her eyes. "The last time I saw Dr. Winterbourne using it, she was reviewing an article with Dr. Fenwick in his office," she managed through her tears.

"That's a great start," I said. "So maybe it's still there."

Elise's shoulders slumped. "The only problem is that his office is locked, and I don't have a key. He hasn't been on campus all week, and..." Her voice wavered. "I stopped by his house yesterday. No answer." She swallowed hard. "He's got a heart condition. He played it off like it wasn't serious, but..." Her eyes shimmered with worry. "He would've called. He's never gone this long without checking in. I think—I think something might've happened."

Guilt twisted in my gut. Sheriff Jackson must not have told the university about Dr. Fenwick's death yet. He was probably still waiting for the official identification to be finalized. I wasn't about to tell Elise and interfere with an active investigation. Especially not one run by a werewolf with a sharp nose and a short temper.

"Well," I said carefully, "maybe campus security can let us in?"

Elise shook her head. "They won't enter a professor's office without a compelling reason. My boss being mad at me isn't enough, not in this building. Too many sensitive research projects."

"What about the cleaning staff? They must have a key," Sloane suggested.

Elise shook her head again. "Dr. Fenwick was extremely private. The cleaning staff only went in when the office was already open."

I hummed thoughtfully. "Has anyone checked the office recently? Maybe he stopped by, and no one noticed."

"I checked it when you were here last," Elise said. "Nobody's seen him since."

"Then let's double-check," I said, already steering us down the hall. Elise trailed after me, Sloane falling into step on her other side. In a few moments, we were standing outside Fenwick's door. I placed my hand on the doorknob.

Elise's voice rose in a quick protest. "It won't open. He always keeps it locked when he's not here. Always."

"Still, maybe we should—oh." I widened my eyes in mock surprise as the lock gave way beneath a quiet push of my magic. It was much easier the second time around.

"Look at that," I said lightly. "Maybe he forgot to lock it."

"That's strange," Elise said, her brow furrowed.

"Or maybe the lock was just sticky," Sloane added with an innocent shrug.

Elise frowned. "No, I don't think so. I tested the door yesterday, and it was definitely locked."

"Well, he must've stopped by then," I blurted out. And then winced. Lying really wasn't my thing. "Come on, let's take a quick look for your boss's pen."

"I don't know..." Elise hesitated.

"Look, we'll be quick," Sloane reassured her. "You'll be with us the whole time. Three sets of eyes are better than one. I bet we find it in five minutes. Then you can return it to your angry boss-lady and be the hero of the day."

Elise's wide, uncertain eyes darted between us before she finally relented. "Alright, but if you touch anything, you have to put it right back where you found it. Dr. Fenwick is very particular."

"You got it," Sloane said smoothly, flashing me a quick smile and a wink when Elise turned to step inside.

As we stepped into Dr. Fenwick's office, Sloane kept Elise talking, her chatter light and friendly. Sloane must've kissed the Blarney Stone because her gift of gab was strong. She had a way of putting people at ease. Sloane launched into an easy, meandering conversation about the time she lost her favorite pen during a job interview and had to sign paperwork with a crayon.

"It was a terrible first impression," she said, shaking her head dramatically. "I think the recruiter thought I was either a genius or completely unhinged."

Elise, despite her obvious stress, gave a watery laugh. "What happened?"

"Well, I got the job. But I also got a three-month probationary period because, and I quote, 'there's potential, but we're not convinced you aren't a disaster.'"

Elise chuckled, and Sloane shot me a subtle glance, letting me know she had things covered. I was grateful. It gave me the chance to focus on what I'd really come here for, searching for any clues about Fenwick's research, Runar Ironvein, or what had ultimately led to the professor's death.

Moving quickly, I started with Fenwick's desk, scanning the surface for anything out of place. It was overly neat, and I could see at a glance that there was no fancy silver pen in sight. Still, I made a show of rattling the writing utensils as if searching before turning my attention to the drawers. They yielded nothing new. Some unused stationery, extra pens, pencils, and highlighters, and a faculty newsletter. One drawer held research notes, pages filled with sprawling diagrams and scribbles in the margins. I quickly flipped through them, but they all seemed like past projects. There wasn't anything I could see about auravores, wyrms, or treasure-hunting dwarves.

Elise turned, and I casually nudged the drawer shut, pretending not to be interested.

"What's in this file cabinet?" Sloane asked, rattling a locked drawer loudly and drawing Elise's attention away from me.

"Oh, be careful with that!" The assistant exclaimed, rushing over. "Dr. Fenwick keeps all of his more sensitive files in there. He was very concerned about someone sneaking a look at his research before it was ready."

I frowned. For a university professor, Dr. Fenwick certainly had a substantial number of locks. Was he paranoid or smart? Had his research resulted in his demise? I rubbed the back of my neck, glancing around. If the thought of someone stealing my research scared me, I wouldn't hide it in a file cabinet, locked or otherwise. I would use that as a distraction and hide my research somewhere else.

The idea took root. Frowning, I crouched and ran my hand along the underside of the desk, feeling for anything taped there. Nothing. I sat back on my heels. I was running out of places to check.

On the other side of the room, Elise said, "I don't think it's here. Maybe we should go before someone catches us snooping around."

"We're already here," Sloane pointed out logically. "Let's make sure we've checked everywhere, just to be sure. Now, would they have sat at his desk or that table in the corner? The table makes more sense, right? More seating?"

"The table, I guess," Elise said. I glanced up as they both moved to the tidy table. Time was running out. If I was going to find anything, it needed to be now.

I moved to the bottom desk drawer, noting a barely perceptible gap, like it wasn't sitting quite right. I gave the handle a tug, but it was locked. No surprise there. Casually, I leaned against the desk. My fingers brushed the drawer handle as I nudged a thread of magic toward the lock. It was a much simpler lock than the one on the door. A moment later, a quiet click answered me.

I hesitated just long enough to make it look natural, then pulled the drawer open. Inside, a small black leather notebook sat tilted against a white prescription bottle, the faint rattle of pills breaking the heavy stillness. The printed label had started to peel at the corners, but I caught a glimpse of Dr. Fenwick's name, and something about a beta blocker. Strange. Wouldn't he have needed something like that at home, not tucked away here?

I glanced up, checking on Elise, but she was still searching across the room. Heart pounding, I slid the notebook out and flipped to the last page. If Dr. Fenwick had been in trouble, then whatever he had been working on most recently might hold a clue.

The final handwritten entry caught my eye immediately:

Alpha: Failed.

Beta: Unplanned. Possible.

Charlie: Pending.

I squinted at the page. Alpha and beta were Greek letters. But Charlie? That didn't fit. If this was supposed to be the phonetic alphabet, Bravo should have come after Alpha, not Beta. I had heard those call signs all my life on my dad's army bases—Alpha, Bravo, Charlie. The slip nagged at me, a muddled mix of Greek and military that made no sense. I let out a quiet sigh. Academics really should pick a lane...or at least double-check their sources. I frowned and traced the final line with my finger.

What were these referencing? Testing phases? Some kind of experiment? My first thought went to the wyrms, but Dr. Harlow had insisted none of the breeding programs were successful. In fact, based on what she told us, I would've expected more than just three tests. Unless... unless he'd pivoted to something else. Something more dangerous. Something he hadn't told even Elise about.

Like auravores.

I bit the inside of my cheek. If he'd gotten results, would that explain his secrecy? Or worse...had it gotten him killed?

"Did you find something?" Elise's voice was hopeful.

I startled, fingers tightening around the notebook for a split second before I caught myself.

I couldn't just ask her about the notes. Not without revealing that I'd found them in a locked drawer that, as far as she knew, had been completely secure. I doubted she'd take that revelation well. Instead, I snapped a quick photo with my phone and returned the notebook to its place, nudging the drawer shut just as Elise came around the desk.

"I thought it might've rolled under something. If the cleaners don't come in here often, they might've missed it, but I can't find the pen," I said, forcing a regretful sigh as I looked up from where I knelt on the carpet. "Maybe it'll turn up somewhere else?"

Elise sagged in disappointment. "Yeah, maybe."

Sloane gave her a friendly pat on the back. "I'm sure it'll turn up soon. I'd guess that it's buried in a purse somewhere or at the back of a desk drawer. That's where all of my pens seem to end up."

Elise nodded, but she looked unconvinced. "I hope you're right. Thanks for trying. But we should probably get out of here. I need to find someone with the key to lock the office again."

"Unless Dr. Fenwick showed up to work today. That would explain the unlocked door. Maybe he found the pen and already returned it to the dragon lady, but you just haven't seen him yet," Sloane suggested.

"Maybe," Elise murmured. "It would put my mind at ease if he were here."

As she ushered us out of the office, I clutched my phone tightly, my heart pounding with the thrill of discovery. I might not have found a fountain pen, but I had something even better—another lead.

What had Dr. Fenwick been testing? And what part of the Charlie test was left pending?

Locked Doors and Loose Ends

 Dr. Fenwick's office, leaving Dr. Harlow to figure out how to secure it. I knew I wouldn't get anything more from her in her current state of agitation over Dr. Winterbourne's pen, so instead, Sloane and I decided to poke around the science building to see if we could dig up any leads on Runar.

Back in Havenwood, snooping around the university had felt like a good idea. But now that we were actually here, surrounded by unfamiliar hallways and hundreds of students who all seemed to know exactly where they were going, the enormity of the task hit me. The university was massive, and it wasn't as if Runar had left us a trail of breadcrumbs to follow.

We tried the obvious places first, peering into classrooms, poking our heads into lecture halls, and even peeking into a student lounge and asking the undergrads who sat hunched over laptops if they'd seen a suspicious dwarf. A quick glance into the faculty lounge revealed only a couple of professors engaged in quiet conversation over half-empty cups of coffee.

Locked areas, like faculty offices and lab spaces, were off-limits unless we planned to break in. I might've been able to do it, but some of the locks looked like they were biometric or needed an ID tag to swipe. This type of security was much harder for me to navigate. Given our already questionable presence on campus, it didn't seem like the smartest idea anyway.

"Remind me again why we thought this was a good plan?" I muttered as we stood at the end of yet another hallway filled with students mingling after a class, scanning for any sign of Runar.

"Because we're stubborn and overconfident?" Sloane said, running a hand through her short hair.

I sighed, rolling my shoulders as frustration settled in. "Yeah, well, overconfidence is looking a lot like wishful thinking right about now."

Unfortunately, I wasn't wrong. Not that we were really expecting to find him hiding out here, but with so few leads, it made sense to search the campus, ask around, and see what we could dig up. A paper trail. A pattern. Anything. And if Runar happened to be lurking in a hallway or lab somewhere? Even better.

But he was nowhere to be found. No sightings. No rumors. Not even a stray whisper. Just silence.

Sloane folded her arms across her chest and frowned. "If only we could get into the security office."

I gave her a surprised look. "That took a turn. What do you mean?"

She lifted her eyes to the ceiling and jerked her chin. "Haven't you noticed? This place is riddled with security cameras."

I glanced up, spotting the small black dome mounted on the ceiling. My stomach dropped. "I hadn't, actually."

"They're everywhere," she said, stuffing her hands into her pockets as she strolled down the hall like she didn't have a care in the world.

"That seems a little...extreme, doesn't it?"

She shook her head. "Not really. Especially in a university like this. I get not having CCTV in, say, the English department. I mean, worst case scenario somebody steals The Great Gatsby, and life goes on. But based on what we saw in Fenwick's office? Some of the research going on around here is pretty hush-hush. I doubt they'd want that getting out."

A sharp wave of unease rolled through me. Cameras. Watching. *Recording.*

I'd broken into Dr. Fenwick's office twice this week. What if security had caught that on camera?

My dad's voice echoed in my head, firm and steady. "*Harper, integrity isn't just about doing the right thing when people are watching. It's about doing the right thing even when they aren't.*"

A pang of guilt twisted in my chest. I hadn't technically done anything malicious, but I had crossed a line. And, thinking back on scoping out the high-tech security locks, I'd been contemplating going even further. Was campus security after me even now? Or would that happen later, when they reviewed all the footage? More importantly, if I got arrested for breaking and entering, what would Dad say?

I exhaled slowly and forced myself to refocus. No one had come after me yet. On a campus this size, there were likely hundreds of cameras. Would security be checking them without cause? Unlikely. Even if they did, it's not as if mundane cameras could see magic. Most likely, it would look like I enjoyed holding doorknobs for an inordinately long time before opening a door. But from here on out, I needed to be a lot more careful.

I bit my lip, trying to refocus my thoughts as we navigated the throngs of students heading to class. "But Dr. Fenwick's research was, you know, *magical* in nature." I whispered the last words.

Sloane shrugged. "Probably not all of it. He had to have some kind of cover for the mundane faculty. But given the proximity to Havenwood, I'm not surprised most of his work leaned toward the supernatural."

I narrowed my eyes. "What's that supposed to mean?"

Sloane glanced at me. "Havenwood is special, but it's not one of a kind. There are places all over the country where supernaturals gather. Some are more open, like Havenwood with all the tourists, and some are a lot more private. I've even heard of a town in the Rockies that only allows supernaturals. But our types of people need somewhere to go where they feel safe despite all the humans and their camera phones. Not everyone can or wants to fly under the radar in big cities."

But before I could push the matter further, she switched gears. "Well," she said, stuffing her hands into her pockets, "I doubt campus security is just going to let us waltz in and review their footage."

I exhaled slowly, scanning the area for anything that might help. "Not even if we ask really nicely?" I asked, only half teasing.

Sloane smirked. "You can try, but I see that as a distinct impossibility."

I let out a soft laugh and shook my head. "Alright, so what's the next move?"

Before Sloane could answer, a clipped voice interrupted us from behind.

"Excuse me, but what exactly are you two doing here?"

I turned to see Dr. Winterbourne watching us, her arms folded and staring us down with the most disapproving look I'd ever seen. The effect was immediate. My back straightened like I was fifteen again, caught talking in class by the one teacher who could make students freeze with just a glance. She had the presence of someone who never needed to raise her voice to command a room. She simply existed, and people fell in line.

Her expression remained unreadable, but something about the way she carried herself elicited a thread of guilt in my stomach as if she'd threatened to call home and let my dad know exactly what I'd been up to.

Sloane recovered quickly. "Oh! We, uh, we got a little lost. Do you think you could point us toward the exit?"

Dr. Winterbourne didn't blink. She narrowed her eyes and studied us long enough that a cold prickle of sweat rolled down my spine. What would my dad say if she called home? The thought was ridiculous. She wasn't my teacher, and I wasn't a wayward teenager, but I still had to actively resist the urge to shift nervously under her gaze.

Eventually, Dr. Winterbourne spoke again. "What are you two doing wandering around here?"

Words dried up on my tongue, withering under the stern look she cast in my direction. Sloane, of course, had no such problem. She beamed. "We're visiting! A friend of ours goes here, and she raves about the place, so we're considering transferring. But she's in class right now, and we got turned around. Could you help us find our way?"

Dr. Winterbourne frowned. "Your friend," she said coolly. "What's her name?"

Sloane didn't hesitate. "Sarah. You probably wouldn't know her. She's not really into all this science stuff. Just taking Geology 101 to fulfill a credit requirement. You know, Rocks for Jocks."

I had to bite the inside of my cheek to keep my jaw from dropping. Sloane was smooth. If I tried lying like that, I'd probably break into nervous laughter and give us away instantly.

So, I did the smartest thing possible. I kept my mouth shut, nodded, and let Sloane do the talking.

Dr. Winterbourne's expression didn't soften. If anything, it sharpened, like a blade catching the light. "Geology is a valuable discipline," she said, her voice clipped. "And Eastford University takes great pride in cultivating serious students. I would hope, should you consider applying, that you approach your education with diligence and focus."

I swallowed and gave what I hoped was a convincing nod. "Of course. It's a great university."

Sloane, unfazed, grinned. "And gorgeous! But it's so big. Easy to get lost. And I think we missed lunch." She pressed a hand to her stomach. "Any chance you can point us toward the cafeteria? Anywhere we could grab a sandwich and a coffee while we wait for Sarah?"

Dr. Winterbourne regarded us for another tense moment before stepping aside and gesturing down the hallway. "Take the stairs or the elevator to the ground floor. Turn right at the end of the hall, then left out the main doors. The brick building on your right has a small café. If you continue another two blocks, you'll reach the main dining area. That's where most students eat."

"Perfect! Thanks!" Sloane chirped, looping her arm through mine as we strode off down the hallway.

I kept my eyes forward, matching Sloane's casual pace, but the prickle of unease at the back of my neck refused to fade. I fought the urge to check behind me but lost the battle as I glanced over my shoulder.

Dr. Winterbourne was still there, standing rigid in the hallway, her piercing gaze fixed on us. Her fingers idly traced the chain of her silver necklace, the glittering pendant catching the light as she watched us go.

I quickly faced forward again, my pulse kicking up a notch. "She's still watching," I muttered under my breath.

Sloane didn't turn around, just let out a low chuckle. "Yeah, well, I'd be suspicious of us too with the way we've just been hanging around. Probably best if we take our search elsewhere for the time being."

Once we were outside, I stole one last glance over my shoulder, expecting to find Dr. Winterbourne's piercing gaze still locked onto us. But she was gone, the glass doors reflecting the bright midday sun. A breath I hadn't realized I'd been holding eased out of me. The tension in my shoulders didn't completely fade, though. The unusually warm March air hadn't quite erased the lingering chill that settled in my spine.

Sloane turned to me. "So? What do you think? Stay here and keep looking?"

I ran a hand through my hair. "I don't know," I admitted. "There doesn't seem to be anything here and even if Runar was hiding out here, we'd never find him. It'd be like searching for a needle in a haystack."

Sloane exhaled, clearly frustrated. "Agreed. A campus this size? If he knows the layout, he could stay hidden for weeks."

"I don't want to admit it, but I think we're at a dead end," I said.

Sloane let out a low groan. "I hate dead ends."

With nothing else to go on, we trudged back to the car. The afternoon sun had warmed the pavement, but the chill from our fruitless search still clung to me. As we climbed in, I fastened my seatbelt, already mentally shifting gears to what came next.

Sloane, however, snapped her fingers. "Wait. I just remembered something my cousin said."

I turned to her. "Yeah?"

"He mentioned this fae woman who runs a jewelry shop in Havenwood. Ellen Wispdale, or something like that?"

"You mean, *Elowen* Wispdale?" I asked.

Sloane nodded enthusiastically. "That's the one. He said she might know something about enchanted jewelry. Do you think she might know something useful about the items Runar sold Liam?"

I shrugged as Sloane started the engine. "Only one way to find out."

Sloane grinned. "Then what are we waiting for?"

With that, we pulled out of the parking lot, leaving Eastford University behind and, hopefully, heading toward answers.

Old Magic, New Leads

SLOANE AND I STEPPED into Elowen Wispdale's jewelry shop, the delicate chime of the door announcing our arrival. The space quite literally glittered. Each display case was filled with beautifully crafted pieces. Silver, gold, and gemstones caught the light in an impressive spectacle of creativity and beauty. Elowen had a gift, not just for creating jewelry, but for displaying it to full effect.

The fae shopkeeper looked up, a flick of lavender hair catching the light. "Harper! What a lovely surprise. You've caught me just in time. I was headed out soon for an appointment." Her gaze shifted to Sloane, curiosity sparking in her eyes as she noticed the leprechaun's ears. "And you've brought a friend. How wonderful! I'm Elowen Wispdale." She extended a graceful hand, smile polite but welcoming in a guarded sort of way.

"Sloane O'Shea," Sloane introduced herself, shaking Elowen's hand briefly. I couldn't be sure, but there was the slightest hint of coolness between them.

"She's Liam O'Shaughnessy's cousin," I added in way of explanation.

Something in Elowen's stance shifted ever so slightly, the coolness melting just a fraction. "One of the lucky folk," she mused, dipping her head in a shallow bow and pressing a hand to her heart. "A lady leprechaun is always welcome in my shop."

"Kind of you to say," Sloane replied, her tone softening, if only slightly. The two women considered each other thoughtfully. I didn't think there was animosity between them, but there was definitely *something*.

I spoke up, filling the silence. "Elowen, I have a bit of a strange request. There have been some bizarre things happening around town."

"Ooh, color me intrigued," Elowen said, eyes alight with curiosity. "Stranger than what happened last month around Valentine's Day? Is this the kind of conversation where I need to lock the door and draw the shades?"

"Not exactly," I said with a small smile, "but probably best if we don't talk too openly if a tourist walks in."

Elowen's gaze flicked to Sloane, considering. "You don't say."

I plowed ahead. "I was hoping you might be able to help us. Liam's been dealing with some trouble. This dwarf named Runar Ironvein showed up with some enchanted jewelry, including a very cursed ring. We're trying to trace where these pieces came from, who might have enchanted them, and how they ended up in Runar's possession before they got to Liam."

"Not to mention what the enchantments might be," Sloane added. "After all, unknown magic can be dangerous."

Well, there it was, right out in the open. Elowen pressed her lips together, considering. Her gaze shifted between us, as if weighing her options. I waited, letting the silence settle. I had a feeling that pushing her wouldn't get me answers at the moment.

She seemed slightly on edge in Sloane's presence, but I couldn't figure out why. Still, from what I knew of Elowen, she was an upstanding member of the Havenwood community. If she understood the risk of unknown enchanted jewelry circulating through Liam's shop, I could only hope she'd be willing to help.

Finally, she exhaled. "I don't know how much assistance I can be, but I do have something that might shed some light."

She turned to a small cupboard behind the glass display cases, retrieving a key from her pocket. Inside, neatly arranged binders of various colors lined the shelves. Humming softly to herself, she selected a thick purple one, pulling it carefully from its place. Holding it between both hands, she gave me a measured look.

"What I'm about to show you, I'd really prefer it not become public knowledge," she said carefully. "But if I can help you stay safe or return items to their rightful owners, I will."

I frowned. "What do you mean?"

Elowen hesitated, tension flickering across her face before she finally set the binder on the counter.

"I'm not the only supplier of enchanted jewelry," she admitted. "But in addition to the mundane pieces I sell to tourists, I do a brisk trade in those types of pieces."

Sloane grunted, but I just nodded. This wasn't new information to me. Elowen had been included among the jewelers who had supplied enchanted items at the annual Silverthorne Ball last December.

Elowen held up a hand. "I should say that I don't deal in anything dangerous. Nothing that's big magic. Just little enchantments. Spells to keep silver from tarnishing. A charm to ward off the common cold. That sort of thing."

Sloane nodded. "And you keep records of every item you sell? The enchanted ones, I mean."

"I do," Elowen confirmed. "Even though the charms are relatively small, if I hear that someone has passed away and their estate is being liquidated, I try to buy back any items before they fall into the wrong hands. It doesn't happen often, but every once in a blue moon, an heir won't know what they have. Or worse, the items will be sold at auction where anyone, magical or not, could get their hands on them."

"What happens then?" Sloane asked.

Elowen shrugged. "Usually, it gets stuffed in a family safe, or the heir passes on, and I can buy it back then. Supernaturals live longer than humans, after all. But typically, those who own enchanted items usually ensure they're passed down properly. I have heard of cases where a lineage ends, or an heir doesn't know what they're dealing with. I do my best to get those pieces out of circulation as quickly as possible."

"So," I glanced at the binder. "What can we expect to find in there?"

Elowen tapped her fingers against the cover before flipping it open. "This is a record of every enchanted item I've ever made, who I sold it to, contact information, and a photograph or description of the piece."

My pulse picked up. This could be the break we needed.

"If any of the enchanted items in Liam's shop came from my shop," she continued, "they'll be in this ledger. If you can confirm they came from here, you'll know they're safe to handle."

My eyes lit up. "Are you serious? That's incredible."

Elowen hesitated. "Yes, but again, I'd prefer this not become common knowledge. I enjoy helping my friends, but if word got out, I'd have every supernatural knocking on my door looking for rare, enchanted items. And honestly? Jewelry is my passion. The magic? That's just a side hustle."

Sloane tilted her head. "Do you ever have to, you know, undo the magic?"

Elowen hesitated, her fingers brushing lightly over the leather cover of the ledger. "If it's something I created? Yes. It's simple enough to unravel my own work. Part of the responsibility." She paused, considering. "But breaking someone else's enchantment?" She shook her head. "That's an entirely different matter. You either need rare materials, artifacts that resonate with the original magic, or an intimate knowledge of how the spell was woven from the start. Otherwise, trying to break an enchantment is like pulling at a thread and unraveling the whole tapestry."

She gave a small, rueful smile. "And even then, it doesn't always work." She turned to Sloane. "In fact, just to be sure, I'd like the opportunity to buy the items back if he wants to sell."

Sloane nodded. "I'm sure he'd appreciate it. But in the meantime, would it be okay if we took this to Liam's shop? You know, to compare the pieces? Or maybe just a copy of the ledger?"

Elowen frowned, her fingers tightening slightly on the book. "I'd rather he brings the items here." Her tone wasn't unkind, but there was an unmistakable edge of hesitation.

Sloane's expression didn't shift, but I caught the slight flicker of tension in her stance. "I get it. I'm a stranger. But you know Harper. And if I call Liam, would that set your mind at ease?"

Elowen's gaze lingered on me for a beat, as if weighing her decision. She clearly wasn't thrilled with the idea, but at least she trusted me.

Before she could refuse, Sloane pulled out her phone. "I'll call him right now. You can talk to him directly and settle any concerns." She stepped away, the phone already faintly ringing.

Elowen exhaled, then gave me a small nod, her fingers still resting protectively over the ledger.

I offered an apologetic smile. "It would really help, Elowen."

She hesitated, then sighed. "I don't want to be uncharitable, but I don't know her," she admitted, nodding toward Sloane. "However, if you're there the whole time, and if Liam agrees..."

Sloane held out the phone. "Liam wants to talk to you."

Elowen took the phone and stepped away for a brief, hushed conversation. When she returned, she still didn't look entirely pleased, but she set the ledger on the counter between us.

"All right. Liam and I have agreed. You can take the book to compare the pieces. Normally, I'd ask that you do that here, but I have an appointment I can't miss, and I can tell this is important to you, so Harper," she said, tapping the cover once, "you're responsible for it."

I nodded, catching the unspoken meaning. Elowen trusted *me* with this, not Sloane.

"No copies," she added. "Digital or otherwise. And it needs to be back before the end of the business day."

"Understood," I promised. "And thank you. I have a feeling this is going to be really helpful."

Elowen nodded, though the seriousness in her expression remained. "Anything I can do to help. That's the Havenwood way."

I glanced at the ledger, feeling the weight of both responsibility and trust. Havenwood had always been a place where people looked out for each other, even if it meant stepping outside their comfort zones. Elowen didn't have to help, but she had. Because that's what people in this town did.

"Thank you," I said, meaning it. I lifted the ledger, balancing it against my hip.

Sloane eyed the thick binder. "Great. Thank you, Elowen. C'mon, Harper. Let's see what we're working with."

As we stepped outside, the crisp air filled my lungs, clearing my thoughts. We finally had something solid to go on. Now, all we had to do was figure out what it meant.

Bling with a Backstory

THE WEIGHT OF ELOWEN'S ledger felt heavier than it should have as I carried it into Liam's secret back room, tucked behind the Pot o' Gold. I set it on the counter with a quiet thud, nervously running a hand over the cover. There was something about holding a file detailing magic-infused jewelry that made it feel more significant—more powerful—than just paper and ink.

Sloane ran a hand over the cover. "What do you think all these do?"

"Only one way to find out," Liam said, setting down three steaming mugs of coffee and a few small bags of chips that looked crumpled and possibly close to their expiration date. The three of us got to work.

Luckily, Elowen's notes were meticulous. She had categorized her pieces by type, neatly cross-referencing everything in an index at the back. She wasn't just creative, but methodical and efficient. It was a rare combination in an artist, and one I had to admire.

We worked through the list, jotting down names and phone numbers of original purchasers when possible. Soon, we had two piles: one of items crafted by Elowen, and the other was made of items of unknown origin. To my surprise, the first pile was much larger than I'd expected. Elowen had severely underestimated her influence in the magical jewelry trade.

I picked up a delicate silver ring from her collection, running my thumb over the faintly carved runes along the inner band. According to her notes, it was meant to help with focus. An ideal item for scholars, overthinkers, or anyone prone to second-guessing. A nearby bracelet had been enchanted to boost confidence in social settings, while a necklace was designed to shield its wearer from minor hexes. Practical, everyday magic. Nothing world-altering, but still fascinating. It made me wonder who had worn them and why they might have wanted such items in the first place.

When we finally matched the last piece, I leaned back and stretched my arms. "So, what do we do with all this?"

Sloane sighed. "Should we talk to the original owners first? It might be that Runar legitimately bought some of these."

Liam snorted. "I doubt it, the scoundrel."

Slone shot him a look. "Well, we should do our due diligence before going to the police, don't you think?"

"Absolutely," I agreed instantly. "We wouldn't want to make any unfounded accusations. Maybe Runar bought the whole collection from someone else and didn't even know that your friend's ring was in there."

"Fine, ye make a good point," Liam grumbled. "I'll need to reach out to a few people. See if these ended up in the wrong hands or if there's an explanation. If they were stolen, I'll loop in Sheriff Jackson. But first, let's talk to the owners."

Sloane stood and stretched. "While you do that, I need a refill. Do you want one?" she asked me, pointing at my coffee mug.

I glanced at my half-empty cup and shook my head. "Better not. Caffeine this late would be a mistake. But I wouldn't say no to a glass of water."

"You got it." She gave me a thumbs-up and followed Liam into the front of the shop.

Idly, I flipped through the ledger again, letting my fingers trail over the pages. It was a glimpse inside Elowen's mind, a record of magic woven into metal.

A bracelet designed to steady the tremors of Parkinson's.
A necklace meant to keep a singer's throat warm and strong.
A pendant to help a fae camouflage when threatened.

I didn't recognize any of the names next to these items, but Liam might. Probably best to wait for him. I paused, tracing the intricate silver filigree in the sketch of the last piece. The enchantments on Elowen's creations reminded me of why Havenwood mattered. It wasn't just a quirky little town full of odd traditions and ley line magic. It was a sanctuary, a place where supernaturals didn't have to hide.

The soft creak of the door pulled me from my thoughts. Sloane stepped back inside, holding two bottles of water. She tossed a bottle of water to me before hopping up onto a stool. "Liam's got it covered. Based on what I overheard on his end of the call, I don't think it's looking good for Runar."

Liam stuck his head back into the room and waved his phone at us. "I think I'll be at this all night. I don't want you girls to be bored. Why don't you head on home and let me take care of this?"

I stood and rolled my shoulders. "I'm not going to say no, but before we call it a day, we need to return the ledger to Elowen."

"I'll drive," Sloane offered. "One book return, coming up."

Liam led us through the shop, shutting the secret room before unlocking the front door.

He gave us a grateful nod. "Thank you for helping with this. I won't rest until I get some answers."

"Anything for you," Sloane said, giving him a one-armed hug.

I smiled at the pair of leprechauns. "I just hope it was actually useful. I feel like we didn't accomplish much."

"You did more than you think," Liam said. "We might not have found Runar, but we took important steps today. Sometimes, all you can do is keep moving forward, even if you don't know where the path leads yet. Just take the next right step, and trust the rest will unfold."

Sloane clapped him on the shoulder. "Spoken like a true sage."

He grinned. "Well, I try. A lifetime of experience ought to count for something."

His words stuck with me as Sloane and I headed out to return Elowen's ledger. By the time we pulled up outside the jewelry shop, the sky had darkened into that dusky twilight where the streetlamps cast long, golden pools along the cobblestones. I hopped out, clutching the ledger, and handed it over to the fae owner with a grateful smile.

"Any luck?" she asked as I handed the ledger over.

"Yes and no, but this was incredibly helpful. Liam's making some calls, and hopefully we can sort this situation out," I said. "And don't worry, we were incredibly careful. I know how important discretion is."

Elowen inclined her head. "Then I'm glad it was of use."

Beside me, Sloane offered a respectful nod. "You run a tight ship. That ledger was meticulous."

Elowen's gaze sharpened, but after a brief pause, she offered the barest hint of a smile. "Coming from a leprechaun, I'll take that as something between a compliment and a challenge."

Sloane's mouth twitched. "Probably accurate."

The two regarded each other with wary acknowledgment. Not warmth, but something careful, old, and shifting. The kind of detente that came from centuries of mutual skepticism and the rare surprise of earned respect. But maybe, in a place like Havenwood, even old grudges could learn to thaw.

Sloane and I waved goodbye as Elowen stepped back into the shop. As the door shut behind her, Sloane stretched, letting out a groan. "Alright, it's been a long day. I don't know about you, but I could use some real food and a sleep. Let's get you back to Spellbooks."

The ride was quick, and before I knew it, we were pulling up in front of the bookshop.

"Thanks again for today," Sloane said as I climbed out.

I gave her a tired but sincere smile. "Anytime."

She winked. "I'll call you if we learn anything new."

I waved as she pulled away, then turned toward Spellbooks, only to catch movement in the window next door.

Finn.

He was inside Wildwood Ink, straightening up a display. As if sensing my gaze, he glanced up. Our eyes met through the glass.

Without thinking, I raised a hand in greeting. His face lit up with an easy smile as he waved before turning back to his work.

I lingered a moment outside Spellbooks, my mind still half on the exchange.

Finn and I had once danced on the edge of something more, but fate had other plans. And that was okay. We'd settled into a solid friendship, and I was glad for it. Especially now that I was with Gabriel, and Finn and Seraphina seemed to be reconnecting.

Seraphina.

I almost smacked my forehead. Why hadn't I thought of her sooner? Elowen wasn't the only one in Havenwood who could enchant jewelry. Seraphina might have insight into the enchantments that were on the jewelry that hadn't been from Elowen's shop. I should really give her a call or, better yet, go see her.

I sighed. Between that and my need to visit Ignatius, my to-do list wasn't getting any shorter.

Liam's words echoed in my mind: *Just take the next right step, and the rest will unfold.*

Hopefully, that was true.

Majestic. Graceful. Absolutely Not Suspicious.

Through Spellbooks' front window, I spotted two figures lurking near the shelves, hunched over as if they were trying to make themselves smaller. One was short and stocky, built like a particularly aggressive pumpkin. His bushy mustache dusted gray with what looked suspiciously like talcum powder. The other was as tall and bony as a heron, oversized sunglasses covering most of her face.

They were both dressed identically in jeans, sneakers, and oversized hoodies bearing the logo of Harvard University, the hoods pulled low over their faces. I froze, wondering if Spellbooks was part of some prank about to happen when I recognized the pair.

Ah. Of course.

The Puddletons.

They were rifling through the display books when I pushed open the door. Cassandra drifted over, greeting them with her usual friendly warmth.

"Welcome to Spellbooks! Let me know if I can help you find anything."

The two figures stiffened. Oswald Puddleton, the shorter of the two, slowly turned toward her, clearing his throat and adopting an accent that wavered somewhere between bad French, worse German, and chronic indigestion.

"We are here," he announced, "to find ze best bookshop in all of Connecticut."

Hortense nodded eagerly, affecting an Eastern European accent with stilted, broken-English. "Yes! Look! Bookshop."

I nearly bit my tongue to keep from laughing.

Cassandra, ever polite, smiled. "Oh, wonderful! Are you looking for something specific?"

Oswald rubbed his hand over his powder-dusted mustache, which left a streak of white on his sleeve. "Ah-ha! Shopping. As patrons. Of the arts."

Hortense clasped her hands dramatically. "Books."

Cassandra hesitated. "Well, you've certainly come to the right place. We've got lots of those."

I stepped forward, folding my arms. "Oh, don't worry, Cassandra. The Puddletons are very familiar with finding books."

Oswald and Hortense jumped as if they'd been struck by lightning.

"Harper!" Cassandra said, clearly relieved to have backup. "You're back."

"I sure am." I glanced between the two shop lurkers. "And look who showed up."

Oswald bristled. "Ah-ha! No, no. We do not know this...Harper."

Hortense shook her head. "Never heard of her."

I arched a brow. "So, you just happen to be in my shop, wearing disguises?"

Oswald sneered, dropping his accent. "These are not disguises. They are...fashionable."

Hortense nodded sharply. "Trendy. Not that I would expect you to recognize such a thing," she said with a sniff.

I tilted my head. "Ah, I see. The bad fake mustache and sunglasses at night are trendy fashion statements now? You're right. I had no idea."

Hortense muttered something unintelligible and turned back to the books, flipping through one with a little too much force.

Oswald, however, lingered, watching me like I had personally wronged him. "We were merely curious," he said, his voice no longer sporting its strange accent. "You seem to be doing well for yourself. You have another author coming to visit, I see."

I leaned against the counter. "That's generally the goal of a bookstore, yes. To do well."

Oswald's mustache twitched. "But *how* are you doing so well?"

I sighed. "Ah, yes, the age-old question. Could it be my excellent selection? My fantastic choice in coffee? Stellar customer service?" I tapped my chin and then shrugged. "It's a mystery."

"Personally, I think it's the customer service," Cassandra chimed in.

"This week? Absolutely," I said, wrapping an arm around her shoulder. "By the way, I don't think you've met. Cassandra, this is Oswald Puddleton and his wife Hortense. They run the other bookshop on Arcadia Avenue called the Dusty Tome."

"If you ever want a real job at an established and reputable shop, all you have to do is call," Oswald said, stepping forward and producing a card from the kangaroo pocket of his hoodie.

Cassandra's eyes went wide, and my jaw dropped at the cheek of the man. To imagine! Propositioning my employee to come work for him right in front of me! We exchanged disbelieving looks.

"Well?" Oswald said, shaking the card impatiently at her.

Cassandra folded her arms over her chest, refusing to take the proffered card. "I'm good. Thanks," she said dryly.

Hortense's mouth twisted. "Hmph."

Oswald jabbed a finger at me. "We'll find out what you're up to."

I blinked. "You do that."

Hortense exhaled sharply. "Come, Oswald. We're wasting our time."

I moved to the door and held it open. "Have a wonderful day, Mr. and Mrs. Puddleton," I said brightly.

They both scowled.

Oswald hesitated, clearly torn between storming out and getting the last word. Finally, he huffed. "The Dusty Tome is superior. And soon, everyone will know it."

With that, they marched outside, throwing dirty looks over their shoulders. Hortense swept through the doorway, then deliberately snatched the handle from my grasp and gave it a theatrical slam, her nose tilted skyward as she flounced away. She looked far too pleased with herself for such a ridiculous victory.

The bell above the frame gave a pitiful jangle, like even it was embarrassed for her. The moment they were gone, Luna's velvety voice carried from her hutch.

"Cabbage catastrophe, that was a tragic display."

I started, glancing toward her. "You knew they were here?"

Luna hopped gracefully onto the counter, twitching an ear. "Of course. I heard them whispering like stage villains the moment they walked in. But I was curious how far they'd take it. Besides, Cassandra seemed to be handling it," she yawned.

"You could've spoken up," I pointed out.

"They're fortunate I didn't. If my headband was in my hutch, I would've given them what for! Lucky for them, I left it at training," Luna sniffed.

"Where does one do ninja rabbit training?" I asked.

Luna arched a brow. "Wouldn't you like to know?" She turned without another word and hopped back into her hutch.

Cassandra exhaled. "Okay, what was that?"

"Luna being Luna," I muttered.

"No. Not her. *Them.*"

I sighed. "My best guess? They were trying to see if I was using magic or something to increase business. That way they could report me to Vivienne Silverthorne. They've been trying to run me out of business since the day I opened. And now that Spellbooks is thriving?" I nodded toward the window, where the Puddletons were still whispering to each other down the street. "I bet it's driving them absolutely crazy."

"Good," Luna called from her hutch. "They deserve to be miserable."

Cassandra's eyebrows lifted. "And they came in disguise to snoop around? That's...honestly kind of sad."

Luna hopped out, munching on a radish, and gave a dramatic sigh. "If they had an ounce of self-awareness, they'd be mortified. But alas, self-reflection is not their strong suit."

I grinned. "Agreed."

Cassandra let out a breath and turned back toward the counter. "I thought you were kidding about them when I took the job."

I shook my head. "Nope. The Puddletons are real. And just as ridiculous as advertised."

Luna stretched luxuriously. "Oh, they're worse. But at least they're entertaining."

Cassandra let out a breath. "Well, I can't say it was fun, but it was definitely an experience."

I chuckled. "Welcome to working at Spellbooks. Every day's an adventure."

"I'm starting to believe it." She grabbed her bag from behind the counter. "I'll see you tomorrow?"

"Bright and early," I promised. "Thanks for holding down the fort."

With a wave, Cassandra headed out, and I locked the door behind her, flipping the sign to "Closed" before making sure the shop was in order for the morning. I swept the floors, checked the register and sales logs, did some marketing work on my computer, and set out extra water for the animals.

A yawn crept up on me as I leaned against the counter. It had been a long day, but there was still so much to do. I needed to get Seraphina's number and talk to her about enchanted jewelry, ask Ignatius for any insights about wyrms, see if there was anything else I could turn up about Dr. Fenwick's death, and try to figure out how Runar tied into this whole mess.

My stomach growled, reminding me it had been a while since my last meal, which had been an unappetizing bag of chips and half a cup of coffee at Liam's shop. It looked like I needed some sustenance before I got any answers.

With a sigh, I turned off the lights and headed upstairs, where I made myself a peanut butter and jelly sandwich. It wasn't fancy, but it was one of my go-to meals when I was too tired to cook anything real.

As I ate, I pulled out my phone and shot Finn a quick message.

Hey, do you have Seraphina's number? Need to ask her about something.

I waited a few minutes, but there was no response. He was probably busy, or—let's be honest—ignoring his phone, as usual.

With nothing else to do, I settled onto the couch and grabbed the book I'd borrowed from Liam. Dr. Fenwick's thick tome on magical creatures was full of fascinating tidbits, but it was also dense.

I flipped through the pages of mythical beasts, absorbing details about their magical properties, habitats, and ancient stories. The words started to blur as exhaustion crept in, but I stubbornly pressed on, determined to learn something useful.

At some point, my eyelids grew too heavy to fight, and I drifted to sleep on my couch. My dreams twisted into a bizarre montage. Dragons with shimmering emerald scales coiled around mountaintops, phoenixes burst into flame and rose anew, chimeras prowled through misty forests, their eyes glowing in the dark.

And then...there were the Puddletons.

Not as themselves, of course. That would have been too normal.

No, my subconscious decided that Oswald and Hortense had infiltrated my dream as an extremely unconvincing Pegasus. Their "costume" was made of mismatched fabric patches, the wings were lopsided and flapping at different speeds, and a crinkled paper unicorn horn had been duct-taped to the forehead.

Oswald's mustache bristled through the nostrils of the horse head like a pair of aggressive caterpillars, twitching with indignation. Hortense's long legs stuck out the back, her sneakers clomping noisily with every step. It looked like a first-grader's art project had come to life and immediately regretted its own existence.

It was a calamity of costuming. A travesty of transformation. A fraud of a flying horse. It would've made far more sense for Hortense to take the lead and Oswald to bring up the rear, but logic and my subconscious weren't on speaking terms.

"We are...I mean, I am...a majestic creature," Oswald declared, his voice booming as though he was addressing a royal court.

"Yes," Hortense agreed, her voice muffled inside the atrocious costume. "Nothing suspicious here. Just a perfectly normal, completely natural horse-with-wings."

A nearby dragon gave them a flat, unimpressed stare. The phoenix circled above, then landed next to me, tilting its head as if to ask, "Are they serious?"

"I don't know," I muttered. "They aren't good at disguises in real life either."

The chimera choked on its own laughter.

"I heard that," Oswald huffed, adjusting his fake Pegasus mane with a dramatic toss of his head. "We are blending in flawlessly."

Behind him, Hortense whinnied in agreement.

A gust of wind blew through the dreamscape, and their entire "costume" gave way. A shower of felt, duct tape, and what looked suspiciously like actual horsehair exploded into the air.

Oswald tumbled forward, rolling across the ground in a flurry of fake feathers, while Hortense sprawled in the dirt, tangled in the remains of her Pegasus legs.

The chimera chortled, the phoenix buried its head under its wing, and the dragon shook its head and flapped away, muttering, "This is exactly why I don't do group projects."

I exhaled. Even in my dreams, the Puddletons were exhausting.

A Tiny Dragon for Tea

Morning arrived far too quickly, dragging me out of sleep like an overenthusiastic cat demanding breakfast. Scratch that. It *was* an overenthusiastic cat demanding breakfast. Mr. Wigglesworth meowed pitifully from outside my apartment door as I fought my way to consciousness. I blinked at the ceiling, brain still foggy from a night of surreal dreams and questionable life choices, like staying up too late reading about magical creatures with a peanut butter and jelly sandwich as my only companion. Somewhere in the depths of my subconscious, a chimera was probably still side-eyeing a very poorly disguised Pegasus.

To be fair, the Pegasus had it coming.

I groaned, and rolled out of bed, pulling on a sweatshirt and padding downstairs to pacify the cat. Mr. Wigglesworth eyed the scoop of kibble in his bowl pitifully.

"Don't give me that look. You know what the vet said. You're on a diet," I admonished the cat.

He flicked his tail in the air, daintily picking one piece from the bowl. That didn't last long though, and he dove face first into his breakfast with gusto. I chuckled. The big orange lump always brought a smile to my face.

I headed back upstairs to get my phone. If I was going to be up at this hour, I might as well be productive.

Finn had sent me Seraphina's number last night, and while I wasn't sure if she'd be awake this early, I figured it was worth a shot. I sent off a quick message asking if she was in town or away on business. To my surprise, a reply popped up almost immediately.

Hey Harper! Good to hear from you. Yes, I'm in town. How can I help?

I blinked. That was convenient. I typed back, quickly explaining the situation, outlining the issues with the unknown enchanted jewelry and what I was hoping to find out. I watched eagerly as the three dots indicating she was typing bounced on my screen.

Meet me at the Pot o' Gold? I've got a lunch break around noon.

My heart leapt. Perfect. I quickly tapped out a response.

Sounds great. Lunch is on me. Consider it a bribe for your expertise.

Seraphina sent a laughing emoji. *You certainly know how to sweeten a deal. See you then.*

Feeling unexpectedly optimistic, I fired off another message, this time to Mason.

Morning! Any chance you're back? I could use some dragon wisdom today.

Mason's reply was almost as fast as Seraphina's.

Morning. We're back, and he's here. Swing by anytime.

I grinned and sent a quick *"Be there soon"* before bustling around my apartment, all thoughts of the preposterous Pegasus of pure, unbridled absurdity fading from my mind.

By the time Cassandra arrived at Spellbooks, I was already showered, dressed, and finishing off a few emails in preparation for the upcoming author visit. She greeted me cheerfully.

"Are you okay?" she asked as she hung up her coat. "You look lost in thought."

I hesitated, then smiled. "Just a lot on my plate today."

"Anything I can do to help?"

I shook my head. "You're already covering the shop so I can run errands. You're a lifesaver."

She beamed. "I try."

Grabbing my coat and bag, I checked my phone one last time. With two promising leads lined up, today felt like it might actually be productive.

"I'll be back in a few hours," I told Cassandra. "Try not to let the Puddletons throw you if they show up in disguise again. Especially if they show up as a Pegasus."

"What?" Cassandra asked with a surprised chuckle.

I waved a hand. "Bad dreams. Don't mind me. Have a great day."

She waved. "You, too."

With that, I headed out the door, feeling something I hadn't in a while. Momentum.

With Cassandra settled in at Spellbooks and Seraphina tied up until noon, I headed straight for Mason Forham's Auto Repair Shop. As I expected, Ignatius was hanging out in the forge and listening to audiobooks. His usual pastime when Mason was working on cars.

The dwarf and the tiny book-loving dragon had formed an unexpected but close friendship, bound by their shared love of literature. Ignatius still visited Spellbooks frequently, and I made sure to bring him books I thought he'd like. But with Mason's extensive audiobook subscriptions, Ignatius had found new joy in listening along with him, particularly when they could discuss the stories together. Still, he remained an insatiable reader, tearing through books at a pace that made me envious.

I knocked loudly on the shop door, hoping to be heard over the blaring music that often accompanied Mason's work. A moment later, the music cut off, and the door swung open to reveal Mason himself. His craggy face lit up with a smile, his Scottish brogue as warm as ever.

"Ah, Harper, here you are!" he said, stepping back to let me in.

"Hi, Mason. Good to see you too."

"It's been too long, lass! How are you keeping these days?"

"As well as can be expected," I said with a shrug.

"Well, glad to hear it. Me, I'll be happier when the warm weather comes for good. But I've seen too much of Connecticut's fickle weather to believe this last week means spring is here for real. Mark my words. We're due for another cold snap before the season truly settles."

I smiled. "I'll take your word for it."

He gave me a shrewd look. "I see that look in your eyes. You're not here to chat about the weather."

"You caught me."

"Aye, thought so. The wee lad's in the back." He jerked a thumb toward the forge. "Knowing him, he's curled up by the coals. You go right on through. Don't mind me, I've got a carburetor to fix."

"Thanks, Mason. I appreciate it."

I entered the forge, where the glow of embers cast a flickering light across the space. Sure enough, Ignatius was curled up near the warmth, flipping through a book with one careful talon. His iridescent purple scales shimmered in the dim glow, catching the light as he turned another page.

I was pleased to notice he wasn't wearing his enchanted bracelet anymore. The emberite and lavastone steel cuff Mason had forged to help him control his fire breathing had done its job. Not a single curl of smoke rose from his nostrils as he focused on his book. Pride and hope swelled in my chest. His control had come so far, and it seemed like he was really settling into life in Havenwood outside of being a statue.

"Hi, Ignatius," I called, shrugging out of my coat.

His head snapped up, golden eyes brightening as his sharp little teeth flashed in a delighted grin.

"Harper!" he exclaimed, his voice still a little disjointed from all those extra teeth, but much more fluid than when we'd first met. "Happy see you."

"It's good to see you too, buddy. How are you doing?"

He uncoiled slightly, stretching his wings before folding them neatly along his back. "Happy. Warm. Reading. Harper bring new book?" he asked hopefully.

"You know I would," I said, pulling a cozy mystery novel from my bag. I'd chosen the one Mindy Hart was promoting. I was curious what Ignatius would think of it. The little bibliophile had a shrewd insight into literature. If he could manipulate a keyboard, he'd probably make an excellent book blogger.

"Ah! Looks good." He reached out, accepting it with careful claws. "Thank you."

"Anytime."

I ran a finger lightly along the spiny ridge on his back, greeting him the way he liked. He let out a contented hum, rubbing his head against my hand before marking his place in his current book and setting it aside.

But then his eyes narrowed. "Mason said you want talk. What's up?"

I sighed, shifting to sit on a nearby stool. "I've run into a bit of a problem, and I was hoping you could help me out."

Ignatius straightened, all traces of relaxation gone. He focused his entire attention on me, from the tip of his nose to the tip of his tail.

"Tell me."

I filled him in on everything relating to the wyrms. The stolen books, Dr. Fenwick's notes, the cryptic "Charlie: Pending" clue, and my growing suspicions about the wyrms.

Ignatius's tail flicked, his claws tapping absently against the book's cover. When I finished, he shook his head.

"Wyrms not great," he said, his wings extending like he wanted to take flight.

"What do you mean?"

"Not great," he repeated, then tipped his head, reconsidering his words. "Well, great scavengers, but not nice."

I frowned. "So why do you think Dr. Fenwick was so interested in them?"

Ignatius shrugged his small shoulders. "Like you say, maybe waste problem?"

I chewed my lip. "Do you really think they could be a long-term landfill solution? Maybe they could break down waste faster?"

The tiny dragon lifted a shoulder. "Maybe? But wyrms not crossbreed. They eat. They eat *everything*."

"Right, so why..." I trailed off, considering.

Was I even looking in the right direction? Had Dr. Fenwick figured that out on his own or through trial and error? Based on what I'd learned about his research, it seemed as if the wyrm crossbreeding was a lofty goal and one that could have distinct benefits for the world. Especially if the hypothetical hybrids had been sterile. No chance of overpopulation or invasive semi-magical species. Just a voraciously hungry animal to turn garbage into fertilizer. Theoretically.

But it hadn't worked. I thought back to Dr. Fenwick's book and the clue I'd found. He'd obviously started some kind of trial. Something with only three tests so far. Had it been an old note? Or possibly a new trial? My mind flashed to Grumbert and his latest sale. Dr. Fenwick had purchased auravores. Had he discarded the wyrm idea after the failed experiments and moved on? I couldn't be sure, but it seemed like an avenue worth exploring.

"Ignatius, what do you know about auravores?"

His entire body went still. "Not much. Why?"

"Because Dr. Fenwick was interested in them. He is a professor and wrote a book on magical creatures, including wyrms and auravores. I also found a note about what I assume to be early tests. Maybe he gave up on wyrms and switched to auravores?"

Ignatius made a low humming sound, curling his tail around himself. "Book? Ignatius read?"

"Oh, I'd love to share it with you, but it's at my shop. I thought you might know something more about the wyrms, but if Dr. Fenwick wasn't even into them anymore, then..." I trailed off and shrugged. "I don't want to interrupt your day."

Rather unexpectedly, the tiny dragon flapped his wings, landing lightly on my shoulder.

I blinked. "Ignatius?"

"Come with you," he said, curling his tail around my neck for balance.

"What?" I turned my head slightly to look at him.

"I come. I read. I help"

I hesitated. Ignatius rarely left Mason's forge unless it was to visit Spellbooks. But... he had already shifted my perspective. Maybe having a dragon's insight would help me connect the dots.

"Are you sure?" I asked, stroking his scales.

"Harper needs help. I come," the tiny dragon repeated. Then he gave a thoughtful hum and flicked his wings. "But first, tea."

I huffed out a laugh. "Tea?"

Ignatius nodded solemnly. "Mason makes tea. Ignatius now likes tea."

I raised an eyebrow. "Did Mason start a new hobby, or...?"

"Agatha's tea," Ignatius said, as if that explained everything. To be fair, it did. "Very relaxing. Good for digestion."

I couldn't help but smile. "Alright, tea it is. I'm pretty sure I have some back at Spellbooks. Then I can show you Dr. Fenwick's book on magical creatures and the slip of paper I found as well."

"Good. Tea, books, helping friends. This is the Havenwood way," Ignatius declared.

I chuckled, running a finger along his scales. "I can't argue there, buddy."

We made our way back to Spellbooks, where the scent of old paper and freshly brewed coffee welcomed us home. Cassandra glanced up from the counter as I walked in, her brows rising at the sight of the small dragon around my neck as I took off my coat.

"Oh, my stars," she said, eyes lighting up. "Is he your new reading buddy or a good luck charm?"

"More like a research assistant," I said, setting my bag down. "And a tea enthusiast, apparently. Ignatius, this is Cassandra. She works in Spellbooks now. Cassandra, meet Ignatius, the smallest bibliophile I know."

"It's a pleasure to meet you," Cassandra said, dipping her head in a shallow bow.

Ignatius returned the gesture. "Likewise."

I was grateful Cassandra was a mage and clued into the magical world, or I would've had to do a lot more explaining. As it was, I just grabbed a couple of Honey's biscotti as I headed for the stairs leading to my apartment.

"I've been instructed in no uncertain terms that Ignatius needs tea. Are you okay down here?" I asked.

Cassandra made a shooing gesture. "I've got it. There's been no flying horses or nosy neighbors. Mr. W and I have the shop. You two enjoy your tea."

I gave her a little wave and took the stairs two at a time. Before I flipped on the kettle, I made sure Ignatius was settled with the book about magical creatures. He curled up on the kitchen table, wings tucked close, scanning the pages with sharp golden eyes while I made the tea. I selected Agatha's Ember and Ivy Elixir. It was a specialty blend she made herself. The mixture of herbs and spices was designed to warm the soul and sharpen the mind. Her words, not mine, but it was one of my favorites.

By the time the tea was ready, Ignatius had already read the section on wyrms and the one on auravores.

"Very acceptable," he declared as he took a sip of his tea and nibbled on his white chocolate and raspberry biscotti.

"Glad to hear it," I said, settling down with my own mug. "Have you found anything?"

Ignatius nodded eagerly and laid a taloned foot on the page. "Reading reminds me of friend long ago who talked about auravores. They different from wyrms. Smarter. Sneakier. Not aggressive. Possessive."

"Possessive." My mind flicked back to the entry in Dr. Fenwick's book and the almost clinical scientific description of auravores storing enchanted objects, even hoarding them into hidden troves.

"Don't other creatures hoard things? Magpies? Dragons, even?" I asked, gesturing at him.

Ignatius shook his tiny head. "Not same. Auravores...relentless. Chase magic, dig through stone, follow magic across miles. Never stop. Never enough."

A prickle of unease slid down my spine. If they'd chase a coin or trinket for miles, what would happen if something larger or more powerful caught their attention? Havenwood had more than one kind of powerful presence. And Eastford wasn't all that far away. Not to mention, Dr. Fenwick's body had somehow ended up in the woods on the outskirts of town.

My thoughts churned as I pieced it together. Dr. Fenwick was an expert on magical creatures. He had ties to Grumbert, the exotic mythological animal dealer, and had even obtained a pair of auravores—the very creatures that hunted and hoarded enchanted objects. Then there was the note indicating early success. I reminded myself it could have meant anything...but I couldn't shake the possibility.

My mind flashed to Runar. Was this the missing piece? The link connecting him with Dr. Fenwick?

I tested my theory. Dr. Fenwick has this creature that can track down and hoard enchanted items. Now he has valuable items, but as a respected professor, he possibly fears to sell them himself. Enter Runar Ironvein, a known middleman and shady dealer. The dwarf takes the professor's ill-gotten gains and sells them at the Pot o' Gold.

I sighed. It fit, but it might not be the truth or perhaps not the whole truth. Still, I couldn't discount the enchanted items Liam purchased as mere coincidence.

Had Runar and Dr. Fenwick been partners? The timeline made sense. Runar's last sale to Liam had been right around the time Dr. Fenwick died. Maybe the dwarf got greedy, and they fought over the auravores or their latest haul. Maybe that fight had ended with Fenwick dead.

I chewed my lip. A memory from the vision the heartwood sapling sent me flickered in my mind.

A cage tumbling into the wishing well.

My breath caught. Could that explain why Runar hadn't surfaced with more to sell to Liam? If he'd lost his source, he'd have to start from scratch. And if he was sniffing around the university, maybe he was hunting for new treasures. But when Gabriel and I had surprised him in Fenwick's office, we might have scared him off for good. Who knows? By now, he could've fled the state. Or the country.

Or we had made ourselves his next problem to solve.

I sat up straighter, and my stomach twisted. This wasn't about scavengers. It never had been. This was about treasure hunters.

"Runar Ironvein," I murmured.

Ignatius's head snapped toward me. "Runar Iron-what?"

I was startled. "Sorry, was thinking out loud."

He hopped onto the counter, tail twitching. "Strange name. What you thinking?"

I let out a slow breath. "It's just...if Dr. Fenwick shifted away from wyrms and was experimenting on auravores, it makes sense why a treasure hunter like Runar Ironvein was involved. Maybe he got greedy. Maybe he wanted Fenwick's research for himself."

Ignatius's claws tightened on his book, his golden eyes darkening. "Dangerous." He tapped a claw against the book. "Auravores. Not like dragons."

"No?" I tilted my head.

"They not hoard like dragons," he said. "Not for protect. Not for love. They take. Take more. And magic not last."

"What do you mean it doesn't last?" I asked.

Ignatius' voice dropped lower. "They feed. Slow, but always."

That sent a ripple of unease through me. "So, they don't just collect magic."

Ignatius gave a slow blink. "No. They strip it."

"And do what with it?"

Ignatius put his taloned forefeet together and then spread them apart. "What anyone does with food. They grow. They adapt."

A shiver crawled up my spine.

Red Flags and Ring Boxes

THE TWO BAGS OF sandwiches and fries bumped against my leg as I made my way toward Liam's antique shop to meet Seraphina. I'd offered to grab lunch from the Hobbit Hole, and everyone had happily accepted.

The sky was its usual lazy blue, and Havenwood bustled in that sleepy, magical way it always did, but my thoughts were far from calm.

Ignatius's words lingered in the back of my mind on a repeating loop. *They feed. Magic not last.*

If he was right, and those auravores had escaped near the wishing well, then my little heartwood sapling might be in danger. I nearly stopped in my tracks as another thought hit me like a punch to the gut. What if the ley lines themselves could be affected? Could auravores eat that magic? And if they could, how would tapping into a nearly limitless supply of ancient dragon magic affect them?

I gripped the bag tighter, unease prickling at the back of my neck. This wasn't just about lost treasure and Dr. Fenwick's death anymore. If those creatures were still out there, chewing through magic like moths through wool, then Havenwood had much bigger problems on its hands.

Seraphina pulled up in a sleek silver sedan just as I turned the corner. She switched off the engine and hurried towards me.

"Oh! I wish you would've told me you were walking! I could've come to pick you up," she said, offering to take a bag.

I handed her the one with the massive helping of fries. "It's not a problem. I don't mind."

"Don't be silly! I have the car. Just give me a call next time," Seraphina insisted, tossing her long blonde hair over her shoulder and smiling brightly at me.

Unable to help myself, I smiled back. She really was the nicest person. Even though every trope in the world said I should be jealous of her beauty or her relationship with Finn, I just couldn't find it within me. She was so sweet and genuine that it was impossible not to like her.

"Well, buying you a sandwich is the least I can do to say thank you for giving up your lunch break," I said, lifting the bag I still held.

Seraphina brushed my words away. "Think nothing of it."

Liam swung the door of the Pot o' Gold wide for us.

"Ladies," he said. "Lovely to see ye. Please be welcome."

"Very kind of you," Seraphina murmured, slipping into the shop.

I followed her, and Liam shut the door behind us, flipping the open sign to closed and drawing the shades.

Sloane was already inside, perched on a faded velvet stool behind the front desk. "About time," she said, looking up. "I'm so hungry I was about to eat the paperwork."

I held up the bag I carried. "Trust me. You're going to be glad you waited for the sandwich."

"It's awfully kind of ya to bring lunch and come round to check out these trinkets," Liam said, sticking out his hand towards Seraphina. "When Harper told me you were willing to make a house call, so to speak, I couldn't believe me luck!"

Seraphina shook his proffered hand. "It's the least I can do. Harper has helped me out more than once."

I set the bags down and slid out of my jacket. Liam let out a little yelp of surprise and actually jumped backward a pace when he saw Ignatius curled around my neck.

"When did you start accessorizing with dragons?" he demanded.

Ignatius looked up. "Ignatius *not* an accessory," the dragon grumbled.

Liam grinned. "I like him already." The leprechaun pressed a hand to his chest and bowed slightly. "Forgive me manners. I didn't expect to see one of the dragonkin this fine afternoon. 'Tis a pleasure to meet ye."

Mollified, Ignatius dipped his head in return. "Pleasure is mine."

"Nice to meet you," Sloane said.

"Likewise," said Seraphina, dropping into a little curtsy.

I could tell the gesture made Ignatius feel important because he preened a little from his perch on my shoulder.

Liam clapped his hands together and rubbed them. "Well, what should we do first? Take a look at these items or eat lunch?"

"I'd like to examine the items," Seraphina said decisively. "If there's anything complicated in those pieces, I'll need time to go through them before I head back to work. But that shouldn't prevent you from enjoying your lunches."

Liam nodded. "Okay. I'll get you set up in the back. Harper, you, Sloane, and the wee dragon can get lunch unwrapped at that maple table in the corner. Might as well put it to use while I'm waiting to sell it."

Liam opened the secret door and got Seraphina started while Ignatius and I set out lunch. Sloane sauntered over, snagging a few napkins and setting them on the table with theatrical flair. While the tiny dragon practically vibrated in anticipation for his sandwich.

"Patience," I said, nudging him lightly. "Let's wait for the others."

Ignatius huffed but obediently curled his tail tighter around himself, though he still sniffed the air longingly.

After a couple of minutes, Liam wandered out of the small back room. "She says she's going to be another fifteen minutes or so, but we should get started without her."

"Are you sure?" I asked. "We can wait."

"No, we can't," Ignatius muttered.

Liam chuckled. "I wouldn't dream of keeping a dragon from his meat. You dig in, wee fella."

Ignatius didn't need to be told twice. He dove into his sandwich with gusto, making happy smacking sounds as he gobbled down his sandwich. Sloane and I chuckled at his enthusiasm.

He'd gone for Beorn's Feast. The sandwich was a towering stack of roast beef, smoked bacon, and melted cheddar, finished with horseradish aioli on toasted sourdough. It was the kind of meal that demanded commitment. I had no idea how the little dragon could fit it all in, but he attacked it with the gusto of a dragon three times his size.

Sloane's sandwich was a St. Paddy's Day twist on a Hobbit Hole classic: roasted turkey, sharp white cheddar, spinach pesto, and cucumber ribbons were tucked into a soft, herb-infused roll. It smelled like springtime in sandwich form.

"So, how are things going?" I asked Liam, tipping my head towards the tiny secret room as Sloane took a huge bite and moaned in gustatory ecstasy.

"Not bad," Liam said, pulling up a chair. "She says most of it looks like pretty innocent enchantments like the first lot but wants to confirm."

"Speaking of that first batch we identified, any luck tracking down the owners?" I asked.

Liam groaned, rubbing his face. "That's been a nightmare."

I frowned. "What do you mean?"

"Most of the owners Elowen jotted down have either passed on or vanished. A lot of the numbers are disconnected, and I'm having a devil of a time tracking down their heirs." He sighed and popped a fry into his mouth, shaking his head. "It's not like there's a yellow pages for lost jewelry owners, you know. I'm having to rely on my knowledge of the community, word of mouth, and just cold-calling people, hoping someone picks up."

I winced. "That's unlucky."

"Frustrating for sure, but not unlucky. Trust me, I know a thing or two about luck," Liam said, laying a finger alongside his nose and winking at me.

I frowned. "I don't know, Liam. This whole situation has felt like nothing but bad luck."

Liam gave me a sidelong glance. "I don't know about that. I think, with a little time, good luck might be turning your way. But if you are really worried about bad luck, you can always try and counteract it."

I tilted my head. "With what? A bad luck reversing charm?"

Liam shrugged. "Sure. Or something simpler. People carry all sorts of things to attract good luck or counteract the bad. Four-leaf clovers, a rabbit's foot."

I smirked. "I somehow doubt Luna would lend me a foot."

Liam snickered. "Probably not. But there are other things. Lucky coins, horseshoes...even a leaf from the heartwood tree."

That made me stiffen. The heartwood tree wasn't common knowledge, but it wasn't exactly a secret either. However, I wasn't ready to divulge that I was the heartwood's new guardian, so I tried to keep my voice light when I asked, "A heartwood leaf? What's that? Are they lucky?"

Liam tilted his head to the side. "A magical plant and no, it's not inherently lucky. Not many have heard of it, but legend says that wrapping an item in the leaves from the heartwood tree will soak up any residual magic—good, bad, whatever."

I blinked. "Wait... really?" My curiosity warred with the prickling unease at the back of my neck. "And then what happens to the magic?"

He shrugged. "As far as I know, it returns the magic to its neutral state. You know, raw potential."

I swallowed, trying to mask the sudden tightness in my chest. "Huh. I didn't know that."

"Not many do," he admitted as he turned away to get us some bottles of water to go with lunch.

Exactly. Not many did.

So how did Liam?

I reached for my sandwich. I'd been looking forward to the Tookish Delight since I saw it on the menu. Roasted turkey, creamy brie, spiced cranberry chutney, and peppery arugula, all tucked into a toasted whole wheat baguette. It should've been the highlight of my day.

Instead, I used it as a distraction.

While the others chatted, I slipped into stillness and stretched my awareness toward the heartwood, sending a quiet question down the bond: *Was it true? Could the leaves really absorb magic?*

The tree answered with a gentle pulse, warm and sure. Knowledge settled in like falling leaves. *Yes, its foliage could neutralize lingering enchantments. Minor hexes? Gone in a day or two. Deeper spells? Slower to unravel, but not impossible.*

I bit my lip. If that were true, it meant I could potentially remove the bad luck from Liam's ring with the heartwood's help. I pushed aside the rising questions and let the warning about the auravores ripple out, hoping the tree could sense my urgency.

The heartwood acknowledged me with a shimmer of magic along the connection we shared, as if it were brushing its leaves in salute. Then, a flicker of new magic bloomed. I understood instantly. It was a signal. If danger came near, the tree would flare a guardian's call. One only I would feel. For now, its communication seemed to only come from the main heartwood tree. The saplings were too young to shout, and honestly, that was fine by me. One voice in my head was plenty.

Liam strode over with bottles of water in hand. Seraphina joined us as well, brushing a few specks of dust off her skirt. "Well, I've checked everything out," she said. "They're all innocuous. Nothing major, just some protective spells and sentimental enchantments. I've made you a list so you can keep track, but you can handle any of them without fear."

Sloane smiled at her, tension almost visibly slipping from her shoulders. "That's a weight off my mind."

Liam exhaled in relief. "Agreed. Thank ye so much. Yer very kind."

"Glad I could help," Seraphina said.

Liam handed her a neatly wrapped bundle. "Me too. Now, let's eat before you have to run back to your work. I wouldn't want ya to go hungry on my account."

Seraphina carefully unwrapped her lunch, spreading a napkin neatly on her lap to avoid any mishaps. Ignatius was still working his way through his mound of meat. Despite his assurances, I wasn't convinced he'd finish the whole thing, but he was giving it a good try.

Seraphina took a bite of her wrap and gave an appreciative hum. "This is lovely."

She'd chosen the Rivendell Garden Wrap. Grilled zucchini, bell peppers, and mushrooms were layered with goat cheese and basil pesto in a spinach flatbread. It looked like something that belonged in an enchanted forest and smelled just as magical.

Liam had opted for something more robust. His Dwarven Miner's Melt was filled with juicy grilled chicken, caramelized onions, and smoked gouda all pressed together with a slather of roasted garlic and a secret sauce on a ciabatta roll.

Liam took a hefty bite of his own sandwich and groaned aloud. "Now that," he said, pointing at it, "is what good luck tastes like."

As we ate, the conversation drifted easily, and I found myself unexpectedly comfortable.

When she finished her wrap, Seraphina neatly folded her napkin and stood. "Thank you for lunch, Harper, but I should really get back to work."

I nodded. "Of course. And thanks for meeting me on such short notice."

She gave me a warm smile. "Anytime. Let's try for a less urgent lunch next time."

"I'd like that," I said with a smile.

She waved as she walked off, and I watched her go, a warmth settling in my chest.

Liam nudged me. "See? Told you. I can always tell when luck's turning someone's way."

I huffed a laugh, shaking my head. "We'll see about that."

But as I glanced at Ignatius happily gnawing on his sandwich, I had to admit that maybe Liam was right.

I snapped my fingers as I suddenly remembered my epiphany with the heartwood leaves from earlier. "But speaking of luck, I think I might have a way to remove the bad luck from your friend's ring."

Liam shot me a wary glance. "It's not Luna, is it? Because I can tell you right now that her foot would come with more sass than luck."

I chuckled and shook my head. "No, it's not Luna. It's..." I trailed off. Even though I'd been the guardian of the heartwood for a few weeks, I still wasn't ready to be proclaiming that in the streets, especially since, most days, it didn't feel like I had a clue about what I was doing. Liam was looking at me strangely, so I hurried to add. "Look, I'm not sure it will work, but I'd like to try something."

"If you think that you can remove the curse, I'm willing to give it a try," Liam said enthusiastically. He quickly ducked through the secret door into the hidden room and returned a moment later with the small, unassuming lead box. He placed it carefully on the table between us, tapping the lid with one finger. "You're serious about this?" he asked.

I nodded. "If there's a chance I can get rid of the curse, I'd like to try."

Liam tilted his head to the side, considering me. "Alright. But fair warning, don't put it on. And keep the lid closed as much as possible. Lead blocks most magic, and this little box is the best containment unit I've got. You don't want to be carrying a bad luck magnet around with you."

I hesitated, a little surprised he was willing to hand it over. "You're really okay with this?"

Liam exhaled through his nose. "I'd like to return it to his family. But I can't do that with the ring as it is. It's too dangerous. If you can scrub the curse off, that'd be mighty kind." His jaw tightened slightly. "And if I could get my hands on that no-good dwarf, I'd rattle some sense into his head. Or better yet..."

He trailed off, his expression darkening.

I narrowed my eyes. "Better yet what?"

Liam glanced up at me and blinked. "Oh. Right. I'd love to get my hands on his boss."

My stomach dropped. "Boss? He had a boss? What boss?"

He tilted his head as if it were obvious. "Yeah. Didn't I say?"

I lowered my sandwich and sat up straighter. "No. You definitely didn't."

Liam winced, rubbing the back of his neck. "Ah. Well, that might be important, then."

"You think?" My tone was sharper than I meant it to be.

He held up both hands. "Look, I didn't think much of it at the time. Runar said he was just the middleman. Claimed his buyer was 'a right demanding sort.' Wanted a steady stream of magical goods but didn't like dealing with people directly."

A chill swept down my spine. "And you didn't think to mention this before?" I asked.

Liam's brows lifted. "I figured the dwarf was the real problem."

I didn't answer. I was too busy calculating just how much trust I'd given a man I barely knew. A man who'd conveniently shown up with a cursed ring, asked for help, and now seemed to know far too much about heartwood leaves.

I reached for my bottle of water, if only to hide the frown tugging at my lips.

Red flags were stacking up like Spellbooks' teetering display table during a clearance sale.

"Did he give you anything else? A name? A description?" I asked.

Liam shook his head. "Not much. Just that they were from the university up in Eastford."

My breath caught. That narrowed down my suspect pool significantly.

"Did Runar say who it was?" I pressed.

"No, he was pretty cagey. Didn't like it when I asked too many questions. But…" Liam's eyes took on a faraway look, like he was replaying a memory in the cinema of his mind. "Now that you mention it, he said she knew about magical stuff. I got the impression that she had some sort of research angle up there."

"She?" Sloane asked excitedly. "Runar's boss is a female?"

My pulse quickened. Dr. Harlow was a woman, and she worked at the university in a research capacity. Not only that, but Dr. Fenwick was somehow tied to Runar Ironvein. Could the link between the two be Dr. Harlow?

She had been defensive when I asked about Fenwick. She had access to the lab. And if she had been sneaking resources out, it would make sense for her to use a third party to offload anything too obviously tied to the university.

I forced a smile. "Liam, thanks. This helps."

"Anytime," he said.

I turned, offering a polite nod to the others. "I should really get back to Spellbooks. Keep me in the loop if you find anything."

"We will," Sloane assured me.

I tucked the small lead box into my purse and scooped up Ignatius, who'd finished his sandwich and was looking pleasantly drowsy. But Liam's sharp gaze tracked me all the way to the door, lingering until I slipped out of sight.

My thoughts spun like a coin spinning nearer the edge of a table, wobbling, humming, seconds from tipping.

It all fit. But why didn't it feel right?

What if this were all a distraction?

What if *Liam* was Runar's partner? Or worse, the mastermind?

He and his cousin had shown up out of nowhere, cursed ring in hand, asking for help. He knew too much about heartwood leaves. And now, conveniently, he was pointing the finger at a vague "woman from the university" which was enough to set me chasing someone else.

Had I just been played?

What if this wasn't a plea for help at all, but a setup? A neat little scheme to get me to carry the cursed object myself?

My breath hitched. Was I just a magical mule? Or was it worse than even I could imagine?

I shook my head, trying to clear it. Maybe I was overthinking. Spinning shadows out of dust. But still, with a murderer on the loose, and a cursed ring in my bag, now was a spectacularly bad time to be wrong.

I needed answers, and fast.

Calling in Reinforcements

IGNATIUS CURLED AROUND MY throat, his snout just poking up between my scarf and neck. To most passersby it probably looked like I was either talking to myself or on a Bluetooth call. In order to help maintain the cover, I pulled out a wireless headphone and popped it into my ear as Ignatius asked, "What Harper do now?"

"I don't know, buddy," I said under my breath. "If Liam's telling the truth, then Harlow's the next logical step."

My fingers brushed the strap of my purse, where the cursed ring nestled inside its lead-lined box. "But if he's lying..." I glanced over my shoulder, half expecting to see Liam following me down the street. "Then talking to her might actually be the safer option. If she's innocent, maybe she can help, then this whole thing might point back to Liam. Either way, I need to have a talk with her."

"Not by self!" Ignatius exclaimed, his little voice outraged.

"No, of course not," I said quickly, even though, if I was honest, I hadn't thought that far ahead. But now that he mentioned it, he was right. I needed backup.

I pulled out my phone and dialed Gabriel. The phone barely rang once before he picked up.

"Harper? Is everything okay, amaryn?"

"Yes, everything's fine," I said quickly. "But I think I just figured out who's behind this. Everything. You know..." I dropped my voice to a whisper. "Dr. Fenwick."

A beat of silence. Then, Gabriel's tone shifted, his curiosity piqued. "I'm listening."

I ran through everything quickly—the book, the cursed ring, Runar, and finally, the bombshell Liam had dropped about Runar working with a woman from the university.

"You see it, right?" I said excitedly. "Dr. Fenwick was on to something with his hybrids, but when he started working with auravores, he must've created a treasure-hunting creature attuned to magical artifacts. That's why Runar was showing up with a ton of enchanted items to sell to Liam. However, Dr. Harlow must've gotten wind of the experiment with the golden touch and decided she wanted in. Maybe she borrowed the creatures or stole them from Dr. Fenwick. Either way, he finds out about her treasure hunting with Runar and tries to put an end to it but winds up dead in the process."

Gabriel took a deep breath and blew it out slowly. "That's quite the theory. Not to throw a wrench into your hypothesis, amaryn, but Fenwick would have had plenty of university contacts who do research."

"Anyone female and with knowledge of his experiments," I corrected.

"That still could be a number of people," Gabriel pointed out.

"But isn't the most likely person usually the one who committed the crime?" I asked.

"I don't know the crime statistics on that, but I'd be inclined to say usually. Which is a far cry from always," Gabriel said gently.

I pressed forward. "Think about it. The sheriff said these crimes are usually committed by someone the victim knows. Who would know Dr. Fenwick better than Dr. Harlow? She had access to his research. She knew what he was working on. And she's the one who told me about the wyrms. What if that was a misdirection? What if she was only giving us the pieces she wanted us to have?"

Gabriel didn't answer immediately. I could practically hear him working through the logic. Finally, he let out a slow breath. "Alright. Let's say you're right. What's the next step?"

"We need to confront her. To get her to confess," I said instantly.

Gabriel sighed. "Harper, if you're right, then either Dr. Harlow or Runar Ironvein is likely behind Dr. Fenwick's death. We can't just storm into her office and demand answers. She might be dangerous."

"You have a point," I admitted. "But if we wait too long, she could destroy Fenwick's research and cover her tracks. She could be shredding papers or wiping hard drives right now."

Gabriel paused and then surprised me with his next words. "You're right. We can't afford to not investigate, but we're going to do this right. I'll call the sheriff and then come pick you up. Where are you?"

"I'm walking to Spellbooks," I said.

"Great. I'll meet you there in fifteen minutes, and I'll call the sheriff on the way. Hang tight, amaryn." He ended the call.

And just like that, things were moving.

I slipped my phone back into my pocket and exhaled, my breath curling in the cool March air.

"Please, please let me be right about this," I muttered.

Because if I was wrong, then what?

If Dr. Harlow wasn't involved, I'd wasted time chasing the wrong lead. And worse, I might have scared off the real culprit by poking around too much. That thought settled in my stomach like a stone.

I rubbed my temples. I was overthinking again, second-guessing myself before I even had a chance to prove my theory. But wasn't that the problem? That this wasn't a strong theory. It was more like a series of assumptions stacked on top of each other, each one just plausible enough to fit. I needed a confession. Proof. Something that made this more than just a gut feeling.

Ignatius shifted against my neck, the warmth of his tiny body comforting against the breeze. "Harper worried?"

I huffed a soft laugh, reaching up to stroke his scales. "Yeah, I guess I am."

"You smart," he said, his little voice muffled slightly by my scarf. "Harper think. Harper find answer."

"That's the plan," I said, but my voice wasn't as confident as I wanted it to be.

Ignatius poked his snout out from my scarf and tilted his head at me. "But?"

I hesitated. "But...what if I *don't* have this figured out? What if I'm wrong, and Dr. Harlow has nothing to do with this?"

Ignatius flicked his tail, considering. "Then Harper look again. That what smart people do."

I bit the inside of my cheek. "It's not that simple. If I'm wrong, I could ruin someone's reputation. I could lead Gabriel and the sheriff on a wild goose chase."

Ignatius thought for a long moment, then gave a small, determined noise. "Harper no give up."

"That's not the same thing."

"But it is," he countered. "Bad people no want truth found. They make things messy. Confusing. That does not mean Harper stop. No wait for luck. Go make it happen."

I let that settle. It was a perspective I hadn't considered. Not really. Yes, I was worried about being wrong, but what if all the confusion was intentional? What if someone was making it harder to put the pieces together? If Dr. Fenwick had discovered something and someone wanted it buried, then making the investigation seem like a dead end was the best way to make everyone stop looking.

I straightened, rubbing my arms against the cold. "You know what, buddy? You might be onto something."

Enthusiastic, But...

As Gabriel eased the car into a parking spot outside Eastford University, I closed my eyes, focusing as hard as I could. If I blocked out everything else, I could just barely sense my connection to the heartwood tree. The link between us was faint, barely more than a whisper at this distance.

I exhaled and opened my eyes. It was possible to sense the heartwood, but not easy. With any luck, if something went wrong, I'd feel it. At least, I really, really hoped I'd feel it, but hoped even more that the heartwood wouldn't have to send out the distress call.

"He's here," Gabriel murmured, interrupting my thoughts.

I glanced behind us. To my surprise, it wasn't Sheriff Jackson in the police cruiser that pulled up behind Gabriel's sleek black sedan.

I stepped out of the car. "Officer Reggie?" I asked incredulously.

Reggie beamed as he stepped out of the cruiser, adjusting his belt like he was about to embark on the most important mission of his career. "Harper! Gabriel! Fancy running into you here."

Gabriel crossed his arms, giving him a pointed look. "I called the police station and asked you to pass the message on to the sheriff to meet us here."

"Oh, right, yeah." Reggie nodded enthusiastically. "And it's a good thing you did! Lucky for you both, I was available."

I frowned. "Where's Sheriff Jackson? I thought he was the one coming."

Reggie's expression flickered for a moment before he waved a dismissive hand. "Oh, he's, uh...occupied. Some big old mess over by the fairgrounds. Something about an enchanted goat getting loose? Or maybe it was an enchanted coat? The radio was kinda fuzzy and Bill sounded like he was running."

I exchanged a look with Gabriel. An enchanted goat? Havenwood really never had a dull day.

Reggie continued. "Anyway, the sheriff told me not to bother him. However, I figured since this sounded urgent, I should take the initiative. So, I told him I was on the case." He beamed proudly.

Gabriel sighed, rubbing a hand over his face. "Reggie, please tell me you at least talked to him before showing up here."

Reggie hesitated just a bit too long before answering. "Well...not directly," the scatterbrained officer admitted

Gabriel groaned. "Reggie."

"It's fine! It's *fine*," he assured us, waving a hand. "I left him a detailed note on his desk. Right where he'd probably see it. Maybe. Eventually."

Gabriel looked skyward, probably praying for patience. "So let me get this straight. You left a note—"

"A very *detailed* note," Officer Reggie emphasized.

"A note," Gabriel repeated, unimpressed, "and then just drove here without waiting for confirmation?"

Officer Reggie grinned. "That's called initiative, my friend."

I looked up at the officer. "Aren't you a little outside of your jurisdiction? What if Sheriff Jackson needs to be here to coordinate with the local authorities? What if this is bigger than we realize?"

Reggie's grin faltered. "Oh. Huh. Didn't think of that."

Gabriel exhaled. "Of course you didn't," he murmured, so low that only I could hear him.

Officer Reggie brightened again. "But you know what? No worries! If it turns out I do need backup, I've got my radio right here. One call to Bill, and boom! Instant cavalry." He patted the radio on his belt as if it was some kind of magical problem-solver.

I looked at Gabriel. He looked at me with a shared understanding that Officer Reggie's enthusiasm sometimes outpaced his competence.

"Umm, will that radio work to connect you all the way back to Haven-wood?" I asked carefully.

Officer Reggie frowned and scratched the back of his head. "You know what? Now that you mention it, probably not. Good thing I brought my cell phone too. I forget that some days, but I'm pretty sure I remembered it today. It's here in one of my pockets, I swear," he said, patting himself down. He pulled it out triumphantly and waved it at us before fumbling the device, barely catching it just before it crashed to the sidewalk. "Whoa! That was close. But I'm all set. Let's go catch a criminal! Uh, remind me again, who are we looking for?"

I pulled the small lead box out of my purse and flipped it open, showing the bad luck ring to Officer Reggie. "This is one of the items Runar sold to Liam O'Shaughnessy. Our current theory is that Runar Ironvein and Dr. Elise Harlow might be working together to find and profit from selling enchanted items like this ring."

"That's one shiny ring!" Officer Reggie exclaimed, reaching for it.

I pulled it back, snapping the lid closed. The last thing we needed today was for the genial but less-than-competent police officer to be cursed with bad luck.

I continued quickly to alleviate any hurt feelings. "However, given what happened to Dr. Fenwick, Gabriel made the very logical point that it might be prudent to have a police presence when we confront her in case things turn ugly."

Officer Reggie nodded sagely, like he was already envisioning himself heroically breaking down Dr. Harlow's office door. "Right, right. Could be dangerous. Good call notifying the police. Alright, let's move!"

Before I could tuck the lead box away, Officer Reggie took off at a light jog toward the university's main entrance.

I quickly shoved the box deep into my pocket. "I really wish he wouldn't charge in like that," I muttered, picking up my pace to keep him in sight.

Gabriel kept stride beside me. "At least he's eager," he offered dryly.

The university quad stretched wide ahead of us, students moving in small clusters between buildings, some heading to class, others breaking for coffee. A group had started tossing a Frisbee near the main walkway, and I tried to skirt around them while keeping one eye on Reggie.

Unfortunately, I didn't see the students stepping out of a lecture hall directly in my path.

I collided hard with one of them, stumbling back as my shoulder smacked into solid muscle. "Oh! Sorry—" I started, but the short guy I'd knocked into just grunted in annoyance and hunched his shoulders. He pulled the hood of his sweatshirt lower over his eyes and angled away, muttering something under his breath.

"Are you okay, amaryn?" Gabriel asked, grabbing my arm.

"Yeah. I just bumped into—" I turned to point, but the hooded figure had already melted into the crowd.

"Come on," Gabriel said, tugging on my hand. "Officer Reggie's nearly at the science building."

Something prickled at the back of my mind, but I didn't have time to dwell on it. Gabriel was right. Reggie was still trotting ahead. Left to his own devices, it was probably a fifty-fifty chance that he'd somehow spook Dr. Harlow before he figured out who she was. Scratch that. More like seventy-thirty, with the odds not being in our favor. I shook off the moment and hurried after them.

I was practically vibrating with nervous energy as we strode through the university halls, my heart pounding with anticipation as we hurried to confront Dr. Elise Harlow. If she'd been working with Runar, then she had to know something about Fenwick's murder.

Gabriel kept pace beside me, his expression carefully neutral, but I could tell he was bracing for whatever was about to unfold.

"We need to be careful," he muttered under his breath.

"I know," I said.

"Careful," Ignatius murmured next to my ear.

The research wing smelled faintly of disinfectant and aged books, and the air held the quiet hush of academia. Our rushed footsteps sounded loud in the echoing hallway leading to the lab Dr. Harlow showed us earlier. Officer Reggie barely knocked before pushing against the locked door to the lab, nearly running face first into the door in his eagerness to apprehend Dr. Harlow.

A sharp click sounded from the other side, followed by the metallic rattle of the push bar. The door swung open, and Dr. Harlow nearly tripped over herself as she took in the sight of Gabriel, Reggie, and me standing there. Her eyes went wide, a flicker of shock darting across her face.

"I—oh, goodness, what's happening now?" she asked, her tone frayed at the edges. "Did you forget something? Why are the police here again?" Her voice rose to a squeak at the end.

"We just need to ask you a couple more questions, miss," Reggie said briskly, stepping into the lab.

I followed close behind as Gabriel eased the door shut behind us with a soft click of the lock. Reggie launched into a line of questioning so convoluted that even I had trouble following.

While he rambled, I looked around the lab more thoroughly. Most of the equipment looked the same as before. Beakers, burners, a microscope surrounded by neatly stacked slides, but something new caught my attention.

A door.

Somehow, I'd completely missed the unmarked door tucked into the far wall. From what I could see, it was locked with no keycard reader, just an old-fashioned lock and handle.

I sidled toward it as Officer Reggie continued talking, placing my hand casually against the knob. A small pulse of metal magic rippled through my fingers, seeking out the locking mechanism. It was simple, old, and mechanical.

Easy.

I let the magic flow into the tumblers, clicking them into place one by one until I felt the mechanism give. I didn't open the door. Not yet, anyway. I just needed it unlocked.

Keeping my voice low, I murmured under my scarf, "Ignatius, slip inside and take a look around."

The little dragon wriggled slightly against my neck. "Snoop?"

"Just a little," I whispered. "See if there's anything out of place."

His tail flicked against my collar in agreement. "Quick like dragonfire," he promised.

I stepped back, turning just in time to see Dr. Harlow throw up her hands. "I don't understand why you're so fixated on me! I've done nothing but try to help!"

"You gave Harper misleading information," Gabriel said coolly. "You told her Dr. Fenwick was studying wyrms. But the notes we found suggested he'd moved on to another, rarer creature."

Dr. Harlow let out a choked noise, her fingers clenching the edge of a nearby table. "You think I—?"

"Yeah," Officer Reggie chimed in. "And what about the dwarf? We know *all* about him, don't we? Spill. Where is he and what has he done with the goods?"

Gabriel shot him an exasperated look as Dr. Harlow shook her head. "What dwarf? What creatures? None of this is making any sense. I've never heard of either of those."

"Exactly what a guilty person would claim," Officer Reggie said triumphantly, folding his arms over his chest and attempting what I think was meant to be an intimidating scowl. He leaned on the edge of a nearby table.

This was my chance. I inhaled slowly, letting the familiar pull of the metal magic hum through my fingers. With a flick of willpower, I nudged the microscope just enough to tip the stack of glass slides beside it.

The clatter was immediate and gloriously effective. Slides skittered across the tabletop, a few flying off the edge like startled birds, shattering against the floor.

"Careful!" Dr. Harlow cried, leaping back.

"Watch out!" Gabriel shouted, diving to keep one from slicing across his shoe.

Reggie staggered upright, arms flailing. "That wasn't me!"

I barely glanced at him. I was too focused on the tiny flicker of movement at my collar as Ignatius darted down my sleeve and slipped under the table, headed straight for the previously locked door.

"Quickly," I whispered to Ignatius, easing the door open just a crack. He darted from the shadows beneath the table and slid through the opening. I silently shut the door behind him before joining in the cleanup effort.

"Oh, this is a mess!" I exclaimed as I positioned myself between the research assistant and the locked room. "Dr. Harlow, you wouldn't happen to have a dustpan, would you?"

Reggie, ever helpful, straightened and beamed. "Oh, don't worry! I got this." He pulled out a notepad and cleared his throat dramatically. "Dr. Harlow, please state your full name for the record."

Dr. Harlow blinked at him. "You...you want me to do that now?"

"Yes," the officer said seriously. "It's very official."

Gabriel pinched the bridge of his nose. "Reggie."

"What? This is what we do, right? Question suspects?" Reggie asked.

"I'm not a suspect," Dr. Harlow snapped. "Am I?"

Reggie hesitated, flipping open his notebook. "Well, we're asking questions, so... maybe?" He cleared his throat. "So, Dr. Harlow, are you familiar with a dwarf named Runar Ironvein?"

She let out an exhausted groan. "No. Like I told you before, I have never met him."

Gabriel crossed his arms, fixing her with a scrutinizing stare. "An antique dealer who received a load of what may be stolen goods from Runar confirmed that he was working with someone from the university. A woman."

Dr. Harlow let out a choked noise, completely forgetting about the mess in front of her. "You think I—?" Her mouth opened and closed like a wind-up toy running out of juice as she looked between us. "No, this can't be happening. I've never heard of this Runar guy, and I'd *never* participate in theft. Never ever!" Her eyes lit up. "You're accusing me because I'm a woman? There must be hundreds of women working at the university, let alone the students. How can you be sure this dwarf was talking about me?"

Officer Reggie stepped forward. "It's what we in the law enforcement field like to call the guilty trifecta. Motive, means, and opportunity. You've got those. Or at least some of them. And because of that, you're going down for the murder of your boss."

Dr. Harlow's mouth fell open. Her expression crumpled into raw horror.

"M-murder? He's...*dead?* I thought he was just missing!" she gasped. "No. No, no, no! This can't be happening. There's been a mistake—a huge mistake!"

Reggie pulled out a pair of handcuffs. "You can tell it to the sheriff."

She let out a wild, half-sobbed laugh. "Oh, of course. Of course this would happen. First Dr. Winterbourne tells me the grant paying for me to assist Dr. Fenwick has been pulled, and now I'm being accused of murder?" Her voice cracked.

I exchanged a glance with Gabriel, a flicker of doubt curling in my gut. Something about her reaction felt...off.

Dr. Harlow wasn't just distressed. She was unraveling.

"I didn't kill Dr. Fenwick," she cried. "To be honest, I barely even liked the man! He was arrogant, dismissive. He mocked my research in front of the entire board, but I wouldn't—I couldn't—" She shook her head hard, curls flying. "You can't really believe *I* killed him?"

"You can explain yourself at the station," Reggie said, guiding her toward the door.

Gabriel pulled out his phone. "I think the sheriff needs to hear about this before Reggie finds a way to bungle it," he muttered as he stepped out.

"Absolutely. We should contact the sheriff. I'm right behind you." I said, taking a step in that direction. However, Gabriel was already engrossed with the phone pressed to his ear. I dashed back towards the side door and opened it a crack.

"Ignatius?" I whispered.

"Reading. Busy," came the hushed reply.

"Buddy, we've got to go. Whatever it is, bring it with you, and we'll get out of here."

A moment later, Ignatius appeared, dragging a small notebook with him. I scooped them up and settled the notebook in my purse as Ignatius curled around my neck in his usual spot. I re-locked the door with my magic and dashed for the main entrance to the lab. It swung shut behind me as Gabriel turned to glance over his shoulder, hanging up his call.

I smiled weakly at him as I hurried to catch up, torn between stopping Officer Reggie from mangling the investigation and finding out what was in that notebook Ignatius had discovered.

A Run of Bad Luck

I HURRIED AFTER GABRIEL, and together we followed Officer Reggie as he ushered Dr. Harlow towards his police cruiser. I noticed he hadn't actually used the handcuffs, which was probably a good thing, given the number of stares thrown our way as we walked across the campus quad. However, as we neared the cruiser, the attention on us seemed to drop instead of increase. Before I could comment on it to Gabriel, a sight stopped me cold.

Runar Ironvein, the dwarven fence and all-around pain in my investigation, was sitting on the curb with his wrists cuffed behind his back, looking like he'd lost a fight with a blender in the middle of a discount party store. Sheriff Jackson stood over him, arms crossed, looking equal parts smug and exasperated.

Runar was drenched in what looked like beer, coated in neon powder—was that from a color run?—and somehow had an entire strand of cheap plastic beads tangled in his beard.

"What in the world happened?" I asked, glancing between the sheriff and Runar.

Before the sheriff could answer, Officer Reggie appeared, marching Dr. Harlow across the quad.

"Sheriff!" Reggie called out, his chest puffed up like a proud golden re-triever who had fetched the wrong stick but was very sure it was important. "I got her! Dr. Elise Harlow! All safe and sound!"

Listening to him made it seem like she'd been missing, not the missing piece of a murder investigation.

Dr. Harlow threw up her hands. "I don't even know what he's talking about!"

Sheriff Jackson slowly turned toward Officer Reggie, blinking like a man processing a very long day. "Reggie. I was gone for an hour. Sixty minutes. That's it."

Reggie grinned. "Yeah! And look at all the good police work I got done in that time!"

Sheriff Jackson pinched the bridge of his nose and muttered something under his breath before exhaling. "You do realize we're out of jurisdiction, right? Did you plan on telling me you were heading out here before causing a jurisdictional nightmare?"

Officer Reggie hesitated. "I left a note?"

"A note," the sheriff repeated flatly. "You mean that scrap of paper on my desk? The one I could barely read? It was hardly legible. I had to get Bill to translate and even he said it looked like a chicken tried writing with its feet." He grumbled, shaking his head. "That's not communication, Reggie. That's graffiti."

"Well, you were busy! And there was a lead, so I took the initiative. Isn't that what you wanted me to do more of?"

"Not in someone else's juris—" Sheriff Jackson paused and tilted his head up to the sky like he was asking the universe for patience. Finally, he shook his head. "We'll deal with that in a second."

Runar rattled his cuffs with a sly grin. "Look, Sheriff, I can save you the headache. No one wants the paperwork. You cut me loose, and we all walk away happy. Eh?"

Sheriff Jackson rolled his eyes. "This might be technically out of my jurisdiction, but fleeing a scene and causing property damage? That's fair game anywhere. Campus security and local PD can sort out the paperwork later."

Runar's grin slid right off his face. He slumped against the curb, mut-tering darkly under his breath.

Gabriel spoke up. "How did you find Runar Ironvein, Sheriff?"

The sheriff lifted an eyebrow. "You know this hooligan?" He jerked a thumb at the dwarf, whose wet sweatshirt was stained with a veritable rainbow of eye-hurting neon colored powder. "Care to explain why he took off running like his life depended on it the second he saw me and managed to crash through half a fraternity's spring event? I'd love to hear a logical explanation because he ain't talking."

Runar scowled, his dignity in shambles. "Not my fault! I was—" He hesitated, shooting a glance at the sheriff before deflating a little. "—minding my own business," he mumbled.

Sheriff Jackson didn't even blink. "Right. And then you just happened to barrel through an obstacle course, get tangled in a streamer net, take out an entire tray of Jell-O shots and a keg, and—oh, my personal favorite—set off the foam machine and stumble into the barrels of colored powder they planned to use at the party while trying to escape through a back alley."

I bit my lip hard to keep from laughing. That explained the powder clinging to his clothes along with the color seeping into his skin. It was absurd. It was cartoonishly unlucky.

"I don't deserve this," Runar muttered, spitting out a stray piece of confetti.

"Yeah?" Sheriff Jackson mused. "Then you won't mind explaining the suspicious items you had on you when I caught up."

Runar's face twisted into a scowl. "They're mine! Every single one."

The sheriff crossed his arms. "So you keep saying." He held up a notebook with rainbow cats on the front from a small pile of items on the curb next to Runar. "I find it hard to believe that this is your style and," the sheriff flipped open the cover, "that you are taking Design 101: The Evolution of Fashion." He eyed the soggy dwarf skeptically. "Unless the kids are right, and I really don't get fashion these days."

I exhaled, ready to let the sheriff deal with this mess, when a nagging thought prickled the back of my mind.

This wasn't just bad luck. This was catastrophically bad luck.

And Runar was a thief.

I reached for my jacket pocket—and my stomach dropped.

The ring.

I patted my coat frantically, my fingers searching for the familiar shape of the lead-lined box. It was gone.

My eyes snapped to Runar, who had the audacity to look smug as he met my stare.

"You stole it!" I hissed at the dwarf.

His face didn't even twitch. "Dunno what you're talking about."

I cleared my throat. "Umm, sheriff? Is there a small metal box there, by chance? With a gold ring inside?"

The sheriff frowned at me but crouched next to the pile, sifting through it and coming up with Liam's lead box a moment later.

"Is this yours, Miss Sullivan?" he asked.

"Not exactly. It's Liam O'Shaughnessy's, but I'm holding on to it for him. As a favor." The sheriff arched a brow, but I hurriedly asked. "Is the ring still inside?"

The sheriff flipped the lid of the box open. It was empty, which I'd already guessed.

I nodded at the confirmation of my hypothesis. "Check his hands, sheriff. I'd bet that he's wearing the gold ring I got from Liam. That would explain all the *bad luck*." I emphasized the last few words, widening my eyes, but the sheriff didn't need me to spell it out for him. He'd worked in Havenwood long enough to recognize a hidden meaning when he heard one.

He shifted around behind the dwarf and tugged on something out of my sight. A moment later he held up a ring.

"Hey! That's mine!" Runar protested.

"Trust me, I'm doing you a favor," I muttered. I gestured toward the lead-lined box. "Sheriff, probably best to get that ring back where it belongs."

Sheriff Jackson raised an eyebrow but dropped the ring inside and quickly shut the lid. He eyed the box warily. "I should take this into evidence."

I hesitated. "You could, but this ring is cursed with bad luck." I waved at Runar. "Exhibit A."

Sheriff Jackson glanced at the dwarf, who was now scowling as a bead of water dripped down his nose.

The sheriff growled at the dwarf. "Is this stolen property?"

"No!" Runar exclaimed.

"The ring belongs to Liam," I insisted. "You can't let Eastford PD touch it. They don't have the protections Havenwood does. That curse is nasty and won't wait for jurisdiction to get sorted."

Sheriff Jackson's nostrils flared, his expression thunderous. I could see the calculations behind his eyes. The last thing he needed was Eastford officers stumbling into cursed magic they couldn't even recognize.

Finally, he grunted. "Fine. But it stays in Havenwood hands. You'll take it straight to Liam and nowhere else."

"You have my word," I said.

"And tell him I'll be by later," he added grimly. "I want to see that ring locked down with my own eyes."

"Of course," I assured him.

He turned to Runar. "Now, about that stolen property charge…"

Runar groaned. "This is the worst day ever."

Sheriff Jackson nudged him toward the cruiser. "Keep talking, I might find a way to make it worse."

Officer Reggie pushed his hat back and scratched his head. "Wait a minute, if he's the bad guy, does this mean we don't have to arrest her?" He motioned toward Dr. Harlow. "Or are they, like, in on this together?"

Dr. Harlow glared. "I don't even know who this is."

Runar seized the opening, voice rising. "Oh, come on! Sheriff, if you cut me a deal, I'll tell you all about this lady and her shady deals."

Harlow blinked at him, visibly thrown. "What?"

"You're the one who stole from your own lab!" Runar barked. "Don't try playing innocent now."

Dr. Harlow's jaw dropped. "Stole? Stole what?"

"The creatures!" Runar cried. "You took them right out of Fenwick's lab. You concocted this whole scheme. I've been fencing stuff for you for weeks. Expensive stuff. Don't act like you don't know."

"I—what? What creatures?" she stammered. "I haven't taken any-thing!"

Runar shook his head, scowling in exasperation. "Unbelievable. You can't think that playing innocent is really going to work."

Dr. Harlow looked genuinely distressed. "I—I have no idea what you're talking about. What creatures? I haven't taken anything!"

Runar let out a bitter laugh. "Oh, sure. I guess it was some other lady with big glasses hauling cages out of the lab two weeks ago and then contacted me about being a fence for some expensive goods. 'Cept you didn't say 'fence,' of course, but that's what you meant. "

Gabriel narrowed his eyes. "Two weeks ago?"

Runar nodded emphatically. "Yeah, I remember because that's the night I was…well, never mind where I was. Let's just say I know it was her lugging those cages."

Dr. Harlow looked like she was going to be sick. "This—this is absurd. I was home two weeks ago! I had the flu all week!"

By now, people had started gathering. A handful of students had slowed down to watch, while two members of campus security approached cautiously, their hands hovering near their radios.

One of them stepped forward. "Everything alright here?"

Sheriff Jackson nodded at them. "Actually, you're just the people I need to talk to." He pulled out his phone. "I need to make a call to the local authorities, but I'd also like to take a look at your security footage from the night in question." He gave Dr. Harlow a measured look. "You're coming with me."

Dr. Harlow paled but didn't argue, though her posture was stiff as she followed Sheriff Jackson away.

Officer Reggie frowned. "Uh…what do I do?"

Sheriff Jackson jerked a thumb toward Runar. "Put him in the back of your vehicle and wait for me."

Reggie hesitated. "But he's a mess. It's going to take an age to clean the upholstery."

Sheriff Jackson clapped the officer on the shoulder. "Exactly why he's not going in mine. And when we get back to Havenwood, we're going to have a talk about your note-leaving abilities. A long talk. Then you can start cleaning your car."

Officer Reggie groaned but did as he was told, muttering under his breath as he led Runar toward his car.

I watched them go, tension slowly draining from my shoulders.

Maybe we'd finally gotten it right. Runar's accusations had been frantic and mean, but also oddly specific. And Dr. Harlow… well, for all her horror and confusion, maybe guilt looked a lot like disbelief under pressure.

I let out a slow breath.

Okay. One disaster down.

Now I could focus on cleaning up the rest. Like returning the cursed ring, figuring out where the missing creatures had gone, and then there was the small matter of my business. I had a book signing coming up, a to-do list longer than the fiction section, and at least three emails flagged "urgent" that I was pretending not to notice.

Normal chaos. Familiar chaos. I'd take it.

Charlie Pending

Gabriel and I sat on a bench beneath the sprawling limbs of an old oak, the cool March breeze teasing at the ends of my scarf. We weren't exactly warm, but after everything that had just gone down, I didn't mind the cold. The air felt clean. Settled. For the first time since we discovered the body in the woods, so did I.

"Well," I said, exhaling hard. "That was a mess."

Gabriel chuckled and stretched his legs out in front of him. "And yet, not the worst mess we've dealt with."

"True." I leaned against him, letting my shoulder rest against his. "Still, I didn't expect Runar to throw Elise under the bus that fast. I almost feel bad for her."

He arched a brow. "Almost?"

I shrugged. "I'll save the full sympathy package for someone not accused of murder."

Gabriel wrapped his arm around my shoulders, and I sank into his side, grateful for the warmth.

"So," he said after a beat. "What now?"

I sighed. "Maybe I should apologize to Liam for mentally accusing him of artifact smuggling."

Gabriel smirked. "If you didn't say it out loud, I'm not sure he'll even notice, but I'm sure he appreciates your internal remorse."

"I still think he knows more than he's saying about the heart-woods. But fine. He's officially downgraded from prime suspect to suspicious-but-tolerable."

"That's progress, amaryn," Gabriel said, pressing a kiss to my temple.

I let my eyes drift to the sky. The breeze rustled the oak leaves gently overhead. For the first time in what felt like days, the chaos had paused.

Ignatius wiggled under my scarf. "Harper?"

"Not now," I murmured, stroking his scales. "Let me enjoy my moment of closure."

"Harper," he said again, his tiny claws gripping my collar with more insistence.

"Buddy—"

"Notebook!" Ignatius finally scrambled up to my ear, pressing his snout against my cheek. "Check purse."

I frowned, then reached inside, my fingers brushing against something smooth and leather-bound. I pulled it out, finally remembering the notebook he'd recovered from the locked room in the lab.

"Oh!" I exclaimed, giving his scales a stroke. "You clever dragon! Well done!"

Gabriel arched a brow. "Where did you—?"

"Ignatius borrowed it from a locked room in Dr. Fenwick's lab. Allegedly," I explained quickly.

"No 'legedly. I did," Ignatius said proudly.

Gabriel paused and took a deep breath before blowing it out again. "Well, I suppose it's a good thing the sheriff isn't here to hear that confession. He doesn't seem like he's in a forgiving mood today."

I shivered, my eyes drawn to the police car with Runar's silhouette in the backseat. "No, he does not," I agreed.

Ignatius nudged me. "Harper read."

"Okay, buddy. I hear you." I flipped open the cover of the journal. I turned the pages, my pulse quickening. The ink was faded in some places, but the writing was clear. These were meticulous notes on Dr. Fenwick's research with the wyrms, including behavioral observations and experimental pairings. Every detail was recorded in this notebook, from diet to environment to light exposure.

Ignatius made a soft, thoughtful hum but said nothing. He was already curling up under my scarf again, satisfied with his part in the discovery.

I scanned through quickly, my pulse racing. "He wasn't cagey at all in these notes," I murmured. "He writes in detail about every step of his process, every failed experiment."

Gabriel leaned in. "Anything on why the experiments failed?"

I dragged a finger down a column of notes. "The mundane mates—oh. Yikes. The stronger wyrms always ended up eating them before they could... you know. Mate."

Gabriel grimaced. "Charming."

I flipped ahead, my brow furrowing as I saw something that caught my eye. I paused, turning back a few pages. "But look here. It seems like he started shifting focus away from wyrms."

Gabriel read over my shoulder. "Looks like he pivoted toward auravores."

I tapped the page. "Exactly as I suspected. He writes that he made the decision to switch research topics and leaves the question of what to do with the wyrms hanging. No wonder Dr. Harlow thought he was still working on them."

"But if he recently switched, why does he have notes on initial testing?" Gabriel asked, pointing at the next page.

I shifted my focus, scanning through the notes. A piece of information was glaringly missing. "And what did he breed the auravores with?" I asked. "In his wyrm experiments, he was quite clear on his trials."

"Not so here," Gabriel said. "But look. Test Alpha failed, but the Beta test was unplanned but possible."

"Alpha failed? Beta possible?" I asked. The words rang a bell, and my mind flashed back to the scrap of paper that had fallen out of the proof copy of Dr. Fenwick's book. The last two words appeared in my memory.

Charlie: pending.

Quickly, I flipped the page, my eyes drinking in every word. I grabbed Gabriel's arm, my heart pounding in excitement as the realization hit home.

"What is it?" he asked, glancing around as if expecting a threat.

"Charlie pending," I whispered, pointing at the entry.

"Yeah, what about it?" Gabriel asked, squinting at the page.

"Look! Charlie isn't a test," I said in a rush. "Charlie is a *person*. See?" I jabbed at a note scrawled in the margins. "Dr. Fenwick wrote that he was waiting for this Charlie, whoever that is, to confirm the test results."

Gabriel straightened, his expression sharpening. "You're sure?"

"He writes in detail about every part of his process," I said. "But he doesn't name a single collaborator in this entire notebook that we've seen. Except for Charlie."

"Okay, so he consulted a colleague. What's the big deal?" Gabriel asked.

I exhaled. "Fenwick had a confidant. Someone he trusted. Someone who knew about the auravore experiments before anyone else."

Gabriel's eyes lit up with understanding. He locked eyes with me, the weight of the realization settling between us. "Someone who might have a vested interest in how they turned out. Which means if Fenwick's work was worth killing for..."

He let the silence stretch. "Charlie is the one person who might have known why."

"Exactly. Not even his research assistant knew he was working with auravores and yet he told this Charlie person? This person might have the answers to all our questions. They could know what Dr. Fenwick was hoping to gain from the auravore experiments."

"And who might want to stop him," Gabriel added. "Maybe it was even this Charlie person, looking to get their hands on the research."

We stared at the book, realization sinking in. We hadn't uncovered a missing research partner.

We'd found a suspect.

What's in a Name?

SHERIFF JACKSON STRODE TOWARD us, his expression grim, Elise Harlow preceding him in handcuffs. She looked ashen, her eyes darting around as if she still couldn't believe what was happening. He guided her into the back of his cruiser with a firm but not unkind grip, shutting the door before turning toward us.

Gabriel and I stood as he approached.

"What's going on?" Gabriel asked.

The sheriff let out a slow sigh and raked a hand through his hair. "Security footage." His tone was heavy, like he'd rather be anywhere but here. "They got her on camera, clear as day. She took cages full of creatures out of Dr. Fenwick's lab. Must've made off with at least four or five, though it's hard to tell from the angle. They were wriggling all over the place. Looked like dark ferrets or skinny weasels."

I frowned. "And she swears it wasn't her."

"Up and down," the sheriff confirmed. "But it's going to be pretty hard to disprove it. At one point, she looks straight into the camera. Clear shot of her face. No grainy shadows, no hood pulled low. It's her."

Gabriel crossed his arms. "You know, for someone with a doctorate, you'd think she'd remember there are cameras in a university lab."

I let out a half-laugh, but it didn't quite reach my chest. I wanted to feel satisfied—relieved even. But the whole thing nagged at me. Something about it felt too clean. Too easy. Still, I shoved the doubt aside. We had a suspect. We had proof. And for once, things seemed to be moving in the right direction.

The sheriff, however, didn't look satisfied. "Sometimes even the smartest people overlook the obvious. But now we're in a jurisdictional nightmare. Campus security wants to take her into custody. They say it happened on university grounds, so the dean should handle it."

I winced. "That sounds convenient."

He nodded. "Exactly. If it's a theft, especially of university property, it's a police matter. But I don't have jurisdiction here. I phoned a buddy at the Eastford PD. He's coming, but it'll be twenty minutes before he can get here. In the meantime, he asked me to hold onto her so campus security doesn't try to sweep this under the rug."

Gabriel nodded. "Yeah, I can see them wanting to bury this."

"Right?" The sheriff rubbed at his temple. "You know how these university types are. Never want a scandal, always want to keep things quiet. You never know how far some people will go."

I exchanged a look with Gabriel. This was getting messier by the second.

Sheriff Jackson exhaled and then focused on Gabriel. "Listen, I need you to stick around."

Gabriel's brow furrowed. "Why?"

"Because you know these types of people." Sheriff Jackson gestured at the looming buildings of the university. "The powerful people who think they are God's gift. You're more familiar with the internal politics of people like this, who pulls the strings, who's got influence over who. You might see or hear something I miss, and I don't want to trust Reggie with this."

Gabriel considered that for a moment, then nodded. "Alright. I can stay."

The sheriff gave a grateful nod and pulled out his phone, already turning toward his cruiser. "Appreciate it. I need to check in with Eastford PD and make sure their guy's still en route."

As he stepped away, I said, "Well, while you two are dealing with the political mess, I'm going to head over to the science building."

Gabriel turned toward me. "Why?"

"I want to check the faculty directory and ask around. See if there's anyone named Charles or Charlie."

"You could just do that online," he pointed out.

I shrugged. "Sure, but what if it's not a professor? What if it's a janitor or a lab tech? Someone who wouldn't show up in an online directory?"

Gabriel gave me a look. "Harper. Do you really think Dr. Fenwick was consulting with a janitor?"

I folded my arms. "You never know. Maybe it was a retired scientist who took the job for the pension. Maybe it was someone with access to something he needed."

"Maybe," he admitted. "But it's still unlikely."

"Okay, fine, maybe you're right." I tilted my head. "But so am I. It's just a quick trip across campus. I'll poke around and see if I turn anything up."

Gabriel sighed, already resigned to the fact that I wasn't backing down. "Alright," he said. "But I need you to promise me something, amaryn."

"What?" I asked.

"Don't go chasing after this Charlie person on your own." His gaze was steady, his voice warm but serious. "If you find something, call me first. I couldn't bear it if something happened to you."

A gentle warmth spread through my chest. "I'll be careful," I promised. "I'm just looking."

"Looking turns into investigating, and investigating turns into trouble," he said wryly.

I grinned. "Sounds like you know me."

He gave me a pointed look but then pulled me in for a quick hug. "Just stay safe."

I squeezed his arm. "I will."

Gabriel turned back toward the sheriff, and I started across the quad, Ignatius shifting against my collar.

"We find Charlie?" he whispered.

I nodded. "That's the plan."

"Good," he said.

And with that, I headed toward the science building.

I paused at the directory posted near the entrance and skimmed the list of names. No Charlies. No Charles. Nothing that looked even remotely close.

Unwilling to give up so quickly, I approached the reception desk, where a student in a university hoodie sat behind a computer.

"Hey, quick question," I said. "Do you have any faculty or staff named Charlie? Or Charles?"

The student squinted at me. "You mean, like, a professor in this building? I don't think so."

"Are you sure? A research assistant, maybe? Anyone who might go by Charlie?"

She shook her head. "Not that I've ever heard. I can check, though."

I waited as she tapped on her keyboard. A minute later, she frowned. "Nope. No Charlie or Charles in our system. Sorry."

I sighed. "Okay. Thanks anyway."

As I turned away, Ignatius squirmed under my scarf. "Try another place," he whispered.

I frowned. "What do you mean, another place?"

"Another department," he said, sounding proud of himself. "Maybe Charlie not Science-Charlie. Maybe Math-Charlie or English-Charlie."

I gave him a baffled look. "Ignatius, why would Dr. Fenwick be consulting someone in one of those departments? What would be the point?"

"Maybe they have magic," he suggested.

"Okay," I admitted slowly. "I suppose that's a possibility, buddy. But I'm not sure I see it. If Fenwick was doing magical research, wouldn't it make more sense that he was working with someone here? In science?"

Ignatius huffed. "Maybe."

"Maybe?" I asked, crossing my arms.

"Maybe not in university at all," he offered. "What if Charlie somewhere else?"

I groaned and flopped onto a nearby bench. "So now we're opening this up to all the Charlies in the sciences? That's got to be tens of thousands of people, Ignatius. How do we even narrow it down?"

Ignatius went silent, and I sighed, staring blankly at the directory board across the hallway. Then a thought hit me.

"I've been thinking about Charlie like it has to be short for Charles," I muttered. "But what else could it be?"

Ignatius perked up. "Like what?"

"I don't know... Charlton? Charleston? Charlize?" I scanned the list again, my eyes drifting automatically down the column of C's. "Maybe it's not a guy at all. Maybe it's a girl's nickname. Charlene is a variant of Charles, right? It could be—"

I froze, my eyes snagging on a familiar name.

"Charlotte," I whispered.

Ignatius blinked. "Charlotte?"

I shot to my feet and pointed at the board. "Look at this—Dr. Maxine *Charlotte* Winterbourne! Dr. Harlow told us she hates her first name. Maybe she went by Charlie with her peers."

Ignatius tilted his head. "You sure?"

"Nope," I said. "But there's only one way to find out."

Maybe fate had dealt the cards, but I was the one who had to figure out how to bluff with a two and a seven.

With renewed energy, I spun on my heel and rushed towards the stairs, determined to find Dr. Winterbourne and, hopefully, some long-overdue answers.

Peer Reviewed and Panicked

I STRODE DOWN THE hall, the polished floors reflecting the overhead fluorescent lights. The walls were lined with framed research posters. Some featured complex diagrams; others were full of equations that made my head spin. A few students lingered outside classroom doors, chatting in hushed voices or scrolling on their phones.

Ignatius peeked out from my scarf. "How find her?"

"Good question," I muttered. I had been so caught up in my realization that I hadn't actually thought through the logistics. Dr. Winterbourne could be anywhere—teaching, in a meeting, or even off-campus.

I slowed as I reached an open study lounge, scanning the space for any sign of her. A few professors were seated near the windows, sipping coffee and going over notes with students. No Winterbourne.

"Library?" Ignatius suggested.

"Maybe," I murmured. "Or—"

A flash of movement caught my eye. A woman in a tailored blazer and crisp white blouse with her hair swept into a sleek bun exited a lecture hall.

Dr. Winterbourne.

My pulse quickened.

She walked with purpose, a manila folder tucked under her arm, her heels tapping softly against the tile. I adjusted my pace, keeping just enough distance to avoid looking suspicious. As she passed a cluster of vending machines, she checked her watch and pivoted sharply, heading down a side hallway.

I hurried to catch up just in time to see her push open a door and step inside.

I slowed to a stop and glanced at the nameplate beside it.

Dr. Maxine Winterbourne—Faculty Office

"Bingo," I whispered. I hesitated, gripping the strap of my bag. I should probably let Gabriel or the sheriff know, but they were knee-deep in dealing with Elise and the PR nightmare that came with it. And that situation wasn't hypothetical. Elise had been caught on camera, plain as day.

Besides, we were on a crowded university campus in the middle of the day. Even if Dr. Winterbourne had been tangled up in Fenwick's research, that didn't mean she was dangerous. This might just be an awkward conversation with a grumpy scientist.

Still, I wasn't stupid. I fished out my phone and dropped Gabriel a quick message with my location. Just in case.

Finding my courage, I took a deep breath, straightened my posture, and knocked twice. Fate might have written the prologue, but I was holding the pen now.

From inside, a clipped voice called out, "Come in."

As I entered, Dr. Winterbourne looked up from her desk, arching a perfectly shaped eyebrow. Her office was immaculately tidy. Shelves lined with books and framed academic certificates filled the walls. A pot of tea sat beside her, the scent of jasmine curling in the air.

Dr. Winterbourne's sharp gaze flicked up from her desk the moment I stepped inside. She tilted her head slightly, a look of faint recognition crossing her features.

"I've seen you around a lot this week, haven't I?" she mused, her voice smooth but edged with curiosity.

My stomach dipped. I forced a polite smile. "Yes, I've been...investigating."

Internally, I kicked myself. *Too honest, Harper. Too honest.*

Dr. Winterbourne's eyes narrowed. "Investigating?"

"For an article," I said quickly, the words tumbling out before I had a chance to think better of them.

Both her eyebrows lifted. "Really? That's interesting. Because I could've sworn you told me you were a transfer student looking to enroll."

Busted.

I scrambled for a way out, my mind racing for an excuse. "I—uh—" My eyes landed on a stack of books on her desk, and I seized the first thing that came to mind. "I was looking to interview Dr. Fenwick, but didn't know if the university would allow it. I'm interested in his latest book."

Dr. Winterbourne froze. Her fingers, which had been tapping absently against her desk, went still. "Book?" she repeated, her tone suddenly sharper.

I nodded, willing my expression to stay casual. "Yeah. The one about the—" I cleared my throat, lowering my voice, "—extremely rare creatures."

Her eyes flashed, but I couldn't tell if it was surprise, irritation, or something else entirely.

A long moment stretched between us before she gestured impatiently. "Don't just stand there in the doorway, come in. Especially if you're going to be saying things like that."

I stepped fully into the office and shut the door behind me, the click of the latch sounding far louder than I would have liked. My pulse quickened as I settled into the chair opposite her, feeling the weight of her scrutiny.

"Now," she said, steepling her fingers. "Why don't you start from the beginning and tell me exactly why you're interested in Dr. Fenwick's work?"

I hesitated for half a second before launching into the first semi-plausible excuse that came to mind. "I wanted to interview an expert in the field," I said. Was my voice too high? Words tumbling out too fast? I took a breath and forced myself to slow down. "And with his new book set to release soon, it seemed like the perfect time to reach out."

Dr. Winterbourne studied me, her lips pressing into a thin line.

"But just my luck," I continued, "I can't ever seem to find him. Every time I ask around, no one knows where he is." I leaned in slightly. "Do you?"

She let out a small, almost dismissive sigh. "No, I haven't seen him this week either. I fear he may have come down with a rather nasty stomach bug. It has been going around." She tapped a well-manicured nail against the desk. "Why, I believe his research assistant had it only a few weeks ago."

I kept my expression neutral, but my mind whirred. Why would the head of department know about a colleague's research assistant's illness? Was she just a very good boss, or was there something more at play here? Something I was unaware of?

"Oh," I said, forcing a note of disappointment into my voice. "Well, I was hoping to ask him a few questions, but if he's not here..."

"You could interview me," Dr. Winterbourne said crisply.

I blinked. "What?"

Dr. Winterbourne gave me a small, almost amused smile. "I'm his superior and well-versed in," she paused deliberately, "rare creatures. I'd be happy to conduct an interview with you. You know, provide a fresh perspective, maybe shake things up a bit?"

Something about the offer sent warning bells clanging in my head, but I couldn't exactly refuse without raising suspicion.

I gave what I hoped was a gracious nod. "That's...really generous of you."

Dr. Winterbourne leaned back slightly. "Aren't you going to get your notebook out?"

My stomach plummeted. How did she know about the notebook in my pocket? Had she seen a corner of it? Had I fidgeted with it too much?

"Notebook?" I asked, feigning confusion. "What would I need a notebook for?"

Dr. Winterbourne shot me a mildly annoyed look. "For taking notes? Of the interview?" She gestured at herself expectantly.

"Oh, right. Of course," I said, thinking fast. If I pulled out Dr. Fenwick's notes, she might recognize them and clam up. Instead, I grabbed my phone, opening it to the voice recording app. I showed her the screen as I pressed record. "I hope you don't mind me recording our interview, Dr. Winterbourne."

"No, of course not. Anything I can do to help," she said graciously.

I carefully set my phone on the desk, making sure to angle the mic just so before speaking in what I hoped was a professional-sounding manner. "For the record, my name is Harper Sullivan." I winced. I should've used an alias. Too late now. I bulled ahead. "I'm here with Dr. Maxine Winterbourne on..." I glanced at the date on my phone screen. "...Thursday, March 13th, at Eastford University. Thanks for talking with me, Dr. Winterbourne."

Dr. Winterbourne nodded slightly in acknowledgment. "It's my pleasure."

I forced a polite smile as I scrolled through the mental list of harmless questions I could use to beef up my faux-journalist persona. "So, Dr. Winterbourne, how long have you been with the university?"

"Seven years," she answered smoothly, her tone bordering on disinterested. "Though I did my early research elsewhere before settling here."

I nodded. "And your field of expertise is...?"

Dr. Winterbourne arched a brow. "Biological sciences, with a particular focus on rare and, shall we say, *elusive* species."

My pulse ticked up. That was an interesting way to put it.

"Sounds like fascinating work," I said, keeping my voice neutral. "Do you collaborate often with your colleagues in similar fields?"

"When the need arises." Dr. Winterbourne tilted her head, studying me. "Though I imagine you're more interested in Dr. Fenwick's collaborations?"

I barely managed to keep my expression from shifting. "Actually, yes. His upcoming book caught my attention, and I was hoping to get a better understanding of his research. When is it out?"

Dr. Winterbourne leaned back in her chair, fingers steepled. "There's no official release date, last I heard."

I tapped a finger against my chin. "That's a shame. I read part of an advanced copy and was particularly interested in some of the sections I was lucky enough to read."

Dr. Winterbourne's expression didn't change, but there was the slightest pause before she responded.

"You've read part of an advanced copy?" she repeated, her voice perfectly neutral. "That's interesting. Those were supposed to be quite limited."

I gave a nonchalant shrug, hoping she wouldn't press me for details. "I have connections."

Her lips curved into something almost like a smile, though her eyes stayed cool. "Do you now?"

I leaned in ever so slightly, keeping my tone casual. "I found some of Dr. Fenwick's references... unusual. Particularly the sections on the, uh, energy-responsive species."

She poured some tea into her cup and took a slow, deliberate sip. "Unusual is one word for it," she murmured. "Others might say imaginative. Or speculative."

"Sure," I said agreeably. "I just wasn't sure if he was classifying them as newly discovered or simply misunderstood." I tilted my head. "And I couldn't quite tell. Did he consider them a threat?"

She set the cup down with a soft clink. Her fingers steepled over the desk, voice smooth but her expression unreadable. "That depends on your definition of threat, Miss Sullivan. The world is full of things that can be dangerous, given the right conditions."

Silence settled between us as I weighed my next words. Her gaze lingered on mine, assessing. I opened my mouth, but Dr. Winterbourne spoke first, asking almost idly, "Tell me. What else did you read?"

I swallowed, choosing my words carefully. "Not much beyond that. Just some speculation about potential applications." I gestured vaguely. "Harnessing their abilities for controlled magic environments, that sort of thing."

Dr. Winterbourne exhaled softly. "Yes, that sounds like Fenwick."

Something in the way she said his name struck me as odd.

I leaned in slightly. "You don't sound particularly fond of him."

A dry chuckle escaped her. "Oh, I have no strong feelings one way or the other," she said smoothly. "Dr. Fenwick was... ambitious. But sometimes ambition leads people down paths they shouldn't tread."

I stilled. "What do you mean?"

She gave me a sharp look. "You read the book. Tell me, what do *you* think?"

I suddenly had the distinct impression that this conversation had become a game of chess—and I wasn't sure whether I was winning or about to fall into a well-laid trap.

But I wasn't about to back down now. Instead, I pushed forward. "Have you ever collaborated with Dr. Fenwick? His work sounds fascinating."

Dr. Winterbourne smiled, but it didn't reach her eyes. "To a layperson, it must. However, my field of study is almost entirely based in the mundane and much more practical than the far-fetched notions Dr. Fenwick pursued."

"Is that so?" I tilted my head, gaze flicking to her necklace.

It was the same one I'd seen her wearing before—or at least, I was pretty sure it was. But something about it tugged at the edges of my memory, like a word on the tip of my tongue. I'd seen it recently. Somewhere else.

Then it clicked

"Wait. Hold on, I've seen that!" I pointed, heart kicking up a gear. "That necklace. It's not generic, it's custom. And enchanted. Which means..." I blinked, the pieces falling into place. "You're fae, aren't you, Dr. Winterbourne?"

Her hand flew to the pendant at her throat. The intricate silver filigree glinted in the light. It was distinctive and unmistakable.

"I saw that exact piece before," I pressed on. "In my friend's ledger. She makes custom jewelry pieces by enchanting them. That pattern? It's a camouflage charm that helps the wearer slip by unnoticed."

I leaned in, words gaining speed. "Which would be useful, wouldn't it? Especially if someone didn't want to show up on security footage. Like, say... stealing a cage from Fenwick's lab."

Silence stretched between us. A muscle in her jaw twitched. Then—

Dr. Winterbourne carefully set down her teacup. "You have a very vivid imagination, Ms. Sullivan." Her expression didn't waver. "But, for argument's sake, let's say you're right. Camouflage charms aren't illegal."

"No, they're not," I agreed. "But using them to disguise yourself? To frame someone else? That's a different story, isn't it Dr. Winterbourne? Or should I call you Charlie?"

Her shoulders tensed, the first real crack in her composure.

I leaned forward. "I'm guessing Dr. Fenwick spoke to you about his new trial. I don't know if it was greed or jealousy that drove you, but you stole the auravores, didn't you?" I said, voice low.

The air between us felt like a stretched wire, thin and trembling, ready to snap.

She didn't reach for the teacup this time. Her fingers curled around the edge of her desk instead, knuckles pale. The light behind her cast a long, distorted shadow, making her seem taller. Sharper.

"I have no idea what you're talking about," she said smoothly, but her voice was just a touch too measured, her words too deliberate.

I tilted my head. "That's interesting, because you've been remarkably calm this whole time. No real reactions, no surprise about his research or the auravores. They're incredibly rare, you know. But the moment I mentioned your necklace, everything changed."

Her throat bobbed in a slow swallow. "Well, it's quite the accusation."

I smiled tightly. "And yet, you haven't denied it."

Her nostrils flared, her fingers flexing slightly, but she remained otherwise composed. The only giveaway was the subtle change in her stance as she shifted her weight ever so slightly forward, her eyes flashing dangerously.

I knew that look. Predators looked like that just before they pounced.

A prickle ran down my spine. I had seconds. Maybe less.

"You tricked the security cameras using that charm," I pressed, my voice lowering, trying to force her into words rather than action. "It wasn't Dr. Harlow who took the creatures. It was you."

Her shoulders went rigid. The controlled façade cracked. It wasn't much. Just a sliver, but I saw it. A single muscle in her jaw twitched.

Then—

She lunged.

I yelped, jerking back as she shoved the desk with a strength that belied her size, knocking it into me and sending her teacup crashing to the floor. I jumped to my feet and stumbled back, trying to get out of the way, but my foot caught on the overturned chair. Despite a desperate attempt to stay upright, gravity won. I hit the ground hard. Pain jolted through my shoulder and the impact rattled through me, making my head spin.

The office door banged open behind me, and hurried footsteps pounded down the hall, fading with every heartbeat.

"Harper, get up! She's getting away!" Ignatius called, his voice sharp with urgency.

Chasing Charlie

A DULL ACHE SPREAD through my shoulder as I scrambled upright. Nothing felt broken—just bruised. My pride was too, but I couldn't waste time wallowing.

She was getting away.

I scooped up my phone and shoved it in my pocket before staggering into the hallway, my breath coming fast as I scanned both directions. The corridor stretched out, sterile white walls and linoleum floors gleaming under the fluorescent lights. But Dr. Winterbourne was nowhere in sight.

"Where did she go?" I whispered, straining to listen.

"Don't know," Ignatius murmured from inside my jacket. "I was stuck."

I nodded, biting my lip. If I were in her shoes, where would I go? Fight or flight?

After what had just happened, I was betting on flight. She wouldn't linger in the science building. She'd want open space, a clear path to vanish into the crowd before I could catch up.

I bolted for the stairs, taking them two at a time, my pulse hammering in my ears. The fire door swung open with a heavy *thunk* as I shoved through, the scent of fresh coffee and warm spring air hitting me as I stepped into the atrium.

No sign of her.

Clusters of students stood near the elevators, chatting, laughing, coffee cups in hand. Across the hall, another lecture let out, spilling more students into the wide space. The sounds of shuffling feet and distant conversations filled the air.

I hesitated. She had to be here.

Then I heard it.

Click. Click. Click.

The sound of heels against tile. A slow, steady rhythm.

I turned sharply, scanning the students. Hoodies. Sneakers. Converse. Running shoes.

No one was wearing heels.

But the sound—distinct, deliberate—echoed toward the exit.

My breath caught. The necklace.

Dr. Winterbourne's illusion charm could change her appearance. It could shift her height, alter her face, make her blend in.

But it couldn't change reality.

And the reality was, she was wearing heels.

I could track her by sound.

The group of students ahead reached the glass doors, pushing them open and spilling out into the sunshine.

I hesitated, my hands clenching into fists. I could track her until she got outside, that is. Then where she was would be anyone's guess. I surged forward, weaving between students, stepping outside just in time to hear the timbre of the heels change. No more smooth tile. She was on the sidewalk now. But where?

I scanned the crowd, searching the students for something, *anything*, out of place. My breath caught when I spotted a girl with a perky dark bob heading swiftly away from the science building. Except this girl had no backpack and no books, which was strange for a student leaving a class.

Her shoulders stiffened as if she could *feel* me staring. She glanced over her shoulder and our eyes locked. Despite fighting to control an impassive mask, her expression shifted. Then she ran.

"That's her," I breathed, leaning forward into a sprint.

Dr. Winterbourne shoved past two students, sending their coffee cups flying, liquid splattering across the pavement.

"Hey!" someone shouted.

"Sorry!" I called, dodging around them, my heart hammering in my chest. I shoved my hand into my pocket. My fingers closed around the lead box—the same box that held Liam's cursed ring. Hoping no one was paying attention, I flipped open the latch. I could practically feel the bad luck wash over my fingertips. It was a risk, but one I was willing to take if it helped me apprehend a murderer.

Dr. Winterbourne hit the quad, losing speed for a second. The soft grass had hindered her, with her heels sinking into the thawed ground. A moment later, she was back on the sidewalk with solid pavement underfoot, and her speed increased dramatically.

I clenched my jaw. No way was I letting a fae woman in heels outrun me. I thrust my hand forward, using my magic to guide the small gold ring through the air and into her suit jacket pocket. She didn't even notice. However, the repercussion of concentrating on my magic meant my pace slowed. Dr. Winterbourne increased her lead, glancing over her shoulder at me triumphantly as I fell behind.

Students turned to watch the spectacle unfolding. A few pointed. Others just gawked. I ignored them all. Was the bad luck ring enough to tip the scales in my favor? I hoped so.

I pushed forward, forcing my legs to move faster, but Dr. Winterbourne was quick. Unnaturally fast. She wove between students with practiced agility, dodging around a pair of undergrads carrying an oversized project board and vaulting over a low bench without breaking stride. I gritted my teeth and surged after her, but she had a head start, and I was losing ground.

She glanced back, and I saw it. The flicker of certainty in her eyes. She knew she was going to outrun me.

I stumbled, breath hitching. She was too fast. I was going to lose her.

But then, luck intervened.

"Behind you!" a student shouted.

Dr. Winterbourne didn't turn in time. A Frisbee flew past me through the air, spinning fast, and smacked her hard in the side of the head.

She staggered, her steps faltering as she gripped her head, obviously disoriented.

Then came the second disaster.

A low stone wall surrounded the fountain at the edge of the sidewalk. Still rattled from the Frisbee, Dr. Winterbourne didn't see it.

Her ankle caught. She pitched forward, arms flailing wildly as she tried to maintain her balance. The moment stretched agonizingly slow. Then she tumbled straight into the fountain.

Water erupted in a dramatic arc, drenching her as she splashed down, sputtering and gasping.

"Harper! Get charm!" Ignatius whispered urgently in my ear.

He was right. Removing the charm would remove the illusion.

Dr. Winterbourne, still illusioned to look like a college student, coughed and shook her head, wiping at her eyes.

I hurried toward the fountain and reached down, offering my hand. "Here, let me help you," I said loudly enough for anyone to hear.

Dr. Winterbourne batted at me when I reached for her with both hands, sending water splashing up into my face. I reeled back dramatically, raising one arm to shield myself.

The other?

I used that to reach out with my metal magic, snapping the thin chain around her neck easily now that I could see it and yanking the charm through the air toward my outstretched hand. At the same time, I pulled on the ring I'd slipped into her pocket. Both zipped into my palm, and I wrapped my fingers around them, stuffing them both into the small lead box in my pocket and snapping the lid closed before the bad luck from the ring could taint me as well.

As soon as the charm left her neck, the magic surrounding Dr. Winterbourne shimmered, warping like heat over asphalt. The fresh-faced college student disguise vanished, revealing Dr. Winterbourne's sharp features, her mascara streaking down pale cheeks.

The murmurs around us grew louder as students rushed towards the fountain. Recognition rippled through the growing crowd. But thankfully most of them were too busy exclaiming over the Frisbee hit and the fountain crash to realize exactly what they'd just seen.

Water streamed down her suit jacket, pooling at her feet as she struggled out of the fountain. She looked more drenched cat than dignified professor, and the sight almost made me laugh. Almost.

I smiled, meeting her furious glare.

"Dr. Winterbourne," I said. "How nice to see you again."

Multiplying Problems

Campus security arrived on site while Dr. Winterbourne screamed at me about assault and demanded I return her property, which I had no intention of doing lest she use the charm to try to escape again. I don't think the security guys quite knew what to do.

I wasn't a student, but I looked calm. Meanwhile, a senior professor was shrieking like a banshee in the middle of a very crowded campus quad while students pulled out their camera phones, recording the whole incident for later viewing or posting.

So, naturally, they did the logical thing: they took us both away.

I could tell the security guards were relieved when I didn't put up a fight. I allowed them to escort me without complaint. Dr. Winterbourne...not so much.

"Unhand me!" she spat. "I am a senior professor!"

The burlier of the two guards looked unimpressed. "Ma'am, please don't make this harder than it needs to be."

Dr. Winterbourne bristled, water still dripping from her hair onto her drenched expensive blouse, but she must have realized that fighting would only make her look worse. Her jaw clenched, and for the first time, she glanced around, as if checking to see how many students were still watching.

The answer? Too many.

Phones were still out, students whispering, recording, and sharing.

My gaze flicked toward the edge of the crowd, scanning for something—no, someone.

There.

Gabriel stood near the quad, his posture tense and his eyes sweeping the scene with a sharp, assessing look. He took a step forward, clearly about to intervene.

No.

I shook my head. Just slightly. A barely there movement.

Gabriel hesitated. His hands curled into fists at his sides, his jaw working. He didn't like this. Not one bit.

We locked eyes.

Behind the security guard's back, I curled two fingers over my upper lip and wiggled them.

Gabriel blinked.

Then, to my immense satisfaction, he exhaled sharply through his nose, his lips twitching in the faintest ghost of a smile before giving me a small nod. Message sent and received. The sheriff would be on his way.

I let out the breath I'd been holding and followed the security guards without resistance. Beside me, Dr. Winterbourne marched by stiffly, still dripping from her undignified tumble into the fountain. I caught her sneaking a glance at me from the corner of her eye, but I didn't acknowledge her.

Let her wonder.

Ignatius shifted inside my jacket, pressing against my ribs. A silent question. I gave my jacket a tiny pat, keeping him calm and quiet.

The security guards led us through a side door of a nondescript office building. Beige walls, fluorescent lighting, and the faint, stale scent of old coffee.

We were likely in some sort of administrative offices. Good.

That meant fewer prying eyes. And, more importantly, fewer interruptions.

The guards guided us down a narrow hall and into what looked like a break room—metal chairs, a long conference-style table, and an ancient coffeepot holding half a pot that had probably been sitting in it since the early hours of the morning.

I sat without protest. Dr. Winterbourne, on the other hand, glared at the guards like they were a personal offense to her existence before finally dropping into the chair across from me.

The taller guard gave us both a hard look. "Stay put. We'll be right outside."

He closed the door behind him.

Dr. Winterbourne wrung out a section of her blouse with furious movements, then turned her glare on me.

"You," she hissed.

I met her gaze evenly and folded my hands neatly on the table, as if we were about to have a perfectly civil conversation.

Maybe, just maybe, I could turn this to my advantage.

I sat stiffly, watching Dr. Winterbourne as she folded her arms and exhaled sharply through her nose.

Time for a little risk. Luck could sit this one out. I was making my own today.

I leaned back, keeping my expression neutral. "Dr. Winterbourne," I said casually. "You knew Dr. Fenwick had been breeding rare creatures, didn't you?"

She shot me a dark look but didn't answer.

"And you figured out that his latest experiment had...unexpected properties," I continued, watching her carefully. "You decided to take advantage of that. And when he found out, he confronted you. That's why you killed him."

Dr. Winterbourne snapped her head toward me, eyes flashing with fury. "No! That's not what happened!"

"No?" I tilted my head. "Because I'm pretty sure that's how the police are going to see it."

Her lips curled in a sneer. "My lawyers will tie the police up in so many motions, they won't ever get close to me. You can count on that."

"You're right," I said smoothly. "I'm not the police. So why don't you just tell me what happened?"

She scoffed but didn't look away. Her gaze flickered up to the corner of the ceiling.

I followed her line of sight.

An old-fashioned security camera blinked its tiny red light down at us.

Ah.

Eastford University must have updated the rest of its security, but clearly, this office hadn't made the cut. The camera was ancient, but it was still recording. The security guards had left us alone for now, and I doubted they were actively monitoring the feed in real time. Still, if Dr. Winterbourne was going to crack, I needed her to believe she was safe to talk. Maybe I could convince her to talk by showing one of my own cards.

I dragged a chair over to the corner, ignoring her suspicious gaze, and stood on it. Placing my fingers over the camera lens, I let my magic flow. A metallic tingle danced up my arm, and I felt the circuits heat beneath my palm.

There was a tiny pop. The red light flickered out.

Dr. Winterbourne's eyebrows lifted slightly.

I hopped down and wiggled my fingers at her. "You're not the only one with magic."

A beat of silence. Then she let out a soft huff of laughter, shaking her head. "Should have known. A witch, are you? Or a mage? What's your magic?"

I sat back down, watching her carefully. "Something that gives us privacy. How does a fae end up here, anyway?"

She tilted her head, considering me. "Not all of us were built for pretty parties and political intrigue," she murmured. "I love science. But it doesn't pay very well."

"You took the auravores?" I asked, keeping my voice even.

She scoffed but didn't look away. For a long moment, she was silent.

"No one's listening." I gestured at the broken camera. "So why don't you just tell me what happened?"

Then, to my surprise, she sighed and leaned back in her chair. "He was being selfish," she muttered.

I raised an eyebrow. "How?"

Her expression darkened. "He had something extraordinary, and he wanted to bury it. These hybrids—they weren't just scavengers. They had instincts for treasure. Actual treasure, Harper. Not just coins and trinkets. Think of what we could've done with them! Archaeological discoveries, lost relics, maybe even entire civilizations buried beneath centuries of dirt. But Fenwick? He refused. He called it 'irresponsible' and 'dangerous.'"

"Why? What hybrids?" I asked.

Dr. Winterbourne rolled her shoulders. "Dr. Fenwick couldn't offload the wyrms when he switched interest to the auravores. No one wanted to take the beasts, and he wasn't about to turn them loose. But somehow, they managed to break out of their cages one night. To his great surprise, they didn't devour the auravores," Winterbourne continued. "However, it wasn't until later that we discovered what had really happened."

I leaned in slightly. "What are you saying? What happened?"

The faintest smirk tugged at the corner of her mouth.

"They bred. He brought me in to confirm his suspicions. It shouldn't have been possible, but they did."

My mind whirled. "Crossbreeding magical creatures?" I asked in shock. "Isn't that forbidden?"

"That's what Fenwick said," she added, waving a hand dismissively. "But he couldn't see the potential. We had a new creature that could track magical artifacts. Not just track them—but retrieve them. Trainable with food. Reliable. *Controllable.* The perfect treasure hunter. And he wanted to lock them away before any more could be impregnated and their numbers grew."

I forced myself to nod, trying to encourage her to continue even though my stomach sank. If they bred, would they be sterile? Probably not. This was bigger than one professor's rogue experiments. Dr. Fenwick had been right.

I hesitated and then took a shot in the dark. "But... I don't get it. What about Ironvein? And why impersonate Dr. Harlow?"

Dr. Winterbourne let out a dry laugh. "You think I was going to sell magical artifacts under my own name? I needed a fence. Someone with connections who wouldn't ask questions. Ironvein was perfect. He's greedy, reckless, and already has magical black-market contacts. I passed him the goods as Harlow. She had enough clearance to access what I needed, and I could mimic her signature well enough to slip past suspicion."

"Did you give him the hybrids too?"

"No. I'm not stupid," she snapped. "He would've cut me out. I used the hybrids to find the treasure, then gave Ironvein the relics to sell. Clean, simple, no trail to me. Or it would've been. But Fenwick figured it out when he caught me using them. That's when he tried to shut everything down. After that, I couldn't risk being caught again. I waited until he wasn't looking... and took them back."

I kept my face blank. "And when he tried to stop you?"

Dr. Winterbourne's expression wavered. She scoffed bitterly. "We're scientists. Our job is to push boundaries. But he was too afraid." Her hands curled into fists.

I bit my tongue, nodding slightly in the hope she'd continue. She didn't. Not right away. The silence stretched long enough for me to wonder if she'd changed her mind.

When she spoke, her voice was tight. "I didn't mean for it to happen. I just...I had a sedative. The hybrids responded to it. They liked it. It calmed them, made them easier to transport. I had it with me. And I had my thermos of tea."

My stomach twisted. "You slipped the sedative into his drink."

"It wasn't supposed to hurt him," she snapped. "Just slow him down. Make him stop fighting me. I didn't know it would kill him."

I exhaled slowly. "Because you didn't know about his beta blockers."

Dr. Winterbourne stiffened. "How could I have known?" she hissed. "I didn't find out until it was too late. He should have told me. We were colleagues! Friends!"

"He didn't want anyone to know. From what Dr. Harlow said, he kept the news pretty private."

Her face twisted with frustration. "He was stubborn. He stumbled away, took the cage, and I tried to stop him, but—" She hesitated. "He dropped it. I couldn't reach it."

I gasped, something clicking together from my memory of what the heartwood sapling had shared. "You were there that night. By the wishing well. Your necklace camouflaged you."

Dr. Winterbourne froze. The shift was subtle, but it was enough. Her eyes flicked to mine, sharp and calculating.

"I never mentioned a well," she said, voice low and tight. "How did you know about it?"

A long silence stretched between us.

Finally, I spoke. "You shouldn't have stolen from him."

The door burst open. Sheriff Jackson strode inside, filling the doorway like a storm cloud, Gabriel following close behind.

"Miss Sullivan. Dr. Winterbourne."

"I'm not saying a word without my lawyer," the professor said haughtily, crossing her arms and leveling a stare at the sheriff. It might've been intimidating if she hadn't been dripping like a half-drowned kitten.

"That's okay, Sheriff," I said, digging my phone out of my pocket. I'd never stopped the recording from her office. "I've got it all right here." I stopped the recording and slid my thumb across the playback bar and pressed play.

Dr. Winterbourne's voice, muffled but still clearly hers, echoed from my phone's tiny speakers. *"I didn't know it would kill him."*

Her gaze darted to me. "That recording is illegal. I didn't consent. That's inadmissible!"

I scrolled back to the beginning of the audio file and hit play.

"For the record," my own voice came through, crisp and clear, *"my name is Harper Sullivan. I'm here with Dr. Maxine Winterbourne on Thursday, March 13th, at Eastford University. Thanks for talking with me, Dr. Winterbourne."*

Dr. Winterbourne's voice rang out over the speaker. *"It's my pleasure."*

Sheriff Jackson raised an eyebrow as he glanced at the professor. "Now I might not be as smart as you, but it certainly sounds like you not only knew you were being recorded, but you were okay with it."

Dr. Winterbourne's jaw tightened, and she stayed silent.

Sheriff Jackson turned to me and nodded. "Good work, Harper. I'll take things from here."

I watched as the sheriff cuffed Dr. Winterbourne and led her away, her proud shoulders sagging under the weight of consequences she couldn't dodge.

It wasn't luck that saved the day. It wasn't fate, either. It was a healthy dose of stubbornness, caffeine, and a refusal to let things fall apart just because the universe got lazy.

Turns out, stubborn beats destiny every time.

On the Loose

THE MOMENT DR. WINTERBOURNE was secured in the back of the police cruiser, I turned to Gabriel. "We need to go. Now."

Gabriel blinked. "What? Aren't we following them back to Havenwood? Or better yet, heading out for a celebratory meal?"

I shook my head. "No. Let the sheriff and Reggie deal with the legal mess. We have bigger problems."

His eyes narrowed. "What kind of problems? We closed everything. The sheriff sniffed around and found the wyrms and auravores in a separate lab. Every single one is accounted for."

I exhaled, scanning the trees lining the edge of the campus, a familiar unease creeping up my spine. "Apparently, the auravores and wyrms from the previous experiment somehow bred. Dr. Winterbourne stole the hybrids and was training them to find and retrieve treasure. However, I don't think she realized how much the wyrm side of them played into their genetics. In fact, I wouldn't be surprised if that's what happened to poor Dr. Fenwick."

He stared at me. "You're saying—"

I nodded grimly. "I think the cage opened when he dropped it, the hybrids escaped, and..." my stomach twisted as I said it, "they ate him."

Gabriel's jaw tightened. "Which means—"

"They're still out there," I finished, my throat going dry. "And they're loose. In the woods. Near Havenwood."

A gust of wind cut through the campus quad, colder than it should have been.

Gabriel didn't hesitate. He dug his keys out of his pocket and started jogging. "Brainstorm on the way?"

"Only if you drive fast," I confirmed, already sprinting toward his car.

We threw ourselves inside, and Gabriel gunned the engine, tires screeching as we peeled down the road.

I ran a hand through my hair, my thoughts racing. "Alright, let's break this down," I said, shifting into crisis mode. "The hybrids are part wyrm, which means they'll be aggressive, always hungry, and quick to breed."

"And part auravore," Gabriel added, drumming his fingers on the steering wheel. "Which means they'll be able to sense magic and be instinctively drawn to it."

I swallowed. "And if they see magic as a food source..."

"They'll be drawn straight to any number of things in Havenwood," Gabriel said grimly. "The ley lines, people, things. Who knows what they'll go after?"

"And with the wyrms' appetite and ability to eat nearly anything, that could spell disaster," I finished.

The realization settled between us like a stone. A carnivorous, treasure-seeking species was about to run rampant in Havenwood.

"How long do you think it would take for an invasive species like that to take root?" I asked.

Gabriel's expression darkened. "With wyrm appetites and auravore instincts?"

"Not long," Ignatius muttered from inside my coat.

Gabriel's grip tightened on the wheel. "We need to find and contain them. The sooner, the better."

I closed my eyes, trying to recall that flicker of a memory from the vision, the way Dr. Fenwick staggered, the desperation in his movements.

"I saw it," I whispered. "In the vision. He dropped the cage. He was trying to keep them from escaping, but the fall knocked the door open."

Gabriel swore under his breath. "Then they could be anywhere."

A tiny shuffling noise came from my coat. "I help!" Ignatius whispered. "We find hybrids!"

I exhaled. "Yeah, buddy. We're going to need all the help we can get."

Gabriel pulled onto the highway, speeding toward Havenwood. "We'll need a containment plan. I can take care of that part."

"Then I'll work on a way to lure them out," I said.

Gabriel shot me a look. "How do you plan on doing that?"

"I'm going to talk to an elf about some enchantments," I said.

Faster than was probably legal, we zoomed past a sign welcoming us to Havenwood. Gabriel pulled over on the side of Arcadia Avenue, and I hopped out.

"You find her as fast as you can," he said. "Take care of your side of the plan. I'll meet you at the wishing well."

"Got it."

He barely waited for me to shut the door before peeling off down the road.

Finn was outside his shop, hanging up some last-minute decorations for St. Paddy's Day. He looked up as Gabriel sped away.

"What's going on?" Finn asked.

"No time to talk, but let's just say your girlfriend might hold the key to saving Havenwood." I said, dialing Seraphina's number.

Finn blinked, mouth half-open as I turned away, but I didn't have time to explain it all. Not when we had bigger problems.

Seraphina picked up on the second ring. "Hi Harper, how are you?"

I was so on edge, I jumped right to it. "I need your help, Seraphina. And it's time sensitive. Can you meet me—like, now?"

A slight hesitation. "I'm at Elowen Wispdale's shop, helping her with something. Do you want me to come to Spellbooks?"

"No. Stay put. I'll come to you."

"Alright. I'll be here."

Seraphina was already waiting outside when I arrived, her phone tapping anxiously against her palm. As soon as she saw me, she strode forward.

"What's going on?" she asked.

"I'll explain, but not here," I said, grabbing her wrist and pulling her into Elowen's jewelry shop.

Elowen looked up from behind the counter, immediately clocking the tension on my face. "Do you need me?" she asked, her posture stiff. "Or shall I make myself scarce?"

I hesitated. "Actually, you might be able to help."

Elowen nodded and flipped the sign to "Closed" before locking the door. "Alright," she said. "Tell us everything."

Maybe it was dumb luck that the very people I needed to make this crazy plan work were both in Havenwood and willing to help. Or maybe, just maybe, I was starting to make my own luck. I quickly explained the situation—the hybrids, the breeding risk, the fact that if we didn't contain them now, Havenwood was in for an infestation unlike anything we'd ever seen.

Seraphina's lips pressed into a tight line. "How soon is soon?" she asked.

"We don't know. Wyrms breed quickly, but who knows with a hybrid species," I admitted. "If they're already reproducing, we could have a major problem on our hands."

Elowen exhaled. "Well, that's terrifying."

"So, what do we do?" Seraphina asked.

I took a deep breath. "I need you to enchant something. Preferably something expensive and full of magic. Something that will be impossible to ignore. We need to lure them out and contain them."

Seraphina frowned. "I don't usually do enchantments like that, but...I *might* have an idea for something that could work." She glanced at Elowen. "Do you have anything in your collection we could use?"

Elowen gestured toward her shop. "Take whatever you need. If it stops these creatures, it's yours."

Seraphina rolled up her sleeves. "Alright. Let's get to work."

An hour and a half later, I stared at the results of Seraphina's impressive work.

Three glistening, opulent brooches lay on the counter, sparkling under the shop lights. Each one was striking—large, intricate, and gorgeous. But the real magic was hidden in the delicate runework along the back.

Seraphina swayed slightly as she handed me the last one, her fingers trembling from exertion. "That's the best I can do in the time we have," she admitted, rubbing a hand over her face. "I'm drained. I don't think I can do another."

I carefully accepted the bundle wrapped in black velvet, my stomach twisting. "This is more than enough. Thank you."

Seraphina's expression darkened. "Stop! Don't let them touch your skin."

I stopped mid-motion and turned only my head to look at her. "Why?"

"They're infused with a freezing spell," she explained, her voice tight. "Nothing permanent, but if you touch them with your bare hands, you'll freeze in place."

"Like a human popsicle," Elowen added dryly. "But without the sugar."

I swallowed hard. One misstep, and I'd be just as stuck as the hybrids we hoped to catch.

"The spell will only last about an hour," Seraphina warned. "After that, they'll be free to move again. You need to trap them before time runs out." She held up a silver vial. "If you want to dissolve the spell early, just sprinkle them with a little of this."

"What is it?" I asked, accepting the vial.

"Salt water," Seraphina said simply, handing it over.

"You'll also want this," Elowen said as she stepped forward and pressed a heavy security bag into my hands. It was double-padlocked, with a set of small keys attached.

I frowned. "What's this?"

"Bait," she said. "I stitched all the enchanted items I had onto a black velvet cloth inside. You can spread it out so the hybrids can sense the magic, but they won't be able to actually remove anything except the brooches. The moment they latch on to those, *bam*—frozen."

The breath left my lungs. "That's...brilliant."

Elowen crossed her arms. "It's necessary." Her voice was steady, but there was a quiet resolve in her tone, the kind that came from someone who understood just how bad things could get.

Seraphina slumped into a chair, rubbing her temples. "If this doesn't work, we're out of options."

I gripped the bag tighter, my pulse pounding. This *had* to work.

"I don't know how to repay you both," I said, looking between them.

Elowen's lips twitched in something that was almost a smile. "This isn't just for you, Harper. It's for Havenwood. It's what we do here."

Seraphina nodded, exhaustion written all over her face. "Don't waste time. You've got to catch them."

I exhaled sharply, then gave a single, firm nod. No room for doubt. No second chances. No more waiting for luck to show up. This was it.

With the bundle clutched close, I said. "Thank you both. Truly." Then I hit the door at a run.

Cobblestones blurred beneath me. The night was cold, and the stakes had never been higher. The hybrids were out there. Hunting magic.

And this time, I wasn't leaving my fate to luck.

The world didn't owe me a happy ending, but I was determined to write one myself.

Will Luck Turn?

THE PILE OF TREASURE glinted under the sliver of moonlight filtering through the trees. I crouched low, my breath shallow, fingers digging into the cold earth beneath me. My heart pounded so hard it felt like the hybrids might hear it.

Gabriel and I crouched behind trees at the edge of the glade, cloaked in shadow, using a scent-masking spray courtesy of Sheriff Jackson. He'd sent backup as well, in the form of Officer Johanna, whose speed nearly rivaled his own. With the full moon cresting the next day, he couldn't risk shifting around humans.

I shivered as I remembered his words. He'd called it the Worm Moon. He said the name came from old magic, the kind that warned of hidden things stirring below the surface, of bad luck. I'd laughed at first. But tonight, with the soil loose underfoot and something slithering just out of reach, I wasn't laughing anymore.

I barely caught glimpses of my teammates through the shifting shadows, but I knew they were there. Silent. Watching.

Waiting.

The seconds stretched, long and brittle. I swallowed, willing myself to stay perfectly still.

Inside my jacket, Ignatius shifted, his tiny claws pressing lightly against my ribs. He was silent, but I could feel his tension, the subtle way his body coiled, ready to move.

Not yet, buddy. Not yet.

A rustle in the underbrush made my breath catch. Then, a flicker of movement and the dry crackle of leaves. Something *slithered* through the underbrush.

My pulse thudded in my throat as one wyrm-auravore hybrid crept into the clearing, its elongated body undulating, scales catching the light in a sickly iridescent sheen. Then another. A third. And finally, a fourth.

I tensed.

Four.

We only had three enchanted brooches.

A cold thought slid through me. The hybrids devoured magic. What would happen if they reached the heartwood sapling nearby? Would it wither? Would they be able to siphon magic directly from the ley lines themselves? If so, what would happen? I didn't know, and that uncertainty made my chest clench harder than almost anything else.

A bead of sweat trickled down my spine as the hybrids crept across the black velvet cloth, their sleek bodies gliding over the glimmering spread of enchanted trinkets like liquid shadow. One paused, nose twitching, then slithered toward a glinting pendant sewn in place near the edge. Its needle-like teeth scraped at the metal, testing.

Come on. Take the bait.

One hybrid chittered as if in response to my thoughts. It snatched up a brooch in its claws. The others writhed forward, their beady eyes snapping toward it in eerie unison.

The moment stretched, tight as a wire as the first hybrid stopped moving.

It was as if someone had pressed a button, locking its body in place mid-motion. Its tail twitched once before going completely still. Only its eyes moved, blinking in slow, confused realization.

A surge of relief rushed through me.

One down, three to go.

The second hybrid hesitated, watching its unmoving companion. Then, slowly, it reached out and plucked another brooch from the pile.

The moment its claws curled around the metal, it, too, froze.

Yes. Yes, yes, yes.

I barely dared to breathe.

The third hybrid let out a sharp, alarmed chitter and lunged forward, grabbing at the second one as if to shake it loose only to freeze itself in place.

My stomach clenched.

Three down and only one left.

The fourth hybrid recoiled, its body twisting into a defensive position. Its beady eyes darted between its frozen kin and the treasure pile. It knew something was wrong. It wasn't taking the bait.

Panic shot through me.

I leaned forward. If it ran, we'd never find it again. It would burrow into the woods, perhaps even multiply, and spread, devouring everything in its path from meat to magic. Even one getting away could spell disaster for Havenwood.

Inside my jacket, Ignatius stirred. I felt the tension in his tiny frame, his awareness mirroring mine.

"We can't let it escape," I whispered.

Sweat slicked my palms. My nails dug into the dirt. I was seconds from springing forward when a warm, familiar weight shifted inside my jacket.

"I trust you. Free me," Ignatius murmured from inside my jacket.

I felt him shift, wriggling to escape from the cloth. "Ignatius, wait—" I hissed.

Then, before I could stop him, he launched himself into the air. My stomach dropped as he flashed through a silvery moonbeam, headed straight for the hybrid.

"Ignatius—*wait*—"

Too late.

The hybrid whipped toward the movement, its long body tensing, and scanned the darkened woods for the threat. Its mouth opened, rows of needle-like teeth glinting in the moonlight as it searched for danger. A whisper of wings and then Ignatius was there. He dove from the shadows above, a blur of claws and fury, wrapping himself around the hybrid's torso in one swift, practiced motion.

Johanna swore under her breath. Even Gabriel flinched.

The hybrid screeched, thrashing violently. Its tail lashed, slamming against the ground in a frenzy. Ignatius held on, claws catching, his small frame taut with effort as the creature twisted and bucked beneath him.

It was stronger than I'd expected. Fast, brutal, and wild, but Ignatius didn't let go.

I lunged to my feet, ready to run, but Johanna was already tearing through the clearing. A blur in the darkness. However, I could tell she wouldn't reach them in time.

My pulse pounded in my ears, every breath shallow and sharp.

Ignatius had one shot.

He coiled his tail, muscles tensing like a bowstring. Then it flicked out, swift and precise. The tip of his tail barely brushed the frozen wyrm closest to him.

A sharp grin flashed across his tiny face, satisfaction gleaming in his eyes.

Then—stillness as the spell took hold.

Ignatius and the final hybrid locked in place, frozen mid-motion—claws embedded, jaws parted in a snarl, the hybrid's spiked tail a breath away from impaling my little book-loving dragon. My heart lurched. Was he hurt? Was he—?

I gasped, my breath stalling in my throat. For a long, agonizing beat, the world seemed to hold its breath with me.

Then I exhaled in a sharp, half-disbelieving rush. My chest burned with the force of it, and suddenly, everything crashed into place.

A wild laugh burst from me. A sharp whoop of relief, disbelief, and sheer victory.

Gabriel and Johanna skidded into the clearing, their eyes darting between me, the still-frozen hybrids, and Ignatius, suspended in his triumphant pose.

By unspoken agreement, we moved fast, adrenaline surging, hands shaking as we carefully transferred the frozen creatures—including my tiny, reckless dragon—into the enchanted containment cage Gabriel had obtained while I was with Seraphina and Elowen.

Seraphina's saltwater shimmered in the vial as I opened it with trembling fingers. The liquid rippled in my shaking hand. With a steadying breath, I tilted the vial and let a few drops spill over Ignatius' frozen form.

Nothing happened.

I bent closer, heart thudding. A shallow gash sliced across his side. It wasn't fatal, but deep enough to make my stomach drop.

"Come on, come on," I whispered, carefully scooping him into my hands. "Buddy? Please."

His body was limp in my hands. A raspy wheeze rattled from his throat as his wings flared weakly and crumpled again. He shuddered, eyes fluttering open, then tucked his head against my wrist with a faint whimper.

Relief hit me like a crashing wave.

He stretched once, shaking off the remnants of the spell. His gaze met mine, his expression smug and triumphant.

"Was heroic?" he mumbled. "Felt heroic."

A watery laugh escaped me. "Yeah, buddy. You saved the day."

The hybrid he'd taken down twitched.

I didn't hesitate.

"Lock it! Now!" I yelled.

Clutching Ignatius to my chest, I scrambled backward just as Johanna slammed the iron door shut with a sharp clang. Gabriel immediately clicked the lock into place.

Silence.

We'd done it!

Officer Johanna tested the weight of the cage, her fingers tightening around the handle as she cast a wary glance at the one slightly thawed and three immobilized hybrids inside. "I'll get these to a secure location," she said, her voice still taut. "The sheriff knows a place where they won't be able to cause any more trouble."

Gabriel and Officer Johanna exchanged glances, the tension that had kept us all wound tight for hours finally beginning to uncoil. Their shoulders slumped as exhaustion crept in, the kind that only hits when the adrenaline starts to wear off.

My legs gave out, and I slid down to the ground, resting against the rough bark of the nearest tree and letting it support my trembling frame. A shuddering breath left me, my heartbeat still hammering against my ribs, unwilling to slow down. My fingers tingled from gripping the vial too tightly.

We had them.

A pulse of warmth stirred in the earth beneath me. The faintest whisper from the heartwood brushed the edge of my thoughts. *"You protected the sapling. I knew you were the right choice for the guardianship."*

I blinked fast, throat tightening.

Ignatius stirred in my hands, still curled around my wrist. "We did it!" he crowed triumphantly, his little chest puffed out. He shook himself, scattering droplets of saltwater. "I was very brave, yes?"

I let out a breathless laugh and reached up to scratch under his chin. "You were reckless, is what you were."

Ignatius preened, clearly taking that as a compliment. "Yes. Reckless and brilliant. Like hero in stories."

My laugh caught in my throat as my gaze fell back to the shallow gash on his side, blood smearing faintly across his scales. It didn't look serious, but it was enough to make my stomach twist.

"Let's get that cleaned up before your 'hero moment' turns into an infection," I murmured, cradling him closer. "No more reckless moves for you tonight, buddy."

Gabriel crouched beside me, nudging my arm. Without a word, he tore a strip from the hem of his shirt and gently tied it around Ignatius' wound. "You were reckless too, you know, amaryn," he said, giving me a pointed look. "But I guess that's what makes you, you."

Officer Johanna let out a low chuckle. "At least this time, no one ended up held at gunpoint."

I groaned, tipping my head back against the tree. "Don't jinx it. The night's not over yet."

Johanna adjusted her grip on the cage and shot me a dry look. "Then I suggest we wrap this up before it is."

She turned, moving toward where she'd left her police cruiser, but I caught something else in her expression. Was that a flicker of respect?

As she headed down the path, Ignatius craned his neck around. He tilted his snout upward, sniffing the night air like a sommelier judging a particularly questionable vintage. Then he gave a tiny grunt and squinted at the forest's edge.

"No just...pass through," he muttered, lips struggling to fit the words around his teeth. "They *linger*. Stay. Hide...things."

Gabriel turned toward him. "You smell something?"

"Not *smell*," Ignatius huffed, clearly offended. "I *know*. Feel it. In claws. In bone. Something here...*precious*. Maybe hoard. Maybe nest." He scratched the ground with one curved toe, nose twitching.

"A hoard?" I asked, pulse quickening.

"They are small," he said. "Sneaky. But they stayed here lots. Why? Must be reason. I think they hide hoard."

He spun in a tight circle, then scrambled into the brush with surprising speed. "Come! Come! I find!"

Gabriel and I exchanged a look and followed. Our footsteps were near-silent on the forest floor, softened by moss and years of fallen pine needles. It was hard to see in the dim light, but I trusted Ignatius.

He paused next to an ancient, gnarled oak, its roots twisted deep into the earth like a titan's grip. Beneath it, half-hidden beneath fallen leaves and tangled ivy, a small, dark tunnel yawned open.

Gabriel crouched, running his fingers along the entrance, brushing away damp soil. "A tunnel?"

Ignatius shook his head. "A network. Big, from what I smell. I go look."

I stiffened, instinctively reaching out, but he was already gone, swallowed by the darkness.

We waited, the silence stretching taut.

Minutes ticked by, each one heavier than the last. My nerves thrummed with restless energy, my muscles tight, ready to act. The woods around us felt too still now, as if the night itself was holding its breath.

Then, finally, a flicker of movement.

Ignatius emerged, his tiny form silhouetted against the pitch blackness of the tunnel's mouth, his wings fluttering as he scurried back onto solid ground. Clutched in his claws was a gold ring, its surface dulled with age but still gleaming faintly in the moonlight.

"There's more," he announced, shaking dirt from his scales. "Lots more. I told you. A hoard," he said proudly.

"Is there anything we can do to help?" I asked.

Ignatius shook his head. "You too big. No worries. I do it."

Gabriel spoke up. "While you're down there, check to see if there are any more hybrids. I don't want to discover we missed some in a few months."

The thought sent a chill up my spine. If we didn't stop them tonight, if they spread further...well, I didn't even want to imagine it.

I pressed my palm to the ground, feeling for the subtle pulse of the heartwood and the ancient magic that connected every root and leaf across Havenwood.

"Are there more of them? More of these hybrids or anything like them?" I asked silently, thinking of the wyrms and auravores.

There was a pause. A sense of the forest stretching its awareness, like light threading through deep soil.

"None remain that I can sense. Not the hybrids or anything that feels like them. You've done well, guardian."

I let out a slow breath, my shoulders sagging with relief. "The heartwood says we got them all," I murmured. "No more hybrids. Nothing like them anywhere nearby."

Gabriel pulled me close and kissed my temple, his voice low. "Good. I don't want to go through that again anytime soon."

Ignatius gave a sharp little nod. Then he promptly turned and scampered back into the tunnel. One by one, he retrieved items from the hoard and brought them to us. There were coins, necklaces, gemstones, and enchanted trinkets. Some were caked in dirt, others were eerily pristine. The air around them shimmered with residual magic, sending a tingle across my skin.

I stood and walked over to the heartwood sapling, its slender form glowing faintly in the moonlight, leaves rustling even though there was no breeze. I crouched beside it and placed my hand gently on its trunk.

"Mind if I have a few leaves?" I asked silently. *"Some of these items feel off. I'd like to cleanse them before we pick them up if possible."*

For a moment, nothing happened. Then, a few leaves shimmered and loosened from their stems, drifting into my open palm. I whispered my thanks and returned to the pile, settling beside it once more.

One by one, I rubbed a heartwood leaf over the coins, necklaces, trinkets that Ignatius retrieved just in case they were steeped in any lingering enchantments. With each pass, I imagined the magic unraveling like smoke caught in sunlight, the heartwood's gift lifting curses and clearing as much old magic from the hybrids' hoard as I could.

Ignatius gave a satisfied nod as he set down the final piece. "No more hybrids. No more tunnels. They didn't spread. I double checked."

A slow exhale left me, tension unraveling at last.

Gabriel ran a hand through his hair, shaking his head. "Good thing we caught them now." His voice was tight, the reality of what could have been finally settling in. "Imagine if we hadn't. We could've had a full-blown infestation under Havenwood."

"Don't even joke about that," I muttered, shuddering.

I stifled a yawn, exhaustion creeping in now that the adrenaline had faded. Now that the excitement was over, the night's events weighed heavy on my limbs and dragged at my thoughts. The first streaks of dawn painted the horizon in muted shades of violet and rose, casting long shadows through the trees.

"I don't think I can stay awake much longer, but I'd really like to go through these with you. How does a late breakfast at the Enchanted Oasis sound?" I asked, already picturing the warmth of the café, the scent of fresh bread and rich coffee drifting through the air.

Gabriel let out a quiet chuckle, shaking his head. "I think that's the best idea I've heard all night. Let me take you home for at least a few hours' sleep. Shall I pick you up around eleven?"

"Eleven sounds great," I said as a yawn crept over me.

We made our way back to the car. I glanced once more at the now-empty tunnel, then at the bundle of treasure in my arms. The hybrids might be gone, but their remnants still lingered.

Sleep, then breakfast with my guy.

And after that, we'd figure out what to do with the rest of the treasure.

The Luck We Make

THE SCENT OF FRESH-BAKED pastries and rich, dark coffee wrapped around me like a warm embrace as Gabriel and I stepped into the Enchanted Oasis. Sunlight slanted through the windows, casting golden streaks across the polished wooden floors. The usual hum of the bed-and-breakfast felt softer at this hour. Most of the guests likely had their breakfast hours ago and were blissfully unaware of the night's chaos.

Bella was already waiting at our usual table, one hand wrapped around a steaming mug, the other flipping idly through a dog-eared copy of *Havenwood's Weekly Gazette*. As we approached, she looked up and arched a brow.

"If you two were trying to be mysterious last night, you succeeded spectacularly," she said, setting the paper aside. "Your text messages were wholly inadequate. I expect a full debriefing."

I sighed dramatically and nudged Gabriel toward the buffet. "Fine. But I'm talking while eating, or not at all."

Bella waved a hand magnanimously. "By all means, the saviors of Havenwood are welcome to help themselves. But if you skimp on the details, I'm switching your coffee to decaf."

I pressed a hand to my chest and laid the back of the other against my brow, feigning a swoon. "Not decaf! We'll tell you everything! I promise!"

Both Bella and Gabriel laughed at my dramatics. Bella waved me towards the expansive breakfast buffet set along one side of the room. "Help yourselves. Mama made sure that there was plenty when I told her you were swinging by today. I'll go make you a fresh pot of *regular* coffee right now."

"You're a saint," I said.

"I know," Bella replied with a smile and a wink.

Ignatius poked his head out of my jacket. "Coffee and bacon?" he asked hopefully.

Bella started and then smiled at the tiny dragon. "Sorry, Ignatius, I didn't see you there. Yes, and bacon. I bet we can even do some steak and eggs for you if you like?"

Ignatius bobbed his head. "I like. Steak and eggs good. But Bella?"

"Yes?" she asked, turning to face him.

"Hold the eggs please?" he asked plaintively.

She chuckled, giving him a thumbs up. "You've got it. Go on, help yourselves."

We didn't need any more encouragement. Gabriel and I grabbed plates and surveyed the absolute feast Honey had laid out. There were flaky croissants, buttery biscuits, slices of warm apple bread, golden-brown waffles, and a deep-dish quiche studded with bacon, herbs, and cheese.

I went straight for the pecan sticky buns, unable to resist the glossy caramel glaze, while Gabriel, ever the protein fiend, piled his plate with red cheddar waffles topped with crispy bacon and scrambled eggs.

Bella returned a moment later, balancing a fresh pot of coffee and a covered plate. She slid the coffees across the table and deposited the plate in front of Ignatius, who perked up instantly.

"Steak and bacon, just for you," she said, whisking off the cover and bowing.

Ignatius' golden eyes lit up like a sunrise. "You are angel," he declared, immediately digging in.

Bella preened. "I know." She turned to face me and rolled her wrist in a get-on-with-it gesture. "Now, don't keep me waiting in suspense. Get talking, Sullivan."

I blew on my coffee, savoring the rich aroma before taking a sip. "Okay, fine," I said, reaching for a fork. "I'll tell you everything. But don't blame me if you start wishing you hadn't asked."

Bella's grin lit up the room. "Oh, I doubt that."

As we dug into our food, I could already feel the tension of the night before beginning to ease. The coffee, the laughter, the warmth of good food shared with friends—this was exactly the kind of magic I needed after the events of the past few days.

Between bites and the occasional refill of coffee, I walked Bella through everything. The hybrids, Dr. Winterbourne, Ignatius's dive into the tunnel, the purifying properties of the heartwood leaves. Her expression shifted from wide-eyed horror to gleeful curiosity, and by the time I wrapped it all up, she was practically vibrating with secondhand adrenaline.

She clutched her mug with both hands and leaned forward. "You realize this would make an incredible movie, right? I demand casting approval, of course."

"Oh, obviously," I said dryly. "You'd never forgive me if I let someone with tragically bad bangs play you."

"Exactly," she said, satisfied. Then she nudged my foot under the table. "Still, you've got to admit you got pretty lucky, catching those hybrids before they could cause real trouble."

I tilted my head, considering that. "Was it luck?" I murmured, then smiled. "Nah. Just determination and a frankly irresponsible amount of coffee."

As I scraped up the last bit of caramel glaze from my plate, Gabriel set down his mug and stretched. "I'm taking the hoard down to Elowen to check against her list. The heartwood leaves helped, but Seraphina's going to meet me and check them out to make sure nothing nasty is still clinging to them. They're expecting me in about twenty minutes."

I hesitated. "If she thinks more leaves are needed, I'd rather ask the main heartwood than take anything else from the sapling."

Gabriel's expression softened. "That's fair. But let's check with her first. If she needs more, we'll make the trip together." He shot me a knowing look. "In the meantime, there's still plenty of time to drop you off at Spellbooks. Unless you want to come with me?"

I reached out and squeezed his hand. "Cassandra's holding down the fort today, and honestly? She's doing a great job. I'd rather come with you if you don't mind the company. However, I also need to take care of this." I pulled the small lead box from my bag.

Gabriel frowned. "The cursed ring?"

I nodded. "I used some of the heartwood leaves on it, but with all that bad luck built up in it, I'm not sure how quickly they'll work. With some time—and maybe a few more leaves—hopefully it'll be safe enough for Liam to return it to his friend's family eventually."

"I'd say 'good luck,' but given that thing's history…" Bella grimaced, clearly remembering the properties of the ring.

"I appreciate the sentiment," I said dryly.

A soft snort came from my lap. Ignatius lifted his head, blinking sleepily. "I stay here?" he asked. "There's bacon. And books."

I smiled and ran a hand gently over his scales. "Sounds like the perfect recovery plan."

Bella laughed and held out her arms to the tiny dragon. He fluttered sleepily over to her. "Don't worry, I'll look after the little hero. He's earned it."

Gabriel chuckled, then nudged me toward the door. "Alright, let's get this over with. Liam's first, then Elowen's."

The Pot o' Gold was only a short drive away, and Liam looked up as soon as we walked through the door. He seemed much more rested than the last time I'd seen him. He took one look at the box in my hands and visibly tensed.

"D'ya have good news for me then?" he asked, but his voice lacked any trace of hope.

"Actually, yes," I reassured him, holding out the box. "I think I might have found a solution for the luck siphon on the ring."

"Oh?" Liam asked, arching a brow as he accepted it.

"Well, to be honest, it was your idea," I said. At Liam's questioning look, I hurriedly explained. "Heartwood leaves."

His second brow joined the first as he looked from me to the box and back to me again. "Heartwood leaves, you say? Now where on this green earth were you lucky enough to stumble across those?"

I glanced at Gabriel and smiled. "Let's just say I have my sources."

Liam noticed our look and laid a finger alongside his nose, nodding knowingly. "Ah. Right. I get what yer saying, lass."

Gabriel opened his mouth to correct Liam's conclusion, but I jumped in. "Yeah, just let me know if you need some more. I'm sure we can arrange another round should the first set not do the trick." Although I was the guardian of the heartwood, it wasn't something I was comfortable advertising just yet. Maybe someday, but my gut was telling me the fewer people who knew, the better.

Liam let out a breath and nodded, considering the box once more. "That's mighty kind of ya. I really hope you're right."

Behind him, Sloane appeared in the doorway, her suitcase in her hand. "Harper," she said, smiling. "I'm so glad you came by."

I raised an eyebrow. "Are you heading out?"

"Yeah, it's time for me to get back to New Orleans."

"Already?"

She shrugged, adjusting the strap of her bag. "I had an interesting little adventure here, but New Orleans is home, and I have a business to run." She tilted her head. "Who knows? Maybe we'll cross paths again."

I grinned. "I have a feeling we will."

We exchanged a quick hug before she headed toward her rental car. As I watched her leave, I didn't feel like it was goodbye. Havenwood had a funny way of pulling people back when they least expected it, and something told me this wouldn't be the last time our paths crossed.

Gabriel leaned in. "Alright, one loose thread down. Ready for our next stop?"

I exhaled and nodded. "Yeah. Let's go."

Elowen's shop was bathed in warm sunlight when Gabriel and I stepped inside. The glass display cases gleamed, and the faint scent of polished wood and something floral lingered in the air.

Elowen glanced up from behind the counter, where she was tapping on a computer. "And here I thought you two might actually take a day off after saving the town."

Seraphina looked up from her phone as we entered. "Harper? Take a break? Please. Havenwood would probably collapse if she did."

I chuckled as Gabriel grinned and set the bag of recovered items on the counter. "Let's see what our little treasure hunters collected," he said as he set the bag of items we'd borrowed next to the first one.

Elowen flipped open her ledger and ran her finger down the list of stolen pieces. "I should be able to account for most of what was made in my shop. If there's anything extra, I'm not sure how we'll be able to track it."

Seraphina thumbed her phone off and hurried over. "Before you touch any of that, let me have a look to make sure there aren't any harmful enchantments."

"No arguments here," Gabriel said, handing over the lockbox with the items recovered from the hybrids' lair.

Elowen leaned a hip against a display case. "While she does that, fill us in on what happened? I've been dying to know."

I glanced at Gabriel, letting him take the lead. I wasn't sure how much his family, particularly his stern mother, wanted to be public knowledge. To my surprise, he gave a concise, but fairly complete, account of events.

"And so," he concluded, "my mother arranged for a place where the hybrids can be relocated safely. They won't be able to breed of course, but at least they'll have space to live out their days without causing any magical disasters."

Elowen blew out a breath. "That's the best we can hope for, I suppose."

I tilted my head. "What about Runar Ironvein and Dr. Winterbourne?"

Gabriel's lips curled into a satisfied smirk. "Sorry, I should've mentioned this earlier. I had a chat with the sheriff this morning. Dr. Winterbourne's going away for a long, long time. Between the sedative they found in her office and the confession you recorded, the prosecution won't have to work very hard. Runar tried to cut a deal, but he didn't have much to negotiate with. Since he didn't actually commit the murder, he's probably looking at a handful of misdemeanors—smuggling, theft of both Dr. Fenwick's and Dr. Winterbourne's property, obstruction, that type of thing. Nothing that'll keep him locked up for long, but at least he's not walking away clean."

Seraphina shook her head. "All this because someone got greedy."

"Greedy and reckless," I muttered, fingers drumming against the counter. "We're just lucky we caught the hybrids before they spread."

Gabriel nudged my elbow. "Lucky? Or just really, really stubborn?"

I smirked. "Both."

Suddenly, Seraphina abruptly yanked her hand back from the pile of recovered goods, shaking out her fingers with a sharp hiss. "Okay. That is *not* friendly magic," she said, rubbing her fingers and glaring at the pile of treasure.

Gabriel frowned. "What is it?"

"Let me show you." Seraphina muttered a quick incantation and passed her hands over the items again. Most of them glowed softly with what I assumed to be traces of harmless magic but when her fingers hovered over a handful of tarnished old coins, a dark shimmer flickered along their edges.

"What is *that*?" I asked, curiosity prickling at my spine. I leaned forward and reached out a hand.

Seraphina's expression darkened, and she grabbed my wrist, stopping me. "That's a curse. An old one. Deep-rooted. It's going to take time and many more leaves to break. Until we do, no one should touch those coins."

I nodded, tucking my hands behind my back. "Noted. Thank you."

"Where do you think they came from?" Elowen asked, moving to get a better look.

"Your guess is as good as mine," Seraphina said, shaking her head. "But what I can tell you is they're old."

"How old is old?" I asked.

Seraphina hesitated, fingers hovering over the coins again. "Based on what I can sense with my magic, we're talking a couple of centuries at least. Probably less than five hundred years. But this curse is nasty."

Gabriel straightened. "Then we need some protection."

Elowen was already turning toward the back. "Don't worry. I've got a lead lined box that should do the trick. I always keep one on hand," she said over her shoulder. "Occupational hazard."

She returned a moment later with a small, reinforced chest, setting it on the counter with a solid *thunk*.

Gabriel shot me a look as he took it. "Better safe than sorry until we can get the curse reversed. Do you think you can..." he trailed off and waved a hand at the coins.

I nodded, focusing my magic. I usually kept it a secret, more out of habit than necessity. However, I'd told Gabriel about my metal powers, Seraphina had witnessed them in December, and Elowen, being a fae, wasn't about to gossip about anyone else's magic. I carefully lifted the coins into the box one by one with my magic. I tried to focus on the task, but my mind was spinning.

Centuries-old, cursed coins. A deep, lingering magic. Treasure that had somehow been hidden, only to resurface now.

A knot of recognition tightened in my chest.

Could it be?

When I first moved to town, I'd discovered a legend of a cursed pirate treasure hidden by a nefarious sailor named Captain Blackfin. Supposedly, his legendary treasure was hidden along the eastern seaboard, lost to time. When I first inherited Spellbooks, I'd come across an old journal of Granny Bea's detailing how she'd found a way to move the treasure and secure it where no one would ever find it again. She had been adamant that the curse was too dangerous to leave exposed.

But if these coins *were* from Blackfin's hoard...

That meant her hiding spot was somewhere in Havenwood. And it had been uncovered. If even a few coins could still hold this much malevolence, what would happen if the *entire* treasure was revealed?

Gabriel nudged my elbow. "Harper? Everything okay?"

I blinked, dragging myself out of my thoughts. "Yeah, I—yeah. All good."

Elowen watched me carefully but said nothing as I used my magic to lift the last coin into the chest. She latched it shut and handed it to Gabriel, who took it with an approving nod.

Gabriel tucked the box under his arm. "I'll make sure it's secured and see if I can get the curse removed." He shot me a pointed look, one that told me he had no intention of waiting for some official magical authority to deal with it. We were going to take care of it ourselves with as many heartwood leaves as the trees let us use.

I nodded subtly, already guessing his plan. We said our goodbyes, Elowen promising to send over an itemized list of the recovered items as soon as she and Seraphina went through them all. I followed Gabriel out of the shop, my mind still whirling.

When we reached the car, he popped the trunk and carefully set the small chest inside.

"So," he said, closing it with a quiet *click*. "Are you going to tell me what's got you looking like you just solved half a mystery but found two more?"

I exhaled, rubbing the back of my neck. "Just thinking. If these coins are *really* as old as Seraphina says, and if they *are* what I think they are..." I hesitated, then met his gaze. "Gabriel, I think this might be part of the cursed pirate hoard Granny Bea found."

His brows lifted slightly. "The one she supposedly hid?"

I nodded. "But if these coins were buried somewhere *in* Havenwood, and the hybrids managed to dig them up, then that means..."

Gabriel's expression turned serious. "That means her hiding spot isn't as secure as she thought."

A cold knot settled in my stomach.

"I don't even want to *think* about what would happen if the full hoard is still out there and someone finds it."

"Then let's not give anyone the chance." Gabriel shut the trunk, his voice steady. "We'll head out to the heartwood saplings first, and get enough leaves to neutralize whatever's on these coins. Then we figure out where she hid the rest."

I let out a slow breath and nodded.

The treasure had waited this long.

But if Havenwood had taught me anything, it was that secrets never stayed buried forever.

Gabriel opened the passenger door for me, waiting until I settled into the soft leather seat before shutting the door and jogging around to his side. The moment he slid in, I fully expected him to turn the car toward the nearest heartwood tree so we could start gathering the leaves needed to break the curse on the coins.

Instead, he reached into the center console, pulled out a small, neatly wrapped package, and held it out with a mischievous glint in his eyes.

I blinked at him. "Aren't we dealing with the cursed treasure first?"

He lifted a shoulder. "Sure. But those coins have waited this long. Another couple of hours isn't going to change anything. Besides, they're locked away both physically and magically. They aren't going anywhere."

He held out the rectangular package again, and this time, my curiosity won out over caution.

I took it slowly, narrowing my eyes. "If this is another pair of shoes that somehow leads to a murder, I swear—"

Gabriel laughed, shaking his head. "It's not shoes," he promised, his lips twitching. "Or murder. Scout's honor."

I arched a brow but tore into the paper, the crisp sound of wrapping giving way to something much better—the scent of fresh pages and ink.

A book.

A brand-new book, its cover smooth beneath my fingertips. The title caught my eye immediately. I let out a soft breath of surprise. It was by one of my favorite indie authors—the kind of book I would've pre-ordered in a heartbeat if I'd had the time to think about something as simple as new releases this week.

My chest tightened, warmth curling through me. He knew me too well.

"I figured," Gabriel said, watching me carefully, "that after the week you've had, amaryn, maybe we could do something simple. Grab a coffee, find a quiet corner, and read. That way, I can make sure the only murders you get tangled up in are literary."

A slow smile spread across my face. I turned the book over in my hands, running my thumb along the edges before looking up at him. "That," I said, "sounds perfect."

After what felt like the most stressful week since arriving in Havenwood, I finally let myself exhale as we headed to Hocus Mochas, where the scent of espresso and cinnamon filled the air. The café was relatively quiet with plenty of open seats. We claimed a cozy corner table, and Gabriel went to order our drinks while I thumbed through the first pages of my new book.

When he returned, he set my favorite latte in front of me and clinked his cup against mine in a quiet toast.

"To a murder-free afternoon," he said.

I chuckled, but as I lifted my book, my gaze kept drifting to the man sitting across from me. Gabriel, with his effortless charm and sharp mind, who had been by my side through magic, mayhem, and one very chaotic week. My thoughts flickered to the cursed pirate gold we'd uncovered. It was another mystery waiting to be unraveled, but it could wait while I had a quiet date with my guy.

Havenwood would always have its mysteries, but for now, coffee, a good book, and the man across from me were all I needed.

Maybe luck really did have a hand in getting me to Havenwood. But the rest of the story? That was mine to write.

Grab your FREE novella now!

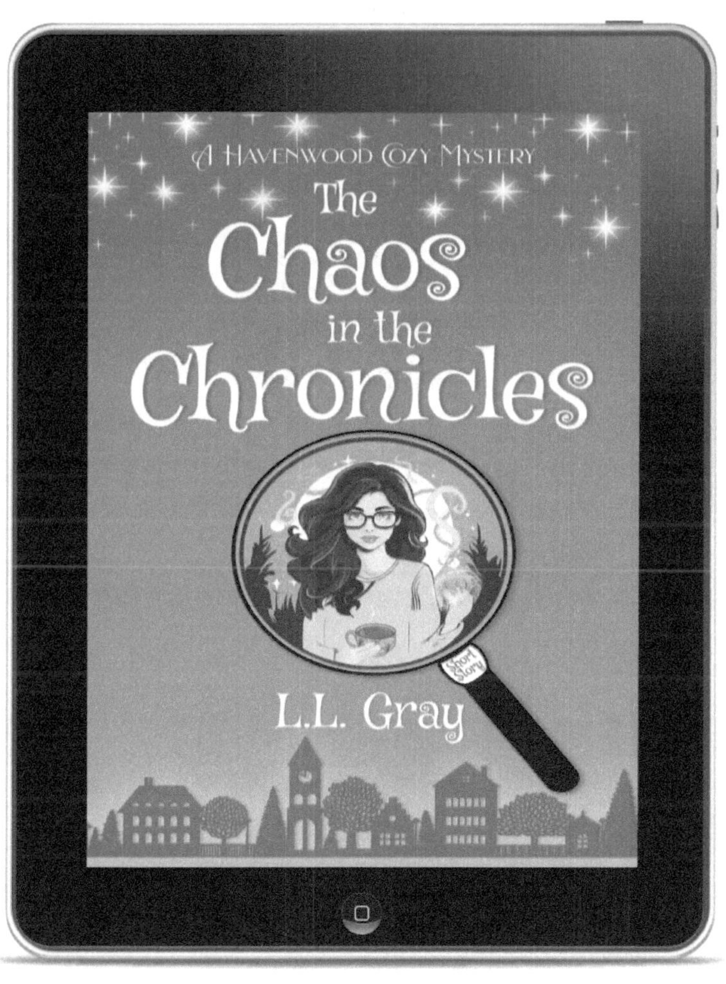

Want a free book?

Of course you do, what madness could possess someone to **not** want free books?
There's no catch - you do sign-up for my mailing list but you can unsubscribe at any time.
There's also no spam.
Ever.
Sign up here to get your free book!
https://www.subscribepage.io/havenwood

Thank you

Thank you for making it this far. I hope you enjoyed the story. Now, I'd like to share another, albeit much shorter one with you, along with a piece of my heart.

Once upon a time, I was a kid with mountains of notebooks, each one bursting with stories and dreams. Writing was my sanctuary, my escape from the world. But as I grew older, reality knocked on my door and whispered, "Writing won't pay the bills." So, I did the "sensible" thing and focused on the real world. For a while, at least.

Then came 2020, a year that turned many of our lives upside down. As an athlete and musician, I suddenly found myself unable to do the things I loved most. In a desperate bid to fight against depression, I turned back to writing. It was like finding a long-lost friend. The stories poured out of me, and I started to feel alive again.

Not that it has been without struggle. Trying to fit writing in around work, kids, and life is like juggling flaming torches while riding a unicycle. But I've kept at it. Since then, I've written and published over 20 books, each one a labor of love and infused with a piece of my heart. I'm not an overnight sensation or a best-selling author, nor do I have a stack of rejection letters from traditional publishers. Instead, I've taken a different path, connecting with incredible readers like you who cherish a good story and a touch of magic.

This is where you come in. Your review is more than just words on a screen—it's a lifeline, a beacon that helps me reach new readers and continue this incredible journey. If you could take just a few minutes to share your thoughts, I would be deeply, deeply grateful. I read every single review, and they touch my heart in ways you can't imagine.

So, if my stories have made you smile, laugh, or brought a little magic into your life, please let me know. Your support and feedback mean everything to me, and they help keep the dream alive.

Thank you for being a part of my story, for believing in my characters, and for sharing this journey with me.

With all my gratitude and a heart full of hope,

L.L. Gray

Also By

Havenwood Paranormal Cozy Mysteries

The Mystery in the Margins
The Chaos in the Chronicles (exclusive novella)
The Puzzle in the Pumpkin Patch
The Secret of the Silver Serpent
The Riddle at the Revelry
The Manuscript in the Moonlight (novella)
The Heist of the Hidden Heart
The Mayhem in the Masquerade
The Legend of the Leaf
The Mischief with the Magnets (novella)
The Conspiracy on the Cruise (coming soon!)

Smoke and Shadows Series

Shadows and Relics
Pixie Pranks (exclusive novella)
Felons and Fangs
Bones and Blades
Tempest and Treason
Daggers and Deception
Sleuths and Scoundrels
Legacy and Lies
Crossroads and Curses

Children's Books

The Secret About Mistakes
Corner of the Sky
To Mom. Love, Me
To Dad. Love, Me
To Grandma. Love, Me
To Grandpa. Love, Me

About the Author

L.L. Gray writes captivating, fast-paced fantasy full of wit, warmth, and magic. Her books transport readers to charming, cozy worlds brimming with lovable characters and whimsical adventures. A lifelong enthusiast of fantasy and myths, L.L. Gray blends humor and heart, inviting readers to escape into her spellbinding stories that feel like home—cozy, magical, and impossible to put down.

Psst, it's me—L.L. Gray!

I love connecting with fellow story lovers and adventure seekers. If that sounds like your cup of tea (or coffee, or whatever magical potion you prefer), come say hello! Visit my website www.llgray.com to join my newsletter, where you'll find exclusive goodies, or join us in my Facebook readers group. And if email is more your style, feel free to drop me a line anytime at info@llgray.com.

I hope you stay in touch!

Acknowledgments

To you, the reader: thank you for stepping into this world with me. I hope you felt the magic, warmth, and wonder woven into these pages. If you'd like to stay up to date with new releases and special content, head over to my website. And if you're looking to connect with a welcoming, book-loving community, join us on Facebook—there's always room for another story lover.

To my fabulous ARC and Street teams: you've become like a second family to me, cheering me on through every twist, turn, and chapter. Your unwavering support, encouragement, and excitement fuel my creative fire—I truly couldn't do this without each of you. Thank you for believing in these stories as much as I do.

Lastly, to my wonderful husband: your support is the foundation of every story I write. Thank you for believing in me, for being my rock, and for making all of this possible. I'm endlessly grateful to have you by my side.

Legendary Acknowledgments

Some readers visit a story.

Legends step into it.

This space is to thank those whose support rises above the ordinary. These are the readers that are quietly extraordinary, steadfast, and full of heart. Their encouragement helps carry the magic forward, even when no one is watching. They aren't just readers, but companions in the cozy, bookish adventure.

Thank you, dear Legends, for standing with these stories. Not behind the scenes, but beside them. Steady, present, and deeply appreciated for all you do to support Havenwood (and me!).

With heartfelt gratitude to:

Linda Woestendiek

From the bottom of my writerly heart (and Spellbooks' slightly chaotic shelves):

Thank you for being part of the story.

www.ingramcontent.com/pod-product-compliance
Lightning Source LLC
Chambersburg PA
CBHW021235310726

48971CB00006B/1838